The Name
I Call Myself

"Moran is a worthy inheritor of Austen's mantel: her writing is witty, engaging, funny, and poignant. She tackles the realities of love, loss, abuse, and redemption with insight; is considered without being heavy-handed, and light-hearted without ever compromising on motional depth. This is chick-lit as it should be — a page-turner whose heroine is transformed and whose journey is not superficial, but edifying and emboldening."

— Anna Thayer

The Name I Call Myself

I Call Myself

BETH MORAN

LION FICTION

Published by Lion Fiction
an imprint of
Lion Hudson plc
Wilkinson House, Jordan Hill Road
Oxford OX2 8DR, England
www.lionhudson.com/fiction

ISBN 978 1 78264 207 7
e-ISBN 978 1 78264 208 4

First edition 2016

A catalogue record for this book is available from the British Library

Printed and bound in the UK, June 2016, LH26

For more about Beth visit: www.bethmoran.org
or her Facebook page: Beth Moran Author

For Joseph –
Who makes me sing

Acknowledgments

Huge thanks again to Jessica Tinker, for her encouragement and invaluable wisdom. Also to Julie Frederick and all those at Lion Hudson who helped put the book together. This would have been a very different story without the lovely Sarah Livestro's invite to visit a Lace City Chorus rehearsal – what an amazing night! Thanks also to Matt McFarlane and Ian Joddrell for letting me ask you lots of questions about police procedure and social work. Please don't cringe at the bits I made up. As always, I cannot thank my King's Church family and the mighty Free Range Chicks enough for their wonderful love and support. For everyone who reads my books, writes a review, or takes the time to let me know you enjoyed them – you make all the difference, and do a great job at keeping me off the Internet when I should be writing. Mum – I am so thankful for the image of womanhood you raised me with. Matthew and Nic, Paul and Reiko, thanks for listening!

Ciara, Joe, and Dominic, thanks for always reminding me what really matters. And to George – thank you for being my biggest fan. I couldn't do it without you.

Chapter One

When, in my younger days, I idly contemplated the time I might one day go wedding dress shopping, it never crossed my mind that it would be a covert operation, accompanied by oversized sunglasses and a floppy hat. Or that I would be the one to cry. And that if I did, those tears would be a combination of stress, fear, loneliness, shame, and feeling buried alive in a gold mine.

It was Marilyn's idea. She bullied me into it. Currently drowning in the domesticity brought on by nine-month-old twins, and representing the closest thing I had to a best friend at that point – or any point in my mixed-up, disaster-strewn, battle-scarred life – she ignored my protestations that it was a waste of time.

"No arguments, Faith. I need some romance! I'm going to remind myself what life was like before existing on four hours' sleep a night and leftover mushed-up vegetables. And you need to show that bag of Botox Larissa who's boss. Get your jacket."

Marilyn and I had met three months earlier, at my first meeting with the Houghton Country Club Committee, known to its members as HCC. Most of the sleek, silky, skinny women greeted me with patronizing smiles, before dismissing me as irrelevant. None of them recognized me from my time serving on the other side of the bar, but they had no doubt heard the gossip. Marilyn, on the other hand, grinned at me across the table. "Nice to meet you, Faith. Although, I have to say the service in here isn't what it used to be. Someone told me their best waitress ran off with a millionaire playboy."

I smiled, and declined to comment. I didn't know if Perry was a millionaire or not, but he certainly deserved the playboy reputation. Until now. I hoped.

After two hours discussing such grave matters as, at the top of the list, whether or not to ban non-organic cucumber in the cricket teas, Marilyn invited me for coffee at her cottage of chaos. I accepted, consuming enough cheesecake and hilarious HCC committee stories to send me home with a stomach ache and sore ribs. And now, here we were, sneaking through Nottingham Lace Market on the hunt for a wedding dress.

The assistant in the first boutique we stopped at smoothed out my skirt, before standing back to reveal my reflection.

I gazed at the woman in the mirror, at her dark auburn hair peeking out from a vintage-style veil and her miraculously cinched-in waist. It looked perfect. The neckline just high enough to cover the scar running underneath her collarbone. Shimmer and shine to deflect attention from the wan, sunken eyes and hollow cheekbones.

I didn't deserve this dress. I never expected or even hoped for it. People like me don't get dresses like this. In wonderment and awe, forgetting the complicated reasons behind the whole need for a wedding dress in the first place, I stepped out of the changing room to show Marilyn, who was lounging on a stripy sofa with a glass of Buck's Fizz.

"Hooten tooten, Faith. You. Are. Beautiful." She screwed up her round face and let out a honking sob. At that point I too burst into tears, pressing my fingers against both cheeks to prevent hot, salty water dripping onto the most beautiful dress in the world.

Marilyn blew her nose, producing more honks. I thought about the frightful, flouncy frock hanging up in its layers of protective wrapping in my wardrobe, and cried even harder. Thick, hiccupy, non-bride-like gulps. Sheesh. I had to pull myself together. I hadn't cried in eight years. Where was this coming from?

My friend wiped her eyes, before offering me her orange, baby-food-stained handkerchief. With a look of horror, the shop assistant dived to intercept, handing me a pure white tissue from a lilac box. Marilyn shook her head. "You have to have this dress. Or another one like it. The last one you tried on, or the one before that. Even the dress in the window with the purple bow and the weird frilly train. All of them are better than the Ghost Web. You have to do this, Faith! If you can't stand up to her, destroy it! Rip it! Burn it! Spill red wine on it! Give it to Nancy and Pete!" Nancy and Pete were Marilyn's twins, currently being looked after by her sister. "I'll do it for you. I'll destroy the Ghost Web."

The Ghost Web is Marilyn's name for my future mother-in-law's wedding dress, because it droops like a sorry, lonely ghost and is covered in peculiar grey net like a cobweb. I know this dress well because, despite having only met my mother-in-law-to-be Larissa four times, she has decided that sometime next year I'll be gliding – or shuffling, one or the other – down the aisle in it. That is, the aisle of her choosing. That is, the aisle of the Houghton Country Club. No, I didn't know either that anyone in twenty-first-century Nottinghamshire belonged to country clubs, until I got a job there a few years ago.

The dress is too long, as at barely five foot three I am seven inches shorter than the original owner. The bodice also needs serious alterations, as I have what fashion stylists call an hourglass figure, and what my charming mother-in-law terms "nothing a bit of hard work and self-control couldn't rectify". The reasons why Larissa insists I wear it are manifold, layered like an onion. The layers include control, selfishness, family pride, and superiority. I wonder if at the centre of this onion is the hope that when her son sees me walk down the aisle in that dress he'll do a runner out the side door.

Perry, my fiancé, wants to think it is a touching gesture, symbolizing my warm welcome into his family.

He hasn't seen the Ghost Web.

* * *

Mission accomplished, Marilyn and I stopped off at a nearby tea shop. She sighed, shaking the equivalent of about six teaspoons of sugar into her full-fat latte. "What are you going to do?"

I shrugged. "I don't know. It's only a dress. I'll talk to the seamstress doing the alterations and see what changes she can make."

"That's not the issue here, and you know it. If this woman decides your dress, she's going to be hovering over you the rest of your marriage. Like a ghost. Or a spider in a web. You have to stop this now! You need your own wedding dress, or how are you going to be your own woman?"

I did. I needed my own dress. The problem was I had no money to buy my own dress and no idea what kind of dress I even wanted. The truth? I had lost control of my life a long, long time ago. I still had the scar on my stomach from the last time I pushed to be my own woman.

"I'll talk to Perry, see what he says."

"You do that. Bat those gorgeous eyelashes at him. Now, what's next on the list?"

Next on the list was a church. I would rather get married in a wheelie bin than HCC. Having slept in a wheelie bin once, it might be more appropriate. Except nobody on the face of this earth except me and a drunk old man knows I slept there.

"Brooksby."

An hour or so later, pressing on with the fake wedding plans, we drove into the village where I spent the latter part of my childhood. Avoiding the road passing the House of Hideous Memories, Marilyn parked in the tiny car park next to the central square of shops. Houghton's poor neighbour, Brooksby had grown rapidly since the initial slump following the pit closure. Well on the way to becoming a commuter town, the old, independent shops were being slowly replaced with high street chains – a bakery, a chemist, a newsagent, and two decidedly non-super supermarkets. Coming to a stop outside the tiny chapel, I paused to look at the dark red brick, the one stained-glass window, and the ugly car park.

Marilyn frowned at me. "Here?"

I nodded. "It was my mum's church."

"She got married here?"

"No. She never got married."

"Will it fit an Upperton wedding?" Perry's family, the Uppertons, would be planning an extravagant guest list.

"Well, given that this is my fantasy wedding, in which the sum total of guests equals five, including your family, I think we'll manage it."

She nodded her head. "Excellent. I need plenty of room since my body seems to have forgotten that it no longer requires the space for two extra people inside it. Let's have a butcher's."

Marilyn must have been curious about my lack of fantasy wedding guests, and why four-fifths of them were made up of a family I had only known for a few weeks. But she didn't ask. She never asked. And I loved her for it.

I tried the front door, which was locked. We could see lights on, however, in the adjacent hall, so after knocking and waiting for a couple of minutes we walked round and rang the bell by the side door. A moment later it opened, and an older woman with hair like a shiny black helmet, a black pencil skirt, and a starchy cream blouse stood in the doorway. She looked us up and down, then at the path behind me.

"Is it just you?"

"Um. Yes."

"There isn't anyone else?"

"I don't think so." We checked behind us, to be sure.

"No one at all?" She sounded incredulous now, her face stiff, lips barely moving. "Well, you'd better come in. The others are waiting."

She turned around and marched off. Slightly at a loss, we followed her up the steps, through a dark porch, and into the church side hall. It had been redecorated since I had visited as a young girl. The cracking plaster had gone, exposing soft pink brickwork covered in bright paintings of outdoor scenes. Instead of the tired carpet the floor now gleamed with light oak boards, and the rows of chairs lined up in the front half of the room were no longer cheap plastic but a combination of wood and red-cushioned seats. The woman strode to the front of the room, coming to a stop next to an upright piano. About a dozen other people sat dotted along the first three rows.

"Well, come along then. You've already missed the warm-up. Find a seat please."

"Excuse me?" I asked, as Marilyn plonked herself down on one of the chairs, shuffling about to get comfortable as she winked at the person beside her.

The helmet woman ignored me, addressing the wooden beams above our heads. "Everybody back in positions. From the beginning, Rowan."

An older teenager, presumably Rowan, cleared her throat. As the rest of the room stood up, Marilyn gestured for me to move next to her before opening her bag and pulling out a packet of toffees.

Helmet woman blew out a large puff of air. "When you're ready, Rowan!"

Rowan, five foot two inches of scrawny nothing, jerked her head at Marilyn, who offered her a toffee. "Who's that, then? I don't wanna do it with them gawpin' at me."

Helmet closed her eyes, momentarily. "You know this is our open afternoon. Would it make you feel better if our new recruits came to the front and introduced themselves? Then perhaps we can start. *Seven minutes late.*"

I answered from where I was. "Um, sorry, but we're not here for this. We wanted to look at the church. I'm getting married."

She stared at me for a good long moment, eyes hovering on the massive chunk of rock I wore on my ring finger before seeking out Marilyn. "You – put that disgusting bag away. No food until we're finished. None of that fake food *ever*. Now, repeat after me." She let out a long, high, clear note that bounced off the stained-glass window and rattled our eardrums.

Marilyn stood up. About half a semitone lower – in other words, painfully flat – she sang, "I'll eat fake food if I want to, thank you very muuuuuch!"

Helmet waited for her to finish, and turned to me. "Aaaahhhhhh," she sang, low like sweet, dark treacle.

I looked back at her. *Really?*

"Come on. Put that pre-wedding stress into it. Aaaaahhhhhhh."

She marched up to me as she sang the note, eyes piercing beneath beetling brows.

I shifted about and glanced over at Marilyn, who smiled at me and stuck another toffee in her mouth. "Aahh."

"Louder! Come on. You've got more to give than that!"

"Aaahh." I upped my volume, minutely.

Helmet stood about four inches in front of me, and thrust her face forwards. "Let go your tension!" she sang. All on the same deep note. "From here, here, and here." She pointed to my shoulders, the centre of my chest, and my stomach. "La, la, la, la, let it gooooo!"

Having a stranger stick her finger at me and sing accusations about my stress levels (however true) in my face did stoke my inner furnace. I had learned how to be tough. To be a survivor. Fierce even. I could happily have kicked my mother-in-law to the kerb weeks ago. Gone back to a life of grot and grime and struggling to keep my head above water rather than compromise my independence. But it wasn't about me. And I would shut my mouth, swallow my anger, scoop up all my doubts, and carry them down the aisle dressed in a dishrag if it kept my brother alive.

People singing in my face? Not happening.

"Baaaaaccckkkk ooooofffffff!" I sang. Helmet closed one eye, backing off slightly.

"Baaaack oooooff. Like that, hold the nooooote. Ooooff. Release all your emotion into it. Oooooff." She sang back every word at me.

"Oooooff," I repeated, mentally adding a word in front of it that I wouldn't say out loud in church.

"Once moooore – ooooooff. Sing it with meeeeee."

We sang together, and I allowed into that note about five per cent of the frustration, fear, and helplessness squatting in my stomach. It seemed to be enough. A tiny crease flickered at the corner of her mouth. I guessed it was a smile. I did not smile back.

"Alto. You can sit with them while you wait for the minister to arrive. He'll be here at four." She gestured towards the women on the right hand side. "You," – she pointed at Marilyn – "feel free to keep plugging your mouth with those sweets. For now."

I took a couple of steps towards the alto section, then another one back towards the door. Helmet spoke as she returned to the front. "Take a deep breath. Let it out slowly. Notice how light you feel. Has a tiny portion of stress been carried off by that one note? That's just one. Think about what a bar, a line, a verse, a whole cantata will do. The power of music. One glance at those shoulders tells me you are a woman who needs to regain some personal power. That's what we're all about here."

She was right. I did need to regain some personal power. It had felt good la-ing out some emotion at the strange woman. I wanted to la some more, sing out some of the twisted, scrunched-up feelings so they could stretch and spread their wings. Maybe they would even flap out the door and never come back.

Marilyn sat down again, pulled out an emery board, and started filing her nails as she whispered to the girl beside her. To be fair, it was as good a place as any to wait for the minister to arrive. I stole around to the alto seats, where a black woman who looked to be somewhere in her thirties moved along to make room for me. Helmet turned her attention back to Rowan, the skinny girl with hair like a Disney princess, and this time, instead of arguing, Rowan began to sing.

How someone could flip from a coarse, jagged whinge to the voice of an angel, I had no idea. If I could sing like that, I would never speak. The notes were running water, the sun coming out from behind a cloud, an eagle in flight, a mountaintop. The words weren't English – I guessed it was Latin – but oh, I understood every single mesmerizing, heart-squeezing, aching syllable. Four lines in, the other members of the group joined her. The water became an ocean, the sun a galaxy, the mountaintop a whole range, stretching out into the distance. At once beautiful, majestic, powerful, and mysterious. They sang of loneliness and betrayal, utter sorrow and bitter loss, the harmonies blending together as they gradually grew stronger, building to a crescendo of triumph.

Talk about goosebumps. Marilyn had been frozen, nail file in hand, since the second note. I wanted to clap, but feared the crudeness of the action shattering the glorious, lingering silence, so heavy I could touch it.

Helmet pursed her lips. "Not bad. You're getting it, soprano twos. Soprano ones – drippy. A cold, wet nose. Alto ones – clompy. A drunk, overweight auntie dancing at a wedding. Alto twos – timorous. A bunch of morose mice. Again."

They sang again, and again, with little rest between Helmet's metaphors (sloppy rice pudding, faded tea towels, anxious bluebottles). Individuals were asked to repeat phrases, relearn melodies, copy strange mouth positions, and breathe in the right places. They broke up into the four different parts for group work and went over everything again.

An hour later, as the choir closed by performing the whole piece one last time, somebody behind me did start clapping. Turning round, I saw a man, leaning on the wall at the back of the hall. He nodded his approval, a thick mop of dark, unruly curls flopping, shadowy jawline definitely more couldn't-care-less than designer stubble or hipster beard. Dressed in a scruffy jacket, with paint-stained hands and a tool belt strapped to his ripped trousers, I assumed he was the caretaker.

Helmet dismissed the choir, and the group began murmuring as they checked their phones, two of the women opening the serving hatch into a kitchen where refreshments stood waiting.

The man wandered over to where I sat, still slightly spellbound by the music, and nodded hello. "Are you going to join?" He had a faint Yorkshire accent, the solid vowels complementing his capable appearance.

I shook my head. "I'm not exactly sure. I sort of ended up here."

He grinned, white teeth gleaming in his swarthy complexion. "I don't think anyone actually chooses to join the choir. More like the choir chooses you."

"I was hoping to speak to the minister."

"Oh?" He raised an eyebrow and started walking over towards the serving hatch. "Coffee? It's filter. Or there's tea. But the coffee's better."

I glanced around the room. With no minister-type person yet appearing, and Marilyn helping herself to a custard cream, I figured I might as well have a drink while we waited. Plus, I was freezing.

"Tea, please."

He leaned forwards to speak to the person inside the hatch, and I noticed a streak of cobweb tangled in his curls. I thought about the Ghost Web, followed by a ripple of disappointment.

I hovered for a moment while someone topped up the teapot, waiting for the leaves to brew. The caretaker chatted easily with the rest of the women, flashing that brilliant smile, making a joke about the poor quality of the biscuits. When he turned to hand me my drink, one of them reached up and plucked out the cobweb, shaking her head at him before pretending to put it in her pocket like a souvenir. He ignored her gesture, nodding politely as he moved away.

"I'm Dylan." He handed me my drink.

"Faith."

"Pleased to meet you, Faith. A perfect name for a choirgirl." He smiled at me over the top of his mug.

"Maybe. Shame I haven't got the perfect voice." I looked away, disconcerted by his open gaze. Disconcerted about feeling disconcerted. I had learned the hard way not to let a handsome man's smile get to me.

"Oh, Hester'll find it in there somewhere. She knows what she's doing."

18

"Hester? Ah – right. The conductor. Choirmaster. Mistress!" I pretended to concentrate on drinking my tea.

Dylan kindly ignored my flustered demeanour – probably well used to his effect on women, engaged or otherwise. "Yes. She talks tough, but she loves her choir. Refuses to let them settle for anything but the best."

"The best singing?"

"That too."

We pondered that thought for a minute. Helmet – Hester – stood on the other side of the room, frowning as she listened to a young Asian woman wearing a headscarf and a long, black cardigan with grey jeans.

"You wanted to see the minister?"

"Yes. I'm looking for a wedding venue."

I pretended that I imagined the micro-flash of surprise on his face. I tried with reasonable success to believe my new, swanky haircut and expensive clothes hid the underlying truth about my utter lack of respectability, but the rapidly concealed expression was a punch to my guts. First Hester, now this bloke. Was this a magic church that revealed my hidden secrets to all of the staff? Did God tell them?

"This isn't most brides' first choice. Not those that aren't members anyway. They tend to prefer the C of E. It makes better pictures. And fits more people in. Why did you pick Grace Chapel? You don't live in the village, do you?"

"Not currently, no. And I'd rather discuss that with the minister, when he finally turns up." I heard the snap in my voice, and tried to wind my wedding-plan irritation back in. This was supposed to be a fun day. And it was only my fantasy wedding, after all. "Sorry. I don't mean to be rude. It's just... private. And churches make me nervous. I can't help finding all that holiness a bit creepy."

He shrugged, smiling to indicate no offence taken. "Why don't I show you the chapel?"

"Thank you. That would be great. I'll grab my friend."

We spent a few minutes wandering around the hall while the

caretaker pointed out the relevant features: where the bride and groom usually sat, where the register was signed, and so on. The room didn't look ugly as much as boring. Plain white walls and ceiling, with one faded banner hanging in between the two narrow windows on one side. More red-cushioned chairs – ten rows of eight; a parquet floor and another piano. Some shelves at the back stuffed with books and that was about it.

Marilyn prowled up and down the centre aisle. "Okay. We can make this intimate rather than cramped. Put some candles in the windowsills, hang fairy lights in the beams. Tiny bouquets of flowers on the ends of the rows?" She carried on describing her ideas for how we would turn this from "dull to quaint" and from "soulless to romantic sophistication".

Dylan, now sprawled on a chair with his legs stretched out into the aisle, straightened up. "Excuse me? Soulless? A more sensitive man could get offended by that. This is a church."

Marilyn flapped her hand at him. "Oh, you know what I mean. Is this minister bloke single? A crusty old bachelor?"

Dylan shook his head. "I'm not sure that's relevant."

"It's absolutely relevant as to why this place is so… stark."

"*Stark?* That's a bit harsh."

"The room's all about functionality. Where's the heart, or the comfort? Anything that would make people other than cyborgs feel at home?"

"*Cyborgs?*"

"Sorry mate, this just isn't the type of place anyone would want to spend time in if they didn't have to. Ask the congregation."

Dylan frowned and looked about, as though seeing the room for the first time. Marilyn was right, but we were strangers here, and her comments were pretty disrespectful.

"Well, thanks for showing us round. It was very kind, considering you've probably got much better things to do than listen to wedding plans. It doesn't look like the minister's going to show. Perhaps I'll call and make an appointment."

"Although," Marilyn added, "if he's always this late, it doesn't bode well for the big day, does it?"

My embarrassment grew. "I'm sure he's not, Marilyn. Ministers must have to deal with important unexpected issues all the time. Maybe somebody died. Or had some terrible news. Or, or... maybe Hester made a mistake."

Dylan shook his head. "No, Hester doesn't make –"

At that moment the door opened and a man dressed in a dishevelled suit, one trainer, and one house slipper burst into the room, instantly followed by a potent cloud of alcohol fumes. "Dylan!" he slurred. "My car's been stolen again!" He shuddered, violently, and let out an anguished wail. "Why do they do it? Why me?"

Dylan strode over, putting his arm around the man's shoulder. "Hey, now. Steady on. We'll find your car. Sylvie's probably driven it home. Let's call her and find out."

As he steered the weaving man out of the door, he turned and pulled an apologetic smile at us. "Sorry about this. If you look online you'll find our website. The contact details are all there if you're still interested. Nice to meet you, Faith. And Faith's friend."

Marilyn watched him leave, then winked at me. "What d'ya reckon? *Interesting?*"

"Behave yourself, married woman with many babies at home. There's only one man I'm interested in, as you know full well."

"You're not married yet. Haven't even set a date. Still plenty of time to avoid shackling yourself to the Ghost Web, and the Ghost Web's previous owner."

We began to leave, too. "I can put up with both of those, if it means marrying Perry. No marriage – or man – is perfect."

"No, but take it from one who knows – no marriages are easy, either. I love you, Faith, and will support you whatever, but this is supposed to be the fun, exciting, head-over-heels bit. If things are tough now... I don't know. My brain is frazzled. I'm probably transferring my own frustrated feelings onto you."

We reached the car, and my good friend Marilyn looked at me before unlocking the doors. "You should be happy. Despite the family and all that goes with it, being with Perry should make you happy. Just make sure you're happy, Faith. That's all."

Happy? What the heck did that even feel like?

* * *

We finished our fantasy wedding plans with a trip to an Italian restaurant on the banks of the River Trent, just outside a village four miles from Brooksby. Housed in a large Victorian country manor with a conservatory wrapped around three sides looking out onto the water, it boasted a huge riverside garden with chairs, tables, and assorted sofas on a canopied patio. Simple, rustic, relaxed, run by a family who had emigrated from Italy only six years before, it was everything I would have dreamed of in a reception venue, had I ever dared to dream of one. At the end of the garden was a wooden area for dancing. I could picture laughter, and music, twinkling lights strung between the trees, great food, and even better wine. A place to let down your hair, sit back, and watch the moon kiss the water. A place where good friends were reunited and new friends were made.

I thought about the HCC function room and its stuffy decor. The fussy menu full of food most people had never tried, and never wanted to. The strict dress code, the ban on children, the uncomfortable chairs. The fact that some there knew I had once been "staff" and now seethed at my crossing over to become one of *them*. Ugh. Dress. Service. Reception. I didn't know which one of the current non-fantasy plans I hated most.

Marilyn gazed out over the water as a barge glided by, slow and easy. She looked as though she wanted to hop onto that boat. I wished I could join her. "This is it, Faith. It's *you*."

I hugged her, vainly attempting to hide my tears. It was not me. It was the me I wished I could one day be. And now almost certainly never would.

Chapter Two

Marilyn dropped me off at Perry's house on her way home. After keying in the security code to let myself into the gated mini-mansion, I found him pacing up and down the sitting room, blond hair standing up on end where his hands had raked through it.

"For goodness' sake, Faith. Where have you been? I was worried sick."

"I was out with Marilyn. Wedding shopping. Why didn't you call me?"

"Your phone was off."

Ah yes. That would be because I had turned it off, in order to enjoy my fake wedding plans in peace.

"Sorry. But I'm a big girl. I do go out by myself sometimes. You don't have to worry."

"Yes, well, I *am* worried. Dedicoat can't make Saturday. He's coming to finalize the Baker deal tonight."

I felt as though a shard of ice had been rammed down my windpipe. Perry had been working on the Baker deal for ten months. I'd agreed to cater a dinner party for Perry and his colleague Eddie, to soften up the notoriously hard-nosed business guru Lucas Dedicoat before they signed on the dotted line. "What time are they coming?"

"Seven."

"Are you still expecting me to cook?"

"Well, yes."

"I haven't got the ingredients yet. I mean, it's all planned out but I need a trip into Newark, and to the farmer's market. The berries need to soak up the liqueur overnight. I could ditch the dessert, make something simple instead, and rethink the mains... But an hour and a half! And you never have anything in the fridge. You should have called me... you did call me but my phone was off. Oh, pants. Do you think a take-away would do?"

Perry sighed. "No. A take-away will not do. You used to work in a Michelin-starred restaurant. Can't you rustle up something?"

"I guess I'll have to try. But I really need to shower and I'm not exactly dressed for a dinner party." I looked down at my casual skirt and T-shirt. "I can probably find time to brush my hair, but that's it. Can you sort the dining room? Get some wine opened?" I looked around the room, at Perry's shoes kicked off by the sofa, an empty beer bottle and crisp crumbs littering the glass coffee table. This morning's newspaper was in pieces all over the rug, and various other man detritus lay scattered throughout the ground floor.

"What time did you get in from work? Have you been sitting around waiting for me?" I waved my hand across the mess, and Perry smiled, a glint in his eye. He quickly crossed the living room and wrapped his arms around me, firmly kissing the top of my head. "I've been waiting for you my whole life. And you're really sexy when you're up against a challenge. I know you'll do something incredible."

* * *

Two hours later, after thirteen emergency texts to Marilyn on posh business deal-making dinner party etiquette, I was hiding in the vast kitchen, trying to arrange on a serving tray six goat's cheese soufflés that neither tasted like goat's cheese nor looked like soufflé. I had cobbled together a meagre salad out of a few carrots, an old, soft beetroot, and some frozen French beans. A sort-of paella bubbled on the stove, again full of mainly frozen ingredients and a packet of instant spice mix. I picked up the tray just as Perry poked his head in at the door. "What are you doing? We'll have no time to discuss the deal if we don't eat now."

"I'm doing my best." Perry looked at me, at my face mimicking the beetroot, my crumpled skirt, and unwashed hair. My eyes, no doubt wild-looking and bloodshot, scrunched shut. It was only a matter of time before Perry Upperton realized my best was not good enough.

He took three strides into the kitchen, and placed his hands either side of my face. Leaning down to kiss me gently, he murmured, "You look so gorgeous, all steamed up and dishevelled. Don't worry about the food. Dedicoat's girlfriend just told us she likes fried chicken because it's fun to eat out of a bucket, and all Eddie's interested in is getting this deal done. Just come and sit down, try to enjoy yourself."

I would have enjoyed myself more had I been eating cold baked beans out of the tin, hiding in the back of a musty wardrobe. I know this to be a fact, because I have done it.

"So." Five minutes later, Eddie's wife Fleur gave up pretending to nibble her soufflé. "You're the one who finally managed to tame Perry Upperton. Wherever did he find you?"

I took a deep breath, but before I could reply, Perry answered. "We met at HCC. About two years ago. But it took more than half that to persuade her to come for dinner with me."

"Really? How fascinating. You're a member of the Club?" Her eyes flicked across my faded T-shirt and back to my never-been-facialled face.

"Yes." I am now. It was an engagement present. I think my in-laws-to-be probably bribed someone to let me in.

"How very old-school. Are your family from around here?"

"My mum grew up in Brooksby. How about you?"

"Well, you could say that. Do you know Teppington Hall?"

Yes, actually. I worked there as a cleaner once…

As we slogged through our starters, I struggled to pay attention.

Eddie and Perry swapped increasingly flash stories about their triumphs in the business world, name-dropping and backslapping as they tried to impress Lucas Dedicoat. Fleur, no doubt an expert at wooing one's husband's boss, batted her eyelashes, simpered, and even stooped to titter at a particularly unamusing story about beating a rival company during an award ceremony dance-off. We all pretended not to notice Lucas spoon-feed the soufflé into his girlfriend's mouth, shuffling his chair around so his back was turned to the rest of the table, and murmuring into her neck repeatedly as she giggled and told him to behave. A faint, bitter, scorched smell began to waft out from the kitchen. However, unsure of the dinner party rules, and unable to find a natural pause in Eddie's current monologue about how the company's core competencies included cost containment, I stayed put, hiding my agitation behind a fake smile.

Eventually Eddie finished, muttering something about not having the distraction of girlfriends next time so they could actually get some work done. Leaping up, I dove into the kitchen to find a dried-up, hissing disaster where the paella used to be.

"Oh no, no, no, no, no." I whipped the pan off the hot hob and grabbed a spoon to inspect the damage. Scraping beneath the surface of the rice I found a thick black layer of carbonized sludge.

I skimmed off the top layer, dumped it in a serving bowl and chucked in some water from the kettle, stirring it maniacally in a vain attempt to rehydrate the non-scorched rice.

"Argh!" Some water splashed out of the bowl and landed on my pale blue T-shirt in a greasy, grainy splodge, right in the middle of one breast.

"Well. At least I hadn't boiled the kettle first." I used a teaspoon to scoop up a rice blob and taste it.

"Hmm. Well. It'll taste better hot."

I shoved the bowl into the microwave, taking a frantic minute to figure out how to turn it on before realizing it wasn't plugged in, and then sponged at the mark on my top with a dishcloth.

Lovely. I now had a much larger brown circle covering my chest. For a second I contemplated adding a second circle to the other side to balance it out, before a wave of forced laughter through the dining room wall yanked me back to the situation at hand.

The microwave pinged. I dumped the now sizzling bowl back on the side, plucked a few leaves from a shrivelled basil plant on the windowsill, and scattered them across the top.

"Perfect. No one will even notice."

I looked at the leaves bobbing about in the grey liquid, surrounded by flecks of ash.

"It's a new trend. Scorched – no – *seared* paella. Yum. Only someone totally out of style would admit to not loving it!"

Hot humiliation prickled my eyes. This wasn't funny. It was Perry's big deal-making dinner, and I'd fried it to a frazzle.

Perry smiled at me as I brought through the bowl of charred slop, carrying it awkwardly in an attempt to hide the stain on my shirt. I looked at the guests in their chic smart-casual outfits, their nails manicured and teeth bleached. On the wall behind the table a huge mirror reflected back my fraught face: red cheeks, out of control hair, a smear of sauce on the side of my nose, eyes red rimmed. For a second I was back in the pigeonhole I had put myself in for so many years – one of *them* not *us*.

Huh. I glanced down at the bowl and back up again. I have a lot to hide. A burnt paella and messy top don't even register on the secrets scale.

I placed the bowl on the table, slightly harder than intended.

"Okay. This is burnt, and is, quite frankly, inedible. There's nothing else in the cupboards except for dry pasta and a sachet of custard. Charlie's Chips, however, is open until eleven. They do an excellent battered sausage. Oh, and the stain on my boob is burnt paella juice."

The silence hung above the table for a couple of seconds. Then Lucas coughed and said, "I'll have a haddock and chips. Lots of vinegar and mushy peas, please."

Fleur blinked a couple of times. "Um. Do they do anything gluten-free?"

"The kebabs are pretty good." Perry winked at me. "Or how about a pickled egg?"

* * *

In the end, the men decided to walk to the chippy together. To my surprise, Fleur and Dedicoat's girlfriend Starr came to help me clear up, equally outraged, sympathetic, and impressed when I told them how I'd created a three-course meal out of leftovers in under an hour.

"And Eddie's rambling anecdotes meant it got ruined. I apologize on his behalf, Faith. Usually I kick him under the table to shut him up but he'd warned me to be on my best behaviour in front of Dedicoat. Having said that, if he sprang a dinner party on me with less than forty-eight hours' notice I'd be kicking more than his shin."

"The only thing I can cook is pizza and Pot Noodle." Starr marvelled at my desserts chilling in the fridge. Individual Irish cheesecakes made using an old packet of ginger biscuits, a tub of cream cheese, Perry's secret chocolate stash, and a splash of Baileys.

Starr lent me a spare top. "I always carry a couple, 'cos I sometimes end up staying out all night, and I might have a meeting at work."

"This is what you wear to your work meetings?" The top was low-cut and completely transparent. I decided to wear it over my T-shirt rather than instead of it. The blotch of sauce still showed through the netting, but at least the crystals and picture of a dog in a onesie provided some distraction.

The men returned, boisterously banishing plates and cutlery in favour of tiny wooden forks and chip paper. Lucas made me feel a lot less self-conscious by accidentally squirting ketchup over his shirt, and we ditched any lingering trace of formality along with the table.

Lounging on the sofas, cans of pop in their hands, Lucas and Eddie toasted a done deal over their empty wrappers, while Perry rummaged through his dresser looking for a pack of cards. Starr and Fleur giggled as they googled wedding paraphernalia on their phones, swapping stories of the best and worst ever in various different categories: bridesmaid dresses, best man's speech, first dance.

Amongst all this merriment, I sat back and gave myself a mental pat on the back. If this was how posh married people's dinner parties went, I could handle it. I could even look forward to it. Perhaps next time I'd think up a fast-food menu – do a home-made pizza with chintzy paper napkins and a tablecloth you could colour in while you waited.

The doorbell rang. Feeling quite the hostess with the mostess, I wandered through to answer it.

And there, standing in the porch, soaking wet, reeking and dishevelled, was the reason I had finally given in and said yes to Peregrine Upperton.

* * *

I quickly pulled Sam into the kitchen, searching his face for the telltale signs of drugs or alcohol. Flicking on the coffee machine, I pushed him into a chair. "Don't move."

I threw the cheesecakes onto a tray and carried them into the living room. Perry stood handing out pens and pieces of paper. "Who was it?"

I hesitated, causing the guests to look up at me, suddenly interested.

"It's Sam."

"Ah." Perry had only met Sam once, the day he left the treatment centre. As Perry had paid for it, I figured the least I could do was introduce them. What I had chosen not to mention was that the centre didn't only treat mental health issues – which had crippled Sam for years. It also provided rehabilitation for those suffering from addictions. And my poor, lost, smashed-up brother ticked that box too. In the three months since then, Sam had moved back into his flat half a mile from me in Houghton, kept up his medication, and willingly attended his support group once a week. He had even talked about painting again – his rickety means of earning a living. But I had been waiting for the crash. Expecting it. I had been through this too many times before to hope the cycle was broken. I knew the symptoms of my brother's plunge into the black whirlpool of mental illness all too well. The shadows in and under his eyes. The self-obsession, the increasing fixation on trivial matters like a dripping tap or the pigeons on the neighbour's roof. The inability to sit still or keep the thread of a conversation, the escalating chaos both external and within.

And then, inevitably, the crash.

"Is everything okay?" Perry stood to take the tray from me. "Sam is Faith's brother. He lives the other side of the village."

"Oh, how lovely!" Starr looked up from her phone. "Bring him in so we can meet him."

"Well, I would, but he's not feeling great. I'll just be a couple of minutes. Please start without me."

Perry met my eyes, his unanswered question hanging in the space above the tray. I gave an infinitesimal nod, and left them to their world, rejoining mine in the kitchen.

Sam slumped onto the breakfast bar, his arms over his head. I poured him a coffee and brought it over. "Drink this."

He ignored the cup, and me.

"Sam."

Pulling his head up from under his arms, he looked at me with utter bleakness, eyes swimming in despair. "He's coming out, Faith."

"What?" An invisible, icy hand clamped itself around my neck and began to squeeze.

"In two weeks. They're letting Kane out."

The last things I heard were the smash of the coffee mug into a thousand shards on the Italian tiled floor, and, a split second later, me crashing down with it.

Chapter Three

Sam started drinking almost as soon as the trial finished, eighteen years ago. We were living with our grandmother, back in Brooksby, and still reeling from the hideous shock of our mother's death. At six, I had been more sheltered from the horrors of what had come before, and the night that ended it all. It was only as I grew older that I began to grasp what both my mother and Sam had shielded me from. This being, primarily, the monster we called Kane.

Upon moving to Grandma's house Sam continued his role as protector – coming to hold me when the nightmares came, brightening my days with silly stories and surprise presents like a flower, or a piece of paper twisted into the shape of a mouse, coaxing me out of my hiding place in the wardrobe. He walked me to school every morning, before sprinting to reach his secondary school on time. He helped me with my homework, took me to the park or the library when Grandma needed a rest, and every single day made sure I felt safe, loved, and that I was not alone.

But the previous years had taken their toll – done deep damage that refused to heal long after Sam's physical scars faded. Grandma tried, but she was hopelessly ill-equipped to deal with the anger and hurt of a boy with Sam's level of trauma. When I remember that time, I still feel my growing distress as my hero began to disappear – frequently staying out well into the night, retreating into his bedroom the rare times he remained in the house, and meeting Grandma's worried questions with silence.

It was only when I got the unexpected invitation to a classmate's party, held in a pub, that I realized the smell accompanying my brother was alcohol.

By fifteen his attempts to drown out the pain had progressed to cannabis, pills and, soon after, cocaine. He scraped through school for my sake, still surfacing enough to be a surrogate daddy as best he knew how. But the stealing and the lies, the fights and the increasingly bad reputation were more than Grandma could cope with. The week after his seventeenth birthday, when a man showed up at the door with a baseball bat looking for money, she finally cracked. Sam came home the next day to find his meagre possessions waiting in a suitcase in the hallway.

For the next three years my big brother was a fleeting shadow in my life. Without him, I felt as though I had lost a lung – every breath a challenge, I clambered through the days exhausted, faint-hearted, a whimper of a girl. The days I would exit the school gates to find him slouched against the wall across the street were like brief bursts of oxygen.

We would hug, for a long, long time, before setting off to walk around the village, or find a seat in the café if it was too cold or wet.

"How are you?" he would ask, eyes hungry as he searched my face.

"I'm fine. I got an A in English."

He smiled. "Good for you. You look taller. Have you grown again?"

"I'm taller than Grandma now."

"Is she being okay? Managing to take care of you? Does she give you enough money for clothes and things?"

I felt too anxious to tell Sam that for weeks now I had been the one doing all the shopping and paying the bills.

"Yes. We're fine."

"Good." He sighed, and I caught a whiff of the toxins on his breath.

Look closer, Sam. Look at me. I'm not fine! I need you. Grandma keeps forgetting things and getting tired all the time and I'm trying to keep everything tidy and make her pension last till the end of the week, but it's so hard. I need you. Come home. Come back to me.

We would chat a little longer, but soon his hands would start to twitch and eyes wander beyond me to the café door. Sometimes before going he asked if I could lend him money. Other times he would offer out a fat roll of notes. I didn't take them. Those notes scared me. They were tainted with the unmentionable things he must have done to get them. Instead I would lie about how Grandma had doubled my pocket money that month (which could have been true – zero doubled is still zero), or how I'd babysat for a neighbour.

But even when the months stretched past without a visit, every night I went to sleep thinking of my brother. Praying for his safety, wishing he would come home, imagining the dark and dangerous places and people he dwelled amongst.

And then, one morning, I woke up to find Grandma cold on the bathroom floor.

And I learned my wildest imaginings hadn't come close.

* * *

Sam fled before the coffee had cooled on the tiles, but by the time Perry had carried me to a sofa, tidied up the mess, and said a charming, if brisk, goodbye to the guests, I felt recovered enough to get up again.

Perry found me in the kitchen. I turned from loading the dishwasher, a thousand apologies on my lips.

"Leave that. I can do it. You need to sit down."

I mustered a weak smile. "No, I'm fine. Just embarrassed. I didn't think I could top that meal, but…"

Perry leaned against the countertop, his hands in his pockets. "What happened with Sam?"

"It wasn't Sam. I'm really sorry he came round – he does that sometimes when he's not well. And when he texted me earlier this evening I mentioned I was here. But I must have had a weird migraine. Or maybe the residual smoke overpowered me. It's been a really busy day."

He walked over and took my hands in his, lifting one to kiss it. "I'm sorry I caused you so much stress. You were amazing tonight. You saved the day. And the Baker deal. I'm so glad you were here. Will you come to all my disaster parties?"

"If you give me a couple of days' notice, they might not be a disaster."

He gazed at me. "Fifteenth of August."

"Now that should be enough notice."

He was no longer laughing. "Marry me on the fifteenth of August. Come and live with me and you can burn my dinner every night."

"You expect me to cook you dinner every night when we're married?"

"You can do whatever you darn well like. Just marry me."

I took a deep breath. "The fifteenth of next August?"

"The very next one."

"HCC will be booked up right through the summer."

"They had a cancellation." He quirked one eyebrow, knowing I would guess his hefty sway at the club would have had something to do with that.

"Let me think about it."

While Perry drove me home, I thought. About Sam, and my empty bank account, pathetically dependent on Perry since my income had been slashed. About how this rich, charming man had laughed off the disastrous evening, allowing me to avoid answering his questions about my wreck of a brother. About the fun we had together, the simplicity of our relationship. Then I considered the alternative to marrying him, which made me shudder.

Perry walked me to my door, which wasn't far, the front path of my tiny terraced cottage stretching three steps from pavement to porch.

"Are you sure you're okay? I could come in for a bit."

"No, honestly. I just need to sleep."

He waited while I unlocked the door, then kissed me goodnight. "Sleep well. I've meetings until late tomorrow. But I'll call you."

I took a deep breath as he turned to walk down the path.

"Yes."

He froze, spinning slowly back around to face me.

"The fifteenth of August. Next year. Yes."

Perry burst into a grin, scooping me off the doorstep and swinging me around a couple of times before jigging down to the street and back again, kicking his heels up. "Fifteenth of August!" he roared. "Eleven months and she'll be mine! Hallelujah!"

He let out a whoop as I stepped inside, smiling. "Keep it down! It's nearly midnight."

"I don't care! I'm getting MARRIED!" He fist-pumped the air as the upstairs window opened next door and my neighbour called out.

"Fer mercy's sake, Faith. Can't you just invite 'im in like a normal person?"

"Ah no, kind neighbour," Perry replied, ever the gentleman. "Surely you know there is nothing normal about Faith Harp?"

I said goodnight and closed the door, leaning on it for a moment while my brain slowed down enough to think.

Perhaps my fiancé knew me better than I thought, because he'd got it spot on. Nothing about me, or my life, had ever been normal.

I certainly didn't feel normal as I lay awake, listening to the creaks and groans of my ancient house, shuddering with terror at the thought of the evil that was Kane, prowling the streets, hunting for revenge.

The next morning I stuck my game face on and went to see Sam. I took the bus to the supermarket first, loading up with bags of ready meals, cereal, fresh juice, fruit, and other simple food a sick man could eat with minimal preparation. Upon letting myself in, I did a quick walk-through of the flat, searching for the all-too-familiar paraphernalia that accompanies drug use. Finding nothing in the living area but empty cola bottles, ten thousand cigarette butts, piles of dirty dishes, and sticky filth coating every surface (pretty impressive since I had cleaned the entire flat only five days previously), I moved on to the bathroom.

Yuck.

I left the bathroom to its grossness and began to unload the shopping. I was placing a tub of fresh soup in the fridge when the bedroom door opened and a naked cheese string walked out, pointing a six-inch knife at me.

"What are you doing?" The cheese string, who on closer inspection appeared to actually be a woman the width of a cheese string with an enormous head of greeny-yellow dreadlocks, jabbed the knife in my direction.

I wasn't intimidated. The scars on my collarbone and stomach were caused by a knife, and person, about twice the size of those in front of me. Six inches would never pierce my toughened hide.

"Unpacking some shopping. Do you want a cranberry muffin?"

She waved the blade a little less convincingly. "Who are you?"

"Clearly no one for you to worry about. I'm bringing stuff in, not taking it away. Reverse burglary." I carried on emptying the bags. "Put the knife down and get some clothes on. And while you're in there tell Sam his sister's here."

She obeyed me, even coming back in a scruffy tracksuit and making a token gesture at washing up while introducing herself as April.

Sam shuffled out a few minutes later, olive skin wan under his black beard. I handed him a bacon sandwich, set down a mug of tea, and tried to hold back my newly resurrected tears, and my temper.

"Would you mind leaving us alone for a few minutes, please, April?" I asked.

April, one of the many, many sorry young women to fall for Sam's brooding good looks and artistic talents, ducked her head. "Is it all right if I have a shower, Sam?"

He ignored her. April disappeared, and I took a seat opposite my brother.

"Tell me."

He rubbed his face, took a gulp of tea, and started to weep.

A short while later, having read the letter from the probationary service explaining that Kane would indeed be free in two weeks' time (unless something miraculous happened like he murdered someone else or tripped in the shower and broke both legs and arms), we were wrung out like damp washing.

We had no reason to believe Kane could find us, even if he tried. Sam and I both took different names after the trial – and no one alive knew save for the original Family Liaison Officer assigned to the case and a couple of social workers we hadn't seen in over a decade. While we did currently live in our mother's home county, we were several miles from Brooksby, one hundred and nineteen miles from where we had lived with Kane, and two hundred and fifty from the prison that would release him. It had been eighteen years. He would be on probation for the rest of his life, one of the conditions being that he never attempted to contact us. He had other things to worry about, scores to settle.

Did all this make the slightest bit of difference to the lightning bolt of terror that had struck the centre of our brains?

Nope.

I called Sam's mental health nurse and told her he was struggling. She promised to be round after wading through the other reams of dangerously distressed patients on her books, most of whom were without a sister with bucketloads of free time to care for them. I sat with Sam through a couple of hours of daytime quiz shows, then double-checked for hidden booze stashes. Before leaving I firmly told April her new boyfriend was an addict with serious mental health issues, and in no fit state to offer any sort of relationship. If she did insist on hanging around, and did anything – *at all* – to empower his addictions I would take her teeny, tiny knife and chop her fingers off one by one.

Yes, I was feeling fairly angry and defensive that morning. My past-life ferocity had been awoken from its recent slumber. I was talking the finger-chopping talk. Would I walk the walk? Probably not. Definitely not. Nah.

I paced the streets around Sam's flat, ending up on a bench near to the cemetery. Having brought my hyperventilating under control, I called Marilyn.

"Faith! How are you doing? Did you destroy the Ghost Web?"

Least of my problems.

"Hi Marilyn. I need cake. And a baby to cuddle. Are you busy?"

"I have nine-month-old twins, I'm always busy. Yet never too busy for cake. I'll leave the door on the latch in case I'm feeding. Or just too knackered to get off the sofa."

I spent the rest of the afternoon tickling fat tummies (Nancy and Pete's, not Marilyn's) and eating millionaire's shortbread, which Marilyn found amusingly appropriate.

Halfway through the afternoon Perry texted to say he'd booked the wedding with HCC.

That led to a wrestling match with Marilyn while she prised my phone away and started typing a reply saying I wanted to get married in Grace Chapel and have my reception at Mirabelli's on the Water.

"Marilyn!" Nancy chose that moment to throw up on her activity centre, allowing me to get the phone back. "I don't care. I just want things over with with as little fuss as possible so I can get on with being Perry's wife."

"As little fuss as possible? And you see that happening at HCC? Have you met your future mother-in-law Larissa Upperton? Have you been to a committee meeting? Did you not used to work at HCC as events manager? Short-term pain for long-term gain, Faith. That man appears to be bonkers about you. Why do you think he would object?" She paused in her cleaning up of Nancy's sick and waggled the muslin cloth at me.

I waggled my hands back. "Hello? Have *you* met my future mother-in-law Larissa Upperton, the Achilles' heel?"

"You need to come back to the choir with me next week. Get some personal power."

"You're going back to the choir? Hester didn't even let you sing." I sat back, surprised.

"I don't care. I liked listening. And my sister doesn't have to know that when I ask her to babysit again. Two hours without my delightful children. Three if you count the journey there and back. And once James is gone again the chance of a breather might be the only thing keeping me from going bananas."

James, Marilyn's husband, worked as a consultant geologist. This meant frequent long stretches away while he mined for valuable minerals in places like Antarctica or at the bottom of the ocean. Marilyn told me that before the twins had been born, she had found this lonely and frustrating, but coped with it as part of the deal. Judging from the state of the cottage of chaos while James was around, I didn't want to think how she would cope alone with two demanding, exhausting babies added to the equation.

At least she wouldn't have time to feel lonely.

* * *

The following Wednesday afternoon, we headed back to Grace Chapel. I'd put my fantasy wedding plans on hold for the week, but this seemed as good an excuse as any to meet with the minister. Assuming, of course, he showed up this time.

We arrived just as the rehearsal started. Hester gave me an unsmiling nod as I slid in beside the other altos. When Marilyn, who had lingered in the corridor to message her sister, sauntered in after me, the choir director's eyebrow twitched. Translate: gobsmacked.

"Good afternoon, Marilyn. I didn't expect to see you here."

"Well, it's a wonderful surprise then, isn't it?" Marilyn waved at everybody.

"This is a serious choir rehearsal. Last week's open day was a one-off. We don't allow just anyone to sit in."

"Lucky I'm not just anyone."

"Please don't make this difficult."

Marilyn sighed. "All right. I'll go. As long as the choir agree."

Hester tutted. "Well, I can't think why they would object."

Marilyn opened up the canvas bag in her hand and took out a tin. Removing the lid, she released the warm, sugary, cinnamon smell of freshly baked apple loaf. Several pairs of eyes darted to the serving hatch, where a plate of plain biscuits sat forlornly on the counter.

Hester pulled her spine even tauter, flaring her nostrils. It was high noon at the O.K. Corral, formidable personality versus home-made cake. Rowan was the first to speak up. "Let her stay, Hester. Apple cake's one of my favourites."

"It does smell pretty good," one of the Asian women, Uzma, said.

"I chipped a tooth on one of them biscuits a couple of weeks ago," an older lady in the soprano section called out. "Look." She opened her mouth wide and pointed into it. "Can you see it, Millie? There, at the back, next to the gold filling."

"I can't see it, Janice." Millie, who walked on two sticks and wore a bobble hat even though it was one of the hottest Septembers on record, peered in.

"There, look." Janice's words were muffled by her finger, pointing out the hole.

"Ooh, I see it. Right in the middle of your molar. That's a biggie, Janice. You should sue for compensation."

"No! Not there. A chocolate peanut from the Vicky Centre market did that one. You know, that stall with the man who wears the monkey T-shirt. It used to sell peanut brittle, but then that dog from the –"

"LADIES!"

Janice and Millie snapped to attention at Hester's command.

"There is no time to discuss this any further. We are already four minutes late. Put the tin in the kitchen and sit down *quietly* at the back. We shall take a vote at coffee time."

"Probably a good idea," Melody, whom I had sat next to last week, whispered in her lilting Jamaican accent, loud enough for everyone to hear. "We can see if it's any good before we vote."

Hester gave another nod, at the same time making a tiny circling gesture with her hands. Everybody stood up.

"Eyes closed!" We closed our eyes, including Marilyn. Then, for the next section of the rehearsal, we did no singing at all.

Accompanied by the soft notes of a violin wafting out from a music player, Hester began to talk. She first told us to take a few deep breaths in and slowly release them, then listen to our bodies.

"What is it telling you today? What can you hear? Is it overworked, exhausted? Uptight and crunched up? Hurting? Weighed down? Sluggish? Does your body feel loved? Whole? Vibrant? Breathe in some love for yourself, ladies. Sigh out that tension. Out, out, ooouuut! Release the troubles and the to-do list. Let it go. Breathe in strength! Let go of your fear. Blow out all that anxiety and angst. Blow it out! That's it, keep blowing…"

About halfway through, as we sighed out all the things we didn't want to have, and be, and breathed in the stuff we wished we did, I felt an overwhelming urge to laugh. What was this? What on earth was I doing here, surrounded by strangers, with my eyes closed, "blowing out disappointment"? I didn't need this. Fine, my life had some issues. But I coped with them pretty well. And how could I be disappointed when I had never expected life to be anything but hard?

And then, suddenly, I felt two warm hands on my shoulders, and realized the choking, hiccupping sobbing was from me. Big, fat, snotty sobs. Like the dam of tears just broke where the leak had formed a week earlier in the wedding shop. I didn't even know why, or where it came from. Melody held me, whispering words of comfort as she rocked me back and forth and stroked my hair. By the time I'd finished, wiped my face, and blown my nose a couple of times, the rest of the choir had moved on to vocal warm-ups, la-ing up and down the scale.

Melody patted my arm. "How do you feel?"

Strange question to ask a woman who had spent the last ten minutes howling. I felt self-conscious, bewildered, and worn out. But not as much as I expected. Mostly, I felt sort of clean.

"What is this place?" I muttered. This place where people see into my soul and guess my deepest feelings, and somehow I'm safe to feel them?

Melody laughed, a deep rich melody. "This is the house of grace."

Following the warm-up, where Hester insisted we stand, breathe, and start to think and sound like singers – "*chins up, lungs open, shoulders back!*" – we moved on to the piece the choir had been working on last time. I had heard some of the alto part, but not all, and had no idea what most of the words were, my knowledge of Latin being non-existent. Hester asked Melody to coach me through it for thirty minutes, and I did all right until we moved back to singing all together. The sopranos, who sang the main tune, kept confusing my brain and knocking me off course. Hester rapped her knuckles on top of the piano.

"Faith! Stop being distracted by women you cannot compare to and were not created to be like! You are an alto – learn from other altos. Listen to them, tune in to them. Focus, focus, focus! You spend too much time worrying about the wrong things, eyes and ears wandering. Find your tune, lady, and hold on to it. From the beginning, last time!"

I tried. I tried to ignore the sopranos with their trills and piercingly beautiful dipping and soaring, focus, focus, focusing in on the depth of the rich, resonant voices around me, earth and deep water, strong and sure. And for a moment – maybe a line, a little longer – I got it. I joined these women in their song.

Wow.

Wouldja believe it?

I helped create something beautiful.

And I would not start crying about it. We'd had enough of that for one day, thank you.

Seriously, though. That was something else.

Rehearsal over, nobody mentioned my earlier "moment" during coffee time. Neither did Hester mention a vote regarding Marilyn, once she'd eaten a tiny, perfectly square piece of her scrumptious cake. Dylan appeared a couple of minutes later, and I tried to ignore the uncomfortable urge to go and check my face for blotches in the women's toilets. Many years of struggle had drummed all potential vanity out of me. I didn't want my new millionaire-fiancée lifestyle to start pumping it back in. I certainly didn't want to feel the need to impress the chapel caretaker, like a desperate housewife swooning over every handsome, rugged man who pays her attention and looks her in the eye when he asks her how she is, as if he actually means it. I fiddled with my engagement ring until the urge scuttled away back where it belonged, deep in the corner of my imagination.

After a couple of minutes of small talk, Dylan asked me about the wedding.

"Did you make any decision about using the chapel?"

"Um, no. Not yet."

"I suppose your fiancé wants to have a look at it."

"Mmm."

"Do you have any more questions? I could show you around again, if that helps."

"No, thanks. I do need to see the minister though, to see if it's okay to get married here when we don't actually come to the church. And if the date's free."

"You've set a date?"

"Yes. August." I still wasn't quite ready to declare the actual day.

"Next year? Not long, then. And the middle of wedding season. You might want to get in there quick."

"Well. If the minister shows up, as Hester said he always does after choir practice, I'll ask him. Although he wasn't here last week. Unless he's so unnoticeable I didn't spot him. Not known for their charisma, generally, vicars, are they?"

Oh dear. I seemed powerless to prevent the torrent of awkward wedding-related verbal diarrhoea…

"Usually quite mousy. Sort of hunched. A bit insipid, like watery custard." I was, in fact, merely describing the minister who showed our class round the chapel fifteen years ago. I didn't actually think all men of the cloth fit the soap opera stereotypes, but I couldn't stop. Dylan made me nervous, looking me in the eye like that. Talking about my wedding made me nervous. When I get nervous my brain gives up and my mouth takes over. "All polite and bland. Maybe he blended into the background. Like a chameleon! A watery, hunched…" I stopped as a horrible realization dawned. "Oh no. It's *you*, isn't it?"

Dylan looked at me. His eyes were a Celtic blue – bright and clear in contrast to his pirate's stubble and shaggy black hair. A muscle jumped in his jaw as he clenched it.

For a brief moment I hoped the combined heat of my hideous embarrassment and Dylan's steady gaze would cause me to melt, so I could ooze between a crack in the floorboards.

"I am so sorry. I didn't actually mean that. I mean, I know not all ministers are like custard." *Did I really say that?* "I'm sure most aren't, even. Hardly any. None! I bet no ministers even slightly resemble custard. At all…" I petered off into a mortified squeak.

Dylan took his eyes off me and stared hard at his shoes. Navy blue Converse. Now, surely *nobody* would guess that a man in those shoes could be a minister? Aren't they supposed to be on a higher plane, above all earthly things like designer labels?

"I suppose you won't want me getting married here now. Totally understandable. You don't want to be marrying someone who's prejudiced against ministers. Ministerist. Shouldn't let them in the chapel, really. And what would God think? You're like, his man on the ground, and I've just called you insipid, in his house of worship. I'm a bit scared, actually, that I've offended God. I think I might see if Marilyn's ready to go home."

I craned my neck, making an exaggerated display of looking for Marilyn.

"Having said that, the tool belt and overalls would have fooled anyone. And you had plenty of opportunity to tell me who you were, instead of all 'call me Dylan', not Reverend Dylan or Pastor Dylan. And aren't people like you supposed to wear dog collars and black shirts, not ripped jeans? Right. Well. I'm going to shut up and leave now. Nice meeting you. I probably won't be seeing you again." I scurried a couple of steps away, before looking back at him. "And you're not, by the way. Unnoticeable. At all."

Dylan's shoulders were shaking. He reached up a hand and wiped both his eyes. Good grief! I knew people in his line of work were supposed to be sensitive, but had my ridiculous babbling made him *cry*? I would definitely never be able to set foot in here again. Stupid, clumsy idiot. It was only because he made me flustered that I even —

He lifted his head and smiled at me, his face bubbling over with mirth. When I tore my gaze away from those blue eyes, sparkling like mountain streams and as wide open as a cloudless, February sky, I saw he held out a card. "Give me a ring. Let me know which date in August and we can set up a meeting with your husband-to-be. I'd like to meet him. And we can discuss your requirements for the service."

I took the card, hoping he didn't notice the tremor in my hand. "Really? Even though I've proven myself to be a terrible, rude, and judgmental heathen? You'll marry us?"

Dylan nodded his head, another smile tugging at his mouth. "Yes, I'll marry you, Faith. Call me."

I gathered up my bag and jacket and located Marilyn, nattering away to Rowan, her hands waving wildly as she talked. She caught my gesture and nodded, giving Rowan a brief hug before coming to join me. On our way to the door, we walked past Dylan, two women now clucking around him like chickens. His eyes met mine as I passed. He shook his head slightly in mock disappointment and mouthed, "*Watery custard?*"

Blushing, I pushed Marilyn out of the door and nearly sprinted to the car. As always, my friend kept schtum. But I knew what she was thinking. I thought the same.

Watch out there, Faith. You could be heading for big trouble.

Chapter Four

That Friday, I ironed my white shirt and black skirt, dug out my least snagged pair of tights, and put on my work shoes. Since my enforced resignation from HCC, life had returned to a desperate sprint from the poverty wolf snapping at my heels. I survived, just, on meagre savings, Perry's generosity, and three or four shifts a week doing waitressing work for a temp agency. The work was back-breaking drudgery for pitiful pay. I missed some of my workmates at HCC – the waitresses and bar staff. I missed regular customers, knowing who would tip generously and who would complain. I really missed being recognized as someone good at their job, who worked hard and could think on her feet. I didn't miss the sixty-hour weeks, the two-mile hike through country roads at all hours and in all weather, or being ordered about like a second-class citizen on a daily basis by a boss with an ego problem.

Temping suited me because it required no commitment beyond the next twenty-four hours, little brainpower, and if Sam needed me I could drop everything and go to him without facing another reprimand, verbal warning, written warning, or final go-before-you're-fired warning. Perry and his family strongly disapproved, stating their expectation that once married I would turn my attention to more suitable occupations (like playing tennis, shopping, and producing babies). I don't think they could imagine a world where not working meant not eating. For this reason, I rarely mentioned my job unless absolutely necessary.

This evening's gig consisted of a private party held in the grounds of a local mansion. As two hundred guests swept their way up the drive in a dazzling array of cars, I worked frantically in the steamy kitchen pouring out glasses of champagne and plating canapés. Thirty minutes into the party (two hours after my shift began) the manager sent me for a quick break prior to serving the first course. I gladly stole outside for a few minutes, escaping the heat. Things were bubbling towards boiling point as the chef heard the guest of honour hadn't arrived yet and, with much cursing and banging of pans, put dinner on hold.

Always anticipating a call from Sam – even more so since the horrifying news about Kane – I dug my phone out of my jacket, dumped in a side-room off the kitchen. Flicking the screen, I wandered outside into the balmy September air.

My heart clenched as eight missed calls registered on the display, easing off slightly when I saw four were from Perry and the rest from Marilyn. I walked over to a bench seated an unobtrusive distance from the nearest group of partygoers. One of them I had waited on regularly at HCC, but I often saw old customers at temp jobs, and the recognition was never mutual. Leaning onto the back of the bench, I dialled my answerphone. Six messages.

"Hi darling. I'm taking you out tonight. Put on your fanciest dress and biggest smile. I'll pick you up at seven-thirty."

"Just checking you got my message. I'll be there in half an hour. Text me."

"Faith? Where are you, darling? I'm outside your house. Call me!"

"Hi Faith, it's Marilyn. Perry called. He can't find you. Are you okay?"

"Right, Perry didn't want me to tell you but he's got this big surprise planned. You really need to call him now, Faith. He's freaking out."

"Faith? For goodness' sake, where are you?"

My heart unclenched, and sank like a stone to somewhere at the bottom of my bowels. I checked my watch. Eight-fifteen. Should I pretend not to have seen the calls until my shift finished? With a sigh, I phoned Marilyn. In the huddle of guests a few metres away, a ringtone went off. It was "Fat Bottomed Girls", the Queen song.

What? That was Marilyn's ringtone. I hung up, sweating. A voluptuous figure in a 1950s-style dress with her back to me rummaged through her clutch bag and pulled out a phone. As she twisted to the side, I caught a glimpse of the baby in her arms. As she leaned over to the man standing next to her, swiping the phone with her free hand, I saw a matching baby in a papoose strapped to his back.

Right. That's fine. Marilyn knows I waitress at functions. Probably best for me not to stroll up and say hello, but there is no problem here.

A teeny, tiny horrible thought suggested otherwise. Before I could tell it to shut up and get lost, my phone rang. I hurriedly answered before the connection became obvious, and slipped behind the trunk of a nearby tree.

"Faith! International woman of mystery. Where are you?"

"I'm at work."

"Oh dear. That's bad. When do you knock off?" she asked.

"I don't know; at least midnight." I felt a prickle of sweat on my back where it pressed against the tree.

"Ah. Have you called Perry?"

"Not yet. I wanted to find out what's going on first." I risked a quick peep around the trunk, scanning for anyone else I might recognize.

"I think you might need to have a sudden attack of diarrhoea and vomiting."

"At a catering job?"

"Well, you'd better think of something. There's a party you need to be at."

As I suspected.

"Is it at White Cross Manor?"

"Yes! Did you figure it out? If you did that was pretty low of you to go to work. I know you're trying to be assertive, but still." I could hear her growing breathless as she jiggled a restless baby up and down.

"I didn't know I was invited! I need this job, Marilyn. I'll call Perry and tell him I'm ill. He won't mind. There'll be other parties."

"Er – not where you're the guest of honour there won't."

"Excuse me?" The party sounds faded into the background, overpowered by the hammer in my head.

"It's a surprise engagement party. For you and Perry. I can't believe you hadn't guessed. You need to get here as soon as possible."

"Right. Well, that's not the problem. I can be there really quickly. *In no time at all in fact.*"

There was silence on the other end of the call for a few seconds. Then Marilyn began to turn slowly around as the truth dawned. I stepped back out from behind the tree and gave her a small wave.

Speechless, she hung up the phone and handed Nancy to James, swapping her for a glass of champagne. Downing it in one, without taking her eyes off me she handed the glass to a waiter and headed to the side of the manor house, where a back entrance offered some shelter.

I joined her moments later.

"Well this is a fine crock of pickle," she said.

"Yep," I nodded.

"What the Jiminy Cricket are you going to do?"

"If I disappear from work, I'll not be hired again and this company provide over half my bookings. Plus, one of the other waiters is bound to notice when they serve me my smoked venison."

"Look around you, Faith. Champagne, swanky dinner, semi-famous swing band. This party probably cost five figures. If you don't turn up, you'll bring shame on the Uppertons. People will gossip about it for years. They'll be a laughing stock." She waved her hands in the direction of the marquee.

"I can tell them I had an accident and had to go to A&E."

"Without telling Perry? He'd be straight over there. You can't pretend to them all you had an accident when you didn't. And are you really going to be able to hide from them all evening?"

I checked my phone. "My break's nearly over. I need to figure out what to do. Whose house is this, anyway?"

"Perry's aunt. Eleanor Upperton. The whole family are here to meet the woman who finally snagged golden boy." She grimaced.

I tucked my phone back in my pocket and folded my arms. "What if I told them the truth? I'm not ashamed of being a waitress."

"Are you sure? Are you brave enough? And if you did, you can hardly expect them to let you keep on waiting on them all at *your party*. You'll have to be introduced to everyone, in your uniform. That'll be it for getting any work done. And, no offence, but you stink of fish and could really do with five minutes in front of a mirror."

I shrugged. "Then I'll explain to the manager. No one could expect me to keep working at my own party. I'll tell her while you race home and grab me a change of clothes. I can call Perry and tell him I'm at work, but on my way."

At that moment, the catering manager opened the door, bursting out with a tray of salmon entrées. "There you are! Your break ended five minutes ago. We've been given the go-ahead." She rammed the tray into my chest, forcing me to grab hold of it.

"What are you waiting for? We're twenty minutes behind schedule, I'm half blind with a stress migraine, and Richard just sliced his hand open on a broken glass. We're already one man down thanks to that loser Karen not turning up. Do I give a filet mignon if her daughter's fallen out of a window? Get those on the tables and be back here in two minutes. I want to see you harassed, pressured, in crisis mode. Go!"

"Errr…"

"GO!" She whipped out an inhaler and started puffing on it furiously.

I glanced at Marilyn. "Will you call Perry?"

She nodded. "Keep your head down, and serve the back tables. You won't be recognized there."

The manager took a break from her wheezing. "If I catch you

engaging the guests in a conversation I'm docking your pay. NOW WHAT ARE YOU STILL DOING HERE?"

Adrenaline pumping, I hurried over to the marquee as fast as I dared, the plates slipping back and forth across the tray. Ducking into the side entrance, I whipped each starter onto the table, trying to keep within the boundaries of professionalism so as not to draw attention from the guests.

One of them leaned back as I plonked the plate down in front of her. "She's not even turned up!" she drawled. "Gone AWOL. How utterly ungrateful."

"It's Larissa and Milton I feel sorry for," another woman said, a tiny bit of bread roll flying out of her mouth. "They've waited all this time for Perry to find a wife, and now this! And nobody knows anything about her. How are you to know she's suitable if you don't know her family?"

"I heard she's only nineteen. Fifteen years younger. And she hasn't got any family. It's a classic – trashy young trollop ensnares older man with her sleazy seduction techniques."

"She's a gold-digger? Poor Larissa. She must be relieved the girl hasn't turned up."

I placed the last plate in front of a middle-aged man with a bushy moustache, trying to prevent my hands from shaking. He looked at me. "Thank you."

"You're welcome." My voice cracked.

He spoke louder as I topped up his water glass, so the whole table could hear. "Any young woman prepared to take on the Uppertons deserves a medal, in my opinion. And you should be ashamed of yourselves, sat here accepting their hospitality while you spout forth poisonous speculation and distasteful gossip. Peregrine is a grown man with a sound mind. Give the fellow some credit. At least wait until you've met the girl before you damn her. And she's twenty-five, not nineteen. Not that it matters."

I resisted the urge to plant a kiss on the top of his balding head before rushing back out.

"Pssst!" Marilyn hissed at me from the side of the catering van.

"Did you phone him?" I pulled her behind the van, out of sight.

"Yes. I said you'd run out of battery so had to use a payphone. He knows you're at work but will be here ASAP. I've sent James to go and fetch you a change of clothes."

"James?! You've sent your husband to go rummaging through my wardrobe for a party dress!"

"Chill, Faith. He's a man of the world. I need to stay here to co-ordinate the mission." She frowned at me, but her eyes were dancing.

"I knew it. You're enjoying this. If you'd heard what they were saying about me on table twelve…"

"Pah. Table twelve is full of the Woodbridge witches. They wouldn't have a kind word to say if you were Kate Middleton. And we're here now, might as well enjoy it."

I shook my head in disbelief. "I've got to go. Let me know when James gets back. And when you figure out what on earth I'm going to do when he gets here, Mission Commander."

I dove into the kitchen, grabbing another tray before heading back into the breach. On the third run, I passed another waitress. Wiping the sweat off her forehead, she clutched my arm. "One of those needs to go to the top table. Someone missed out the bloke's mum."

"Okay, take one of these."

"Not a chance." She took a step back. "That woman is like a scorpion in a bad wig. She's already sworn to have me fired. No way I'm going back there."

I felt as though a clammy hand squeezed hold of my spine. "I'll give you all my tips if you do it."

"If you think your tips are going to reach one hundred thousand pounds, you might have a deal. Otherwise, not a chance. Better hurry up, Faith. The scorpion's waiting."

She sprinted off back in the direction of the kitchen. Frantically looking around, there wasn't a single member of staff to be seen. I entered the tent and offloaded all the contents of the tray but one onto a table. Taking a shaky breath, I swiped a scarf from the back of an unoccupied chair as I swept past. Ducking behind one of the disco lights, I emerged the other side with the scarf wrapped around my head. Head high, plate clattering on the tray in time to the quaking in my shoes, I glided past Larissa's table, practically throwing the starter in front of her before racing away. Glancing at my future mother-in-law out of the corner of my eye she appeared rigid, livid, puce. I was going to be severely punished for missing a party I knew nothing about. Goodness me, if she knew the truth of the matter, she'd never let Perry forget it.

A week of no sleep due to my terrifying secrets, no dinner, the evening's ridiculous antics being far from over, and the thought of spending the rest of my life as an Upperton all combined together to create a whirlwind in my stomach. I smoothly exited the tent, whipping off the scarf and draping it on a nearby bush before watering said bush with that day's lunch.

James arrived shortly afterwards. He carried a bag containing a knee-length black dress, plucked from among the jeans and T-shirts taking up ninety per cent of my meagre wardrobe. To give him credit, he also remembered to bring some matching shoes. I dove behind a bush, Marilyn whispering me instructions while she kept guard.

"You've fifteen minutes until it's time to clear the first lot of plates, according to the head waiter. Get in there and start schmoozing. And here…" She grabbed my ponytail, yanking out the elastic before fluffing the locks about my face. "If you keep your hair forwards and keep smiling none of the staff will recognize you."

I took a deep breath. "Do I have to go in there?"

My friend began pushing me over to the marquee.

"Your shirt is in the bag behind the holly tree. You can slip it on over the dress when it's time. Go, go, go!"

Together we entered the tent. Breathless, I wove my way between the tables up to the empty seat of honour. Perry spotted me a few steps in, his face breaking out into relief as he rose to greet me with a kiss.

"You made it! What a mix-up!"

"I am so, so sorry." I turned slightly to address the rest of the table, including Larissa and Milton. "I had no idea – and my phone ran out of battery. I hope you haven't been waiting too long."

Larissa humphed, and opened her mouth to say something, but her husband interjected. "Not at all. Perry should have warned you – at least checked if you would be available. Imagine if you had been away for the weekend, or out of the country?" He shook his head. "The whole thing could have been a complete fiasco."

Perry's hand turned rigid in mine.

"No, really. Perry called me hours ago but I didn't get his message. I don't think anyone's to blame. And I'm here now, so no harm done. Is this my seat? Oh, and you've saved me some salmon. Wonderful. It looks delicious."

I sat down and took an enthusiastic bite, trying to smile simultaneously. At the far end of the tent I spied two waiting staff beginning to clear some of the plates. I chewed harder, gratefully accepting the glass of water handed to me by the woman to my right.

Perry slid into the spare seat on my other side, gesturing politely at the woman. "Faith, may I introduce Eleanor Upperton, my aunt and our generous hostess."

I choked, grabbing my napkin in time to prevent crumbs spraying out of my mouth, at the same time using it as an excuse to both duck my head and hide behind the linen. Eleanor had spoken to me twice already that evening.

She stared at me, nose slightly wrinkled. "I think you need a moment to compose yourself, dear. You can introduce yourself properly later."

I nodded gratefully, and wiped my mouth, leaving the remaining salmon on the plate. "I'm so sorry, if you'd excuse me for a minute. I arrived here in rather a hurry and didn't get a chance to tidy myself up."

"You can say that again!" Larissa muttered, as I pushed back my chair. "And let's be honest, it might take more than a minute."

I bolted back into the open air, straight over to the bush, where I donned my shirt, tucked it into my belt to give the appearance of wearing a skirt, and shoved my hair back into a ponytail. Scooting over to the door of the marquee, I snagged one of the other waitresses.

"The top table's finished – you need to clear them first."

"Feel free. I'm not going back there if I can help it." She began to move away.

"I can't – I've been asked to fetch some more bread. If you don't, and she complains, I'll remember we had this conversation."

"Whatever!"

I waited long enough to see her stomp up to the top table before re-entering, keeping my back to Perry and his parents as much as possible as I cleared the remaining plates at the furthest end of the tent. Three trips back and forth to the kitchen, a swipe of Marilyn's lipstick to feign some "tidying up" and I was back as Faith. And so it went on… My phone conveniently rang when it was time to serve the mains, thanks to Mission Commander, and I left to mop up the accidentally spilled wine on my dress when it was time to clear them away. I simply skived serving dessert, dropping a fork under the table so I could duck down to avoid the waiter, and Marilyn dragged me off in the guise of introducing me to some friends as we finished our chocolate parfait.

I was exhausted, fraught, and coming across as an idiot, embarrassing Perry and irking his mother. This was preposterous.

But the worst was yet to come.

As I carefully poured out coffee for table eight, shielding myself behind a large bunch of flowers on a plinth, the tinkling sound of a fork on crystal caused the chattering to fade into silence.

Oh, no.

Perry stood to his feet, glass in hand. He was going to make a toast.

"Right, where's my beautiful fiancée?" He peered around the tent, where I stood, immobile, behind the flowers.

"Excuse me, miss!" An old man resembling a turtle smiled at me across the table. "May I please have a cup of coffee?"

Everyone, at that moment looking around and waiting for the missing fiancée, turned to stare at the man.

Marilyn called out, "I think she went outside for some fresh air. I'll go and find her. Hang on."

She caused a bit of a distraction, pushing and shoving needlessly through the tables, elbowing people in the head, and knocking over a water glass as she went, but it wasn't enough.

I glanced at the turtle man, still smiling as he pointed to his cup. Then back to Perry, watching us while he waited for Marilyn, no doubt wondering why the waitress hadn't moved.

I straightened my shoulders, desperately tried to clutch on to some perspective, and stepped out from behind the bouquet. Pouring the man his coffee, I quietly leaned over and asked the table if there was anything else I could help them with. There wasn't. I declined from enquiring if anyone happened to have a teleporter. Standing back up again, I turned to catch Perry's eye. He coughed, and tapped his glass again.

"Well, while we're waiting – and please, do excuse Faith for needing a moment, she's had a very tiring day – I would like to thank Aunt Eleanor for hosting such a fabulous party, and my parents, Larissa and Milton, for all their help with the wedding plans so far. And, if any of you happen to have August fifteenth free, we might have another little do to invite you to."

His voice faded away as I rushed out of the tent and into the bushes for the last time. Trying to yank myself together, I ran my fingers through my hair, slipped into the dressy shoes, and went back to the tent. Marilyn caught up with me at the entrance.

"Deep breaths."

"No time."

"Yes, time. Three deep breaths. Think about choir rehearsal.

Breathe out the panic and breathe in the cool, calm, courageous Faith who is loving her engagement party."

"He saw me."

"And covered for you. Breathe."

I took a couple of trembly breaths.

"Better. Now, go knock 'em dead.'"

The marquee burst into applause as I stepped back in, again apologizing with a smile as I made my way to join Perry.

"Morning sickness," one of the Woodbridge witches hissed as I passed. "That would explain a lot."

Larissa pursed her lips, her eyes glittering stones. "If your girlfriend has quite finished serving our guests their coffee, Peregrine, could you please get on with it and make a toast."

Perry's eyes darted back and forth between his parents and me, as the guests collectively held their breath.

"Um, right. Yes. Of course. So, Faith is, well, a very... I mean, I'm very happy to say that, um..."

Peregrine Upperton, millionaire businessman extraordinaire, floored by the steely gaze of his mother. "Well, Peregrine, what precisely *are* you happy about?" she asked, with a voice that could crack a walnut.

"Hold on a minute." Eleanor stood up, brandishing her glass at me like a weapon. "You're not Faith. You're the staff."

My brain tried to scrabble for something to say, but the words were like leaves being tossed along the pavement, always a gust in front of me.

"She's an imposter!" Eleanor tried to push her way around the table to where I stood, frozen, my back to the room. Her chair went flying as two hundred guests gasped as one.

Milton began squeezing round the table to intercept. His wife remained firmly seated.

"Where is Peregrine's real fiancée and what have you done with her?" Eleanor ducked her head around Perry, attempting to shake off his restraining hands.

"Good question," Larissa muttered, smirking at nobody in particular.

"No, Aunt," Perry implored. "This is Faith, my fiancée. She sat and ate with us, remember?"

"Yes! All part of the scam, no doubt! Look at her, Peregrine. She's clearly nothing more than a common desperado. Masquerading as a waitress, masquerading as a fiancée!"

"Hear, hear!" Larissa made her own personal toast, chugging down the rest of her wine.

"She's after the family fortune! Somebody call the police!" Eleanor cried. "What have you done with poor Faith, you evil trickster?"

"Stop it!" Milton, reaching his sister, took hold of both her shoulders and gave her a shake. "This is Faith. Who happens to work as an... in... as a, erm..."

"Events manager," Perry said.

"Waitress," I corrected him. "I'm a waitress," I repeated, to the room at large. "And an excellent one. Usually." Despite gritting my teeth together so hard I thought they'd snap, it was only the friendly face of Marilyn as she stood up, yanking James with her, that gave me the gumption to hold back the tears.

"An excellent fiancée, too, isn't she, Perry?" Marilyn called. "And she'll throw the best parties." She raised her glass. "To Perry and Faith. Proving the law that opposites do indeed attract, and adding some much-needed class, beauty, and brains to the Upperton clique. I mean *clan*. Woohoo!"

Amidst many murmurings, knowing looks, and Milton's repeated attempts to reassure Eleanor I wasn't a con artist hoodwinking them all, the crowd stood to return the toast. I slid into my seat, eyes on the table, and braced myself for Larissa's onslaught. Perry sat down next to me, taking hold of my hand as he leaned to whisper in my ear. "Do you want to get out of here?"

I nodded, whispering, "I'm sorry."

I saw his smile out of the corner of my eye. "Don't be. I take full responsibility. And I can't begin to imagine what you've been up to this evening, but I'm very impressed. Come on." He started to rise to his feet.

"One moment, Peregrine." A voice like a glacier pushed him back down again. "I think the guest of honour has some explaining to do."

Yep. Mission failed.

Chapter Five

Sam called me at least twice a day. I usually dropped by his flat three or four times a week, but had left it longer than usual this time due to work shifts, an HCC committee meeting, and a need to summon up enough strength to face the beast of his illness again.

I found him up, which was surprising, and dressed, which was near miraculous. Sprawled on the sofa, yes, but the flat wasn't quite as messy as it had been, and he held a cup of tea.

"How are you, Sam?"

He lay back, staring at the ceiling. "I'm losing it, Sis. Waving goodbye to all the lovely money your billionaire boyfriend spent on my rehab. Poof, gone."

"Have you taken your meds?"

"Yes."

"Well that's something." We sat there in silence. I reached out and took hold of my brother's hand, the spectre of Kane leering over our shoulders.

"April's still here, then?"

He nodded. "She's driving me crazy. Nagging all the time. Fussing."

"Does she drink?"

He shrugged. "Not much. Not any more." He sighed. "I don't want to be saved, Faith. I wish she'd leave me alone. I've told her to go and find a man who wants looking after."

"But she stays."

"She's a fool."

"Where is she now?" I glanced around, but could see no sign of her.

"I don't know. Jobcentre."

I took the mug from his hand, pushing aside some old food cartons to place it on the stained coffee table. "Is there anything you need me to do?"

He closed his eyes. "No. The nurse is coming later on."

"Try and help yourself, Sam. Don't let him do this to you."

He laughed. An ugly, hollow sound. "He already did."

*　*　*

The following Thursday, I took Perry to look around Grace Chapel. A couple of nights earlier we had managed a serious – well, serious-ish – conversation over dinner.

"I don't understand why you need to do that work."

"What do you want me to do? Live off benefits? I need a job, Perry."

"I want you to marry me and let me take care of you. If we're going to be legally joined anyway, why not set up a joint bank account now? You've got enough to worry about with the wedding and Sam. Let me take care of the finances."

"I need to be earning my own money. I know it's hardly anything, and the work is a slog and embarrasses your family, but I need some independence. That is non-negotiable. Plus, if I don't work I'm going to end up bored out of my mind. Planning a wedding and being on the HCC committee isn't a full-time occupation. I'm not about to spend my life having manicures, planning centrepieces, and shopping. It's not me."

"Couldn't you find something better, though? You used to manage the whole events team at the club. Why go back to being just a waitress?"

"Okay. Firstly, there is no such thing as *just a waitress*. Being a waitress saved my life. Secondly, I can't manage the responsibility of a full-time job with Sam. This works. I choose this. Please respect my choice."

I hadn't told Perry I had no qualifications, or that HCC had told me to resign or be sacked, with the promise of no references. I felt ashamed of both those things, and to begin to explain the reasons why would open a truckload of worms I didn't want to go near.

"You're right. I'm sorry. It just seems pathetic for you to have to work a double shift to earn what I can make in less than an hour."

"Thanks. That makes me feel better."

"Sorry! I'm sorry." He reached across the table and squeezed my hand. "You are an amazing, intelligent, talented woman and I hate thinking about how that catering manager treats you like a skivvy. What can I do to make it up to you and demonstrate how much I respect your choices?"

I considered that. Ghost Web. Wedding service. Reception.

"Anything?"

"Well… within reason."

Right, then scrap the possibility of the Ghost Web and HCC being booted out of our wedding.

"There's a church I want you to look at. It's really important to me. My mum used to go there."

* * *

So, here we were, looking almost like a normal, happy couple choosing a church for their wedding.

Dylan met us at the door, his jeans and long-sleeved T-shirt a striking contrast to Perry's tailored suit. As we wandered through to the main hall where the service would be held, I couldn't help seeing the building through Upperton eyes. Even with Marilyn's decorations, it would appear too drab, too simple, too small.

"I'll give you a few minutes to look around. Come through to my office when you're ready," Dylan said, smiling as he left us to it.

Perry was not smiling.

"Faith, what...? I mean, I know your mum used to come here, but, well... It's horrendous."

"Excuse me?"

"We can't possibly get married here, darling. You must see that." He went to take hold of my hand, but I pretended not to notice, pressing the hand to my flushed neck.

"Why not?"

"It's tiny, for one thing." He shook his head in frustration.

"So we invite fewer people to *our* wedding. What are the other things?"

"The other things don't matter because we can't invite fewer people. I don't want to invite fewer people. I'm not going to cull the list, or offend anybody, or make it look as though we have a reason not to have as many people as possible see you become my wife."

"What does that mean?"

He sighed. "Nothing. It means nothing. It means this church is too small."

"I'm not picking a wedding venue on the basis of you having a point to prove about not being ashamed of me," I said.

"Faith!" He glanced over at the door to the office before lowering his voice. "It is not about that. This is the twenty-first century. Nobody thinks like that any more. But this room can't seat more than a hundred. I have thirty-eight relatives I want to celebrate my wedding with, and that doesn't begin to cover friends, or guys from the office. How is that going to work if we only have room for fifty guests each?"

"I don't need room for fifty guests. You take ninety and I'll have ten," I said, wrapping my arms around me.

"That's ridiculous. You can't have ten guests. And I'm sorry, but this place just isn't what we want," he snapped, like a managing director instructing his underling.

"What who wants? *I* want this place! And I'll invite however many guests I like."

Perry looked around again at the bare walls, the scuffed floor, the sagging banner hanging next to the window. "No. I'm prepared to compromise on the wedding, but not this."

"*Compromise?* How have you compromised? I don't even get to pick my own wedding dress!"

"Well buy your own dress then! Or perhaps you should just get married in your jeans and that ratty T-shirt? My mother has made an incredibly kind gesture. Don't throw it back in her face. I'm giving you the kind of wedding every woman dreams of – no limits, or budget. Most brides would be thrilled. Or at least grateful. And all you can do is make impossible demands that mean half my family can't even come. I'm not having it, Faith. The answer's no."

I closed my eyes for a long moment. "I'm sorry. I am grateful. And I understand. But this is a really big deal to me. You can pick everything else – do it all how you want. Have the hugest, most ostentatious reception with five hundred guests and a nightmare wedding planner. I don't care. But I'm getting married without my mother, and I can't tell you what that feels like. I'm asking you, please, give me this."

Perry looked at me. He knew how hard I found it to ask him for anything. Sticking one hand in his pocket, he held out the other to me again.

"Come on then, let's have a proper look round. But we'll have to think up a way to sell this to Mum without her disowning us."

Disowning us? A potential unexpected bonus.

We agreed on a simple wedding service, with immediate family and close friends, followed by a massive party during which we would repeat our vows at HCC. I weighed this compromise on one hand, the Ghost Web heavy on the other, and my heart sank a little. Then I remembered again who I was and where I had come from and mentally gave myself a big slap. It was one day, one dress.

Get over yourself, Faith.

I was trying. Boy, was I trying. And, yes – I was so, so grateful.

We spent twenty minutes in Dylan's office, sitting on comfy

sofas rather than at his desk. He went through various practical details, most of the answers to which were, "We're not sure yet."

Then he moved on to a whole other type of questioning.

"So, why do you want to get married in Grace Chapel?"

I shifted on my seat, guard automatically clanging up.

"My mum used to come here. I grew up in the village."

"Oh, great." Dylan smiled at me. "Did you come here with her?"

"No. She left Nottinghamshire before I was born. And died before I came back."

"I'm sorry. I can understand why you chose here, then. But how about you, Perry?"

Perry had slipped out his phone and was scrolling through messages. "Excuse me? What?"

"Why do you want to get married in a church? What does it mean to you personally?"

Perry briskly put his phone back in his jacket pocket. "It means Faith is happy. And that's the most important thing."

"Okay. Well, one of our requirements for getting married in Grace Chapel is that you attend a marriage preparation course. Marriage is a serious thing. I take the responsibility of marrying you in this church seriously. I won't do that unless I know you've done the same. No offence – as I said, it's standard practice."

Perry smiled his businessman smile. The one that failed to reach his eyes. "Of course. Pass the dates on to Faith and we'll sort something out."

"Excellent." Dylan stood up. "Well, that's it for now. Let me know your plans as you make them. We'll do everything we can to make it your day, but it helps if we have as much notice as possible." He held out his hand to shake ours, but found Perry busy reaching into his pocket again.

Before I could either stop him, or die of shame, Perry scrawled out a cheque and held it out. "We really appreciate this. I want to give Faith the wedding she deserves. Maybe buy a few tins of paint, couple of new pictures for the walls, or something, yeah?"

Dylan accepted the cheque, and to his credit, there was only the tiniest flicker on his face when he read the obscene amount. "Thanks. That's very generous of you." He glanced back up, blue eyes sparking. "We've actually just opened up a food bank. This could feed a lot of hungry families."

Sorry, mate, you can waltz in here and wave your fat chequebook around, but neither I – nor my church – can be bought.

Perry paused, one hand on the door handle. It felt like a wrestling match without any actual wrestling. "Well, it's your church, vicar. Whatever you think is best."

Spend it on what you like – there's plenty more where that came from.

"Thanks, Dylan. I'll see you Wednesday." I barrelled Perry outside before his testosterone levels rose any further, pulling the door closed behind me.

* * *

I will never forget my sixteenth birthday, for several reasons, none of them sweet. Life settled into a sort of pattern after Grandma died and Sam came home. He found work in a factory near Mansfield, a bus ride away, and with the odd double shift we managed to budget for the occasional take-away pizza. I spent my days at school and my evenings and weekends either doing homework, housework, or washing pots in the local pub kitchen. I relished being the woman of the house, sorting our money and cooking dinner for Sam every night without anybody telling me what to do or how to do it. I had no friends, no social life, and no plans for my future, but in many ways those were the most contented days of my life. I lived for Sam – put all I had into making him happy, believing if I loved him enough, took care of him, was a good enough sister, it would keep his demons at bay. Maybe he was only that way before because of Grandma. It was different now, wasn't it?

Then my sixteenth birthday arrived. It was November, and a

thick layer of frost lined the outside of the window when I woke that morning. Sam had an early shift, so I got ready for school in an empty house, pausing to grab a couple of pounds out of the money pot to treat myself to a hot dinner. The pot was empty. Momentarily startled, my mind flashed back to Sam stumbling in through the front door while Grandma wept about her stolen pension. And the safe she bought to keep her valuables in, until she found the back forced off and her jewellery gone.

Then I remembered about my birthday. Of course! Sam had taken the money to buy a present. I was sixteen. That needed a special present. I hugged myself inside as I put the lid back on the pot, wondering what he could possibly have bought with all that money.

Later that day I found out. He had bought me a foul-mouthed, violent, out-of-control brother.

My sixteenth birthday also happened to be ten years to the day since Kane had killed our mother. Something in Sam snapped. I was no longer a child. He had done his duty and seen me through to adulthood. The bomb of rage and pain and guilt and grief exploded, blasting away the delicate shoots of the life I had been nurturing for us, my dreams, my security, and the last lingering wisp of my innocence.

My old brother disappeared, rapidly consumed by his addiction and anguish. He lost his job a few weeks later. Not long after that he began selling off Grandma's remaining possessions. I bought a money belt, wearing it under my clothes twenty-four hours a day to protect my paltry earnings. He broke down the bathroom door while I showered and took it. I started working longer shifts – cramming in homework during breaks and before school. I often had to choose between heating or electricity, food or sanitary towels. Sam vanished for days at a time. I could never relax, never switch off, never take a break. But, lowering my head like a mountain goat, I ploughed on, determined to finish the last few months of school and keep some hope of a future that didn't include all the knives and forks being sold at the local car boot sale.

And then Snake slithered in.

Snake was a parasite. Sam let him stay because he sold drugs from the back door, paid rent in the form of heroin, and Sam was too weak, too lost, too messed up, and too scared to make him leave. He got his name from a tattoo of a python that started on his ankle and coiled itself around his leg, up past his groin, and in a loop around his torso before slinking up his neck to end in an open mouth enveloping his bottom jaw and one side of his skull as if the snake was in the process of swallowing his head. I wished a real python would swallow his head.

I bought two solid bolts for my bedroom door, and for the bathroom. For three weeks I stayed away as much as possible: at school, at the pub where I worked, in the local library, the café, on the streets, anywhere but at the place I had called home. I still feel ill when I think about it. The stench of vomit and sweat and filth, the wizened, grey bodies passed out on the living room floor, the fights and the moaning and the girls, some younger than me, who came round trading their dignity for a fix. The night after night after night when I lay awake with the fear and the misery pounding in my head in time to the banging on the door and the creak of broken bedsprings.

I cried to my brother, wept and cursed and threw empty bottles. Swore I would call the police if he didn't do something. The men disappeared, and most of the girls. Snake stayed, his eyes glittering hard when we crossed paths in the kitchen, or on the stairs. But then he started talking to me, asking how my schoolwork was going, when my exams started, what I planned to do afterwards. I would answer in shaky monosyllables, darting out of the room to the sound of his rasping laughter. In the new-found quiet, I felt no less afraid.

I felt watched.

I was being watched.

By an evil snake.

Chapter Six

The third Saturday in September, Hester arranged an outing for the choir. The heat of summer had begun to fade, replaced with the faint whisper of autumn carried along on crisp air, and I dressed in dark grey tracksuit bottoms and a long-sleeved top for our outdoor adventure day. This was no fun trip, but a necessary requirement, according to our choir director, to get us "working together in time, rather than bumbling along like a herd of blind sheep who happen to randomly knock into each other but have no idea what any of the others are doing". She insisted on settling for nothing less than us being able to read our fellow choir members' minds.

Fair enough. We would give it a go.

Having said that, if anyone managed to read the depths of my mind that lurked beneath how petrified I felt about the challenge ahead, I would have to resign from the choir forthwith. I stuffed my waterproof jacket into my old rucksack and waited for Marilyn to pick me up. As she wasn't, strictly speaking, a member of the choir, Marilyn was going to watch from the sidelines and supervise refreshments.

Having parked in Brooksby, we boarded the church minibus with the other choir members. Dylan had agreed to be our driver. I sat near the back, away from him, still cringing about Perry's behaviour at the chapel. It took an hour to reach our destination, the landscape changing dramatically from the rolling fields and forests of Nottinghamshire to the Peak District's craggy moorland.

Eventually, the road narrowed to a winding trail that ended up as a rough car park surrounded by nothing but coarse grass and enormous rocks. In front of us rose a cliff face, which I reckoned stood slightly lower than Mount Everest. There were a few brightly coloured spots dotted along the cliff, which I suspected were climbers, and a couple of other cars parked up. That was it.

We scrambled out of the van into a brisk wind that whipped the hair out of my ponytail, stealing my whimper away before the others could catch it. Two tanned, athletic, hardy-looking men jogged over carrying ropes and metal things that I assumed were going to prevent us from falling off the cliff face and splattering into smithereens.

"You the choir?"

Hester, wearing a black, belted trench coat and brogues, nodded briskly. "We are. We are here to learn trust, courage, and each other's secrets. Working as a team is not good enough. I want these women as one organism. Can you do that?"

The tallest man, with a thick blond beard and very broken-looking nose, grinned at her. "I'll give it a flaming good go, ma'am, so long as they're game."

He moved his gaze to us, eyes crinkling in the breeze. None of us looked game. The others appeared exactly how I felt: like clueless wimps. That is, except for Janice and Millie, our older choir members who had kitted themselves out in full-on outdoor gear – skin-tight Lycra leggings and tops, climbing shoes, and fingerless gloves. "There was an outdoor special at the market!"

They looked like jelly babies left out in the sun too long. One of them propped up on two walking sticks and wearing a bobble hat.

Also, one of the other altos, Polly, appeared tranquil. She took a folding chair out of the van and created a small nest including a book, a newspaper, an MP3 player, a bag of knitting, a flask of hot chocolate, and a jumbo packet of cheese puffs. Polly was fourteen weeks pregnant, and therefore excused from climbing, but not the trip. She would be keeping Marilyn company and cheering us on from the sidelines in between naps. I didn't know much about Polly, but behind her polite smile and immaculate outfits I suspected she carried as many burdens as the rest of us. She leaned back in her chair, closed her eyes, and breathed in a long, slow lungful of wide open sky. A secretive smile played at the corner of her mouth and within seconds she fell asleep.

What is going on in someone's life when they are so desperate for sleep they can find it buffeted about on a folding chair on the edge of a mountain?

We got through the safety bit, the initial instructions, and were told to choose a partner to hold the other end of the rope for us while we climbed the smallest rock face. *Smallest* being relative, of course.

"Stick to your groups!" Hester ordered, as she marched up and down behind the instructors. "No inter-subsection partnering!"

That made things a little simpler – or more difficult. I shuffled over to my fellow altos. Apart from Polly, now faintly snoring in her chair, there was Rosa – a fifty-something woman from Bulgaria, Melody – exactly the kind of woman I would trust to hold the rope that might potentially save me from serious injury, and Kim. Kim, who had so far spent the whole trip Snapchatting her boyfriend Scotty, had chosen to wear a pair of cut-off denim shorts and a cropped top. If I happened to look up while holding her rope I would get to see a lot more than I had paid for.

Rosa and Kim moved next to each other, like girls pairing up for school sports lessons. Relieved, I joined Melody.

Hester strode over. "Right, Kim, you're working with Faith."

"Actually I'm with Melody." I turned to show my choice of partner.

"Do you think it would be easier to work with Melody, or Kim?"

"Um, well, I know Melody better." I shrugged.

"Precisely! Have you not understood the point of today? Are we here for a jolly up a mountain together? To have a lovely time with our friends?"

I scuffed my shoe against the rocky ground. "I guess not."

Hester barked, "Why do you always look for the easiest option? How is that going to strengthen your spine and destroy your cowardice?"

"I'm not a coward."

Hester stared at me for a minute. "You are a survivor, Faith. I don't suppose most things scare you – hardship, or trouble, being alone. But having to depend on someone else? Trust them with your life? Dare you do that?"

"No offence to Kim, but I trust Melody. I know her better, and to be honest I'm nervous about working with someone wearing gold wedge heels to rock climb."

Kim bristled enough to pull her eyes off her phone. "They're trainers! The letter said wear trainers. These cost sixty quid. I bought them special."

"Faith, if you are going to be in this choir, you have to start by getting to know your fellow altos," Hester said. "You need to love them, respect and depend on them. You need to know that when you jump off a cliff, they will catch you. That when you open your mouth to sing the next note, they will be right there with you to the demisemiquaver. Unless you want to form a duo with Melody, you need to know Kim. And let her know you. Now! Enough time wasted on me repeating myself. We are seven and a half minutes behind schedule."

We were further delayed by fifteen minutes while Kim argued with the black-bearded instructor about her footwear, stomping around the whole time trying to find a phone signal. Hester had brought a spare pair of walking boots which Kim declared too heavy, too small, too filthy, too soaked in other people's sweat, too uncomfortable, too flat ("I can only walk in heels!"), and too ugly. Our patient instructor answered every whine with, "You ain't climbing unless you change ya shoes."

In the end, huffing and puffing and throwing in a couple of snorts, Kim changed shoes and began to climb. She was strong, and fit, and made it up to the top first, seeing as Hester had made everyone start together "as one organism"! Twisting slightly as she gripped the edge of the clifftop she called out, "There. I've done it. Can I get down now?"

"You have to share a secret!" replied Mags, one of the sopranos holding a rope.

"What?"

"You have to tell Faith a secret before you come down."

Kim tossed her head, pretty impressive considering she was clinging on to a rock. "I hate these shoes. There you go."

I laughed. "That's not a secret."

"I hate Hester."

"That's not true. Go again," Hester called.

"I once wet my pants in school assembly."

"No. Go again."

Kim swore. "That's true!"

"Maybe, but it's not what you need to share with us today. Come on, think about it. Faith's waiting. What is the secret in your heart, Kim?"

Kim turned back around and faced the cliff. I waited so long, I thought she wasn't going to answer. Then she spoke out in a voice I strained to hear. "I spend nearly every penny I've got on looking like this. But when I face the mirror I still see the fat girl the boys mooed at. I hate that girl and I hate that it still matters. There. That's the secret in my heart. Can I come down now?"

She came down.

Kim was not the only one to share her heart that day. Oh – the secrets women keep tucked away in there! Melody told us she was awaiting the results of a biopsy – all that fear, hidden behind soft brown eyes and a gentle smile. Rosa had left behind a husband in Bulgaria who didn't know where she was, and she had no plans to tell him.

We cheered as Millie, the last of the initial climbers, eventually reached the top. She clutched on to her rope with gnarled fingers, whooping and hollering as she scanned the horizon. It took her a long time to find a secret to share.

"My husband left me for his personal assistant."

"We know that, Millie. We even know her bra size. That is not a secret," Hester scolded.

"I once went to an illegal rave."

"We know. A secret, please."

"I have an intimate piercing." She wiggled the relevant body part.

"You showed us at the Christmas party. None of these are the secret on your heart, Millie!"

Millie closed her eyes, wobbling a little on her ledge, and clutched the rope tighter. "I'm terrified I'm going to die alone."

Oh my goodness. Janice helped her partner down lickety-split and wrapped her in the kind of hug that says, "You will not die alone; I will be with you. No matter what it takes, or how hard it is, or when or where or how. I am your friend and the only way you'll die alone is if I go first."

Did I mention that I'm crying a lot these days?

* * *

I felt more than a little nervous when it was my turn to climb. Kim had grown bored, and was spending more time waving her phone about to find a signal than listening to the instructor's recap. I stood at the bottom of the cliff face and asked her one last time, "Kim? Are you ready?"

"Yeah." She held the rope in one hand, phone in the other.

"You can't be on your phone while I'm climbing. It takes two hands. If I slip, you have to support me."

"I know that, Faith, but you're not climbing yet, are you?"

I glanced around, searching for the instructors, but they were busy with the sopranos. I thought about asking Marilyn to come and keep an eye on Kim, but she appeared to be snoozing along with Polly. Dylan, sitting on a large boulder enjoying the view, caught me looking around. "Okay?"

I jerked my head towards Kim and shrugged. "Just waiting for Kim to check her Twitter feed."

He grinned. "You'll be fine. I heard someone say you're not a coward."

That irked me. I'm not a coward, but neither am I a fool. Or so I thought, until the need to prove myself to a church minister had me launching myself up a gigantic rock, trying to ignore what Kim may or may not have been doing below me. The climb quickly took all of my focus, finding the hand and foot holds, attempting to combine heaving myself up with my arms and pushing with my feet. I could sense Rosa somewhere to the left of me, hear her humming to herself as she ascended, the pace and urgency of her notes increasing during the tricky spots.

Despite the cold wind whipping into my face and neck, I started sweating by the halfway point, the exertion of using long-forgotten muscles causing my chest to heave as I fought to catch a breath.

Someone in the soprano section had already reached the top. It sounded like Uzma, who called out, "Underneath these boring clothes I wear red lace, purple silk, or leopard print underwear. I hide them in my drawer behind all the respectable white and beige bras and knickers my mother gets me. Sorry to mention unmentionables, Dylan."

I began to slow my pace as a couple more climbers reached the top and shared their secrets. What secret would I share today?

What is the secret on your heart, Faith?

My heart was so squashed with secrets I didn't know where to begin.

My brother is an addict struggling to resist falling off the wagon.

I've done desperate things I am too ashamed to tell the man I'm going to marry.

The monster who murdered my mother is out of prison and I am filled with dread he will find us.

When the minister of Grace Chapel smiles at me, for the first time in my life I feel beautiful.

Faith Harp is the name I call myself, but it is not my name.

As it turned out, those secrets would remain in my heart that day. I placed one worn-out hand on the ridge of the clifftop, my brain churning as the secrets writhed about like a bucket of maggots. My foot, totally drained of energy from three weeks of broken sleep, anxiety, and all my other problems, failed to keep a grip on the narrow ledge it had been balancing on. Caught off guard, my hands slipped, and before my head could process what was happening I tumbled into open space.

Unfortunately, at that moment, a teensy twinge of mobile phone coverage allowed the text Kim's boyfriend had sent her to ping through. Distracted, thinking I had reached the top, she failed to notice the change in slack that indicated me careening down the rock face above her.

I couldn't see this, being lost in terror and adrenaline, but I knew in that second I would surely die.

No, my life did not flash before my eyes. They were closed. I may have screamed. I think I prayed. I hope God didn't mind that my prayer was not altogether wholesome. It wouldn't be the kind of prayer you said in church.

I guess he didn't, because when the splat that marked my doom came, it was more of an oomph. When I managed to gasp in an almighty wheeze of air, open my eyes, and wait for the world to come back into focus, I discovered myself sprawled on the ground on top of someone. Hoping hard I had bumped down slowly enough not to cause them any serious damage, I accepted Kim's panicked hand and turned to see whom I had squashed.

Dylan lay spreadeagled on the rocky earth, face pale beneath his stubble, eyes closed.

"Faith! Dylan saved you! He like, jumped underneath the rope to catch you and you crushed him. It's like Jesus – he sacrificed himself to save your life!" Kim gasped.

Most of the women on the ground were unable to come and investigate, as their partners were still descending the cliff, and no one was letting their eyes off their ropes for a nanosecond after watching me bounce past them. Melody, however, having handed her rope to one instructor, now deftly checked me over, the other instructor jogging back and forth to make sure everyone else was still concentrating on getting down safely.

"What does that make you, then, Kim?" She tutted. "If Dylan's Jesus I think you must be the devil."

Kim burst into tears. "I might as well be! Flip! My hands are shaking so hard I can't even call an ambulance. Dylan's gonna die and it's all my fault! This proves I'm a total loser. A murdering, failed loser! What's Scotty gonna say?"

Melody, satisfied I suffered from no more than scrapes and bruises, kneeled down to examine Dylan. By now the others had begun to gather, although Hester held them back with outstretched arms and blazing eyes. "Keep your distance! Melody is an accomplished medical professional. Everybody stay calm. Kim has not killed Dylan! Although I may yet kill Kim!"

Dylan confirmed this by groaning. He gingerly reached up to grasp the top of his head, opening one eye a tiny slit. "Woah, Faith. You're heavier than you look," he rasped. "But I'm fine. Just winded."

He let Melody help him up to a sitting position. "That didn't turn out quite how I intended."

"Aaah," Uzma said. "Were you supposed to catch her in your arms like a hero?"

Dylan smiled, then winced sharply, clutching his side. "Like a man at least. The beards over there wouldn't have fallen over. Having said that, Faith weighs a heck of a lot for such a shrimp. Even they might've found it a challenge. I'm pretty impressed I didn't drop her." He winked at me.

I didn't say anything. I felt discombobulated. The adrenaline flow was withdrawing, leaving my teeth chattering and stomach nauseous. I swayed a little, causing someone to sit me on a rock while Marilyn poured sweet tea from her thermos. As the rest of the choir returned to earth the instructors checked everyone was all right.

After a few minutes, people drifted away to eat lunch, Kim still sobbing as she swore never to touch her phone again, once she'd tweeted how terrible she felt, and Hester beside herself at the abject failure of our trust exercise. I remained frozen on the rock, my brain in suspended animation.

"I wouldn't have died," I announced, to no one in particular. "I wasn't falling fast enough. Just a broken leg, or arm, maybe."

A broken leg or arm. People with broken legs or arms didn't make very good waitresses. That meant they couldn't work, and therefore couldn't earn any money. No money meant no food, rent, or anything else. It meant no shower gel or toilet paper. No hot water and no way to support my brother, let alone pay off the debts he cost me. No way to be there for him, to keep him from spiralling so far he chose never to come back.

I squeezed my engagement ring tight. Fifteenth of August. Maybe then the anxious ball of dread in my stomach would begin to melt. A fair swap for spending the rest of my life with a decent man I was fond of, loved even, but was not in love with.

I looked up, shaking my head to try to clear the pathetic, self-pitying thoughts. *Buck up, Faith. Pull yourself together. Your bones are unbroken.*

Dylan stood in front of me, his clear eyes serious as he watched my face.

"How are you doing?"

I nodded. "Fine. Thank you. I can't believe you did that."

"Well." He shrugged, with a wry smile. "I happened to be watching just as you fell. It was instinct. You landed on top of me before I even knew I'd moved."

I bit down hard on my lip as my chin wobbled. Dylan leaned down and squeezed my shoulder, briefly.

"I'm just glad you're safe."

Oh boy, how I longed to be safe. And when I thought about how his body had felt beneath me, as solid as the cliff face, his arms wrapped tight around my chest, I wondered how someone could feel so safe, and yet so dangerous, all at the same time.

* * *

On the way home, hoping to avoid both conversation and Marilyn's pointed stares, I asked Rosa if I could sit with her. As we rumbled back down the motorway towards Nottinghamshire, my wits slowly regathered themselves, and I asked Rosa what brought her to the UK.

"My husband. He is not a bad man, but he drive me crazy anyway. Spend all money on his crazy plans to make us rich. All bad plans. Nothing work. And now my girls grow up. One in America with soccer scholarship, one married to nice, boring man no crazy plans. I think, I can't stand this any more. I done my duty. I done more than reasonable. But when I try to go, he cry and kiss me and I feel sorry for him and stay. This happen lots of times. Once I get all way to my sister's house, he follow me there. That man so handsome. Like movie star. When he look at me I am like – what you say – hypnotized. I cannot resist. So, I wait till him off on next crazy plan, and I leave. Take secret money I saved and get bus out of there. Lots of days travelling, bus, car, lorry. I okay on lorry because I have knife. Big one, look."

She pulled out a butcher's knife from her rucksack to show me. "I no let no more handsome men trick me into waste my life. Big knife keep them away."

I didn't ask how she had got that monstrous knife into the country.

"Then I meet man who gets me job in England. I share flat with three women. First we wash cars, then I get job clean offices. Now I work in factory, pack boxes. Not a lot of money but I get to keep it, spend on what I want. No crazy plans like build zoo or make film with Lego or sell pizza made with donkey cheese. I happy now. I miss my husband kisses, and his sexy eyes, but I happy."

"That's an amazing story. Did you have a job in Bulgaria?"

"Yes." Rosa puffed up her chest. "I seamstress. Best in my city. Make clothes for all important people. Dress for daughter of Prime Minister when she got married. I make this dress. Best wedding dress in whole of Bulgaria. I get good money for all these clothes I make, but my crazy husband throw it all away."

"Could you get a job as a seamstress here?"

"Maybe. But I need samples. Need good machine, material, thread, scissors. All that stuff. I'm at factory all day, too tired to think about anything else. If I had good machine in my house, those women sell it. I need break, and no one going to give old Bulgarian woman break. That okay, I happy."

I leaned my head against the window and watched the trees whizz by at the side of the road. A crazy plan, not quite as crazy as donkey cheese pizza, popped into my head.

"Did you know I'm getting married this summer?"

"Yes. We all know this. Janice heard your man shout in church about it too poor and ugly."

"Oh. Right. I don't think that quite… Anyway. Would you like to make my bridesmaid dresses for me? I can't pay you much, but I can chip in enough to buy you all the stuff you need. If we got a decent machine second-hand. And you can have the dresses afterwards, use them as samples."

And me! my heart whispered. *Make me a lovely dress, too!*

Rosa gripped my hand in hers. "You mean this? You let me make dresses for your beautiful wedding, special day?"

"Yes. I would love you to."

"I make you really good dresses, Faith. I not do cheap, bad dresses look like little girl at party or from cartoon. My dresses classy. What you say… tasty."

I smiled. "Tasteful."

"Yes! Good, good dresses. Beautiful, perfect fit. Right shape for each person. Show little bit bosom but not so men look bosom not face."

"Fantastic. I don't want men looking at my bridesmaids' bosoms."

"So, how many dresses you going to need? Who you got for bridesmaid?"

Ah. That would depend upon who was controlling my wedding.

"Can I get back to you on that?"

"Yes, yes, lovely Faith. You get back to me whenever you want. I happy before, but now I really happy. I not even mind those women take my coat any more."

* * *

I dreamed of Kane again that night. Dark, twisty dreams full of cracked, muddled images and dormant memories. My mother, little more than a shadow to me now, calling me, her hands frantic as she scooped up my pathetic pile of clothes into a bag, tossing in my favourite stuffed koala and a book.

"Come on now, Rachel. We have to hurry. Get dressed, quickly now!"

"Where's Liam? I want Liam."

"He's packing. Why aren't you dressed yet? Hurry, we've got to hurry. He's coming, Rachel!"

But it was one of those dreams where no matter how hard I tried, I couldn't get ready, couldn't dress. Every time I looked down I still wore my faded pyjamas. The panic attacked my throat as my mother grew even more frantic, "Quickly, Rachel, quickly. *He's coming!*"

Liam hid me in the wardrobe, right at the back, and made me promise to stay there, stay quiet.

"Just for a little while, while me and Mummy talk to Kane. And then we'll get our bags and go, Rachel. We'll go far away to somewhere he can't get us, and live in a nice new house with a swing and your own bedroom with pink walls. But now, it's very important. Stay here, and don't come out. Don't look and don't make a sound. Promise me?"

I stayed there, even when the screaming and the crashing started. So loud I thought the house was falling down around the little wardrobe where I crouched, huddled, holding on to the promise of my brother.

And then the wardrobe door opened, but in my dream it wasn't my mother, or Liam. Nor the policeman who found me all those years ago.

Snake leaned in, his thin lips glistening, irises bloodshot and bulging. "You can't get away, Rachel." He giggled. "I'm coming and you can't get away."

I leaned back in the wardrobe, burying myself deeper and deeper under the pile of clothes, so deep I couldn't see, couldn't hear his gurgling laughter, couldn't breathe.

And then two steady arms went around me, held me tight, and whispered my new name, the name I call myself. And for a split second before I woke, drenched in sweat and tears, I was safe.

Chapter Seven

The weight of my dream still heavy in my skull, I completed a lunchtime shift at a golden wedding anniversary in a local hotel, then went to see Sam.

I found him lying on the sofa, the state of his clothes and beard suggesting he hadn't moved since the last time I had been round.

I didn't ask how he was doing. Not interested in a lie, and not up to the truth.

"Where's April?"

He shrugged. "Out. Gone to the shops, probably."

"Have you had any alcohol?"

He closed his eyes, pressing the back of his head against the arm of the sofa. "No."

"I want to call Gwynne."

He opened his eyes again, still motionless, but his stillness sharp.

"We can't be left waiting, with no idea where he is or what's happening. You need to get well again, Sam. And I need to sleep for more than two hours at a time, preferably without Kane-themed nightmares."

Sam let out a shuddery breath. I understood. Calling Gwynne made it real again. Hearing where he was, or what he was doing, or any other tiny detail made him even more alive to us. Made the monster real.

"It might be good news." The tremble in my words betrayed the ridiculous lie.

"What, that he's dead already?"

"Or ill, or rearrested, or has to stay within one mile of wherever he was released from. Or has emigrated to Antarctica. It doesn't matter anyway. We need to know where he is and if… if he's looking for us."

"Looking for me." Sam swung his legs off the cushion and sat up. The simple action seemed to sap every last ounce of strength in his wrecked body. "I don't need to speak to Gwynne to know the answer to that question, Faith. You don't either. He's looking. And he won't stop until he finds me."

I sat and buried my head into Sam's shoulder, our bones clattering as we remembered. Bereft, bewildered, traumatized, Sam had testified via video link to a judge and jury about how he had dialled emergency services with shaking hands while in the next room Kane had battered our mother beyond recognition.

Upon much skilful, gentle questioning from Gwynne, our designated Family Liaison Officer, he also recounted the last words Kane spoke before the police broke down the front door.

You're gonna regret this, boy. Keep lookin' over your shoulder. Don't matter how long it's been. As soon as they let me out I'll be coming for you.

I'll be coming for you.

He was coming.

* * *

I left once April returned, Sam still adamant about not phoning Gwynne. It was entirely possible I wouldn't be able to track Gwynne down, anyway. She had been young, maybe late twenties, when it happened, and a thousand reasons could have caused her to move on from the Chester police force. I never questioned whether she would remember us, or want to help. Gwynne spent more time with us than was perhaps wise – or allowed – back then. She sent Christmas cards for the first few years, even made occasional visits until Grandma sat her down and explained how seeing her brought it back – the night terrors, the bed-wetting, hours crouching in the back of the wardrobe. Sam's uncontrollable mood swings.

I did question if she *could* help, but I had to do something. Kane was coming, I had no doubt. My ragged, screaming nerves could do with having some heads up as to when.

* * *

The following Thursday, Perry and I were summoned to a family dinner at HCC. Agenda: The Wedding. Chairperson: Larissa Upperton. Other members present: Milton Upperton, Perry's younger cousin Natasha, Aunt Eleanor, and Hugh, Perry's cousin, also taking on the role of best man. Perry prepared for the dinner by shaving, tweaking his hair in the bathroom mirror for twenty minutes, and donning a suit and tie pre-approved by his mother. As I hurriedly slapped on some lipstick and an olive green shift dress, all the better to hide my pre-*dis*approved of figure, I contemplated how the Uppertons rivalled my warped family for functionality.

I had no illusion about whether or not I had been forgiven for the engagement party fiasco. As we entered the dining room, Larissa smiled – a big toothy grin like one of those fish with massive teeth who live in the depths of the ocean.

Mike, a waiter I used to supervise, brought our drinks, then Larissa called the meeting to order. My in-laws-to-be were not happy about the church, the date, the time, and the bride (they didn't actually list the last one, but I added it to my mental meeting minutes anyway). Wait – amendment. *Larissa* was not happy about these things. Milton was not happy because when Larissa wasn't happy he suffered.

To his credit, Perry did some deft negotiating. At no point did he state that actually, this was our wedding and with all due respect we would do what we wanted. But he stood firm on Grace Chapel and the date. We moved the time back to midday, presumably so the Uppertons could still schedule in most of the day at the club.

"And I may not manage the whole day, Perry. Not with having to entertain so many guests for all that time, quite frankly most of whom are exhausting bores. I've decided to hold a pre-wedding breakfast for those who won't fit in that poky church place. Not for everybody, just the important ones. And maybe some we like."

"Mother, the important guests will be invited to the church service. As will you."

"Well, they may not want to go! And there's hardly any point if you're going to repeat your vows here at the reception, is there?"

"It's fine," I interrupted, leaning back while Mike placed down my starter with a wink. "I don't mind if there's only me, Perry, and enough witnesses to sign the register. Becoming Perry's wife is what matters. Not who sees it, how grand the party is afterwards, or any of that other stuff."

What about a pretty dress? the vain, shallow part of my brain cried. *If you're going to have a swish, swanky wedding, you might as well do it in a beautiful dress! Or at least not a disgusting, ill-fitting one!*

I added it to my mental minutes:

Note – Faith's brain requested a vote on whether or not she should wear the Ghost Web. Overruled.

"Well, that's perfect then, isn't it?" Milton added, through strained teeth. "We can have a breakfast for those who don't fancy the church, and all meet in the ballroom for the photo shoot at one-thirty."

A morsel of crab got wedged in my windpipe.

"Excuse me?" I spluttered, after much hacking, choking, and trying to hide my mortification behind a linen napkin. "The what?"

Nobody said anything. Perry shifted in his seat.

"By photo shoot, I presume you mean photographer, as in a man or woman who will come and take photographs of the wedding that we then privately look through before choosing our favourites to take home in an album? That is what you meant by photo shoot? Perry?"

Additional note – Faith's voice has now entered supersonic frequencies that are near impossible to decipher. There may be some inaccuracies in the minutes after this point. Which may be a good thing all round.

Perry placed a restraining-slash-comforting hand on my leg.

"This is a big day for the Uppertons. And you, of course! We wanted to have an extra special way to remember it by, so *Nottinghamshire Life* are coming to take some pictures, do a small feature."

"Oooh." Natasha clapped her hands together a few times with glee. "It'll be like *Hello!*"

"No."

"Oh, come on now, Faith. Please don't be difficult about absolutely everything," Larissa snapped.

"No." I shook my head, trying to steady the roar inside and focus on Perry, so he could see how much this meant.

"Darling." I could hear the frown. "They won't bother you; it'll be no different from a normal wedding photographer. You didn't think we'd have no photos, did you?"

"I can't do it."

I'm coming for you.

"Why not?"

I felt as though someone had stuck me with an HCC steak knife.

"I'm not being difficult. It's not that… I mean… I can't be…" I took a long, deep breath in. Remembered the technique Hester had shown us at choir rehearsal the night before: *You are in a storm, most of you. It is swirling, churning, picking up bits of your precious, fragile life, and smashing them about. But you, you strong and courageous women, are in the eye of the storm. You watch it rage around you, but it will not destroy you! Breathe in hope, wise women. Breathe out panic and doom! Blow out all your trembling terror. Breathe in calm. Peace. Resilience. A million women before you have braced this storm. Stand up, shoulders back, head high! You cannot control the storm, choir, but you can stop it controlling you!*

I breathed in calm, courage, wisdom. Puffed out a microgram of fear and despair. Did it a few more times while Mike brought our main course, throwing me an encouraging smile as he topped up my drink.

I finally reasoned that if Kane ever read *Nottinghamshire Life*, the chances of which seemed a zillion to one, he'd already reached Nottinghamshire, and was well on the way to finding us. Might as well get it over with quickly at that point. Besides, August was nearly ten months away. Anything could have happened by then.

"Okay. I'll do the shoot." With a mask on? Or my veil in front of my face?

Next item on the agenda: Bridesmaids.

I hadn't been surprised to see Natasha at the dinner. Typical tactics, making it impossible for me to say no. And, honestly, I wasn't bothered. It gave Rosa another dress to make.

Hah. Natasha was just the pre-emptive strike.

"So, Natasha, of course." Larissa gave her a brisk smile. "And Hugh's sister Catherine. We thought of asking Johanna and Geoff's eldest, Marianne or Mary or whatever it is, but she might be in Switzerland. Probably ought to have the chairwoman of the committee. Who is it these days? Margot Pemberley?"

By all means ask a girl to be my bridesmaid that I haven't yet met and you *can't even remember the name of!* And yes, why not throw in a middle-aged chairwoman who treats me akin to a hair found in her dinner?

"For flower girls, as well as Lilly and Felicity, we need Jasmine, seeing as she's your goddaughter, Perry, but that makes an odd number so we'll want an extra. The only person I could think of was Ted's little girl, but she's awfully young, so could very easily let us down on the day."

Perry smiled, his hand still firmly pressed on my thigh. "Now, Mother. Don't you think Faith might want to choose some of her bridesmaids, or a flower girl? I think that's traditional."

Ingenious countermove, Perry. The tradition trump card.

Larissa came dangerously close to a snort. Who knows what excessive pressure could do to such an extensive nose job? "Well. If you think she has anyone suitable. Do you have anyone, Faith?"

"Yes. I've asked Marilyn to be matron of honour. And with Natasha, I think that's plenty."

Larissa rolled her eyes as if to say, *Of course you would have to be awkward about this as well as everything else.*

"We wouldn't want to steal any more guests from your breakfast, after all." I smiled, sweet as cyanide.

"If you're having Marilyn as matron of honour, you need Catherine to balance Natasha out. Otherwise, who will she walk down the aisle with? Besides, I don't want Catherine at my breakfast. Last time she drank too much Pimm's and made a dreadful fool of herself with the gardener. You can keep her under control at the church."

"Fine, Catherine too. But I'm going to ask her myself."

Larissa sipped her wine. "Oh, I don't think anyone holds to all that old-fashioned carry-on any more, do they? A bridesmaid is little more than a token gesture."

As I suspected. My delightful mother-in-law had already asked.

By the time we moved on to coffee, most things had been decided. Added extras like flowers and a cake, cars and invitations were details I happily let Larissa handle. Yes, there was a principle at stake, but every decision I allowed her to control was ammunition in case I managed to breathe in enough personal power to ditch the Ghost Web.

* * *

The following week at choir practice, after warm-up, Hester announced a new song. A buzz rippled down the rows of chairs as we passed along the sheet music: "O Holy Night". A Christmas song. Lovely, for those who loved Christmas. Personally, I thought Christmas was blah. Or bleurgh. Or both.

The Name I Call Myself

Hester asked for silence while she played us a track of the carol "as it was meant to be sung" by some other, famous choir. She then spent the rest of the rehearsal teaching us the four parts for the first section. It sounded beautiful – we sounded beautiful. I nearly felt a tiny twinge of Christmassy joy as we sang. Towards the end of the rehearsal we were feeling pretty good. That hadn't taken long to get to grips with, had it? Next verse, please!

Hester watched our merry chatter with a blank expression. She signalled to Dylan, who had taken up his usual spot leaning on the back wall, and he sauntered to the front.

"Right, choir. We are going to do that one more time."

She counted us in. On the third beat, Dylan held up a tablet and started to film. We finished the song, and dispersed for refreshments. Ten minutes later, we were marched into the main chapel. Here, in a freeze-frame on the big screen at the front, was the footage. Dylan pressed play.

Two minutes later we sat quietly, and waited for Hester to speak. Oh dear.

"Somebody remind us of the sixth line of that song."

We fidgeted about like children in school assembly.

Hester glowered. Melody called out the line. "A thrill of hope the weary world –"

"A thrill of hope! For yonder breaks a new and glorious morn! Rowan, did that sound hopeful to you?"

Rowan shook her head.

"Ebony, was it thrilling? Glorious, Uzma? Kim – did that conjure stars shining brightly, or a sputtering, buzzing strip light in a grimy basement?"

Hester smacked the top of the lectern beside her with the flat of her hand. "I do not expect perfection after one rehearsal! I know you, like the greatest singers in the world, need time and guidance and practice, practice, practice. I know this. Why don't you? What are you aiming for, choir? Adequate? That'll do? Not bad for a bunch of women like us? Not a *proper* choir?"

Nobody so much as breathed aloud.

Hester's hair seemed to be standing up a good inch higher than normal on her head.

"*What are you thinking?* When are you going to aim for the very best you can do? When are you women going to believe you can achieve jaw-dropping greatness? Look at that choir."

She jabbed one finger at the screen behind us. "Slumped! Lazy! Half-hearted! Pretty hope-*less*, wouldn't you say?"

We would. We looked like women with very little hope.

"You are never going to look or sound any different until you become different! No! Change that! You are never going to look or sound different until you believe that you are not those women. Dylan has offered us the chance to sing at the Christmas carol service. I will not let you stand up in front of people and sing like that. You need to start believing in yourselves! To be able to stand, unashamed, and show the world that you are women of triumph! Everyone expects this choir to fail – to be a rubbishy mess."

Do they? Who does?

"And they will be right, until you learn to believe. Until you learn to love yourselves, choir! Like I do. Like I believe in you."

She coughed, and blinked a couple of times. "I want everybody at Marilyn's house: The Old Rectory, Houghton. Seven o'clock, Friday. I will take your non-attendance as your resignation from Grace Choir. And none of you had better dare quit now."

She marched out of the room. We all collectively released our breath.

"Well, wouldn't you know it!" Janice said. "That was a proper racket."

"Terrible," Millie agreed. "Like a herd of elephants being attacked by killer bees."

"Or a pig stuck in a drainpipe."

"Fancy another flapjack?" Millie tugged on her bobble hat.

"Ooh, go on then. They say sugar's good after a trauma."

"We'd best have two then."

I stood alone in the kitchen drying up cups when Dylan came in, bringing the rest of the empties.

"Hi, Faith. How's it going?"

"Yeah, good thanks." I concentrated hard on wiping every single drop of moisture from the cup in my hand.

"No post-traumatic stress symptoms after your near-fatal cliff plunge?"

I smiled, despite myself. "No. Thanks. I've had worse brushes with death and survived."

He turned from where he'd begun washing up the cups and looked at me. "When?"

Pah. I should have known he wouldn't let a casual remark like that slip past.

"A long time ago. How about you? Suffering any lingering back problems from your heroic catch?"

"No, but I have started having this recurrent nightmare about being suffocated under a crushing weight…"

"Very funny."

"Good. You should smile more."

My smile disappeared. Dylan, ever tactful, turned away again and asked, "So how did you meet Perry? I can't imagine you mixing in the same social circles."

"You mean because he's rich and I'm not?" I bristled slightly.

"I've met enough children of privilege to know you're not one of them, and he is."

I didn't know if that was a compliment or not. I didn't know if I wanted it to be one. Part of me felt riled, but he only stated the obvious. I glanced at his easy-going face, hair drooping as he bent over the sink.

"I met Perry when I worked at HCC. His family are wealthy, but he's worked really hard to build up his business. And still does. He isn't a snob, despite sometimes acting like one." I grimaced. "After all, he's marrying me."

"I don't think he's a snob. I'm sure you'll be very happy together."

Really? You might be the only one who is.

* * *

I first met Perry properly at a function he had organized for his business. His family were well known in the club, and during the six months or so I had been waiting tables and serving behind the bar I had observed them many times – grumpy father, domineering mother, son who nearly always left with a woman on his arm on the rare occasions he arrived without one.

Izzy, the events organizer and all-round incompetent whose dad happened to be club treasurer, found me in the smaller of the two private dining rooms, setting out the table for an evening event.

She rushed in, eyes wild, swearing repeatedly under her breath. I heaved a mental sigh.

"What?"

"A mistake's been made with tonight's booking."

"The party of six for that finance company?"

"Sort of."

"What do you mean, sort of?" I carried on laying knives and forks just so.

"That's the mistake. It isn't a party of six."

"Izzy, if you're expecting me to sort out another one of your cock-ups, you'd better tell me what it is."

"A number was somehow missed off the booking form."

"Izzy."

"Sixty guests are arriving in just over an hour." She sank into a chair, lowered her head into her hands, and began swearing again.

At that point, Perry Upperton strode into the dining room wearing a tuxedo.

"Ah. Sorry. My mistake. I'm looking for the Churchill Room."

"Yes. This is it."

Perry looked around. "No. I'm looking for the room where my party is tonight. For PSU Finance?"

I placed the tray of cutlery on the table, and took a deep breath. Izzy had ceased muttering, but now crouched in the chair like a frightened mole.

"Mr Upperton, on behalf of HCC please accept my sincerest apologies. There has been a mistake with your booking which has only just been discovered. Our records made a rather grave error regarding the number of guests."

Perry's eyes flicked around the room, with the one central banqueting table elegantly laid out for six.

"You are kidding me."

"No. Look, I'm going to do my absolute best to sort this. And I'm pretty sure we're only going to charge you for six guests. Did you send through a seating plan?" I took a step towards him.

"I did."

"And talk about the room arrangements, music, centrepieces, stuff like that?"

"Yes. I spoke about all these things with the events manager. Izzy Black. I would like to speak to her. Please."

I tipped my head in the direction of Izzy.

"Ah."

"Right. Here's what I'm going to do. First, I need to speak to the chef. What menu had you ordered?"

He looked back at me. "I can't remember. And at this point I don't really care."

I pulled out my pad and made a couple of random notes. "Okay, we'll see what he says. I'll make sure we bring in the extra staff, and Izzy will print out your function list and get started on sorting the room. The ballroom is empty, but it will need dressing."

"What can I do?" he asked.

"Can you shift some tables?"

"Just point me in the right direction."

* * *

96

Two hours later, only half an hour late, we had a hot buffet for sixty guests, a room decorated with a box of leftovers from a wedding a month before, a free glass of bubbly for anyone who wanted it, and a party saved by the skin of its teeth.

The next day I turned up at work to find a generous bonus, no Izzy, and a promotion. Later on that afternoon I also received a ridiculously flamboyant bouquet from Perry Upperton. The card read, "You blew my mind last night. I'd like to take you out to show my appreciation. Call me." And a business card.

I called using the bar phone and left a brief message of thanks and you're welcome, just doing my job.

At twenty-three, I had never dated. Not since *him*. And that could hardly be described as dating. For multiple reasons, I felt terrified of any commitment other than the one made to myself to never trust anybody, ever. It made for a lonely life, but I was more than used to being alone. Lonely was safe. Safe from shame, rejection, and abuse. I knew that the type of man I might want, if I wanted one, did not want women like me.

I certainly had no interest in going for dinner with the club lothario.

Although I had been pleasantly surprised by his willingness to arrange furniture and flowers rather than yell at other people to do it.

Perry showed up later that week. He had booked a table for two in the restaurant. There you go, I thought; he's moved on to the next poor girl.

The two included me.

I politely declined, due to working.

He had checked. My shift finished at eight.

I declined again. I was tired, and had some things to do. At eight-fifteen, Perry's car pulled up alongside me at the bottom of the sweeping HCC driveway as I made my way home. He crawled along for a couple of hundred metres, using all his charm to try and persuade me to accept a lift. He seemed pretty charming. Funny, and self-deprecating. No mention of the fact I was walking two miles home from work because I couldn't afford a car, whereas his racing green convertible probably cost more than my house.

I climbed over the stile that led to the shortcut through Top Woods, and politely declined once more.

This carried on for a couple of months until he finally got the message – or so I thought. Intrigued and spurred on by the rare resistance to his attention, Perry tried another strategy. He ceased the compliments, the flowers, and the dinner invitations, and instead took to sitting on a bar stool and making conversation.

A few more months went by and, so subtly I hadn't quite noticed it happening, we became friends.

Perry was interesting, and nice. He also made me laugh – not something I did often or easily. Gradually, over the weeks, he chipped away at my armour, so when he asked me to be his plus one at a wedding, making the very valid point that we would have a fun evening together, I accepted.

Three months later he proposed, in a fairly casual way during a moonlit walk along the River Trent.

I laughed it off and said no.

The next four times he asked me I said no.

The sixth time, nearly a year into our relationship, when he got down on one knee and produced the billion-carat diamond ring, I promised to think about it. I thought about it for all of half a day before deciding to decline once more.

Then I got the flu. And three days later Sam took a cocktail of killer substances strong enough to knock him into a coma.

Chapter Eight

Mid-October, at the end of my tether and worried sick about Sam, who seemed to be shrivelling before my eyes, I called the police station where Gwynne had been stationed all those years ago. The Inspector was in a meeting. Could she call me back?

I left my name and number. Shoving on a pair of trainers, my fingers barely managing to tie the laces, I snatched my rucksack from a peg by the front door and launched myself down the front path, automatically turning right towards the woods. I knew these footpaths well. HCC was situated two point two miles from my front door. Not being the kind of place whose customers use public transport, it was quicker (and cheaper) to walk cross-country than take the intermittent bus to the next village and hike the hill the rest of the way. And over the three years I had worked there, I had grown to love walking. I valued the peace, the openness, the beauty. Between long shifts and looking after Sam, the walk to work became my headspace, a chance to relieve pressure, burn up stress, or simply forget about everything but the hum of summer bees, the spring blossom decorating the hedgerows, the frost sparkling on bare branches, the crunch of nuts beneath my feet.

I became no one out here. Neutral and nameless. The robin who perched on the fence post by the sheep field didn't care who I was or what I had done. The squirrels dancing up the oak trees gave not a chestnut if I spent my last penny on my brother's counselling, then ended up using the session myself when he failed to show up. No snail, butterfly, brown rabbit, or toad derided my lack of education, plans, prospects. Neither did they taunt me about the secrets I kept or the shame I carried. Nothing here had a name. Sometimes, on days when the loneliness threatened to crush my heart altogether, when the ache inside made it hard to breathe, I would walk, and walk, and for those long hours, the name I called myself was Rachel.

Today, I turned away from the usual route across the fields to HCC. Instead, I veered off towards the river, where a muddy path ran along the water's edge for a mile or so. The trees along the riverbank showed the first signs of an unseasonably late autumn, flecks of yellow and brown dancing among the canopy of green above my head. I shrugged off my jacket and wrapped it around my waist, pausing to drink from the bottle of water in my bag. As my feet paced the dry earth, I soaked up the sounds of the river splashing over rocks, the chirrups of the birds, the faint hum of a tractor sowing winter crops on the ridge. A large stick bounced in the current alongside me, bumping into rocks and spinning through patches of vegetation. I slowed to match its pace, waiting when it became temporarily snared on a fallen branch or caught in the weeds at the edge of the bank, hurrying when a stretch of faster current sent it careening smoothly downstream.

After a while, it disappeared under the shadow of a bridge and didn't come out the other side.

At the moment I had decided not to scramble down the treacherously slippery bank to set it free, my phone rang. Leaning on the wall of the bridge, I saw the unknown number and felt my heart accelerate.

"Hello?"

"Faith? It's Gwynne."

I gripped the stone wall with my free hand.

"Hi. Thanks for calling me back."

"No problem at all, Faith. How are you, kid?"

I thought about that. How was I?

"Kane is out." That should answer her question.

"Ah. Are you still in Brooksby?" she asked.

"No. A few miles away. Sam's here, too."

"How's he taken it?"

I sighed. "Not great."

"What do you need to know?"

"Where he is. If he's looking for us. If our fear is justified. If we need to emigrate, or hire bodyguards. Or forget about him and move on." I turned around and leaned with my hip on the wall.

"Did the VCS let you know the conditions of his release?"

"He's not allowed to contact us."

"Give me a couple of days."

"Thanks, Gwynne."

"You are very welcome." Her voice softened. "Take care of yourself."

Phew. I was trying.

*   *   *

Sam was in bed when I called in later that day. He didn't want the tea I made, or the sandwich. April lay amongst the debris on the sofa, wearing Sam's tatty dressing gown.

I gave her his rejected tea, and switched off the television.

"What are you doing here, April?"

"I'm taking care of Sam. And the flat."

I looked around. I hoped she was taking better care of Sam than the flat. "Why?"

She shrugged. "I love him."

"How long have you known each other?"

"A few weeks. Long enough." She flicked a dreadlock out of her face.

"So you met him when he was well." I sat down on the seat opposite her.

"Yeah. But you don't just love someone when they're happy, do you? Love means being there when they need you."

"Sam suffers from serious mental illness. He's also been an addict for fourteen years. This could go on for weeks, maybe months. Then he might get better for a while, before another crash. He will probably start drinking again, and smoking whatever he can find to numb the torture. It's going to get a lot worse before it gets better. He needs serious help, April. Major commitment that will grind you down, wear you out, and wring you dry. No one would ask or expect that from someone he's just met."

She stared at me. "I don't care what anyone asks or expects. I want to be with Sam and I'm going to help him out of this. He'd do the same for me."

"No. He wouldn't."

Her eyes filled with tears. "I'm not just another one of those slappers! He told me about them. He's changed since he went in that place. He's not going to do that no more."

"Does it look like he's changed?" I waved my hand about at the mess.

"He told me what happened. Why he's like this."

"*What?*" That stopped me dead. Sam had never, as far as I knew, told anyone about Kane.

"I want to help him."

I sighed, running my hands through my hair. "How are you going to do that?"

"I'm making sure he eats, and takes his meds. I don't drink no more. I listen. I take his mind off it. I try to give him something to live for. You should be pleased you don't have to do it all by yourself."

I nodded. "But you understand Sam is extremely vulnerable? Taking care of him is really tough."

"I know that! I'm here doing it, aren't I?"

I raised my eyebrows. "You're sat watching television in a dressing gown in the middle of the afternoon. Look at this place. Did you live like this in your last house?"

She took a packet of cigarettes out of the dressing gown pocket and pulled one out, lighting it with shaking hands.

"April?"

She ignored me, taking a long drag.

"Where did you live before you met Sam? Do you have family round here?"

Her eyes flicked from one wall of the room to another. "My mum lives in Mansfield. We don't get on. I'd been sharing a house with a couple of mates but that didn't work out."

"So what will you do if this doesn't work out?"

She took another long drag. "I don't know. I'll find something."

"Sam said you were at the jobcentre last week."

She shrugged. "I lost my job when the café closed. Can't find nothing round here since. I'm not proud though! I'm looking."

"Don't let Sam get in the way of that." I handed her an empty mug to catch the ash dropping off the end of her cigarette.

"What, like you?" She grimaced. I didn't hate April. She was way sharper than she looked. I wondered if she might end up being good for Sam. But would she stick around long enough to find out? Not without help. And a truckload of personal power.

"What are you doing next Wednesday afternoon?"

* * *

The following day was Friday, and at seven-twenty I knocked on Marilyn's door with more than a little Hester-induced trepidation.

"It's open!"

I stepped inside, to be engulfed in a haze of baking smells – vanilla, cinnamon, and coffee. Marilyn appeared in the kitchen doorway, looking as though she'd fallen into the flour shaker.

"Faith, thank goodness it's you. I need a pricker."

"Excuse me?"

I followed her into the kitchen, where she shoved a fork into my hand and pointed me to a tray of raw shortbread.

"No time! Prick it! Then whack it in the oven."

I had often been in Marilyn's kitchen while she baked – it was her therapy once the twins were asleep. It had never before looked as though she'd been the one sleeping while Nancy and Pete did the baking.

"What's going on? Did Hester tell you to do all this?" I asked, as I started pricking.

"No." She shook her head, causing a cloud of icing sugar to puff off the top of her brown bun. "I'm nervous. Hester here. The choir here. Why? What's happening? Did I mention Hester will be here? In my house! Her eyebrows peering at my things."

She waved her hands about at the dozens of bowls, pans, spatulas, and food containers. "Peering at this!"

"It's fine. Calm down. You get on with the baking and I'll start clearing up. I don't think you need to let Hester, or anyone else, in the kitchen." I took the tray of shortbread and slid it into the oven.

"Looking at me!"

"So what if she does? So your kitchen's a mess and you've picked up a bit of flour. You've been baking. You've got twins. Your husband is away."

The doorbell rang.

"Help!"

I smothered my smile. "Go upstairs and get changed. I'll let them in and direct them to the living room. Calm down, Marilyn. Do some choir breathing. People'll think that chilled exterior is all a ruse."

She took a deep breath, gave a firm nod, and barrelled out of the room. I found Rowan and Hester on the doorstep, both wheeling suitcases.

I welcomed them in and sat them on one of the sofas. Marilyn had set out some glasses and a carafe of water on the coffee table, along with some cartons of fresh juice. They declined tea or coffee, but Rowan did help herself to the bowl of crisps.

Before I could check on Marilyn, the doorbell rang again, and for the next ten minutes I was letting people in, boiling the kettle, cutting up cake, and trying to keep an eye on the shortbread in the oven while deflecting everyone from the wreckage of the kitchen. To be fair, the rest of the house wasn't much better. While James had been home, things had been fairly *relaxed*. Since he'd left, they'd tumbled into shambolic.

Marilyn appeared as the last arrivals scurried in, depositing shoes and jackets in the hallway. By half seven, fed and watered, fourteen choir members were squished onto seats, chair arms, beanbags, and on cushions on the floor, all eyes on Hester.

"Good evening. And welcome to Marilyn's house. Thank you, Marilyn, for hosting us." Marilyn shrugged, unaware she had had any choice in the matter.

"You women are old and wise enough to know that true beauty comes from within."

"Speak for yourself!" said a couple of the younger women.

"Old?" exclaimed Janice. "That crossed a line, that did. I'm offended."

Hester swivelled her laser beam eyes to look at Janice, whose cheeks turned pink. She mouthed, "Sorry Hest."

"Confidence, poise, grace. A woman at peace with herself. Size and wrinkles are irrelevant. This choir is going to create something beautiful. But it cannot do that if you don't know you are beautiful. How can something ugly produce something beautiful, Leona?"

Leona, a fifty-something soprano, frowned. "Well, my kids are all gorgeous and I produced them."

"Are you ugly, Leona?"

She looked around at us, hoping someone would provide her with the right answer. "Well, I'm no Carol Vorderman."

"Rowan?" Hester nodded at her. Rowan opened up her suitcase, took out a large pink make-up bag, and opened it up. Removing a bottle and a wodge of cotton wool, she passed them to Leona. She then took out a couple more bottles, and more cotton wool, handing them to Rosa and the soprano called Mags.

"Remove your make-up please, then pass the cleanser and cotton wool along."

"What?" There were a few gasps and grumbles. Kim stood up. "Are you telling us we have to take our make-up off?"

"Yes."

"Why?" Kim asked, hands on her hips.

"Because it's part of this evening's exercise."

"I don't want to."

"Why?" Hester shot back.

"Because it took me ages, and I like it."

Hester stared impassively. "I remember clearly stating that participation in this evening is not optional, Kim."

Kim went so red it showed through her many layers of primer, concealer, foundation, powder, bronzer, and blusher. "You can't make me do it. It's not fair. I always wear make-up. I feel wrong without make-up on."

"Why are you getting angry, Kim?"

"Because I don't like people seeing me without make-up on! You know why. You heard me on the cliff. I *am* ugly. That's why. I don't want people to see that! I don't want them laughing at me."

"You think we'd laugh at you, Kim?" Melody asked, who having arrived with no make-up on had quickly passed the bottle along.

"No. Not out loud. But inside you would. You might. That's what they all used to do." Kim plonked back down into her armchair.

Melody shuffled her beanbag up to where Kim sat and took hold of her hand. When Millie had finished wiping her face, Melody took hold of the bottle and the cotton wool and handed it to Kim. "Come on, child. You are with friends. You have nothing to fear."

"Will you do it for me?"

Melody shook her head. "I will not."

Slowly, Kim poured out a drop of cleanser and began removing her armour, wiping away tears along with the cosmetics. "Great. Now I'm going to look all blotchy and red-eyed, too."

When we had nearly all finished, Hester opened the second

suitcase. She took out a pile of white T-shirts and began handing these round, too. "Please change into the T-shirts."

What?

Some of the women were happy to fling off their jumpers and blouses, swapping into the T-shirts without thinking. Millie and Janice gave us all a little striptease as they shimmied out of their Marks and Spencer twinsets. Uzma and her cousin Yasmin asked if they could wear them over their shirts, as they preferred to keep their arms covered. Hester dug through the pile and found two long-sleeved T-shirts for them instead. They ducked behind the sofa to change, giggling. I was disappointed by this. I wanted to sneak a peek at Uzma's fancy red lace, purple silk, or leopard print bra.

Mags, one of the larger ladies in the room, who happened to be sitting next to Marilyn, made a gesture of removing her jumper, making jokes about her sagging breasts and flabby stomach. It didn't stop Marilyn from looking as though she wanted to die as she scrambled out of her own top. In her haste, a button snagged in her hair, leaving her sitting with her top up over her head, one arm flailing, the other desperately trying to cover up her post-pregnancy body before Mags hurriedly set her free, making a kind joke as she did so.

Gradually, the other self-conscious women gave in, until me and Polly, baby bump gently bulging under her maternity clothes, were the only ones left.

"Polly?" Hester asked. "Didn't you find the maternity top in the pile?"

"Yes," she whispered. "But could I have a long-sleeved top, please?"

Rowan, whose baggy T-shirt covered more of her thighs than her dress had, boggled her eyes. "You've got a belly like a beach ball and you're worried about your arms?"

I sat and watched, adrenaline sprinting through my veins. I should have changed when the rest were doing it. Nobody would have noticed. I should do it now, while they looked at Polly.

Get changed, Faith! Whip your sweater off and throw the T-shirt on before you cause a scene. You can do it!

I couldn't. My limbs were lead.

Polly looked around at us all, stricken. "I… it was… I don't want… You don't understand."

"Nobody's looking, Polly. Look." Millie began pointedly staring at the ceiling. Someone else rummaged in their bag for nothing in particular. Animated conversations requiring full-on eye contact broke out across the room as the others caught on. Kim, though, was having none of it.

"Come on, Polly. Nobody's judging you here. Apparently."

Lowering her head, shoulders slumped, positively cowering in her chair, Polly began slowly undoing the buttons on her pretty maternity blouse. Unable to bear her mortification, I sucked in a fortifying breath, stood up, and stripped off my top.

Everybody froze. A couple of people gasped. Janice said, "Wowzers, Faith! Did you get those wrestling a crocodile?"

No, not a crocodile, Janice. The four-inch slice beneath my collarbone and the eight-inch jagged red rip across my stomach were obtained while fighting off a Snake. I put on the T-shirt and took my seat, trying to keep my chin up and hands still. I was not ashamed of having scars. I didn't care that they were ugly. I was very, very ashamed of how I got those scars, and the ugliness that accompanied them.

Polly, meanwhile, had changed too, and now sat huddled in her chair, hands quietly folded in her lap.

Oh my.

Her arms were covered, from the edge of the T-shirt to just above her wrists, with a hideous palette of blue and black, yellow, green, and violet, like monstrous tattoo sleeves. Fingerprints from an evil hand. Polly glanced up at us, her eyes wide with fear. "I fall a lot. Low blood pressure," she muttered.

She knew that we knew.

Hester, who probably knew all this already, using her X-ray

vision, and seemed as unsurprised by my scars as she was by Polly's bruises, clapped her hands together once to call the meeting to order.

Oh yes – we'd forgotten there was supposed to be a point to all this stripping.

"Leona, you're first. Please stand in front of the mirror," Hester said.

Leona, rolling her shoulders awkwardly, twisted until she faced the mirror.

"Now. Rowan, please tell Leona what you see."

Leona stiffened; I think only Hester's grasp of her shoulder prevented her from bolting out of the room. Leona didn't usually wear much make-up, or dress in especially flattering clothes, but white was not a good colour on her.

Rowan pursed her lips in thought. "I see your eyes. They're like, nice. And kind. You don't look at me like you think I'm worse than you 'cos I'm young and I've got a kid and I never passed any exams." She paused before continuing, "Sometimes I wonder what it would be like if you'd been my mum."

Leona jerked in astonishment.

Rosa was next. "I see a woman who always put everybody first. It your fault your children are fine woman and man because you gave all your love to them. Did great job."

Uzma said, "Rowan's right. You look at people as though you really care about how they are. If I had a problem, I'd be glad to have you around."

And so we carried on, right around the circle. By the end, Leona seemed somewhat shell-shocked. In a good way.

Melody went next. And one by one, fourteen women stood in front of that mirror, some of whom barely knew each other, others who had walked shoulder to shoulder through dozens of the challenges women face. There were many smiles, many hugs, many tissues spilling over the edge of the bin by the end of it. To say I felt terrified when I took my place in front of Marilyn's oak-framed mirror didn't begin to cover it. What did these women see when they looked at me? Did I want it to be the truth, or the mask I wore, the pretend Faith? Was she almost the same thing these days?

"I see a woman who is strong as well as tough," Melody told me.

"I see a woman beginning to find out who she really is, and there is nothing more lovely than that," said Mags.

"Faith, I see in your eyes and your crocodile scars a woman who has suffered, but hasn't let it make her bitter," Millie declared.

"Faith, I love your hair. Millions of women would kill for hair that colour and that thick. You must be doing something right to have hair that thick."

"Thanks, Rowan."

"I love that you have no idea how beautiful you are," Kim said. "You catch the eye of most men you walk past, and don't even realize. I even caught Dylan staring at you."

Excuse me? Can we please erase that comment? Not helpful to my embarrassing childish crush.

"You were a survivor," Marilyn said. "But now you're well on your way to being a conqueror. I look at you and I see a kick-butt queen like Boadicea lurking just beneath the surface."

"It's the hair!" Janice said.

"It's not the hair. Well, maybe a bit her hair. But it's more than that. There's something about you that inspires me to fight for what matters. You get what's important. Not many people manage that."

"Thanks, Marilyn."

"You're welcome, buddy."

Polly was last, having been the last to get ready. We all told her pretty much the same thing.

"I see a woman who is beautiful, and kind, and precious, and deserves to be cherished, and treated with love and care and respect *at all times*."

"I see a woman with many friends who love her, who will do whatever it takes to protect her and make sure she is safe and can live somewhere safe. Like my house. I have a spare room with a soft bed and cushions and a cream dressing table. You won't fall and hurt yourself at my house, Polly."

Polly hated every second of it.

She tried to cover up those bruises with her hands, stared at the floor, and looked as though she was trying to shrivel into her shame. I wondered how many times she had stood like that in front of the monster who decorated her arms.

It would be a long road, no doubt, but we were only getting started with Polly.

Hester then tried to move on to phase two of the evening, but we weren't ready. We jostled her into the special place before the mirror and forced her to look at herself.

"Hester, underneath that chain mail you have the biggest heart of anyone I know," said Ebony, a quiet soprano who spent most of the time caring for her elderly parents.

Hester snorted.

"Don't you dare snort. It's our turn now," Janice barked. "I see the woman who brought me dinner and sat and ate it with me every night for two weeks after my no-good, cheating, brain in his pants husband ran off with the tart-with-no-heart. That's above and beyond the call of duty. You go above and beyond."

We carried on around the circle.

I said, "I see a woman who cares more about us than about what we think of her. Who is prepared to be disliked and moaned about if it means we can be better women. That's a rare and courageous thing. You are selfless, Hester."

"Got something in your eye, Hester?" Millie asked.

Hester span around like a soldier on parade. "Enough! We are now twelve minutes behind schedule, thanks to your long-windedness and sentimentality. Please assemble before the mantelpiece in concert formation. Quickly now!"

Our brief mutiny over, we all formed a huddle in front of the hearth. Before we had a chance to wonder why, Hester ordered us to "remind yourself of the most pleasing thing someone said to you in front of the mirror." We did. There was a flash, and Hester took our picture. She handed it to Yasmin, an IT whizz, who took a couple of minutes setting it up on Marilyn's enormous television.

First, she showed a still of the choir practice when we had been recorded. Then she flicked to today's photograph.

Were they the same women? We looked taller, stronger, surer, freer. Beautiful. All of us except for Polly, who looked miserable and terrified. We looked raw, and we looked real.

"Choir. Do you need make-up and flattering colours and fancy fashion to be beautiful?"

No, Ma'am, we did not.

"What do you need?"

We called out the answers: confidence, to feel good about ourselves, to relax, great friends, honesty, to feel proud, to know we're loved, to know we are accepted. We needed each other.

Are all choirs like this?

Or only the great ones?

"Now. This is what makes me mad!" Hester smacked her hands together. Uh oh. "Why did you need a special meeting, bullying, make-up remover, a pile of white T-shirts, and a mirror to discover this? Why are you not telling each other this stuff every week? Every night? Once a year? Why does it take a crisis, or a tragedy, or a birthday – or someone to *die* – before we can spell out what it is that makes them unique, and marvellous? What are you so afraid of?"

She glowered at us all.

"I tell you this. And it is not a threat, it is a *vow*. If we resort back to *them*" – she flapped one hand distastefully at the rehearsal recording – "we will do this again. And full nudity will be required. Rowan."

Rowan reopened her suitcase and took out a bag of hairbrushes, like those you would get in a salon. She then took out straighteners, curlers, rollers, and a load of clips, grips, and other hairdressing equipment.

"Right. Hester said if we did okay I could do your hair. If you want. But I have to get my bus in an hour so it can't be everyone."

"Rowan, if you can sort this squirrel's nest I'll give you a lift home," Leona said.

Kim put up her hand. "I can help, Rowan. I did a bit of styling on my beauty course."

So, the weird evening morphed into a pyjama party, only with white T-shirts instead of pyjamas. Marilyn and I fetched more drinks and cakes while the choir were primped and styled in Rowan and Kim's capable hands. And they did seem more than capable. Rowan instinctively knew what would suit each of us.

"Can you cut hair, Rowan?" Mags asked, while Rowan began a complicated type of chignon.

"A bit. I'm not trained or anything. I just like it. I did all my sisters when they had their prom. Mum said it was only fair 'cos I wasn't allowed to go to mine," she replied through the grips in her mouth.

"Why weren't you allowed to go?"

"I knocked one of the teachers out cold."

"Knocked them out?" Uzma boggled. "How?"

"Punched 'em. They were windin' me up. I used to have a right temper on me, then. Didn't know what to do with all that stress before Hester taught me to sing it out."

"Well, school can be quite stressful." Mags raised her eyebrows while trying to keep her head still.

"Nah. Annabel, my social worker, said it was the baby messing with my emotions. By nine months they're takin' over, like an alien, she said."

"You punched your teacher when you were nine months pregnant?" Uzma's eyes were complete circles.

"Yeah. So I think they should've allowed me to the prom, really. Extenuating circumstances. My nan got me one of those baby slings, in red so it matched my dress and everything. I could've taken her with me. It wasn't fair." She pinned up the last twist of Mags's hair and sat back to inspect her work.

"Perhaps you should train properly, if you enjoy it. Go to college, or get an apprenticeship in a salon?" I said.

"I could, but paying for the childcare would leave me skint. My mum watches Callie for me enough as it is. And it would only interfere with my music career."

"You have a music career?" Mags stood up to go and look in the mirror.

"Not yet. But you can't give up your dream."

Rowan spent a long time on my hair, taming the copper curls into glossy ringlets, then pinning most of them up so I resembled a heroine from a Jane Austen novel.

"Rowan, would you come and do my hair for my wedding? I'll pay you, of course."

She shrugged. "Yeah, s'pose." But I saw the gleam of joy in her eyes when she turned to pick up the comb.

"And my bridesmaids. There's three."

"And what about my work Christmas party?" Yasmin asked. "Will you do my hair for that?"

By the end of the evening Rowan had four bookings. We had a quick run through of "O Holy Night" as we cleared up, flicking our fancy locks and smiling at our new, more beautiful selves. I walked home through crisp moonlight back to my little terraced house, and made it nearly all the way there before realizing with a shock that I hadn't once looked over my shoulder for Kane.

Chapter Nine

The summer I sat my school exams resembled a car crash. How could I concentrate on French verbs and simultaneous equations while struggling to survive? Waking up every morning wondering if my brother would still be alive. Waiting for the police to bash down the door, or social services to come and take me away. How could I find the time or energy to revise when I worked five nights a week, spending my nights off and weekends cleaning up filth, washing my clothes in the bath, and trying to stretch pennies into pounds so I could quell the constant hunger?

When all I thought about was avoiding the Snake.

My exam results were a disaster. I spent the summer washing pots, trying not to think about my prospects, and sinking deeper and deeper into a murky pit of despair.

At some point during the summer, I caught Snake's attention. He started offering me drugs or alcohol. I declined. Any flicker of temptation I may have felt at the chance of temporary oblivion was quickly stamped out by the up close and personal knowledge of what that oblivion cost.

So he backed off a little, and began making me cups of tea. Or a sandwich. Bringing me a take-away. More than a little weird – cosying up in front of a rom-com and sharing a curry with my spaced-out brother and his dealer.

Sometimes I would come home to find he'd cleaned the kitchen. He paid me compliments – not creepy ones, but crafty ones about my smile, or how clever I was, or how he wished he had a sister like me. He told me time and time again that I wasn't like the other girls – he admired my choice to stay clean and work hard. He would give me a lift to the pub if the weather was bad, and wait for me at the end of a late shift in his rusty car.

It took weeks, months even, but my life had shrunk to a very small world with few inhabitants. At nearly seventeen, desperate for any kind of meaningful connection, woefully starved of affection, with no idea of what a real man was like, no compass to assess normal behaviour, I slowly let Snake twist his evil lies around me.

I hated myself for it, but I began to enjoy the feel of his arm when he casually draped it around my shoulders, like Sam had once done. I let him hug me, squealing as he span me around when feeling playful. A couple of times he stuck a CD on and cajoled me into dancing with him in the living room while Sam beat time on the table. I had never danced with a boy before. Never really danced before. He started kissing me goodbye on the cheek before he left, or held my hand as he pulled me out of the pub door and into his car in a rainstorm, knowing my poor, starving heart would take the fake love of a wicked man if it meant I could for a few moments believe somebody actually cared about me.

As Sam grew worse, Snake shared his concern. My brother barely left his bedroom, rarely ate, or changed his clothes. He had lost any remnant of control, and my worry for him was a gnawing beast on my back. Snake suggested he take him to a doctor. I agreed, anxious beyond words to do something, anything. I don't know what he said, or even whether it was the right decision or not, but Sam got admitted to hospital. I now lived alone with Snake.

It was November. The week of my seventeenth birthday. Snake was thirty-two.

For three days I got up, went to work, tried to eat and sleep. My lodger lay low, made sure there was food in the house, and kept the chaos to a minimum. He invited me to eat with him at lunchtimes, which I did, on edge but still pathetically grateful for the attention. *He's not so bad*, I thought.

Wrong. He was worse.

On the fourth day, I had an early shift. I came home to find dinner on the table. Not a sandwich this time, a proper meal. There were candles and a vase of flowers. He had laid out napkins and a bottle of wine.

My heart began to thump, either with nerves or anticipation, I had no idea.

"Happy birthday, Faith." He entered the kitchen, holding out a gift bag.

"How did you know?" I took the bag with trembling hands.

"How could I not know? I care about you, Faith. Open your present."

I obeyed him, unwrapping the tissue paper to find a dress. Bottle green, stretchy, short, and strapless. A dress those other girls would wear – the ones Snake said I was better than.

"Don't you like it?"

"No, it's really nice. Thanks."

He smiled, appearing genuinely pleased. As if it mattered to him what I thought.

"Well, food is nearly ready. Why don't you go and put it on, and I'll dish up?"

I took my time removing my worn jeans and sweatshirt, pulling the dress on and zipping it up before wriggling out of my bra. I shut my brain off, not able to comprehend what Snake might be expecting from all this. Knowing he always took what he wanted, but still desperate to keep pretending that I was different, that I was special. He might even love me. I might even be loveable.

Brushing out my frizzed-up hair, I heard a sound behind me.

Turning, I found him leaning on the doorframe, a smile playing at the corners of his mouth.

"Well, well. Look what's been hiding under those jumpers. You're gorgeous."

He stepped inside, carefully closing the door. My breath jammed in my throat. Snake, in my bedroom, his eyes glinting. Would I do what he wanted? Would I have any choice?

"I thought dinner was ready."

"Not yet." He sat on my drooping single bed. "Come here."

All those touches, the kisses, the compliments, the gifts tumbled around my brain like litter in a storm. With the twisted logic of a neglected child, I felt I owed him this.

I sat down. He put out one hand and stroked my face. "Don't be afraid of me, Faith. I'm not going to hurt you."

He lied.

* * *

Wednesday, I went round early to Sam's to drop off some shopping and clean up a bit before taking April to choir practice.

When I let myself in, the flat appeared tidy. Slightly disconcerted, I went into the kitchen. The Formica work surfaces gleamed. New tea and coffee pots lined up smartly next to the sparkling kettle. Even the floor had been mopped.

I dumped the shopping on the table, and opened the tiny fridge door. It was already full. A half-eaten cottage pie took up one shelf. The others were stuffed with salad, vegetables, a packet of chicken breasts, cheese, fresh juice, eggs, and a chocolate cake.

Oh.

A prickle of irritation skittered up my spine and lodged at the base of my skull.

Squeezing a box of cereal and some tins into a well-stocked cupboard, I left the rest of the shopping and went to find Sam, ducking my head into a spotless bathroom on the way.

I found him in bed, conked out.

"Sam." Shaking his shoulder, not a little roughly, I woke him up.

"Faith. What time is it?"

"Nearly one. Have you been in bed all morning?"

"No." He pulled himself up to a sitting position, running his hand over thick beard. "I went out with April."

"Where?"

"For a walk. The nurse told April I need to get out the house every day, so we walk now. To the river and back. It knackers me out."

"Maybe you shouldn't go so far, then?"

He shrugged. "I like it. It's peaceful by the water. And if I didn't I'd still be knackered."

I tried to squish down my annoyance.

"Have you eaten? I brought some bacon."

"Uh, yeah." He rubbed his head, as if trying to get his mind going. "We had a salad thing, with fish. April's been reading about a diet that can help your mood."

"I think your illness is a bit more than a bad mood, Sam," I snapped. "If food was the issue, someone would have mentioned it by now."

"She's trying to help."

"I can see that."

Sam's girlfriends, if they could be called that, fell into two camps – those that joined him and those that tried to change him. The ones who tried to change him generally lasted a couple of weeks, maybe a month at the most. None of them had the patience, the selflessness, or the strength to persist. That was my job.

"Do you want a cup of tea? Or some cake?"

"No. Thanks. I really need to sleep."

"Where's April now? I'm meant to be taking her to choir practice."

"Oh, um, yeah. She said something about that. She can't come. She's got a job interview."

Right. And how long will the lovely April stick around if she gets a job?

"Where did the flowers come from?" A vase of yellow roses stood on the bedside table.

"I sold a painting." He rolled back over, with his back to me.

He was painting again?

"Don't tell April. She thought I should hold out for a higher price," he mumbled through the duvet.

"Since when did you care what anybody else thought?"

He was painting?

So why did I feel peeved rather than pleased?

* * *

A couple of weeks later, Rosa came round for the first bridesmaid dress consultation. I had taken an alarming chunk out of my Avoid Returning to a Bedsit at All Costs emergency savings, and also borrowed a couple of hundred pounds from Marilyn. This would cover the price of the bridesmaid dress fabric, a good second-hand sewing machine, and all the extras like dressmaking scissors, buttons, and thread. Compared to the kind of outfits Catherine and Natasha would expect if we bought them new, it was a bargain.

I could have asked Perry to pay for the dresses. Or used the credit card he had given me. The teensy, tiny microdot of pride I had left, along with my deep reluctance to feel indebted to a man, ever, forbade it.

Rosa had taken Marilyn's vital statistics at a previous choir practice. She arrived at mine with a bag containing a mocked-up dress in cheap material, a sketch book, and a tape measure.

Catherine and Natasha arrived soon afterwards in a gaggle of flowery perfume, overlarge designer handbags, and pumpkin-spice coffee. I made Rosa, Marilyn, and me supermarket-own-brand cups of tea.

"Right." Rosa beamed at us, perched on my little armchair. "I have some very exciting designs to show you. Marilyn's dress is already begun, but first I need information. Like – what colour is this wedding? What is the theme – the flowers or invitations or location? And – most of all – what is the wedding dress? Otherwise, I cannot make good match."

They all looked at me with expectant smiles. Natasha clapped her hands together a few times with excitement.

I pretended it wasn't weird meeting one of my bridesmaids for the first time.

"Right. So. I haven't really thought much about that stuff yet. I thought it would be nice to have a colour that suited all of you, then we can choose everything else to match."

Three pairs of eyes goggled at me. "You don't have your colours yet?"

"Nope."

"I have my colours picked and I don't even have a boyfriend!" Catherine said. "Everyone has their colours, don't they?" She looked at Natasha for confirmation.

"Mint, sea foam, and yellow."

"Fig, camel, and blush pink," Catherine said. "See? What about you, Marilyn?"

Marilyn grinned. "I had old man underpants and rancid chicken."

"Pardon?"

"Yellow and pewter."

"Right!" Catherine looked back to me. "So, what are you going to choose?"

I looked at my three bridesmaids. "Umm... what colour dresses would you like?"

An hour later, Rosa had taken all the essential measurements, and they had decided they liked blue.

We chose navy for Marilyn as matron-of-honour, as it flattered her mid-brown hair and paler skin, and "dusty aqua" for the others, as they preferred a colour with a fancier name.

"That is good," Rosa said. "I will make beautiful navy dress make Marilyn look like she very sexy lady, and dusty aqua dresses, give you girls shape. We give you nice round hips so men think you make good babies."

"Um, I don't think men are really bothered about that."

Catherine frowned, glancing at Marilyn's ample frame.

"Hah! That what you think. Men all modern now, talking about feelings, wearing guyliner and leggings, don't give up seat on the bus any more. But it there in old bit of brain. What you say? Caveman bit. I don't know proper word for this. Anyway, first we need see wedding dress so Faith look more gorgeous than rest of you. Faith – you go get dress and I pin Marilyn's sample while we wait."

"Actually, I don't mind if their dresses don't match mine."

"What? That make no sense. I'm top-class seamstress. I make match and still look good on these skinny women."

"I know, but I don't think it's fair to make my dress look better than theirs."

"Of course fair! You the bride! Stop being so nice. Go and put dress on."

"Okay, but the other dresses will have to be quite ugly if mine's going to look nicer."

"Fine. Whatever. I don't understand you now. We want see dress please."

I trudged up the stairs and took the Ghost Web out of the wardrobe in my tiny spare room. Yanking it on, I didn't bother looking in the mirror before returning to the living room.

Marilyn shook her head. "It gets worse every time I see it. I always think it won't be as bad as I remember, but my mind can't actually retain how awful it is."

She, on the other hand, looked incredible, having borrowed my bedroom to change into the tight-waisted, three-quarter-length-sleeved sample dress. It had a huge, floor-length skirt of floaty material that would have made me appear like a child drowning in her mother's party frock.

"You look incredible, Marilyn."

"Wish I could say the same to you."

The others stared at me, mouths open.

"I'm trying really hard to think of something positive to say, like, 'It's not that bad; with a couple of alterations we can make it fabulous.'" Catherine screwed up her face. "I'm sorry, Faith. I know we just met, and Larissa is your mother-in-law. But, honestly? That is the worst dress I have ever seen. It doesn't fit you, or suit you. Your shape, style, or your complexion. You cannot wear that dress on your *wedding day*. You can't wear that dress to empty the bin. I think it might be too scary for Hallowe'en."

I was starting to quite like Catherine.

Rosa had turned the colour of pickled cabbage. One of her country's national dishes.

"That is not a dress!" she choked. "It is a... a... I cannot even find the words!"

"It's a Ghost Web," Marilyn said.

"I don't give a *rakia* what it is! Take it off!"

The doorbell rang.

We froze, caught like nuns in their underwear.

"I'll get it." Natasha stood up. "I'll think of an excuse to get rid of them."

Too late. The front door opened and somebody stepped in.

"Hello?"

Oh dear. My nearly mother-in-law.

"Faith?"

And Perry.

"We heard you were having a bridesmaid fitting. Mother thought she'd join you. Hope that's –"

I didn't wait to hear any more. As Larissa's pointy heels tapped down my tiled hallway, no doubt preceded by Perry's Italian leather brogues, I frantically searched for a hiding place. There was only one way into my tiny sitting room, I wasn't going to squeeze into the television cabinet, and if I hid behind the sofa it would end up pushed into the middle of the room. In a moment of crazed panic at the thought of Perry seeing me in my wedding dress – not for superstitious reasons but for hideous ones – I dove under the only available cover: Marilyn's enormous poofy sample skirt. She rapidly shimmied back into the space between the armchair and the window, to provide maximum concealment. I curled into a ball, and waited for the most embarrassing moment of my life to be over.

There was a tap on the door. It squeaked open.

"Oh. Hi, ladies. Is Faith not around?"

"Perry!" Natasha said, judging by the squeal-like tone. "This is a dress fitting, you cheeky man. Get out!"

"Yes!" probably Catherine added (the voices were quite muffled underneath the net petticoat and I was trying not to breathe too deeply due to hiding between a person's legs. Thank goodness it was November and Marilyn had kept her chunky tights on). "What would Faith say if she heard you came bursting in here, knowing full well there were likely to be young women in a state of undress?"

"My apologies." I could hear the smile in Perry's voice. "I didn't think. As you know I only have eyes for one woman."

Somebody snorted. Somebody else said, "Ooh. That's soooo sweet!"

"Is she here?"

"She's upstairs getting on her wedding dress, so you'd better scram." Catherine. I could tell by the way she rolled the r.

"Ah! Best had. As tempting as it might be. Don't want to ruin the big surprise."

Larissa sniffed. "It's hardly a surprise, Perry. A photograph of me in the dress has been hanging on the wall at home for forty-eight years."

"That may well be the case, Mother, but I don't look at you and Faith in quite the same way. I'll be off then. When will you ladies be done here?"

"Ten minutes at most," Rosa said. "No point you staying now. We chose colour and everything, did measurements. Tried sample. Just looking at Faith's dress to make sure it match. Then done."

"Well," Larissa said, "I hardly think you should have made those decisions without me. What if the colour clashes with my outfit? I insist on being filled in on everything. Perry, you can pick me up in an hour."

Sweat pooled in the back of my knees as I tried to remain balanced in a squatting position. The air hung thick and humid like a hothouse, only without any plants to replenish the oxygen. As Perry said goodbye and left, leaving an awkward silence, cramp began burning up my calves.

"She's taking her time," Larissa barked. "One of you go and help her."

"Would you like a cup of tea, Aunt Larissa?" Natasha asked. "Why don't you come into the kitchen while I make one?"

"Why indeed?"

Marilyn, who must have been struggling as much as me from having to balance in one position with a person crouching almost between her legs, began to wiggle her hips, bending her knees as her muscles twitched.

"I'll go and get Faith," she said. "Perhaps she's got stuck in her zip or something."

"Please do!"

No, Marilyn. Please don't.

She took a tiny, exploratory step away from the wall. I jiggled two inches after her, biting my knuckles to stop me groaning as the cramp shot up my legs.

"I'll come with you." Catherine came and stood behind us. "Help you not to trip in this beautiful dress."

"Not beautiful – it is a sample!" Rosa said.

"Well, we don't want her falling down the stairs in it, do we?" Catherine bent down and pretended to hold the skirt up out of the way, in actual fact trying to hide the woman-like shape underneath while not lifting it so high that you could see the woman was me. This obviously failed, as Natasha came to join her as we shuffled forwards, both of them surrounding the dress like geese following a farmer with a bucket of corn.

What Catherine failed to notice, as we bizarrely waddled out of the room, was the bottom of the Ghost Web trailing out from under the thick folds of Marilyn's dress. Marilyn began to speed up as she reached the exit. As I hurried with her as best I could in my squatting position, the hem of the Ghost Web snagged on the bottom of the living room door. I pulled against the resistance, without realizing what it was, and a distinct ripping sound erupted from the bottom of Marilyn's skirts.

"Sorry," she said, nearly falling through the doorway in her haste. "I had cauliflower cheese for lunch."

We all tumbled after her, barely making it to the bottom of the stairs before collapsing in a pile of giggles. Scrambling up and into my bedroom, the laughter died in our throats as we saw the state of my wedding dress. A three-inch-wide section had torn away from the bottom, and now dangled by a thread. The pressure had caused the skirt seam to detach from the low waistband (hip-band, in my short-legged case), leaving a gaping, jagged hole. Never mind the sweat patches on the overly tight underarm sections, or the stretched seams where my hunched-over back had pushed the fabric further than it was ever designed to go.

"Hooray!" Marilyn whispered. "The Ghost Web is destroyed!"

"Not hooray," I hissed back. "Larissa is downstairs waiting for me to come down in it."

"Just tell her it doesn't fit," Catherine said.

"She's already seen me in it. She knows I can get it on."

"Well, you have to do something."

* * *

"I thought you were putting on the dress? Don't tell me. You've changed your mind and decided to wear jeans!" Larissa glowered at me as if to say *I wouldn't put it past you, given the rest of your decisions regarding this wedding.*

"Yes. Well. There is a slight problem there."

She raised her Botoxed brow as far as it would go.

"I seem to have put on some weight since I last tried it on, so, um, it doesn't actually fit me at the moment."

She scrutinized me for a moment, scanning me up and down as if I were a horse at the county show.

"Are you with child?"

"No! No. Definitely not. I'm not walking as much since I stopped working at HCC. It must be that."

"Hmmm. Well. I'll give Anton a call. Set something up. We can't have this continuing for much longer or we'll have to cancel *Nottinghamshire Life*. It's bad enough that…" She glanced at Marilyn and pursed her lips.

"Excuse me!" Marilyn stood grandly in her sample dress. "I am in the room, and I do have two perfectly functioning ears."

"I'm sorry. Did I say something to offend you? I don't recall mentioning your name."

I said nothing. Be "set up" with Anton, Larissa's brutal personal trainer to lose pretend weight I hadn't even put on, so I could squeeze into the ruined Ghost Web and feature in *Nottinghamshire Life*? Or alternatively I could conjure up some personal power and tell Larissa where to stick it.

I swallowed, hard. "Thank you, Larissa. I'll think about it."

"There's nothing to think about. Nobody wants a fat bride. Especially Perry. Now, could you please call him to come and pick me up? It's going to be a nightmare trying to find something blue that doesn't make me look like I'm old enough to be a grandmother. But what do I matter? I am just the mother of the groom!"

As soon as she left I ran upstairs and brought the Ghost Web to show Rosa.

"Can you mend it?"

"No!"

"Oh. Maybe if I took it to an alterations place, they could do something?"

"No, no, no! Of course I have the skills to mend it. I could make this dress look as if it never happened." She started packing her sewing equipment away.

"But you said you can't mend it."

"That's right."

"But you can mend it?" I squinted at her, confused.

"Yes."

"I don't understand. Are you going to mend it or not?"

"Wait for one moment." Rosa took out her Bulgarian/English dictionary and did some flicking about. "Here we are. *Technicality* I can mend it. No problem, easy peasy lemon is squeezing." She flicked some more. "Morally I cannot."

"Pardon?"

"I am an artist! A professional! The best Bulgarian seamstress in UK! I will not repair that terrible, ugly, horrible dress. It does not fit you, Faith. It is made for woman of no boobs and no behind and no tasteful. How can you think of wearing" – she picked up a fold of the dress between one forefinger and thumb as if it was covered in slime – "*this*? *On your wedding day*?"

"It's only a dress. Please, Rosa. Even if I don't wear it, I can't give it back to Larissa like this. Can't you do something?"

Rosa thought for a few minutes, pacing up and down my tiny living room, tapping a pencil against her forehead. Eventually, she stopped.

"Okay. You doing me big, big favour, buy me machine and all these other things. Trust me to make dresses for your wedding. It breaks my heart, but I will do this: mend horrible dress, alter to fit. Also make you dress I design, free of charge. Then you can choose what dress you want."

"Yessss!" Marilyn fist-pumped the air.

"Okay." I am not usually a hopeful woman. I think that's understandable, all things considered. Yet the glimpse of optimism scampering across my peripheral vision wore ivory antique lace and a flower in her hair. There were nine months until my wedding. Larissa could change her mind, or get run over by an HCC golf cart. I could keep on singing, breathing out my fear and sucking in personal power until I told Larissa what she could do with her Ghost Web. Maybe, just maybe, I would find a way to be an Upperton wife and still be me. Once I figured out who that was, of course.

Chapter Ten

Gwynne took a week or so to call me, but she did with a reassurance that Kane was living in a house for ex-prisoners in Merseyside, working part time, and keeping his head down. He would be under probation for the rest of his life, and if he broke that – including missing any meetings or doing something that would land him back in prison – his offender manager would keep her informed.

I was not reassured. In my memory, Kane remained a monster, fuelled by hate, anger, envy, and the need to dominate. How could eighteen years locked up in a high-security prison have lessened that? But living looking over my shoulder, jumping at shadows, and wasting away with the "what ifs" proved too exhausting to sustain. We knew he would come. Now, at least we should have some warning.

* * *

November meandered along frosty footpaths into the twinkly lights of December. Choir rehearsals intensified, if that were possible, as Hester attempted to ready us for the debut performance at the Grace Chapel Christmas carol service. April, still hunting for work, allowed me to bring her along.

Hester expressed her irritation at a newcomer showing up so close to the big night.

"You can stay, but if you aren't ready you won't sing at the carol service."

April shrugged. "Okay."

"Now, repeat after me…"

A clear soprano, I introduced her to some of the others at coffee time. She struck up a conversation with Rowan.

"Enjoy it?" Rowan asked.

"I wasn't expecting to, but it was all right, yeah. It sounded good when you sang it that last time. Dead Christmassy."

"Will you come back then?"

April nodded. "I think so. I might even see if my boyfriend'll come to the service. He doesn't really like Christmas."

"What? Why would anyone not like Christmas?"

I stood, hovering, willing April to say something stupid so I could justify my annoyance at her intrusion into my family. Instead, she shrugged. "It's complicated. Some bad memories. But this year's a chance to make some better ones, I reckon."

Bad memories. You have no idea, I thought. Or did she? Did she know about the Christmases Sam spent in hospital? The squat? Perhaps even more miserable than those he wouldn't remember at all. I usually worked Christmas Day, unable to turn away triple pay, and generally Sam spent most of it in bed with a bottle, or out seeking the hollow comfort of a stranger as lonely and depressed as himself.

It looked as though this year I would be choosing between an Upperton Christmas, or cosying up with Sam and April. I couldn't have imagined anything worse, until Perry suggested we combine the two.

Maybe Marilyn had a spare place at her Christmas dinner table?

* * *

My first scar, the four-inch slash beneath my collarbone, was a Christmas present from Snake. I don't know the official name for what I had become – his girlfriend or lover? His victim? Whatever name I called myself, it didn't disguise that I was sleeping with a drug dealer. A man who controlled me with his mood swings, his money, his raw power, and absolute supremacy. Occasionally his fists.

Christmas Eve, he objected to me working so many hours over the holiday period. I objected to him having sex with all the skanky women who came round begging for handouts. He said he wouldn't need to if I was around more, and ordered me to get undressed even though I had a shift in the pub.

In my head, I knew this was wrong. I knew he treated me like a slave. He was a merciless man who had no more capacity to love me than a cockroach did. But he wanted me, for something, and in my twisted heart that felt better than nothing.

However, some kind of survival instinct kicked in when he told me to skip work. It remained my one tenuous thread to a different reality, to a world where people sat down to eat Christmas dinner with their family, swapped presents, played board games, and talked about where they were going on holiday. He didn't know that half my tips were stashed in a metal box the pub manager let me keep in her office.

"No. I have to go to work."

He sneered at me. "What, because they couldn't possibly cope without you to wash the pots? A monkey could do your job. And probably better."

"I need the money."

"I've got money. Look." He pulled a wodge of notes out of his jacket pocket and thrust them in my face. "Oh no – you won't touch my money, will you? Might taint that perfect white skin of yours. Too good for my money. Except when it pays your rent. Or the electricity. Or the food in your sexy belly."

I tried to push past him, to get my bag and go. He grabbed my hair, yanking me back into the bedroom.

"I said, get undressed."

"I said, I'm going to work." I could hear the fear in my voice, the hint of panic. Snake could hear it too. He laughed, grabbing my shoulders and slamming me against the wall.

"No, darling. You're going to do what I tell you."

I screamed, making him laugh even harder. The couple of people passed out downstairs wouldn't dare intervene, even if they could hear me.

"You're not going anywhere."

The phrase triggered something deep in my memories.

You're not going anywhere.

I had heard those words before, many times, spoken by a snake in a different skin.

I remembered what she said – that night – the night we packed our bags and so very nearly made it. *We're going, Rachel. Starting a whole new life. With a new name. Faith means strong. It's being sure of what we hope for, and certain of what we don't see. We can't see it yet, but there's a new life waiting for us.*

I didn't understand my mother's words. Not then, not now as Snake bored his crusted eyes into mine, daring me to resist him. But I knew, standing here with my back against the wall, what she would say. She died trying to free me from a life like this. She had *died.* Beaten and bloodied on the floor while her baby hid in the wardrobe under an old coat and her son begged the police to hurry.

I thought about all the times Grandma found me hiding in my new wardrobe, my hands pressed against my ears in a vain attempt to shut out the memories. How she held me, rocking me through the night and telling me over and over again that I was safe now. This was a safe place.

I glanced past Snake's head at the wardrobe, old and battered now, and slowly brought a hand up to release one of the grips pinning my hair back. Then as Snake visibly relaxed, easing back a fraction, I raked the grip across his face as hard as I could, and ran.

He caught up with me in the kitchen.

I did not make it to work that day. I stayed a full week in hospital, sleeping in clean sheets and eating three square meals a day while I tried to piece myself back together. It felt like a holiday, despite having to repeat so many times the story Snake concocted to explain my injury. By the time I came home, Sam was back. One look at me and all his new resolve disintegrated. Life carried on as before, me taking care of my brother while we both tried to keep Snake happy. But I kept on working as much as I could. I smiled and filled up customers' water glasses and remembered which one had ordered the medium steak and who wanted the gluten-free bread. The metal tin of tips grew fuller.

* * *

Dylan came and said hello before I left rehearsal. We chatted about Christmas – his plans to visit family the week after Boxing Day, how I would be working as much as possible to pay for bridesmaid dress material.

He asked if any of my family or friends would be coming to hear me sing. I mentioned April and Sam. He asked me where Sam lived, and what he did, and before I knew it I had told Dylan about my brother's illness, stuck in a swamp of depression and going nowhere fast.

I blame it on natural politeness (it would have been rude not to answer all those questions) or the post-rehearsal high. Maybe it was because he was a minister of the non-creepy variety and too easy to talk to. I hoped it wasn't down to those gentle eyes; but for one, or all, of those reasons – or maybe simply because I felt so desperate to tell somebody, and he asked – I spilled more to Dylan about my situation than I had to Perry in the year we'd been together.

Afterwards, feeling a flush of embarrassment at my outpouring, I said, "You won't tell anyone, will you? For Sam's sake. Are you bound by priest-type confidentiality?"

Dylan pulled up his mouth on one side. "No, I'm not really."

"Oh."

"But, Faith – I'd like to think you know I wouldn't speak about this because I'm your friend."

"Thank you. I didn't mean to imply you would. I'm not used to having friends. Still learning the rules." There I went again, spilling my secrets. I grinned, trying to lighten the comment but probably appearing like the kind of person that probably, no, doesn't – and shouldn't – have many friends.

Whoops – try to look normal, Faith.

"Well, I'm honoured you trusted me with this. And, actually, I was wondering if…"

I never found out what Dylan wondered, as at that point my phone rang. Sam.

"I can't remember if I've taken my meds." I could rate how Sam felt by whether he said hello to me or not. Half a second and I knew every time.

My stomach clenched up in the conditioned response to his call.

"It's okay, don't panic. We'll figure this out. Have a look and see if you can find the glass of water you'll have taken them with."

"I can't! She's cleaned everything away."

"Try to remember what you did this afternoon. What you had to eat, if you had a hot drink. Work backwards."

"I can't remember!" His voice rose, hoarse with anxiety. "I had some with orange juice but that could have been yesterday."

"It's all right, Sam. Try to calm down. I'll be there in twenty minutes. Just sit tight until then. Okay?"

The phone hung up. I hurriedly apologized to Dylan and said goodbye before interrupting April's conversation. "We need to go."

"Is everything okay?"

I pulled her to one side, away from the group she'd been standing with. "Sam called. He can't remember if he's taken his meds today. Last time he did this we could count forward from the date he started taking the latest pack. If we can't figure it out I'm not sure what we'll do."

"He took them just before I left. I made sure 'cos he looked tired and I thought he might fall asleep. Anyway, I got him a thing where you put the pills in little compartments to mark off the time and the day. He should be able to check that and see, if he can't remember. I'll give him a ring."

"That's great." I slapped away at the jealousy poking its head out from behind my hurting heart like an ugly goblin. "You can phone him in the car."

"But we don't need to leave if I call him, do we? I haven't finished my coffee and Marilyn won't want to go yet."

I gritted my teeth, stress levels surging. *With all due respect, April, after a couple of months of playing nursemaid, do you really have a clue?*

"The problem isn't the pills, April. Sometimes Sam panics when he's on his own. He's worked himself into a state, and if I don't go, he's going to find another way to calm himself down."

"So, what, you drop everything and come running whenever he calls you a bit upset?"

I took a deep breath. "Yes. That is what I've been doing for the past six years. It's called taking care of my very ill brother. If I didn't, he'd be dead by now."

"Right." April raised her eyebrows as she shrugged into her coat and hat. I resisted the urge to yank that stupid floppy hat off her mouldy dreadlocks and slap her round the face with it.

As I said goodbye to Dylan, he looked at me steadily, creases forming between his eyebrows. "I hope Sam's okay. I mean. I know he's not *okay*. But, well. I'm thinking of you."

I nodded, not trusting myself to speak, sure I would give something away about how I would no doubt be thinking about him, too. Not in an appropriate, concerned friend-type way, either.

Chill out, heart. He's doing his JOB. You should be ashamed of yourself, feeling mushy about a minister being kind to a friend – FRIEND – going through a tough time.

* * *

I spent most of December picking up shifts at Christmas parties, waiting on the kind of people Perry wished I hung around with. In between serving sparkling wine and mini lobster thermidors, I practised "O Holy Night", with and without the rest of the choir, answered Sam's middle of the night and all through the day phone calls, walked miles along frosted lanes and crunchy footpaths, and tried not to think too hard about anything else.

I'd just got back from a walk and was defrosting my toes in front of the fire when Perry called. "Are you coming to the firm's Christmas do?"

"When is it again? I might be working."

"You are not bartending at my Christmas party."

"When is it?" I repeated.

"The eighteenth."

I checked my mental diary. "I'm not working. But I have a choir rehearsal until eight."

"Skip it."

"Can I come along afterwards? It's only three days before the performance. I ought to be there."

"Maybe you ought to spend more than a couple of evenings with your boyfriend all month," he said, voice tight.

"You know I can't afford to pass on the extra shifts. This is my busiest time of year." I held back any comments about his frequent late nights in the office, numerous business trips, and weekends schmoozing clients.

"I miss you, Faith. Come to the party. Drink champagne and slow dance with me. Let's kiss under the mistletoe. I'll wrap you in my tux in the taxi home so you don't get cold. Let's forget about responsibilities for one night and have a wonderful evening."

I thought about that, about which I found more wonderful: a choir rehearsal with a group of mixed-up, semi-crazy women and a drill sergeant for a director, or a night in an awkward dress and uncomfortable shoes making small talk with Perry's work colleagues. I glanced down at the ten billion pound ring on my finger.

"Okay. Yes. I would love to come to your work do. They can manage without me for one evening."

* * *

"What?! And how are we supposed to manage without you for the entire evening?" Hester barked. "You're missing practice for a *party*? Ebony has already backed out. Something about her kids' school play. Would anyone else like to skip rehearsal this week? How about the dress rehearsal on Saturday? How about none of us bother – we just spend the day Christmas shopping or eating mince pies or watching *The Muppet Christmas Carol*?"

"I'm sorry, Hester. I promised my fiancé I'd go with him. We've hardly spent an evening together all month, and this is important."

She stared at me. "Important to him or to you?"

"For us. It's important for us. And me."

She nodded her head briskly before tapping the back of a chair with a baton. "Excellent. Good to see you standing up and making some choices for yourself. Your self-belief is growing. Have a wonderful time. Everybody stand!"

* * *

The party went as I imagined – the swanky restaurant in Nottingham full of men with glowing faces in black tie, women in too short, too tight dresses, and overly bright smiles. I sat next to Eddie and Fleur, from the disaster dinner party, which made the meal bearable, and then Perry dragged me into his arms on the dance floor, and we swayed along to the swing band until we were ready to leave.

He asked the taxi driver to drop us off at the end of my street and we walked the rest of the way beneath a sparkling canopy of December stars. He held my hand as we strolled in silence through the crisp night air, stopping at my front door.

"Would you like to come in for a coffee?"

Perry knew I meant a coffee, as I had mentioned months ago that an abusive relationship had left major trust issues, and I didn't feel ready to sleep with him (let alone show him my scars). I basically considered myself damaged goods in that respect – I would share Perry's bed as his wife, but I certainly didn't expect to enjoy it.

His willingness not to push the matter had been part of the reason I could contemplate him being my husband – although I wasn't ignorant to the fact that our stalled sex life was a contributing factor in his haste to get me down the aisle.

We could make a life together that would be better than anything I ever dreamed of, or deserved. I would do what needed to be done, out of gratitude if nothing more. Shooting stars and violins, trembling kisses and I-think-about-you-all-the-time – that wasn't real life. That faded with putting out the bin and cleaning the bathroom, sleepless nights with screaming babies, and the onset of saggy skin. Didn't it? What we had – friendship, mutual respect – didn't that make just as solid a foundation for a lifetime together?

As my future husband kissed me goodnight, his mouth warm against my frozen lips, I willed myself to lean into him. To wrap my arms around this choice I had made and embrace it.

* * *

The afternoon of the carol service we met in an upstairs room at Grace Chapel. Perry having been called in to the office again, I had grabbed a last-minute lift with Marilyn. The air crackled and popped with built-up tension as the choir changed into the simple black dresses Rosa had whizzed up on her new sewing machine, adding thin silver belts and various different metallic shoes picked up for eight pounds each in a closing down sale. Rowan and Kim hastily curled or straightened hair, pinning in silver Christmassy ornaments. We giggled with bunched-up nerves, squeezed each other's hands, and blotted sweaty make-up. There would be no more than eighty people in the hall below – maybe a few extras standing at the back – but it may as well have been eight thousand. "Does Rosa even have a dress for you?" Mags asked, somewhat bemused at Marilyn's appearance.

"She absolutely does," Marilyn huffed. "I'm one of the choir, aren't I?"

"Well, technically yes. But you don't sing. What are you going to do? Click your fingers? Play the tambourine?"

"I'm going to demonstrate the fine art of lip-synching, my friend. Which is in many ways more challenging than actual singing."

"Why are you going to do that?" Uzma asked, turning around so Yasmin could zip her dress up over her green underwear decorated with glittery candy canes. "Isn't it a bit deceitful? When people lip-synch it's usually to their own song."

"You're like the Milli Vanilli of choirs!" Yasmin said.

"Or the four out of five members of most boybands," Kim added. "There to look good and add some charisma, but with microphone not switched on. No offence, but I don't think one extra person will make any difference. You aren't *that* good-looking."

Marilyn shifted about a bit, and fiddled with her hair in the mirror.

"Your sister's here, isn't she?" I asked. "The one who looks after Pete and Nancy every choir practice. Who believes being in a choir means you actually do some singing, rather than sit about knitting and tapping your feet."

"No comment." She pulled back her shoulders and smoothed down her dress. "But if any of you lot blab, that's the last time you'll taste my chocolate squares."

"Our lips are sealed," Leona called out across the room. "Right, girls?"

Hester burst in, wearing a black suit with a silver shirt underneath. "They'd better not be! No sealed lips here, thank you. Apart from you." She pointed at Marilyn.

We lined up ready to take our places downstairs, skirts rustling with anticipation. Hester stood at the head of the queue and raised her chin. "Sing as if this is the last time you ever will, not the first."

"I hope it is the last time we sing this carol!" Janice said. "I'm right sick of it. Those glowing hearts and angel voices. In all our trials born to be our friend – this'll be a trial if we sing it much longer."

"As I was saying," Hester rapped out. "Sing as if it's the last time you will ever get to sing. And as if it is the first time you truly understand these words. A thrill of hope! O night divine! Think about how the best song you ever heard made you feel. How your heart sped up and your skin tingled and your ears strained to catch every glorious, beautiful note. Ladies, you have the chance to lift eighty spirits out of the mundane clamour and clatter of life. To make them forget their stress and their sorrow, their broken dreams and bad-tempered bosses. To switch off their phone and step into something timeless and magnificent. Give it everything you've got. And do not sing one note like startled chickens, drowning hippopotami, or lifelong losers!"

She paused, looking around at the choir all spruced up like Christmas trees, then whipped one hand out from behind her back and stuck a silver tinsel wig on top of her helmet hair. "Rock it out, choir! You're going to blow their novelty Christmas socks off."

In the candlelit hall, featuring an eight-foot tree decorated with silver bows on one side, and a squished together group of children in tea-towel headdresses and angel wings on the other, we did indeed, ladies and gentlemen, rock it out. I watched carefully, but to my surprise saw no blown-off novelty socks.

The best four minutes and thirty-eight seconds of my life. I looked out at the crowd, on their feet, clapping and cheering, and I felt just about as full of personal power as it is possible to get.

There being no available chairs, we scooted round and leaned against the back wall for the last few minutes of the service. Dylan gave a short talk dressed in a pair of faded jeans and a jumper with a badly knitted snowman on the front. He was engaging and funny, warm and earnest. I felt a pinch of pride at my friend's ability to capture the crowd and hold their attention while he spoke about the power of hope.

Note my casual use of the word *friend*. Not like the rest of the sad and sorry women of Grace Chapel who had a pathetic and ridiculous crush on the manly minister.

I absolutely did not think that the best thing about Dylan's talk was having an excuse to stare at his scruffy hair, crinkly eyes, and broad shoulders for twelve minutes. That never even crossed my mind, no sir.

* * *

I cornered Polly in the side hall afterwards. She was hunched over and huddled up, her baby bump the only part of her that wasn't skin and bones. A man I assumed to be her husband loomed at her side. He had slicked-back hair and a smart shirt on over skinny jeans. When I said hello, he held out one hand to shake mine.

"Hi. I'm Tony. Polly's husband."

"Faith." *Pleased to meet you, scumbag. It's good to remind myself that evil, violent women-haters come in all shapes and brands of denim.*

"Polly, Rosa is leaving in a few minutes and she needs the dress back. Are you able to come and get changed now?"

I caught her eyes darting to Tony, the flash of fear, the need for approval. "Um. Is that okay? I'll only be a couple of minutes."

Tony snickered. It sounded like a hissing cockroach. "Of course. Take your time. I'll be right here waiting."

We excused our way through the clusters of people enjoying their mince pies and mulled wine, and went upstairs.

"Where's everybody else?" Polly made a beeline for her bag, sitting on one of the chairs in the corner of the room.

"Probably enjoying the refreshments. I lied about having to get changed. Rosa's happy to pick up the dresses at rehearsal next week."

"What?" Instantly Polly's shoulders pulled up tight around her chin as she crossed her arms over her bump.

I ignored her. "Can you unzip me, please?"

After a moment's hesitation, Polly unzipped me out of my dress. Shrugging it off, I pulled on my jeans and turned to face her, leaving my four-inch collarbone scar and my terrifying stomach slash-scar on full display. "Did you listen to Dylan's talk, about hope?"

Polly visibly cringed now, her eyes looking anywhere but at my mutilated body.

"I know you feel trapped. You feel as though you have no hope. You think it is your fault. That if you act better, stop forgetting things, listen to his instructions properly, stop being so irritating... then he won't hurt you any more. It is a lie, Polly. He is never going to stop. I know you think you love him, you need him. But you have to think of your baby now. I can help you." My voice broke. "Please let me help you."

She bent down, hands fumbling with the buttons on her maternity dress. "How dare you speak to me like that? How dare you say these things about me? About Tony? He is a good husband. He loves me. You know nothing about it. Or me. I am not one of those women. I am not! Don't ever speak to me about this again."

She ripped off her outfit as she spoke, revealing a glimpse of the purple blotches I had spotted earlier before she pulled on her high-necked, long-sleeved sweater and frumpy black trousers. "Stay out of my business, Faith! How dare you suggest I would put my baby in danger!"

I kept my voice soft, my tears in check. "Don't you think your baby is in danger when he hits you?"

"Shut up!"

"I just want to help you, Polly. I know what it's like. I've been in your situation –"

"I am nothing like you!" she screamed, grabbing her bag and throwing the dress at me as she pushed past. "Nothing."

142

Chapter Eleven

My second scar, the stomach slash-scar, was given to me ten months after the first. Nearly a year of bowing, scraping, surrendering, and disappearing inside myself as Snake ruled our household with a tattooed fist and crack-fuelled temper. Sam lurched from day to day, seeking oblivion from the pain of the past and the present in the only way he knew how. I worked, cowered in my bedroom, and tried, tried, tried to keep the peace, my sanity, and my brother alive.

The money tin grew heavier.

I had to get out of there.

Beside myself with stress, exhaustion, and wretched self-loathing, I began walking. At first, to get away from the poisoned fumes swirling through every room of Grandma's house, to avoid the yellowed, withered near-corpses queuing up for another hit of death. To escape the stench of despair, including my own.

But after a while, as my muscles embraced the miles and my body grew sturdier, my breathing deep again, I found my eyes began to open. To the vibrancy of the rapeseed in the meadow, or the tomato-coloured chest of the robin on a branch. The perfect swirl of snail shells, clinging to verdant hedgerows. The beauty in the butter-coloured cornfields framed with thickets, the silvery-brown stream bubbling by.

My ears, dimmed by the slap of cruel words amid jarring chaos, retuned themselves to the melody of birdsong, the soothing paradiddle of rain on the treetops, the laughter of the river as it cavorted under the open sky.

My expanding, unclogging lungs sucked in the scent of the honeysuckle, the sweet and sour of the autumn muck-spreading, the deep musk of moss upon the chestnut trunks.

Slowly, as the weeks went by, as the fresh promise of spring gave way to summer, I mapped the hills and hideaways with my worn-down trainers and I remembered. I remembered, and in many ways became aware for the first time, that life is not all murky shadows, turmoil, and unravelling ruin. There is life beyond fear and loss and foul menace. I learned to appreciate the caress of sunshine on my skin, treasure the peace of a stunning vista, and relish the anonymity of a summer storm.

Yes, walking saved my life. Pacing, pounding, moving, journeying amongst a million of nature's companions. None of whom demanded anything of me, judged me, or tried to control me.

So after the second scar, walking gave me the strength to walk right out.

Snake decided I was hiding something. He refused to believe my walks were just walking. Every man who crossed my path became a suspect, and as I increasingly developed the strength to avoid his bed, he grew even more distrustful. Pumping himself full of paranoia-inducing, mind-destroying chemicals only made things worse, and he convinced himself I had become pregnant. On a particularly bad trip one night, he tried to destroy the non-existent evidence of my affair with a bread knife.

Snake drove off in a fury, leaving me curled up on the bedroom floor. Sam patched the gash – mercifully shallow but still bleeding profusely – with surgical tape and Disney princess plasters. Once finished, he gathered my paltry belongings and threw them into an old school bag. It was time.

"Come with me, Sam."

"What?" He paused, kneeling on the bedroom floor to tie my shoes.

"Come with me. Start again, just you and me. No Snake and no drugs."

"This is our house. Grandma's house," he said.

"No it isn't. Not any more. You know that. And it's destroyed anyway. The house doesn't matter. We matter. Staying alive matters. Being free from *him* matters."

He lifted his gaze to meet mine, raw fear swirling amidst the desolation in his eyes.

"Come with me, Sam. Don't make me do this alone." I placed my hand upon the top of his arm.

A tear ran down his emaciated face. He bowed his head.

"Please, Sam. We can do this. Please. If I leave you here, you'll die, and then I'll have no one."

He finished tying my shoe.

"You can do this, Rachel. Go and find the life she saved us for."

"I don't want to go without you."

There was a long silence. "If I come, I'll bring this with us. Not Snake, but someone just like him. I'm the problem here. You're better off without me. *You know you're better off without me.*"

Reaching forwards, he picked my phone up off the bed. I stood up gingerly, slowly balancing my bag on one shoulder. For the second time, my brother phoned the police to save me. The last thing I heard as I let myself out was his careful recitation of the long, dangerous list of illegal substances currently stored in Grandma's pantry.

They arrested Sam that afternoon, round about the time I bought my train ticket to London. He eventually got transferred to a secure hospital, where once free of drugs he learned to draw, then paint, to ease the panic in his head.

Snake spent a couple of nights in jail before his evil henchmen posted bail and he got straight back to business. Two months later he skipped town for good.

Would I have returned then, had I known? Returned to the wreckage of my childhood home? The House of Hideous Memories?

Left my current job in London, waiting tables for depraved old men who called me Anna, wearing next to no clothes and a bleak smile?

Perhaps.

I now lived alone, on pennies plus the tips earned allowing greasy, gross men to fawn over me, sleeping in a bedsit with intermittent electricity, reliably non-existent heating, and a bathroom I shared with eight other people, all of whom terrified me to the point of vomiting.

But I thought I was free. Believed myself to be in control, having started again with a new life, calling myself a new name. I would not, and did not, go home to save my life. So why did I go back three years later? The same reason I did most things – to save my brother.

* * *

In the end I spent the first half of Christmas Day with Sam and April. We walked four miles through the fields in the morning before cooking roast chicken and pecan pie in my cramped kitchen while Sam dozed on the sofa. To give her credit, April pulled her weight in between her numerous smoking breaks. She had even bought me a present – a wedding planner book. I had to smile as I pictured myself wrapping it back up and giving it to Larissa, but I begrudgingly appreciated the thought, and what it had cost her.

Perry arrived at four to take me to HCC for a late dinner with his parents. He shook hands with a deflated Sam and grinned at April, waiting for them to leave before saying, "I've got an idea. Why don't we skip dinner and stay here? We can veg out on the sofa watching cheesy Christmas specials and eat junk food until we can't get up again."

"An excellent plan. Let's do it," I said, playing along with the joke.

He pretended to hand me his phone. "You call Mother and let her know we can't be bothered to come while I open the chocolates."

"On second thoughts, I'll get my coat."

Parked outside sat a shiny red car. It had a tiny back seat and a soft top, so I guess that made it expensive.

"Wow. Is this your Christmas present?"

Perry grinned at me. "No. It's yours." He held out the keys. "Happy Christmas, Faith."

My astonishment puffed out in a cloud of wintry vapour.

"What?"

"I'm giving you this car for Christmas."

"But I can't afford a car. I can't afford the insurance, or tax. I can't afford the petrol."

"The insurance is set for the year. As is the tax. And you can finally use the credit card I gave you for wedding purchases to buy petrol. You can't refuse. It's part of the present."

I ogled this ridiculous, ostentatious, flashy car and tried to pull my jaw back up into an acceptable position. Perry could easily afford it. I knew men like him bought their girlfriends things like this for Christmas. I even knew he wouldn't mind a couple of books, a jumper, and a homemade voucher promising to cook him a monthly slap-up meal in return.

"I'm sorry. This car is… something else. But I can't accept it."

"Go on, tell me why. I have a perfect counter-argument for every possible reason you might use to reject this."

"Perry, I can't drive."

He smiled, leaning forwards to kiss me as he opened the passenger door and took out two magnetic learner plates. "First time for everything."

Maybe, but despite his protests, today was not going to be the first time I took the wheel. Let alone the wheel of a fifty-thousand pound sports car. We compromised: he would drive, if I kept the present.

"Fine. But I'm choosing who gives me lessons." I slid into the passenger seat. "And Perry? Thank you. I really, really appreciate this."

"You're welcome. I consider you absolutely worth it."

Really? I consider you absolutely wrong.

Dinner included sixteen Uppertons and me. I managed to wangle a seat near my bridesmaid, Natasha, but that meant sitting opposite Great-Uncle Russell. At least two hundred years old, it soon became apparent that he had lost his inhibitions, his social graces, and quite possibly his marbles, along with all his hair and most of his teeth.

He complimented Perry several times on his fine choice of "filly", declaring redheads to be "red hot like a chilli pepper". This caused my skin to provide a visual demonstration of red-hotness, so when he asked me about my "bloodline" the extreme discomfort was perhaps a little less apparent.

"Yes, Faith," Larissa said. "Tell us about your family."

I had been skilfully sidestepping this question for months. This time I knew I had to say something.

"My mum died when I was six, so my grandma brought me up after that. I also have a brother, Sam. He's an artist."

"Oh, how awful!" Natasha exclaimed. "Not that your brother's an artist. Your mum. How did she die?"

Did Uppertons not do tact or discretion?

"It was pretty sudden. She had an accident." She accidentally decided to run away the night her live-in monster's football match got cancelled, so he came home early and caught her.

"And what about your poor father?" another relative asked, whose name I'd forgotten, confirming the whole table now listened to the conversation.

"Children are better off being raised by a woman." Great-Uncle Russell nodded at me. "Sensible decision, parcelling you off to Grandma's."

"That must have been terrible for him." Natasha looked at me with wide eyes. I tried not to visibly squirm. "Losing your mother and then you moving away."

I took a steadying breath, reciting my rehearsed response in a hollow voice. "We were living with my stepdad. I didn't know him very well, so moving to Grandma's felt best."

"So you don't see your real dad? Where does he live?"

Like I said: no tact in this family. Or ability to read body language, apparently. I scanned the room in panic, wishing fervently to be back on the other side of the bar.

"Um. Excuse me, I need to make a phone call." Pushing back my chair, I made a scrambled exit from the private dining room, collapsing back against the wall outside while my pulse stabilized. I heard Larissa's strident tones sail out after me: "Honestly, Peregrine. It's not too late to reconsider."

I ducked into one of the smaller meeting rooms, leaning my head against the cold glass of the full-length window and closing my eyes.

"Faith!" a man's voice whispered. Turning round, I saw Mike, the waiter, standing near the doorway.

"Hi, Mike. Happy Christmas. How's it going?"

"I'm spending the day serving other people Christmas dinner. Could be better."

"Need any help?"

"Yes. But you're on the other side now. You've made your choice." He smiled at me.

"You're right. I shouldn't be fraternizing with the likes of you any more."

"No. Tongues would wag. Your reputation would be in tatters."

I pretended to consider this. "I'd probably get thrown out of the club. Maybe even have to cancel the wedding."

"Alone, in the Langley meeting room with a member of staff? What are you playing at?" he tutted in disgust.

"You followed me in here! I could have you sacked."

Mike closed the door behind him, his face turning serious. "I wanted to tell you something. It's probably nothing, but, well, I thought I'd let you know, just in case."

"What is it?" A couple of thoughts flashed up: had Perry been here with someone else? Had Larissa changed the wedding plans?

"A man's been in. A couple of nights ago. I noticed him because he isn't a member, and was here by himself."

The hairs rose on the back of my neck. A strange man out here, alone, at any time seemed weird. The week before Christmas? In the past, my first thought would have been that he was scoping the place out for a crime of some sort.

Now? The sudden clenching in my gut told me I knew full well who that man was and why he had been here.

"He asked if a red-haired woman in her twenties worked here."

I slid into the wooden chair next to me, suddenly very aware my body consisted of sixty per cent water.

"I told him no, and asked him to leave. Watched him drive away."

"Could he have spoken to anyone else?"

Mike frowned. "Maybe. Before he came into the bar. But he didn't look like the kind of man most members would stop to chat with, if you know what I mean."

"Can you describe him to me?"

"I can do better than that. Here."

Mike took out his phone, scrolled to the right picture, and handed it to me. I looked at the blurred face of the man on the screen, and to my surprise felt nothing, no flash of recognition or trigger of emotion. This middle-aged, overweight man with a blank expression behind wire-framed glasses could have been anyone.

But it wasn't just anyone.

It was him.

And he was here. Looking for me.

I handed Mike his phone back. "If you see him again, will you call me?"

"Yeah, sure. Do you need me to do anything else?"

"A double whisky would be nice."

I squared my shoulders, took in a few deep breaths of courage and calm, blowing out some of my mind-numbing, raging terror, and went back to eat Christmas pudding and brandy sauce with the least of my worries.

* * *

Perry took a bunch of clients on a pre-deal, no-expense-spared, please-do-business-with-us ski trip over New Year. I spent most days up to and including New Year's Eve working as hard as I could, trying to exhaust myself to a point where my head might stop whirring.

I failed, miserably, and after another night getting twisted up in the bedcovers fighting to escape the beast that hunted me, I started the new year wrapped in a blanket on the sofa, blinking at the dazzle of the rising sun on freshly fallen snow.

My phone rang, and I fumbled for it in my dressing gown pocket, sure it must be Sam. I hadn't yet decided whether to tell him about Kane being at the club. I didn't know for sure it even was Kane, and first I wanted to speak to Gwynne, currently on holiday, to have all the facts. Sam hung on in there. I had spotted flickers of hope that he might avoid a total crash; that his abstinence might last awhile this time; that the shudderingly expensive stint in the hospital would prove worth it. In summary: I couldn't risk the consequences of telling him.

I stared at the dial, displaying unknown caller, for a few rings before jerking my finger across the green answer button. If Kane had somehow got my number, I might as well get it over with.

"Hello?" My voice was a whimper.

"Hello. Is that Faith? It's Dylan."

Is it possible for a human heart to slow down and accelerate all in the same instant?

"Dylan. Hi." I released a sigh of relief.

"Marilyn gave me your number. Happy New Year. Did I wake you up? I know it's pretty early for the morning after."

"No. It's fine. I've been awake for ages. I worked last night."

"Marilyn told me. I'm really sorry to bother you. But do you like turkey pie?"

"Um. Yes." *Is Dylan asking me to dinner? Slow down, heart, and for goodness' sake behave! If he is, I'm obviously saying no. Because you, heart, can't be trusted.*

"You might have heard we're cooking our usual New Year's Day lunch at the chapel. Seventy people who will otherwise be on their own and probably going hungry are coming in for turkey pie and all the trimmings."

What? He thinks I'm alone? And can't afford food? I'd be offended if it wasn't nearly true. Sometimes true. Okay, true.

"Mags and her husband Chris, who run the kitchen, are snowed in on their farm. I've managed to round up a couple of other volunteers, but none of them have done anything like this before, and quite frankly it's going to be a disaster. My culinary expertise reaches its peak at a bacon sandwich. You would be doing me the biggest favour if you came and helped us out. No, scrap that. I mean if you came and took charge. I know you're probably exhausted and fed up with serving people, and you're bound to have plans, but these guests are counting on us. It might be the only decent meal they get all month. Even if you could spare an hour. I'll come and pick you up in the truck. Please. I'm happy to beg."

"Please don't beg. I'd love to help. What time do you want to pick me up?"

"How soon can you be ready?"

I glanced down at my far from fresh pyjamas, running a hand through the frizzy nest on my head.

"Give me forty minutes."

* * *

Three-quarters of an hour later I stood shivering at the end of my street as Dylan came to a stop. I pulled open the passenger door and climbed in. The navy blue pick-up suited him perfectly – scruffy, dotted with the odd rust patch. A toolbox, thermos flask, football boots, and a worn-looking paperback lay strewn about the floor amongst various random bits and pieces. It smelled of paint,

DW40, and other manly man smells. This truck had nothing to prove, didn't care what anybody thought, and may well have run on testosterone. I clicked my seatbelt on and sat back to enjoy the ride.

"Morning."

"Hi."

"I would have come to your house. People talk when the minister picks women up from street corners."

Ouch. Being likened to a street worker, even in jest, rubbed a little too close to the bone. "The snow's a foot deep. I didn't know if the truck could make it."

He grinned, and patted his dashboard affectionately. "This old girl can make it anywhere."

"I don't think I can say the same about my new car."

"You have a car?"

I grimaced. "A Christmas present."

"Right. Nice present. From Perry?" He glanced at me, quickly.

"Yes."

"What type is it?"

"A red one."

Dylan smiled. "Ah. I particularly like the new model of red one. Very fuel efficient. And reliable, so I've heard."

"Yes. And it's easy to find in the snow."

"A very desirable feature." He glanced across at me again, a little longer this time. "And red is my favourite colour."

Well, Pastor Dylan, you can enjoy looking at my face for the rest of this drive then while my treacherously transparent skin tries to out-red my hair.

Grace Chapel was empty when we arrived. Six large slow cookers full of pie filling sat steaming on the work counters, and a pile of individual-sized puff pastry tops were defrosting on plastic trays.

There were three buckets full of new potatoes and two more containing muddy carrot and broccoli. I found shopping bags full of mince pies and chocolate brownies, and a tower of bread rolls.

Dylan hovered while I took stock, poking in cupboards and

examining the contents of the kitchen drawers. "You can phone Mags if you have any questions about what to do."

"Nope. It's fine. How long until the guests arrive?"

"A couple of hours."

I whipped open a drawer and tossed him a potato peeler. "We'd best get started then."

Chapter Twelve

The rest of the day passed in a flurry of cooking, plating up, washing pots, and wiping my brow in the suffocating heat of an overcrowded kitchen. Three more volunteers turned up, and over fifty of Brooksby's needier residents braved the snow. The team dashed about clearing plates, pouring drinks, wiping tables, and being bossed about by me.

By three we had served the last tea and coffee, and the pace began to ease off. Dylan had prepared a quiz, and a few of the other guests set up a card game in one corner. The dozen or so children piled into one of the Sunday School rooms to watch a film with an enormous bowl of popcorn and a heap of cushions. We pulled crackers and set off party poppers, and once it was dark Dylan opened the doors and everybody who could walk unaided spilled out into the car park for a mass snowball fight. I tried to stay out of sight in the kitchen, hiding behind the mountain of dirty dishes, but once someone opened the fire door, a missile whizzing in and splattering muddy snow all over the fridge, I knew it would mean a lot less work if I went to the fight instead of letting the fight come to me.

After an hour of soaking wet, squealing, pink-cheeked warfare, culminating in a last stand between a family of six brothers barricaded in behind a snow-wall and a full-on charge from a group of retired veterans, we trooped back inside for more hot drinks and the last of the cakes.

It was after six before the guests began to leave, fresh flurries of snow spinning down through the orange street light. A couple of volunteers stayed to help Dylan and me with the remainder of the clearing up. Eventually, I declared us finished, collapsing on a chair in the side hall, pulling off my sopping wet boots and socks.

Dylan came out of the kitchen a couple of minutes later. "Right, who's staying for supper? I guessed none of us would have much time to eat earlier."

He was right. I had been too full of adrenaline to manage more than a couple of mouthfuls of pie. The pitiful contents of my fridge back home seemed deeply uninviting.

"As long as it's not turkey pie. Ever again."

He grinned. "I've put a couple of frozen pizzas in the oven."

"Frozen pizza?" I screwed up my face. "Maybe I *could* manage a piece of pie…"

"They're posh ones! Upperton standard."

I hesitated, but not because of the pizza.

"Come on, Faith. Are you a food snob?"

"Yep. Three-hundred and sixty-four days of the year, absolutely. Today, however, if someone else cooks I'll make an exception."

"Great. You round up the others and I'll set the table."

"Actually, everybody else left. They were worried about the snowdrifts."

Did I imagine that charged moment of silence?

"Ah." Dylan looked uncomfortable. *No, Faith. You didn't imagine it. But it wasn't for the reason you thought. Minister, dining alone with an engaged woman while her fiancé's out of the country? Slightly pushing the boundaries there, methinks.*

"It's okay," I said, hastily gathering my socks and shoes together. "I'll go. You probably can't wait to get home, anyway."

He ran one hand through his hair, looking back at the door before making a decision. "No. It's fine. We're friends, right? We both know there's nothing going on. And they are massive pizzas. Even a Yorkshireman couldn't eat all that by himself. Wasting all that food doesn't sit well with the spirit of the day."

"If you're sure?"

He grinned. "Come on. I spend far too many evenings eating alone."

We poured ourselves a drink, leaning against the kitchen counter while the pizzas cooked.

"So, how do you define a posh frozen pizza?" I asked.

"One's got spinach on it."

"Woah! Classy."

"And buffalo mozzarella."

"I'm impressed."

"Maybe even some of those sun-dried tomatoes." He grinned. "It'll be like being back in my old Michelin restaurant."

We ate at a table in the hall. Despite the dour surroundings – although let's face it, I'd eaten in much worse places – and being clear about the whole friends thing, it didn't alter the fact I now sat having dinner with a very attractive man. I took a moment while Dylan fetched napkins to admire my beautiful engagement ring, wonder how my precious brother was doing, and sternly remind myself that if Dylan knew I mentally flapped my hands in front of my face because his hand brushed mine when he passed me a plate he would boot me right back out into the storm. He would not want to be friends with the kind of woman who, being engaged to one man, had immoral thoughts about another while sharing an innocent posh pizza *in the church she planned to get married in*.

I grabbed hold of those bad, bad thoughts with both hands, stuffing them back where they belonged in the forbidden corner of my mind where my childhood hopes, worst memories, and murderous plans live.

Phew. Okay. Everything back under control.

Hah! You keep telling yourself that, Faith, and one day you might actually believe it.

"Cheers." Dylan leaned across the table to chink my glass. "You were amazing earlier. Saved the day."

"Cheers. And thanks for inviting me. You saved *my* day from a potential cheese puff overdose on the sofa. And I enjoyed being in charge of a kitchen."

"I don't just mean in the kitchen. Not many people are comfortable making conversation with some of those guys. You didn't bat an eyelid at their more bizarre behaviour. Or the flirting."

"Err – hello? Nobody flirted. They were just grateful for the pie."

"The bloke with the Doctor Who scarf wouldn't leave you alone the whole time you were clearing tables."

I helped myself to another piece of pizza. "Maybe so, but repeatedly grabbing a person's backside isn't classed as flirting."

"Right. That might explain my lack of success with women…"

"Really? I think there must be another reason you're still single." I mean, come off it, how *did* that happen?

He took a moment to wipe his hands on a napkin. "Yeah. It's a long story."

"I like hearing stories."

He shook his head. "I don't like telling this one. Maybe another time."

"Okay. I'll hold you to that."

We ate in silence for a couple of minutes.

"I meant it, though," Dylan said. "It's a rare gift to mix with people like the Uppertons and some of the guests today and get along with all of them. You should do something with that."

I put the half-eaten pizza slice back down on my plate. "Right. One – I don't get along with most of the Uppertons. I'd tell you what Perry's mum called me at Christmas dinner but I don't want to wreck your high opinion of me. Two – I can mix with messed-up people struggling along the bottom rung of society because I used to be one. I've lived with people like that. And for a short time, I had nowhere to live at all."

He looked at me, deadly serious. "Can you tell me about it?"

Could I? Could I tell someone? Could I tell *Dylan*? I stole a peek at those soft, clear eyes and thought I could try.

"I left Brooksby and took a train to London. I don't know why

London – I thought I'd find work there. But obviously I didn't in the first couple of days, and within a week my money ran out. I spent thirty-one nights sleeping rough." I paused, took another drink of juice. "I did some stuff I'm not proud of, the kind of stuff desperate women do, to protect myself, and in exchange for food and some shelter. It was November. I don't know if I would have survived otherwise."

Dylan's hand slid across the table, towards mine, veering at the last moment to fiddle with the pizza plate. I ignored how badly I wanted to feel the strength of his rough fingers wrapped around mine, and tried to concentrate on the words.

"I had an injury. Not from then; from before. But unsurprisingly it got infected. Eventually, when the fever grew so bad I knew I'd die if I didn't get help, I crawled to the nearest doctor's surgery and passed out on the doorstep. I spent a week in intensive care. Another on a normal ward. One of the nurses found me a place in a women's shelter. That gave me an address, so I could find a waitressing job, and once I had work I found a room to rent."

"How old were you?"

"I turned eighteen in the ICU."

Dylan breathed the kind of word I'm sure church ministers aren't allowed to say. I could see his knuckles turn white where he gripped his glass.

"Who hurt you, Faith? How did you get injured?"

I opened my mouth to answer and found I couldn't speak. Who hurt me? Kane, my mum for staying with him so long, Snake, Sam, the girls at my new school who didn't want to be my friend because I spoke funny and wet myself, the teachers who failed to notice my life falling apart after Grandma died, the man who paid for my body, the neighbours at the bedsit, the boss at the strip club, and his countless clientele. Would that do for starters?

And I hated it. I hated having been a victim. Loathed the power these people had wielded over me. Raged that it still bothered me, that the me I called Anna still lived inside. That it still hurt me. That no matter how hard I fought, or worked, or put the barriers up, they still hurt me.

Whew. I was a mess.

Dylan handed me tissues while I cried, all the same.

* * *

He drove me home soon after that. I felt weird, having told him, and awkward trying to explain why I hadn't told Perry. We rode home in silence. Dylan's face was set rigid in the silver light, and when he said goodnight he barely looked at me.

I remembered the joke about the street corner. Would he still be my friend now? Could he be? Would he tell Hester, or someone else at the church? Maybe they had rules about people like me getting married in the chapel.

Another sleepless night, staring at the ceiling.

* * *

The Monday after New Year I woke up to the doorbell ringing. Fumbling for my phone, the time read seven o'clock. I lay there for a moment, hoping the caller would go away, but the bell rang again, followed by a sharp knock. I tumbled out of bed and crept over to the window, peeping out through a chink in the curtain. A black four by four had been parked behind my new car, but the person at the door stood too close to the house for me to see them.

After another ring, I pulled on a sweatshirt over my pyjamas and went to peep through the front window. A man, about my age, stood on the doorstep. He caught me looking, smiled, and gave a salute.

"Hi. You must be Faith," he said when I opened the door, his accent hailing from somewhere in the southern hemisphere.

I nodded, still too asleep to speak.

"Anton. Your personal trainer. I'm guessing you'd forgotten your appointment?"

That would explain the shorts in January. I rubbed my face with one hand, trying to get my brain going. "No. I really think I would remember making an appointment with a personal trainer. Sorry."

"It was a gift card? From Mrs Upperton? For Christmas?"

Eugh. Now I remembered. I hadn't even bothered to check if an actual appointment had been made, presuming it would be left up to me to call Anton and arrange a session. What a ridiculous presumption, considering whom the gift came from.

"Um. She never told me an actual session had been booked."

"Riiiight." Anton frowned sympathetically, still managing to smile at the same time. He bounced up and down on his heels. "Not to worry. You go on and trackie up and we'll get going. The session's two hours, so plenty of time to work off some of those mince pies."

"Actually, I think I might give it a miss. I haven't slept all that great, and, well, you know how it is. Stuff to do, places to go."

Anton leaned against the door frame and began stretching his leg muscles. "No can do, I'm afraid. I heard you got a wedding emergency. Too fat for your dress. And that was before the holidays. We've got serious work to do."

He moved on to his arms, pulling them behind his head.

"Okay, look. Come in for a minute and I'll explain."

"I'd save your breath if I were you. You're gonna need it. Trust me, I've heard every excuse in the book. There ain't a reason on earth why I'm gonna let any of my clients remain a fatty."

"I'm wearing a sweatshirt! Everyone looks fat in them."

"Trust me, darling, I don't."

I sighed, wondering what would happen if I just closed the door and went back to bed. "If you're not going to go away, then please come in before the house gets any colder."

He grinned and stepped inside, then began jogging on the spot in my hallway.

"Come into the kitchen. I need a drink."

"Just water! No caffeine required to get pumping in one of my sessions."

Ignoring him, I filled up the kettle and switched it on.

"If I tell you something, will you keep it confidential?"

"No worries. What happens in session stays in session. My lips are sealed."

"I don't actually need a personal trainer. I have a physical job and I walk fifteen miles a week. Underneath this sweater I am actually in okay shape. I lied to Larissa about not fitting into the wedding dress any more because I'd ripped it and it's her dress and I didn't want to upset her. So I really don't want to waste your time and undergo fitness-related torture for two hours every week for no reason."

"Two times a week. And it's been paid for. Be unethical not to coach the sessions. And there's always room for improvement in my book."

I poured myself a coffee. "Are you sure you don't want one?"

"Got any oolong tea?"

"Er, no."

"I'll pass, then." He nodded at my mug. "That stuff is poison. Look, have you ever tried a trainer before? Why not give it a go? Most people can benefit from a decent workout. Releases stress, lowers blood pressure. Lotta tension involved in organizing a wedding."

"Thanks, but my choir sorts that. It does give me an idea, though."

A quick phone call settled it. Marilyn greeted us at her front door wearing pink running gear and a matching bandana.

"They're in the high chairs, ready for breakfast. The porridge is on the hob; it'll need another minute or so. Make sure you blow on it. And don't turn your back for a second! Oh, and if they make a mess, don't worry about clearing it up. Changing bag, spare clothes, beakers, Pete's dummy, Nancy's dog, remote control are all in the living room. Anything else?"

"Um, nope. Don't think so."

"Cool. I feel sexier already. Speaking of which! Hell-o!" I followed her gaze to see Anton, now out of the car, doing more stretches. He'd taken his jacket off, the skintight running top underneath leaving nothing to the imagination. Flicking back his blond hair he clapped his hands together.

"That's what I like to see! Something to get my teeth into," he called out.

"I was just thinking the same thing," Marilyn muttered, before I slapped her.

"Behave!"

"Seriously though, Faith. Those arms."

A squealing sound came from the direction of the house.

I braced myself. "Right. I'd better go. Anton – Marilyn, Marilyn – Anton. Please don't work her too hard. She needs enough energy to look after two babies for the rest of the day." I dashed inside, took one look at the bomb site of Marilyn's kitchen, Pete smearing the mess from his nose across his high chair tray with a plastic spoon, Nancy screaming next to him, sniffed the burnt porridge on the splattered hob, and wondered which of us was going to have the less strenuous morning.

An hour and a half later, I declared it a draw.

In my baby-free, magazine-article, rose-tinted spectacles, I had planned to do some tidying up for Marilyn, maybe put on a load of washing or get the iron out while the twins gurgled in their playpen.

My plan hadn't factored in that ninety-nine per cent of the time (eighty-nine of the ninety minutes) one or both of them were crying, pooping, sneezing, smearing, spilling, snatching, poking, or getting their head stuck in the cat flap (a frankly terrifying moment only solved by a lightning-fast Internet search and a packet of butter).

Wowzers. Babies were hard work. I now understood Marilyn's eagerness to join the choir, and to spend an hour and a half slogging round the park in freezing cold rain being shouted at by a half-man, half-golden retriever. She returned red-faced, sweat-soaked, and dishevelled, barely able to stretch her arm up to meet Anton's high five.

"Tea. Cake. Help."

"Green tea, a granola bar, and I'll see ya Thursday. Great job!" Anton jogged back to the car as fresh-faced as when he arrived.

"I can't believe it's only nine in the morning." Marilyn limped inside, pausing to kiss her children on the head before falling face-first onto the sofa.

I made us some tea and fruit toast.

"How was it, then?"

"He's a maniac. As soon as the session started it was like the Incredible Hulk. He flipped into this beast-man. Like an SAS commander or something. Only I'm not a soldier. I'm an obese woman in her thirties who drives to the corner shop on the corner of her own street. He had me doing squats. *Squats!* And pulling a tyre on the end of a rope. Every single inch of me hurts. I threw up twice and at one point went blind in my left eye."

"Eek. Sorry."

"Don't be sorry. It was flippin' awesome. This is the start of the new, improved Marilyn. Marilyn mark two. James won't know what's hit him when he comes home."

So now, along with work, seeing Sam, organizing a wedding, choir rehearsals, and worrying about being hunted by a murderer, I got up at six three times a week and spent two hours trying to apply damage limitation with Nancy and Pete. And in between all that, I walked, pounding through the fields as if eventually I could outpace my problems.

No chance.

Halfway through the month, Gwynne phoned to let me know Kane had been attending all his probation meetings, including one only a couple of days earlier. If he had been in Nottinghamshire, and hanging around in HCC, it had been for a few days at most, and he wasn't there any more. His probation officer would be keeping a close eye on things. I thanked her, and let out a long sigh of relief.

I tried to picture the blurred face on Mike's phone. Maybe the man wasn't Kane. Maybe the redhead he was looking for wasn't me.

Maybe I wouldn't have to tell Sam, after all.

Maybe.

Chapter Thirteen

*C*hoir rehearsals were buzzing. Not only were we learning two new songs, but following the success of the carol service, Hester announced she had entered Grace Choir into a competition.

"The East Midlands heat of the International Community Choir Sing-Off. This is it, choir! A chance to convince yourselves you are a real choir. That you can sing, together, and create something magnificent. That when you put some effort in, believe in yourselves, and embrace the togetherness of the team, you can do it."

"How many teams are in the competition?" Rowan asked.

"Irrelevant!" Hester retorted. "You be the best you can be. Don't think about who you're up against."

"Are they, like, proper choirs that have been together for ages, with, like, people who are musicians and sing in theatres and stuff? How would we stand a chance against choirs like that?" Rowan added.

Hester picked up the folder of music and bashed herself over the head with it a few times. "You. Are. A. Proper. Choir. You are musicians! And none of the choirs in the competition are allowed to hold auditions."

"And none of them have Hester," Mags pointed out. "I bet other choirs don't strip off and climb mountains together."

"Would I enter you into this competition if you weren't ready?"

"No, Hester," we droned in unison, like schoolchildren.

"Incorrect! None of you are ready! You still don't believe in this choir, because you still don't believe in yourselves. Or each other. But you will! We've got six weeks. Both the choir that gets first place and the runners-up go through to the national final. Those of you who talk to God, please start praying. Those of you who don't, now would be an excellent time to start."

The first song we learned was "Stand by Me", by Ben E. King, mashed together with the chorus of "All Together Now", by the Farm. No prizes for guessing what Hester's point was there.

She announced that she wanted us to choose our second song. We had two weeks to offer suggestions, after which she would decide the winner.

"No meaningless slush, sentimental claptrap, or sexualization of women! No whoop-de-do now I've found a man I can stop feeling sorry for myself as I must not be ugly after all, my life finally has meaning and I don't have to worry if there's a spider in the bath."

Millie scratched her bobble hat. "I don't think I've heard that one. Who's it by?"

Hester scowled. "A man wrote it. A stupid one whose wife only married him to stop feeling like a worm. It didn't work. She became a worm with an idiot husband."

"Are you talking about somebody in particular, Hester?" Melody asked.

"Time to stop blethering on and learn some notes! How on earth are we going to be ready for this competition if we keep falling behind schedule? Now, on a count of four…"

* * *

The fourteenth of February fell on a Saturday this year. The previous Valentine's Day had been one of the times Perry proposed: a trip to a planetarium, where he'd bribed some soppy intern to reprogramme the stars so they spelled "marry me Faith". That had been a test of my mettle, saying no while two members of staff hovered hopefully in the corner with a bottle of champagne and some glasses.

This time around, he surprised me with two tickets to Rome the week before. We were eating the second of his Christmas voucher slap-up dinners. The plane left in six days.

"You want me to take the whole weekend off?"

"And all day Friday and Monday. If I can spare the time, running a business, you can manage it."

"I think you get better tips than me."

"Four days, Faith."

"This is really short notice. I think I've got something booked already."

He put down his fork, leaning forwards slightly across his half-finished gnocchi. "Then cancel it."

"I hate cancelling. It makes them less willing to call on me again." And it lets the poverty wolf snap closer at my heels.

"You're the best waitress they've got. They'll always call on you. Come on, Faith. You need a break. You look exhausted."

"Thanks."

"I'm worried about you. Please take the weekend off and come and have a lovely time with me."

I said nothing, trying to sort the reasons I felt such resistance to the idea into a rational order.

"I've booked us separate bedrooms if that's what's bothering you."

"I can't go for four nights."

"Three."

"I don't want to go to Italy."

Perry threw his napkin on the plate. "Well where do you want to go, then? Pick somewhere else if Italy bothers you. Paris, New York, Baghdad? Quite frankly I don't care. I just want to spend a few uninterrupted days with my fiancée, enjoying ourselves. Sorry for being so ludicrously demanding."

I took a deep breath, but Perry hadn't finished.

"What is it with you, Faith? Most women would be delighted to be whisked off to Rome for the weekend. You make me feel like a needy fool, wanting to spend time with you. Is Italy the problem, or is it me?"

"No!" I shook my head. "I'm sorry. It's not you. I don't want to leave Sam for that long."

"So… what? You're never going to go on holiday in case Sam needs you? That's ridiculous. And what about his girlfriend?"

"It's just, right now is a particularly bad time. He's going through some stuff."

"Oh, come off it. It's always a bad time, and he's always going through stuff."

"Excuse me?"

"What then?" He stood up, pushing his chair back. "Tell me, Faith. What stuff is he going through right now – stuff he isn't normally going through – that means you can't leave for three nights?"

Even in my bubbling frustration, I knew I should tell him. About Kane and my mother, moving to live with Grandma. Sam's addictions. If not all of it, then at least something. He stared across the table, eyes challenging me to finally open up and let him into an area of my life that actually mattered.

"I haven't got a passport."

"Then get one. You'll be needing it anyway for our honeymoon."

"I can't afford a passport, Perry. They cost eighty pounds."

He pulled out his wallet, yanked out a pile of twenties, and threw them on the table before storming out of his own dining room, and then out of his own house. I swallowed a couple more mouthfuls of the gnocchi, put the cappuccino brûlées back in the fridge, and cleared up the kitchen.

* * *

In the end we compromised. I booked four days off, and we went to York. If Sam had a meltdown, we would come home. And Perry would also come with me to our first marriage preparation class at Grace Chapel. Three days before the trip we spent an hour and a half in the lounge room at the chapel with three other engaged couples and the older husband and wife leading the class. To our relief, it involved no sharing or baring of secrets – just a video followed by time in our pairs to work through some questions. The topics were listening skills, time together, and conflict resolution.

How apt, considering the weekend to follow.

The couple leading the class were lovely. They asked if they could pray for us before we left.

"No, thanks." Perry smiled his businessman smile. "See you all next week." He took my hand and led me out of the building, but as we reached the car I stopped.

"I think I forgot my gloves. Hang on." I scurried back in, to where the class leaders were tidying up the mugs and stacking the chairs.

"Oh, hi, Faith. Did you forget something?"

"Will you pray for me quickly, please? Perry's waiting in the car."

"Of course." The woman – Zoe – came over and put one hand on my shoulder. She looked at me, and I could see the concern. I didn't say anything. Goodness me. If she knew the truth she'd be a lot more concerned. I knew it, and I certainly was.

She spoke out a brief prayer, head bowed and voice low. I don't even remember what she said, apart from praying for peace. And in that short moment, as a kind woman took my secret problems, my mammoth-sized anxiety, my doubts, fears, loneliness, helplessness, and whirlpool of spinning confusion – as she took these things and handed them over to a higher power, the God these people believed could somehow help, and for some reason cared, the burden on my tired shoulders lifted, a little, and in its place fell a soft, warm blanket of peace.

The blanket shifted soon enough, knocked aside by a ten-hour stint at a weekend wedding reception where the bride passed out drunk underneath the top table and the groom had a fist fight with his best man on the dance floor. They toppled the four-tier cake into the champagne fountain, smashing glasses in all directions, injuring three guests, and covering several more with lemon icing.

* * *

Sam continued calling me several times a day – he couldn't find his jumper, the workmen outside were giving him a migraine, he needed a specific brand of cereal from the supermarket, April had gone out and he didn't know when she would be home. Translation: I'm scared, I'm panicking, I can't cope. I'm teetering on the edge of the abyss and I need someone to pull me back.

I didn't tell him about York. If I called in Friday morning before we left, and again Monday night, he didn't need to know. Nor did I tell April, sure her solidarity lay with Sam. And when Dylan asked me after choir practice if I was doing anything nice at the weekend, I shrugged, mumbled, and changed the subject.

The Friday and Saturday in York were fine. Better than fine, once I'd managed to untangle the knots in my back and begin to appreciate the beautiful cobbled streets and shopfronts dripping with history. We toured a couple of museums, visited the stunning Minster, called in at various tea shops, and dined in the hotel's fancy restaurant.

Perry was, as ever, good company. Affable, amusing, and thoughtful. He let me set the pace, and the conversation. He smiled ruefully and said nothing when I bid him goodnight.

Sunday morning, while we were eating breakfast, Perry's nose in the papers, Sam called.

No hello.

"He's here."

"What?"

"I saw him. Out walking with April this morning. He's here, Faith. He's found me. Oh, man. He's going to kill me."

"Wait. Take a couple of deep breaths," I said. Perry looked up from his paper as I got up and moved into the hotel foyer.

"You have to come round," Sam said. "Now. I need you. I don't know what to do. I can't handle this by myself. What if he comes today?"

"Let's take this slowly and work through it. Okay?"

All I heard for a while was his ragged breathing. "Okay."

"Are you absolutely sure it was him?"

"What? Of course I'm sure. Well… I was sure. He's a lot older. His hair looked different. Longer. And he'd put on weight."

"Did he see you?"

"No. I don't know. I don't think so. He could have."

"Did you see where the man went?"

"He got into a car and drove off. Why are you saying 'the man', like you don't believe me? You don't think it was him?"

"We need to phone Gwynne. Tell her you may have seen him in Houghton."

"Not in Houghton. We were in Brooksby. April wanted to show me where you sing."

"You went to *Brooksby*?"

Sam hadn't been there since I had come back from London, when we sold the House of Hideous Memories and bought his flat.

"April wanted to go."

I spoke very carefully. "Sam, do you think, bearing in mind where you were, your subconscious could have affected you? That there's a chance you made a mistake?"

Your subconscious, plus years of mind-bending, brain-cell frying substance abuse?

"I don't know." I could hear him crying now. "I thought it was him, Faith. I really did."

"I spoke to Gwynne a couple of weeks ago. She said he'd been making all his meetings. She's going to tell us if he stops."

More sobs. "Please come over. I can't cope with this without you."

We both knew what that meant. What Sam did when he couldn't cope.

"I'm in York with Perry."

"What?" When Sam fell off the cliff he never considered anyone else maybe having a life not involving him. "You're coming, though?"

I looked up and saw Perry standing in the doorway. His expression impassive, he took a sip from a cup of coffee.

"Where's April?"

"She had to go to work. She started at the garden centre this week. When will you be here?"

I always came. If Sam needed me, I came. How could I leave my brother on the brink this time, while I lived it up on a mini-break with my millionaire fiancé?

Nobody would do that!

Perry took another sip of coffee.

"Give me a couple of minutes. I'll call you back."

"What? Faith? No! What if he comes?" I could barely understand him now.

"Sit tight, you'll be fine for a couple of minutes. I will call you back."

I hung up, my guts rolling over.

"Sam."

Perry nodded his head, one sharp movement.

"I'm going to call April, see when she can get back." I paused, made an effort to slow down. "I'm sorry. It won't take more than a few minutes."

April didn't pick up. I wanted to call Gwynne, but with Perry standing there glowering I didn't think now was the time to reveal that particular secret.

I called Sam back and asked him for the number he'd been given for the psychiatric crisis team. He refused to give it to me, adamant he would be fine if I came. His problem was Kane, not his mental health.

I hung up, sinking into a yellow flowery sofa near to the reception desk, my head in my hands.

Perry sat down beside me, leaning his elbows on his knees.

"What's happened?"

"He thinks he saw someone from his past. Someone who threatened to hurt him."

"Is that likely?"

"No. But it's possible. And doesn't really matter. If he thinks he saw him, that could be enough to tip him over the edge."

"Over what edge? If you stay here for one more day, what's the worst that could happen?"

He takes a drink, and then a thousand more? He finds a dealer, and scores?

I straightened up. "Sam has tried to kill himself twice. That I know of."

"You're saying that if you don't go home, right now, Sam will attempt suicide?"

"I don't know. Would you take that risk?" I pulled my phone out again. "Hang on a minute."

Taking a few steps away, I called one more number.

"Hello?"

"Dylan? It's Faith. I need your help."

Thirty minutes later, while I was fidgeting and fretting in my hotel room, Dylan called back to say he was with Sam. He didn't fudge the truth: my brother was in serious distress. But if he'd really seen Kane, who could blame him?

Perry knocked on my hotel room door a few minutes later.

"Sam all sorted?"

I gaped at him. "Are you joking?"

He shrugged. "You know what I mean. The vicar's going to stay with him until April gets home?"

"Yes." I stood back so he could enter the room.

He leaned against the desk, gripping the engraved edge on either side. "So we can take the river cruise. Nothing terrible's going to happen if you're not there for the next twenty-four hours. We can head home first thing tomorrow, and at least you'll have had a good rest."

I looked at my suitcase, propped up in the corner.

"For goodness' sake, Faith. You are not responsible for your brother!"

"Well, who is then?"

"You've done more than is reasonable, considering the circumstances. When are you going to stop letting him dictate your every move?"

I shook my head. "That is not what's happening. He needs help!"

Perry stood up, taking a couple of steps towards me. "And you've got him help. Is you being there really going to make that much difference? He seems equally miserable either way."

I looked up at him. "So you don't think I'm any help?"

"Honestly? I think half the time you running round after him probably only makes him worse."

The silence stretched out between us like a canyon in the wooden floor.

"I'm sorry. I shouldn't have said that," he said, his body completely still.

"I'd like to go home, please."

Perry closed his eyes. "There's no point staying here if you're worrying about him, anyway."

I waited until he opened them again before replying. "Thank you."

"Please think about whether there's a better way of doing this. If it's the best way to help Sam. Maybe you need to speak to someone, try to find some balance. You can't keep living like this."

I started putting my things into my bag, my body wound so tight I could feel it humming. I would forgive Perry, not least because he didn't know the truth of the situation.

Was it so terrible that part of the reason I finally agreed to marry him was for his money, if the money wasn't for me?

It certainly felt terrible.

Perry dropped me straight round to Sam's. He made a half-hearted offer to come in with me, but I said no. I couldn't be straight with Sam if Perry was there. I found him on the sofa watching *Band of Brothers* with Dylan.

"You didn't have to come." Dylan clicked off the television.

I pulled a face. "Well, yeah. I kind of did." I shrugged off my coat. "I need a cup of tea. Anyone else?"

"No, we just had one, thanks." Dylan followed me into the kitchen, which was the whole point.

"How is he?"

"He told me everything, talked about it until the panic subsided. I phoned the police, who are going to keep an eye out but can't do much else. I don't know how bad he is usually so it's hard to tell. He did eat some toast."

I let out some of the breath I'd been holding since the call. "Thanks for coming over. I hope you weren't doing anything important."

He smiled, briefly. "It's fine. I'm glad you called me. I'm sorry you had to cut your break short."

"It hardly matters, in the scheme of things."

"Do you think there's any chance he did see this guy? Would he really come after you?"

I took my time answering. "Yes. Yes, he absolutely would. And it's not the only thing that's happened."

I told Dylan about the man asking for the redhead. Only noticed my trembling hands when he handed me some tea.

"Wow." He ran fingers through his messy hair, face pale. "Have you told the police?"

"They're doing all they can."

"Which isn't a lot."

I shook my head.

"Maybe you should think about not living on your own for a while?" He cleared his throat. "You could stay with Perry."

Except Perry knows nothing about this whole situation.

Sam had fallen asleep by the time we returned to the living room. I told Dylan we'd be fine if he left, but the closing of the flat door jolted Sam awake.

"It's fine, Sam. Just Dylan leaving."

He lay back down. "Oh. He's not bad for a priest."

"He's not a priest."

It was only then that it hit me. Dylan was a minister. Of a church. Churches met on Sunday mornings. I knew Grace Chapel met ten-thirty every Sunday morning because a great big sign outside the main door announced it every time I walked past.

Grace Church boasted about sixty members. They only had one minister.

Dylan had missed the church service to come and sit with Sam, a man he'd never met. Because I'd asked him to.

Perry had wanted me to go on a river cruise.

What a good job I had a heart of toughened leather. Otherwise, it wouldn't stand a chance.

* * *

I came back to Nottinghamshire after three years in London. My first ten months in the big city were, to put it bluntly, horrific. Working in a just-about-legal bar and living in a decidedly non-legal bedsit taught me how to woman up. Inside I was still a beaten-down, stomped-on, scar-marked nothing. But I learned how to stand tall, watch my back (and my backside), and fight my corner.

I worked all the shifts I could get, smiled at men who made me sick in order to boost my tips, lived on little more than bar snacks, and counted every single penny. Eventually, I got a new job in a bar that required its staff to wear shirts and trousers over their underwear, and threw out the men who pawed our bodies, instead of giving them a prime position in front of the stage. Like incy wincy spider, I began my slow, slippery, determined climb back up. After a few more months, I scrimped enough deposit together to move into a one-room apartment. On the eleventh floor of a run-down, syringe-strewn, rat-infested block of flats. But. I had my own toilet. I had a shower, a kitchen area with four cupboards, and a two-ring hob. I had something resembling a sanctuary and glorious privacy. A tiny smidge of security behind my locks and bolts and window bars.

I also had no friends, no self-worth, and no peace. What about Sam? What did he have? Where was he? In prison? Dead? Sober?

I thought about him every night as I lay on my wilting blow-up bed, staring at the stains on the ceiling and listening to the gangs of boys laughing and brawling on the concrete beneath my window. Did he think about me?

After another four months, I plucked up the courage to call Grandma's house. Bile rising in my throat, fingers barely able to hit the right keys.

"Hello?"

"Sam." I reeled back, slumping onto my bed with relief.

"Faith? Where are you? Are you okay?"

"I'm fine. I'm in London. How are you?"

"Um. Yeah. I'm good." He took a moment to recover. "I'm an artist now. I paint."

"Wow. That's great."

"Yeah. I'm doing all right. Not enough to make me rich, but it's a living."

"So, is it just you, in the house?"

A short pause. "Snake's dead."

I nearly dropped the phone.

"When? What happened?"

"He got shot. Last year."

"I can't believe it." My head struggled to take this in. What it might mean. "So, what about you? Are you taking care of yourself?"

Are you sober, without him? Did the addict Sam die with Snake?

"Yeah. I said, I'm good. I got some proper help this time. Better medication."

We chatted for a couple more minutes. Sam wanted to know when I was coming home. I said it felt like an if, not a when, and wouldn't be any time soon.

I knew my brother. I recognized the drawl of weed in his voice. And I knew not to trust him. After years of living in a home akin to hell, I had finally got my own place. You would have to drag me back kicking and screaming before I gave that up.

* * *

The day the police called to tell me Sam was in hospital, I didn't kick. But in my head I did some screaming. I packed my precious few possessions into the old rucksack, stuffing the surplus into a carrier bag. My cherished stash of tips bought the coach ticket to Nottingham, where I caught a free bus to the Queen's Medical Centre. He lay in the last bed in the bay, with a view out across the car park and to the sparse trees beyond.

The outline of his skull pressed stark against ghostly green skin. A sharp contrast to his hair, spread out like oil against the pillow.

I shuffled the plastic chair up as close as possible, leaning forwards and laying my head as gently as I could upon his chest. Wrapping his hand in both of mine, I felt the rise and fall of his lungs, the thump of his heart, still beating despite his violent attempt to destroy it.

"You came back."

"Yes." My voice was as weak as my brother's.

"Will you stay?"

"Yes."

"I'm sorry."

"So you bloomin' well should be. Don't ever do that to me again."

He didn't answer. For once, my brother didn't choose the easy lie.

Chapter Fourteen

Over the next few days, Sam failed to improve. The mental health nurse visited, and assessed him for risk of self-harm. The results made me want to crawl into the back of my wardrobe and curl into a ball. I stuffed my pride in there instead, and called Perry.

Sam cried with relief when I asked if he wanted to go back to the private hospital. With a squillion-pound security system designed to keep patients safely inside, it would also keep vengeful murderers safely out. If we'd offered, I think he'd have moved in permanently at that point.

With Sam readmitted, I suddenly found myself with a lot more time on my hands. The end of February offered little in the way of work, and having missed choir practice, the following Sunday I decided to go along to Grace Chapel to thank Dylan properly for skiving church.

I walked to Brooksby. The buses ran intermittently on Sundays, and I had done nothing about the absurd red car sitting in front of my house yet. It took longer than I thought, so by the time I ducked into the back row, the singing had already started.

Hester led from the front, a keyboard player, guitarist, and a teenage girl playing a violin behind her. The style sounded quite folksy – a bit Irish – but it worked, and the congregation sang along with a gusto that more than made up for any lack of musicality. I spotted Rowan with her daughter Callie, to my surprise, and Melody. I knew Janice and Millie would be there, but hadn't expected to see most of the other choir members. No one had ever invited me to the services, and they weren't exactly stereotypical Christians – even Hester. I didn't know churches could include so many mixed-up, non-religious-type people. I had expected to stick out like a sore thumb. Instead, it felt strange I'd never been before.

After a couple more songs, the band sat down. Hester strode to the back row, and took the chair next to mine. I braced myself for the glower, and the reprimand about missing rehearsal so near to the competition. Instead, I felt her rough hand take mine. She lifted it up and gently kissed it, before letting go again.

Listening to those songs about forgiveness, and not being ashamed any more, and hope and peace and God's love never letting go had been bad enough. In the church where my mum had found something worth believing in, this simple gesture was like a tap opening up my tear ducts again. Hester handed me a tissue, and hissed, "Pay attention, Faith. Crack open your heart and mind, and you might be surprised."

No might about it. Mags – *Mags* – spoke for twenty-odd minutes about a kick-butt woman in the Bible called Esther, who although a poor orphan, won the king's heart to become queen, and then by her beauty and bravery and brains managed to save the whole of the Jewish people from genocide, and got the baddie caught red-handed committing sexual assault.

It was a fascinating story. I sort of related to some of it. I thought I might like to read the Bible if it was full of stories about incredible women committing daring deeds, rather than a million lists of don't-you-dares and no-you-can'ts.

We sang one more song before finishing. Afterwards, when I chatted to the choir women over hot drinks and boring biscuits while trying to spot Dylan across the room without staring at him, random lines of the music kept playing, over and over, in the back of my head.

I had been orphaned twice – once when my mother died, and again when I lost Grandma. God hadn't saved me from Snake. Or everything else. He hadn't saved Sam. He hadn't stopped Kane killing my mum.

And yet. I was here. And doing okay for myself. Sam and I survived Kane, and escaped Snake. I had somehow met an unusually generous man, who also happened to be a millionaire and had fallen in love with me, meaning Sam could get help.

I was making friends at this strange little hotchpotch church. Having fun. Finding strength. Proper, in-your-guts, not-faking-it strength. Hmmm.

* * *

As the crowd thinned, I managed to collar Dylan.

I filled him in on Sam, briefly, before bringing up my real reason for walking six miles cross-country on a freezing cold winter morning.

"I wanted to say thanks, again, for last week."

"It's cool. I accepted your thanks the first time." He grinned.

I crossed and uncrossed my arms, suddenly not quite sure where they were meant to go.

"Did you miss the service last week, to be with Sam?"

His face went very still for a microsecond. Then he laughed. "I did. But we had a family service, and it was my turn to end up in the gunge tank again. I really didn't mind missing that."

"But it's your job."

"Taking care of people in crisis is also my job. Our family worker led the service that morning. Apparently it all went smoothly. And Hester quite enjoyed getting gunged."

"Why didn't you say something?"

Dylan looked at me, blue eyes serious now. Something unidentifiable flickered in that look.

"I wanted to help." He shrugged. "It's what friends do. Now, if you'll excuse me I need to speak to that guy over there before he leaves."

After a particularly gruelling choir practice – "Stop lolling! Use your diaphragm to breathe! It's why God gave you one. FOCUS! If you can't make me believe you actually care if I stand by you or not, there is no point entering this competition. Rowan! Is that *gum* in your mouth?" – Rosa asked for another dress fitting.

"I'll text the bridesmaids and see when they're free. When were you thinking?"

"My goodness. When were *you* thinking? Are all brides in England like this? You don't care about your dresses, or what they are looking like. Not even your own dress! What about rest of plans? Cake? Flowers? Decorations for tables? Have you written invitations or will you be sending a text?"

"Larissa has it all under control."

"What, she chooses and you say yes? Why don't you care about your wedding, Faith? It less than six months away." Rosa shook her head in disbelief.

"Last week she phoned me about wedding favours. Did I want the heart soaps to read 'Peregrine and Faith love everlasting', 'Perry and Faith to have and to hold', or 'Mr and Mrs Upperton til death do us part'? How can I plan a wedding with someone who thinks there are people on this earth who would enjoy washing themselves with any of those options? It's being married I'm bothered about, not getting married."

"So you been getting ready for becoming a wife? That's good. What you been doing? Learning how to look after a man?"

"No! Perry can take care of himself. I've been going to the marriage course here on Tuesday nights."

"Ah! So you and Perry learn together."

"Yes."

Yes. When Perry finally turned up. Usually somewhere about halfway through the class. But to be honest, I didn't think Perry was the one who was going to need help making this marriage work.

Saturday afternoon, my bridesmaids gathered. Marilyn brought Rosa and the dresses in her car: four dresses carefully folded in supermarket carrier bags and one zipped inside a professional moth-resistant, polycotton dress cover.

"Marilyn first," Rosa commanded. "You are causing me a lot of trouble with this personal trainer. I going to waste a lot of material if this continues."

Marilyn stripped off her tunic and leggings, squirming. She quickly stepped into her dress. This time, no longer a sample, the fabric shone a deep blue tulle, with delicately embroidered butterflies along the bottom third of the skirt in silver, bottle green, and three shades of purple. Some of the butterflies looked as though they had broken free from the rest, and were flying up the skirt. Marilyn held the dress up while Rosa fastened the row of tiny buttons, in colours to match the butterflies. As it swished slightly, the dress shimmered, giving the impression the butterflies were flying.

"A-may-zing," Natasha breathed. "Like, totally, utterly brilliant. It's the most gorgeous dress I have ever seen. Like, ever. Better than anything at New York fashion week by miles. You look like the queen."

"Pardon?" Marilyn's smile dimmed somewhat.

"No, *a* queen. Not *the* Queen. A queen from a film about an amazing queen who is massively beautiful, and wise and strong and married to a gnarled old king obsessed with power and money who doesn't see the real her, but then she meets a hunksome knight with humble beginnings who rescues her from a terrifying beast and at the start they, like, argue all the time because he thinks she's dead proud and used to people obeying her every command. But really she's just lonely and miserable, and she thinks he's a rough brute with no respect for women. But they fall in love, and the king dies so they're free to be together. Only it's too late. The knight has gone on a quest leading to certain death. But then she goes after him and…"

"Okay! I get it. I think I know how it ends."

"You can't!" Natasha shook her head vigorously. "I haven't made up the ending yet."

"Well, as enjoyable as it was, and complimentary, shall we carry on with the fitting? Leona's babysitting for me. I don't want to leave her alone for too long with Nancy and Pete. It might put her off having them again."

Rosa shuffled Marilyn in front of the mirror I'd carried downstairs. Marilyn gasped at the incredible reflection, letting go of the top of the dress to get a proper look. As she did, the dress slipped right off her to the floor. She carried on staring into the mirror, for once dumbfounded.

"Looks like those training sessions have been paying off," I grinned. "It almost makes six hours a week with the torture twins worth it."

"I thought my scales had gone doolally."

"How much have you lost?"

"Nearly three stone. I didn't believe it, but it must be true. Look at me. I have muscles. And a waist. And look, a bone!"

"You look fabulous."

"But you must have seen in the mirror?" Catherine asked. "Or noticed that your clothes didn't fit?"

"If you got four hours' sleep a night, were five stone overweight, covered in stretch marks, and brushed your hair once a week you wouldn't look in a mirror, either. And I've spent the past year in leggings and tracksuit bottoms. I knew I'd lost something. Even if it was just the gallons of sweat Anton wrings out of me. But. I look…" She sniffed. "Hooten tooten. I look almost *normal.*"

"Normal?" Rosa shook her head in indignation. "You are extraordinary."

"Your dress is extraordinary." Marilyn pulled it back up. "You'd better get measuring. And be prepared. Who knows how skinny I'll be by August?"

Natasha and Catherine's dresses were perfect fits. Both "dusty aqua" as planned. On the bottom seam of Natasha's, Rosa had embroidered tiny shells, some pointy, some curled like snails, others in a fan shape, all in a mix of palest pink, mother of pearl, vanilla, and coral. Catherine's shimmered with starfish, each only a few centimetres long. Deep red, gold, slate grey, and copper, they swam along the bottom of her skirt and the edges of her capped sleeves.

Rosa's creations were like nothing I'd seen before. Striking. Magnificent. Alluring and innocent at the same time.

I looked at those stunning girls, hair sleek and shiny, fresh-faced and glowing, the dress fabric flowing over every curve like water. Steeling my senses, I unzipped the climate-control garment bag in one swift movement, releasing the repaired Ghost Web. Only it wasn't the Ghost Web. Soft, light fabric spilled out of the opening, an antique cream in the sense of antique being beautiful and timeless, not your mother-in-law's horrible old dress.

"It is Nottingham Lace," Rosa said, lifting the dress out of the bag. "I get it cheap from a woman in the paper."

"Where's the Ghost Web?"

She sniffed, jerking her head in the direction of the last carrier bag. "Is it repaired?"

"Yes. And altered to fit. I took some material off the bottom and inserted it into the bodice. It is still the ugliest item of clothing I ever saw. I disinfect my hands after touching that dress. Then I had big glass of vodka and sewed many butterflies to clean up my brain. But here, you try this dress first. Then decide."

I tried on Rosa's dress. The top half was covered in Nottingham Lace, the bottom plain silk. I felt like a movie star from the 1940s. Understated elegance, my curves an asset not a liability, to be celebrated rather than hidden. I felt beautiful. And unlike in the lovely dresses from the bridal shop, I felt like me.

"Do you see the flowers?"

It was hard to find them through my blurry vision, but I did find three rows of daisies winding along the bottom of the hem, in keeping with the embroidery on the bridesmaids' dresses.

"My favourite flowers."

"Yes. I heard you telling Melody. And, see, each row is different."

They were. On the top row, the flowers were in bud, the second row were partly open, and the third in full bloom. And in amongst the flowers were tiny butterflies, shells, and starfish.

"You open up, Faith, like a flower. I even see you smile now, sometimes. Once or twice shoulders relaxing. Your face – how you say" – she hastily consulted her dictionary – "*peep* out from behind your stone wall. This dress tell your story. Like Marilyn's dress tell her story – change from fat caterpillar to butterfly. Natasha like pretty shell – nice outside protect squishy inside, to stop heart get broken again."

"What?" Natasha splurted out a mouthful of coffee.

"Catherine's dress tell her story. You chop off starfish arm, it grow back again. Catherine had difficult things happen, take away part of her that mattered most. Still Catherine, but new Catherine. More careful now, wiser, and watching what really happening. Still a star."

Catherine began to cry.

"Wowzers," Marilyn said. "Are you one of those mentalists?"

"Those what-ists?" Rosa frowned.

"She's wondering how you knew." Was it my imagination, or did I *sound* more lovely and elegant in this dress?

"Aha!" Rosa smirked. "You think I'm brain reader? Tell what going to happen by looking at your hand?" She laughed. "I call your house, your mothers answer. They very happy telling me why their pretty girls not got a man yet. You need to move out, get some privacy."

I tried on the Ghost Web, standing on the other side of my living room from the mirror. Nobody said anything. It felt like a funeral. The dress fit, and the rips had vanished. Marilyn, back in her leggings and tunic, narrowed her eyes at me, the cup of coffee in her hand twitching.

"Don't even think about it." I pointed at the coffee.

"Oh, I will. I will think about it. But I'm not going to slay the ghost until you give the order. It's your decision, Faith. You have to make it. But, when you do, I'm going to enjoy ripping that ghoul to shreds."

"Or neatly packing it away and returning it to its owner."

"Yeah. Or that."

* * *

The first Saturday in March, the Grace Choir assembled in the chapel car park, boarding the minibus in a gaggle of breathless excitement and bad jokes. Our black choir dresses, this time accessorized with a rainbow of coloured belts and shoes from red to violet, lay in sheets of plastic across the back row.

We were ten minutes late. We were waiting for Polly.

Thirty-eight weeks pregnant, we had hoped (and prayed, literally, after every rehearsal and on Sunday mornings) that Polly's baby would wait until after the competition. Increasingly pale, and worryingly thin except for her beach-ball bump, Polly had shrunk more inside herself as the weeks went by. She gave up trying to smile or pretending to be okay, making no more than the barest attempt at conversation. Despite us both being altos, and supposed to know each other's ups and downs, dreams, secrets, and knicker size, Polly had barely spoken to me since the Christmas carol service. And only then, I knew, because to ignore me completely would confirm I'd been right about her situation.

She insisted she was simply tired, worn down from backache, permanent indigestion, and being kicked in the ribs.

I prayed the baby was the only one kicking Polly. I prayed with fervour, and tears, and a swollen heart.

We were half an hour late. We had to go. Hester was vibrating like an overheated washing machine.

Where was Polly?

We rang the phone number she gave when joining the choir. *I'm sorry*, we were told, *that line is not in service.*

"I'll go and get her," said Marilyn, our non-essential choir member. "Does anyone know where she lives?"

After much discussion it turned out that none of us had ever been to Polly's house, dropped her off, picked her up, or even heard her talk about where she lived. Eventually, Janice reminded Millie that her daughter's husband's secretary had been at school with Polly, and they used to be friends once. A load more phone calls, including a five-minute heated discussion with a local plumber, the force of which threatened to blast Hester's helmet into orbit, resulted in a village, a probable street, and a definite description of a red front door, an eight-foot-high leylandii hedge, and gateposts with two lions sitting on the top.

"Hokeycokey. I'm on it. You go, and we'll catch you up."

Marilyn sprinted over to her car (more proof of Anton's amazing fitness powers) and started the engine. Roaring out of the car park, she sped down the road, before screeching to a stop, reversing at about fifty miles an hour back to the chapel, and winding down her window.

"Where's the competition again? Is it Leicester, or Lincoln?"

I shook my head. "Hang on. I'm coming with you."

There were roars of protest from the choir. Polly and I were both singing second alto. Without us, the whole sound would be off-kilter.

Hester looked at me, steadily, as everyone quietened down to see what she would say. I placed my hand on my stomach, across the hidden slash-scar, and Hester's head nodded, the tiniest fraction of an inch. "Well, what are you waiting for? You're blocking the drive. Get! Get! Get!"

We got, got, got to Polly's house.

Sort of. After about four wrong turns, three times up and down the high street, and having to stop and ask a man walking his dog for directions to the house with the lion gateposts.

With or without the lions, the eight-foot hedge, and the red front door, I would have known we had the right place.

The house was immaculate. Every stalk of grass pointing straight up, not one piece of gravel out of place on the driveway. Regimental rows of early flowers – snowdrops, crocuses, purple anemones – lined up along the front wall of the house. Every window was shrouded in drapes. The house looked frozen. Lifeless. It looked like Polly.

We rang the bell, knocked, peered through the windows. No answer.

"What do we do?" Marilyn tried jumping to see over the side gate.

"There's no car. Maybe she's late, so Tony's giving her a lift. Or she's gone into labour and is at the hospital," I said.

"I can't imagine any other reason Polly'd miss the East Midlands heat of the International Community Choir Sing-Off."

Oh boy. I could imagine several reasons. They wriggled in my guts. I hoped those choir girls were praying.

I folded my arms. "We can't leave without making sure she's not inside."

Marilyn squinted at me. "I'd high five that decision, but I'm too worried about Polly. What's the plan?"

"I have no idea. Credit card to pick the lock? Kick the door down? Maybe they've got a key hidden under a plant pot."

While Marilyn hunted for a spare key, I sized up our other options. While I pressed my face against the window, hoping for a clue, a faint moan drifted through the glass.

"I heard something!" I ran over to the front door, pushing my fingers through the bristly letterbox to try to make a peephole. "We're here, Polly. We're coming to help you."

"Should we phone the police?" Marilyn asked, squeezing up behind me on the doorstep.

"We can't call the police because someone isn't answering the front door. Argh. Think, Faith, think." I sprinted over to the side gate, trying to gauge if I could scale it with a boost from Marilyn. "Maybe if we get around the back, we can find a window open, or something."

Crash!

I turned back to see a saucer-sized hole in the front door pane. Marilyn tossed the rock she'd used to one side, wrapped her cardigan round her wrist, and shoved her hand through the hole.

She frowned. "There's no key in the lock."

"Can you see one hanging up anywhere?"

Pulling her hand out, she stuck her eye up to the opening.

"No." She picked up the rock again. "I'm going to smash enough of the glass for you to climb through. What do you think?"

"I think I'm glad you're here. I think I hope Polly isn't inside calling the police. I think I'm going to wet my pants if Tony comes home and finds us here. I think you should be quick about it. And please be careful."

About six minutes later, I stood carefully amidst the shards of glass on Polly's hall carpet. Leaving Marilyn to make her own way inside, I started searching the house.

In the perfectly decorated, tastefully furnished, spotlessly tidy master bedroom I found her. Kneeling on the floor, leaning her shoulders on the bed, one hand clutching at the silk bedspread for dear life. She buried her face into the mattress and released a deep, primal groan.

Forget the blackened eye, the split and swollen lip, the purple palm print decorating her forearm for now. This woman was having a baby.

Like, now.

I gripped the door frame, shook the buzzing out of my head, and yelled for Marilyn.

Chapter Fifteen

An hour later, the paramedics tenderly loaded Polly and her tiny pink baby girl into the ambulance. The midwife had arrived just in time, while the person on the end of the phone gave me instructions to relay to Marilyn, playing interim midwife due to her having actually given birth before.

"It looks a lot different from this end!" she panted, squeezing Polly's hand as another contraction wracked her poor, smashed-up body.

To our shuddering relief, everything had gone smoothly. Polly was too dazed to ask questions. She cradled her baby girl while slow, silent tears spilled out of her puffed-up eyes.

Marilyn and I cleared up the mess while the midwife did her stuff.

"Usually, we'd give Mum a cup of tea and some toast, followed by a shower. Given the situation..." She stopped and cleared her throat. "Given the situation, we're admitting her straight away."

"Can we come too?"

"You can follow behind. We're taking her to City Hospital. Perhaps you can bring her a bag of things?"

Nobody mentioned a possible father, despite the numerous photographs of Polly and Tony hung up around the house. Nobody expressed the slightest concern for the broken window, despite the light rain now falling. There were questions to be asked, and authorities to be contacted, but right now, all anyone cared about was getting Polly and her baby out of that house.

The paramedics, both men, shut the ambulance door and made one last scan of the horizon. Shoulders flexing, jaws locked, they appeared to be half hoping Tony would come zooming up in his testosterone-powered, midlife-crisis machine, so they could show him what they thought of men who beat up pregnant women.

I did not half hope it. I wholly hoped it. And for that, I am finding it really hard to be repentant.

"I can't believe it," Marilyn hiccupped, as we sat in her car, about to drive off. "There was a whole new person. There wasn't a person, and then there was. A. Whole. New. Person. Bam!"

"Bam?" I laughed through my tears. "More like aaaarrgh! Grrrr! Hhhnnnnn! *Then* a whole new person. And when you did it, there were two new people!"

"Yeah, but watching someone else do it is totally different. A new person. Out of nowhere. A teensy-tiny, perfect, rosy, sweet-smelling, yawning person."

"You forgot pooping."

"I didn't forget. My skirt is ruined. I just didn't want to lower the tone. Why would you lower the tone, Faith? That was a hooten tooten, bona fide miracle."

"I'm sorry. I don't want to lower the tone." My voice hitched. "But I'm so, so scared for them. She's so small, and helpless, and beautiful. The thought of that precious baby living with that terrible man. It can't happen. I won't let it happen."

"Shall we burn the house to the ground?" Marilyn started the car.

"He'd take them somewhere we can't find them."

"What are you going to do?" she asked, as she pulled away.

"I don't know." I glanced in the wing mirror, making one last check for Tony.

"Surely she won't go back? She's a mother now. That changes everything."

I thought of my mother, the faint scent of lavender, the tickle of her soft, auburn hair on my cheek as she bent to kiss me. Her gentle voice singing me to sleep.

I shook my head, watched the tears plopping onto my lap. "I just don't know."

* * *

I called Hester. The choir were at the concert hall, about to go onstage.

"I'm so sorry. All that work, and now you're two short," I commiserated.

"Not important! A baby has been born! Why are you talking to me instead of taking care of Polly?"

"We're on our way to the hospital now."

"Good. Make sure you tell that girl what's what. After telling her how much we love her. And that we are all going to stand with her, and do whatever it takes. And take some pictures on your phone. Send them over."

Someone interrupted. It sounded like April. "Hester! We need to go."

"Well, what are you waiting for then?" she huffed. "Go and be spectacular."

I called out my best wishes, and have a fantastic time, and knock 'em dead, but they'd gone.

"Are you gutted to be missing it?" Marilyn asked, as she snuck through a light just as it turned red.

"Remember the whole new person? How could anyone be gutted about that? Besides, we have a job to do. I've got a feeling things might get ugly before all this is over."

Things got ugly about seven that night. Ugly, as in a curled-up lip, bulging veins, and hairy, flaring nostrils.

We were choosing a drink from the vending machine in the hospital reception when Tony strode in. The woman on reception, no doubt used to stressed-out men swinging their weight around, patted her silver bob and repeated the question.

"Who are you here to see?"

"My wife. She's been here all day, and no one even bothered to call me. Don't you have rules about informing next of kin?"

"I presume your wife has a name?"

"Polly Malone."

"One moment please." She narrowed her eyes. "Sir."

"Uh-oh." Marilyn and I sidled across to stand behind a nearby pillar. I faced the reception desk, with Marilyn as my shield, and peeked out to see what would happen.

"I'm afraid I can't help you." The receptionist pursed her lips.

"What are you talking about? I know she's here. My neighbour told me."

The woman's eyebrow rose a millimetre, clearly indicating what she thought Polly not telling him herself implied.

"If we did have a woman here of that name, it would be her choice whether she wanted to see you or not."

He laughed, but it sounded uneasy. "She's my wife. Of course she wants to see me."

"I'm afraid not." Her face set in an instant, like quick-drying cement, as she glanced over Tony's twitching shoulder. "But *they* would like a word."

During the few short minutes the police attempted to restrain the husband of Polly Malone, witness reports confirmed his deliberately aggressive and violent behaviour resulted in his face smashing into a pillar, breaking his nose.

Nobody, and especially not the two witnesses, cheered under their breath, clapped, did a little jig, or saluted the receptionist when she muttered, after the scuffle had moved into the car park, "You had a girl, by the way. I hope she never has to meet you."

Harsh? No harsher than Polly's hammered – yes, *hammered* with an actual hammer – fingers, cracked eye socket, and broken teeth.

We broke the news to Polly during visiting hours in her private room. She said nothing, gazing at the warm, sweet bundle of new life in her arms and nodding softly when we asked if she wanted us to fetch her things and move them to a safe place.

By ten o'clock, we were at Marilyn's house, drinking hot chocolate and waiting for the buzz of adrenaline to subside so we could stop shaking and go to bed. A suitcase and a laundry basket full of Polly's meagre possessions waited in Marilyn's spare room. We'd left most of the baby paraphernalia behind. Polly needed a new start, and with all of the twins' kit still strewn around the cottage of chaos, there was plenty to go around.

"It's a bit different from Polly's house." Marilyn winced.

"Her house wasn't a home. She'll probably love the noise, and the company. And the cake."

"She needs some cake in her."

"She needs a lot of things. It's good of you to let her stay."

Marilyn chewed on her lip. "To be honest, with James gone I could do with the company too."

The doorbell rang, making us both jump.

"Police?" Marilyn asked.

"No. The police wouldn't call at this time unless it couldn't wait."

"Right. I suppose we'd better answer it then."

The bell rang again, swiftly followed by several loud knocks.

She frowned. "Sounds like it can't wait."

Well, how could the runners-up of the East Midlands heat of the International Community Choir Sing-Off possibly wait to crack open the bubbly, coo over the photos of Polly's baby (not of Polly, we kept her bruises quiet), and describe everything that happened – the lights, the applause, the moment Janice tripped up and her wig slipped off? Quite obviously, they couldn't.

Once everyone had piled in like dwarves in a hobbit hole, eating nearly as much and singing twice as loud (waking Nancy, but not Pete, who would sleep through the battle of five armies), we toasted the choir, the judges, Hester, the NHS, new beginnings for Polly and her daughter, awesome women everywhere who find the courage to tell scumbag men they can't visit them in hospital, the handsome driver, Dylan (who looked totally at home sitting up against the wall with one leg stretched out, surrounded by overexcited women), brawny policemen, tight-lipped receptionists, Hester again, and the choir again. Then the champagne ran out.

Somewhere around two I heaved myself up from a beanbag covered in dinosaurs and stumbled to the door. "I give in. I can cope with breaking and entering *or* delivering a baby, no problem. But not both in one day. I'm pooped. See you all soon."

I slipped on my shoes, and started walking down the path towards home. It was a cold night, the stars were out, and the world was draped in moonlight. I huddled into my coat, thoughts turning back to Polly, safe for now, but alone and afraid, facing life with scars I knew would take a long, long time to heal.

The slam of Marilyn's door echoed through the night as someone else left the party. Looking back I saw Dylan jogging up behind me, shrugging into his leather jacket.

"I'm walking you home."

"You don't have to do that."

He moved alongside me, the village path so narrow he had to walk on the street. "Well, my job description was to see all the choir members home at the end of the competition, so actually, I do."

"Ah, just doing your job." I smiled, and glanced over at him, grateful for the distance he'd placed between us, lessening the intimacy of the darkness.

"Yes. But when I ask how you're doing, that's as a friend. Not part of my job."

We walked in silence while I thought about it. After our conversation on New Year's Day, I wanted to take the opportunity to answer honestly. I'd be an idiot if I pretended today hadn't triggered some deep, nasty memories.

"I'm okay. At the moment. Seeing Polly was pretty horrendous. But if we hadn't got there – hadn't found where she lived, or managed to get there in time? There are so many what ifs my head spins when I think about it. But we did get there, and she's made the right decision, for now. I feel grateful for that. And grateful I made the right decision, too, when it was my turn."

I pressed my hand against my stomach slash-scar. "I'll have nightmares tonight. And probably for the rest of the week. But I'm okay. At least the nightmare stops when I wake up these days."

We were quiet for a minute or so, before Dylan started telling me more about the day. How Hester had dedicated the performance to Polly and her daughter. How the women had thrummed with pride when they got a standing ovation. How he shamelessly cried when Rowan sang her solo.

We reached my little front path, and I let out a long sigh.

"Sorry." Dylan grimaced. "I'm rubbing it in."

"No. I want to hear. I'm so darn proud of us all. And I'll be there for the second round. Someone else can take care of any emergencies next time."

He grinned. "They'd struggle to do as good a job as you."

"You didn't hear me squeal when her waters broke." I pulled out my key and unlocked the door.

"Thanks for walking me home, Dylan."

"You're welcome." Turning sideways, hands tucked tightly in his pockets, he nudged my arm with one elbow. "Don't have nightmares. Please."

He strode off into the night, and I quickly closed the door behind him. Leaning back against the frame, my heart thumping, I held my breath, reluctant to exhale the scent of battered leather. I think my arm might have been on fire. I think my whole body was in danger of bursting into flames.

What was I doing? Was this really what a crush felt like?

I had to stay away from Dylan.

My phone beeped with a text:

Just got back from the conference. How'd it go? Looking forward to seeing you tomorrow. I love you xxx

I did have nightmares that night, but not about what I expected.

I dreamed about a wedding, and the Ghost Web, and running

through the blazing corridors of HCC, choking on billowing smoke as I searched for the fire escape.

Good gracious. I had to stay away from that man.

* * *

Despite her newfound fitness levels, I felt increasingly concerned for Marilyn. I spoke to Hester at choir practice.

"I have an idea for another choir activity."

"Go on," she said.

"Polly comes out of hospital in a few days. Marilyn still hasn't cleared out her spare room. James has been away for months and the house is more chaos than cottage. It's gone way beyond homely clutter. I'm worried about her. I think she's overwhelmed, and doesn't know where to start even if she had the time or the energy."

"Have you offered any help?"

"I still babysit Nancy and Pete while she trains with Anton. I hang out a load of washing when I can, or chuck some toys in a box, but when I bring it up she changes the subject."

Hester nodded, her mouth a flat line. "Leave it with me."

Thursday morning, the text went round:

Choir meeting Marilyn's, Sat 9am. Don't tell Marilyn.

Thursday afternoon, I had a phone call.

"Faith. I need a really, really big favour. I've won Anton's trainee of the month. It's a spa day. Eight hours by myself, in a spa, being pampered and steamed and encouraged to wear a dressing gown in daylight hours! But it's this Saturday."

I smiled on the other end of the phone. "What time do you need me?"

"Eight-thirty. If you're sure? You're not working? Or walking? I know it's a big ask."

"I can bring the twins on my walk. Show them the river."

"They're exhausting. And a handful. And quite stressful at

200

times, when they decide to cry in sync." Marilyn couldn't keep the bubbling hope from her voice.

"Your babies are beautiful, and lovely, and hilarious, and I love looking after them."

"I'll pay you, of course."

"I'm pretending you didn't say that," I said.

"You know I hate asking for help."

I pretended to be annoyed. "Do you know I hate not being asked to help when my friend needs it? I have a gaping help-hole in my life right now. I'm going to look forward to spending a whole day with my best buddies Nancy and Pete. Maybe I should pay *you* for the privilege."

* * *

Sixteen choir members, bin bags and dusters in hand, surveyed the mountain of mess open-mouthed. They had thought the skip Hester hired a little over the top, but not any more.

"How long have we got?" Melody asked, stretching out her rubber glove and letting it ping back with a thwack.

"Eight and a half hours and counting," Hester barked.

"What do we even do with all this junk?" Rowan boggled. "We can't just throw away someone else's stuff."

"We can, and we will," Hester ordered. "Five piles. Skip, recycling, give away, keep, don't know. The don't know pile will be the smallest, followed by the keep pile. Two sub-teams. Sort and Clean. Sort will complete the first phase in each room, Clean will then follow. Each sub-team splits itself into pairs."

"Sub-sub-teams?" Millie asked.

"If you insist. Each pair –"

"You mean, each sub-sub-team?"

"Each *pair* tackles one room at a time."

"I thought you said we could call them sub-sub-teams?"

"Call them what you like!" Hester beetled her brows. "Just get going! It is time you ladies learned how to distinguish between what you need to keep hold of, what other people need to take off you, and what nobody wants or needs. Too many of you have cluttered up your life with junk. Unhealthy! Hindrance! Go and master the art of prioritizing. Go!"

No doubt sensing the sizzling tension between us, Hester paired me up with April. We started in Nancy and Pete's bedroom, letting them play in one of the cots together while we sorted through the piles of baby clothes, toys, broken equipment, and four hundred and thirty-seven parenting magazines.

April was a ruthless machine. She displayed no hesitation in chucking away someone else's belongings, refusing to acknowledge the "don't know" pile. We filled two bin bags with clothes that needed washing and two with rubbish. We created an enormous pile of tiny clothes for Polly's as yet unnamed daughter, and made significant contributions to the recycling and give-away piles.

I nearly gagged at the state of the carpet we uncovered. It reminded me of my bedsit in London.

We took down the curtains to wash, changed the cot sheets, wiped the walls with baby-friendly detergent and disinfectant, and scrubbed every other surface until they sparkled.

Two hours later, Hester poked her head in the door. "Are you ready for the Clean team yet?"

"We've already done it." April's face shone pink. "All that's left is cleaning the carpet, but we didn't want to do that with the babies here."

Hester's eyes flicked over every corner of the room. Pete laughed and threw his stuffed kangaroo over the top of the cot bars.

"Right. You're scheduled a fifteen-minute tea break. Then you can start on the conservatory. Good job."

We had our tea huddled on the back step, the only place free from piles, or people sorting piles.

April, who had said barely anything to me throughout the morning, peeked over her mug.

"How is he?"

I blew out a sigh into my tea. "He's a little better. Still a really long way to go, but he's getting there."

I hoped. Oh, how I hoped he would get there.

"Have you seen him?" April asked.

"Only once, for an hour. We've spoken a couple of times on the phone. Too much outside interaction can disrupt things, early on. It puts pressure on him. There'll be more opportunity to visit as he gets stronger."

She kept her eyes down, voice hesitant.

"Did he mention me?"

I took another sip, taking a moment to form an answer. "You remember how he was, before he went in?"

She nodded.

"In his head, it's like full-blown panic mode, every second of the day. He's having to scramble to survive, only the danger is in his head, so he can never get away from or deal with it. He didn't mention you, April. But I was sat in front of him for an hour and he didn't mention me, either."

"Is he angry with me?" she whispered. "For letting him get so bad? For not helping him? Does he think it's my fault?"

"Look at me." Slowly, she lifted her head, eyes skittering all over the place. "Right now he's in some form of hell we can't begin to understand. He's ill. You couldn't have stopped that. I couldn't have stopped that. He couldn't have, either. It's no one's fault. Okay?"

"Okay."

We drank our tea for a few more moments.

"You love him, don't you?"

She nodded, her mouth twisted.

"You know it might not be enough? It's going to be a long time before he can focus on anyone apart from himself. Even if he loves you, it doesn't mean you can make it work."

"I know that. But it doesn't mean I'm not going to try."

We took our mugs into the kitchen, finding a tiny space to

squeeze them onto near the sink before getting to work in the conservatory.

A while later, as we carried a broken futon out to the skip, I watched April's determined face, and considered how hard she'd worked all morning. How hard she'd worked since September. I looked around at the Sort and Clean teams, beavering away in secret because Marilyn hated to ask for help, had tried to carry her struggles alone. I made a decision not to keep trying to carry my load alone. It wasn't heroic. It was stupid. And prideful. And bordering on obsessive. Maybe I could let some of my Sam junk go.

"I can ask if they'll let you visit, if you like."

She stopped, nearly tripping over a plant pot as the momentum from the futon pushed her backwards.

"Are you sure?"

"They might not agree. Sam might not agree. But I can ask."

"Thank you."

I couldn't bring myself to say "You're welcome", but I'd made the offer. Made a start.

Chapter Sixteen

By one o'clock, we were starving, and there were still mountains of work to be done. I rummaged around the kitchen, finding a sack of potatoes in the pantry and a tray of eggs.

Twenty minutes later we had Spanish omelette, flavoured with red onion, chives, and parsley fresh from the garden and a frugal layer of parmesan cheese. Having sent April out to buy a couple of loaves of crusty bread, I added some tomato salsa and finished off with a coconut cake thrown together from Marilyn's amply stocked baking cupboard.

"This is well good," Rowan said, through a mouthful of egg, perched on a cardboard box in the living room. "How did you cook for all of us that quick?"

I shrugged. "I used to work in a restaurant. You pick up some tips."

"You should go into catering or something. Open a café."

"Maybe one day. Right now I couldn't take on running my own business."

"Yeah." Rowan shoved in another forkful. "It's a lot of work. When I open my beauty salon with Kim you could get a place nearby, somewhere for the clients to have lunch once we've got them all spruced up."

"So you're planning on becoming a hairdresser?" I asked. "Is the music career on hold?"

She shrugged. "While Callie needs me here, anyway. I'm trying to find someone who'll take me on as an apprentice but it's tough. Hester says you have to keep trying if you want to fulfil your destiny; it doesn't ever come easy. She said I need to keep my chin up and remember I'm a strong, courageous woman with as much worth as anybody else. One day someone will see the potential inside me."

I smiled. "You know Hester; she's usually right. And in the meantime, you're still doing my wedding hair and other stuff like that?"

"Too right!" She stuffed in her last piece of omelette, leaning over to grab a chunk of my hair.

"Oh, sorry." As I ducked away to avoid her eggy fingers, she reached about for a piece of kitchen roll and wiped her hands on it. "Rosa showed me what your dress is gonna look like, so I've been thinking about what hairdo will suit it best."

"She showed you my dress?"

"A picture. It's amazing, in't it? When I get married, she's definitely making mine."

She tugged out my hairband, and deftly twisted and twirled for a moment behind my head before tying it back up.

"Something like that."

I took a look in the mirror above the fireplace. "Wow."

She grinned, cheeks flushing.

"When you next have an interview at a salon, bring me along."

We were interrupted by Hester clapping her hands together. "Choir, while most of us are here, I will release the details of the Community Choir Sing-Off national final."

There was some jostling and nudging as we prepared to listen.

"The next round will be held in Derry-Londonderry, the City of Culture a couple of years ago."

"Derry or Londonderry?" Millie asked, scratching her hat. "I'm confused."

"Isn't it the same place?" Janice said. "Or are there two now?"

"No. It's one place with two names. Derry-Londonderry."

"What? Both of them together? Why?"

"I don't know why. Because some people call it Derry and some call it Londonderry and nobody wanted to taint a cultural event with a political statement."

"Why not call it Londonderry-Derry? How did they choose which one to put first?"

Hester closed her eyes for a moment, reaching into her head to find the Hester zone of tranquillity and eternal patience. "We have a thirty-minute lunch break scheduled, Millie. Twenty-one minutes of that lunch break are already over. Shall I use the remaining nine to inform you about the competition or answer questions you can easily find the answers to via an Internet search?"

"Sorry, Hest."

"Apology accepted. Now, we will be needing flights, plus two nights in a hotel and transport either side of the airports. Food, outfits, sheet music. That comes to an estimated three hundred pounds each. Or four thousand eight hundred in total."

"Flights?" Rowan asked. "Where is this Derry-dunderry place anyway? Will I need a bikini? Can we have a hotel with a pool? If I'm going to leave Callie with Mum for a whole weekend, I'm gonna make the most of it."

"Derry-Londonderry, which I shall be calling Derry from now on in order to remain on schedule, is in Northern Ireland. We will fly to Belfast. The average temperature in October is ten degrees. By all means bring a bikini if you must. No, we cannot have a hotel with a pool unless you want to pay three times as much. I'm sure we can find a leisure centre."

"Three hundred pounds each?" April had gone pale. "That rules me out, then."

There was some general murmuring and shaking of heads. A couple more people agreed that the price was going to be a big problem, even with several months to save up for it.

Kim said, "Let's face it, Hest. The only person in the choir who can afford that sort of money is the one person who doesn't even sing."

Hester smiled. One eye actually twinkled. "Well. That puts us all in the same boat then, doesn't it? We'd better head back to shore, write it off as an impossible dream." She let out a long sigh. "It was a lovely idea, but of course it couldn't ever really happen. After all, we aren't even a proper choir. Might as well give up now."

"All right! We get the point," Kim huffed. "What are we going to do then? Pray about it? Hope we find a box of buried treasure in the chapel vestry? Buy a lottery ticket?"

"That's your suggestion, Kim? After all this time in Grace Choir? Sit about, hoping the answer to our problem will just come and poke us in the eye?"

Hester looked at us, probably unaware how intimidating the steam whistling out of each ear came across. Nobody moved a muscle as we all waited for someone else to speak.

"We could sell stuff," Rowan suggested. "Like cakes."

"You need to sell a lot of cakes to raise five grand." Mags shook her head. "And by the time we've paid for the ingredients, we'd need to sell twice as many."

"We could do a sponsored something," Uzma said. "Like, a sponsored sing. Or a cycle."

"We could do a full Monty," Janice said. "I saw a film about it once."

"Excuse me?" Melody looked confused.

"In the film, these blokes needed to raise money, so they did a dance and took off all their clothes. It wasn't hard. They weren't professionals or anything. Men pay a lot of money to see women take all their clothes off. If they're anything like my fella, they won't mind a few wobbly bits."

"My fella used to like the wobbly bits best," Millie sighed. "Before that young floozy came along all perked up and toned triceps."

"Stop!" Hester barked. "Nobody is taking their clothes off for men. Have I taught you women nothing?"

"You taught us we're beautiful!" Millie replied. "I'm not ashamed to get my kit off for the sake of the Community Choir Sing-Off national finals." She stood up and began to sway suggestively, playing with the top button of her frilly blouse.

"Well, you should be!" It looked as though a volcano was about to go off underneath Hester's helmet hairdo. Someone needed to do something quick.

"What about a proper concert?" I said.

"Oooh." The choir looked at each other, impressed. Hester smacked herself on the forehead, as if she couldn't believe it had taken that long for someone to suggest it.

"But how many tickets would we need to sell? Even if we charged twenty pounds each, we would need to sell two hundred and fifty tickets. And that means we'd need to hire a venue. When the Guides wanted to hire the Coddington Theatre it cost hundreds." Melody frowned. "And I'm not sure we are a twenty pound concert yet."

"So we make it more than a concert," I said. "A proper fundraising event. With dinner and a raffle."

"A raffle?" Leona grimaced. "What, a few bottles of unwanted smellies, an ugly teddy bear, and a jigsaw with three pieces missing? No one makes decent money from a raffle."

"Okay. So how about a raffle selling stuff people actually might want?"

"That costs money."

"Not if we provide the stuff."

"What have we got that people want to buy?" Rowan asked, causing Hester to screech.

"We could sell half of this junk and make a couple of hundred quid," Ebony said.

"No. No junk." I stood up now, my brain whirring into gear. I could see it – a beautiful hall, round banqueting tables with tasteful centrepieces, full of men and women with more money than sense, bursting to spend it on some local good cause. "We can do better than that. How about a hair and beauty makeover? A privately catered dinner party? A singing lesson from a pro. A bespoke designer outfit from the woman who created the Bulgarian Prime

Minister's daughter's wedding dress?"

"You can't sell one of Rosa's dresses for the price of a raffle ticket."

"An auction." I felt a bubble of excitement begin to grow. This could actually work. "I went to one with Perry once to raise money for a children's hospice. This isn't quite the same, but once the guests got into the party spirit they didn't care. Some of them got into this competitive 'who's prepared to spend the most money because they're the richest?' type of spirit. If we got the right auctioneer, we could make a fortune. Add that to the entrance ticket and we could make five thousand without breaking a sweat."

"Just one problem." Kim pointed at me. "Where are we going to find a load of rich people willing to come along to our dinner/concert/auction thing, where are we going to have it and, no offence to anyone here, but who is going to organize it all?"

I grinned. "Have you met my fiancé Perry Upperton, long-time member of the Houghton Country Club? I met him when I was the *events manager* there. I'll make a few calls, pull in a couple of favours, and get back to you with a date."

"Show-off," Kim muttered.

"And so she should be!" Hester said. "About time the rest of you starting showing off your God-given talents. And the Grand Grace Gala sounds like just the place to do it. Now, fifteen minutes behind schedule, will you lot finally get back to work?"

* * *

It was a good job Marilyn had been de-stressing all day. By the time she came home, the team had dispersed along with the skip, a dozen bags of recycling, and a carload of items for the charity shop. Nancy and Pete were gurgling on the sofa while I read them a story about a family of sausages. The smell of still slightly damp carpets, bleach, and thirteen women working at full pelt for eight hours had been just about replaced with baby-bath, half a dozen bunches of fresh flowers, and the pasta bake warming in the oven.

Marilyn waltzed in, in a whirl of contented spa-day bliss. She plonked herself on the sofa next to Nancy before doing a double-take.

"What?"

I bit my lip.

"Who?"

I gathered up Pete and sat him on my lap, like a human shield.

"When?"

Pete burped. I think I squeezed him too hard.

"Did you do this?" She lowered her eyebrows at Nancy. "Did you help Faith tidy up?"

She looked around a bit more. "Tidy up, and throw out three-quarters of my things?"

I gulped.

"Is it just the living room?" She spoke to me now.

I shook my head. Silently, she got up with Nancy and walked out into the hallway. I sat and listened to various doors open as she checked the rest of the rooms. Her feet plodded up the stairs and we heard her doing the same above us.

"Bah," Pete said.

"I know. Do you think she's pleased, or is she never going to talk to me again?"

"Ppffffff."

"Well, she's your mum. You should know better than me."

"Ack!"

"I don't understand women either, and I am one."

We waited with bated breath until she finished her inspection. Standing in front of the fireplace, she balanced Nancy on one hip and nodded her head at me.

"Hester."

"Yep."

"She thought my house was in no fit state for Polly and Baby Pol."

"Actually, it was my idea. For you as much as Polly."

"You thought my house was too messy. You've been coming here, twice a week, and thinking I can't take care of my own house."

"No. That's not true. I've been thinking anyone in your situation could do with some help."

"What do you mean, *my situation*?" She pulled Nancy's fingers from where they tugged at her hair.

I swallowed. "I mean a mum with twin babies and a husband who works away most of the time. Who has no support apart from a sister who works four days a week. You get no sleep. And hardly any breaks. Goodness me, Marilyn, I look after them for two hours and I'm exhausted."

"Where's everything gone? You must have needed a skip."

I nodded, attempting a wry smile.

"You had a *skip*? How many people came?"

"All of us," I said.

"Poking, sorting, analysing my stuff. My house."

"We didn't go in any drawers or cupboards."

She snorted. "*You* didn't. What about Kim? Or Rowan? She's probably gone straight to the pawn shop and made a fortune."

"No. No one pried. We only threw out what was broken. We mainly sorted, and cleaned and tidied."

"Well," she huffed, looking at the floor, and then the ceiling, and then the floor again. "It looks rip-roaring fantastic. So, thanks. I guess."

"You're very welcome."

"And a bleepin' good job I didn't have any shameful or embarrassing secrets hiding under all that rubbish."

"Ooh, I don't know. Janice and Millie found a pretty snazzy negligee on top of the wardrobe. They got quite excited wondering how it got there." I winked at her.

Marilyn smirked. "They can wonder away. I might be able to fit back into it by the time James comes home."

"Nah. It was covered in mildew. James'll have to buy you a new one."

"Seriously, though. Thanks. I feel like I can breathe again." She looked around at the transformation once more.

"Maybe you should think about getting a cleaner."

"I'm a housewife. I'm supposed to be the cleaner." She came and sat back down on the sofa next to me.

"With all due respect, old friend, you are a rubbish housewife."

"A rubbish everything. I can't keep my house up to basic living standards. My marriage is a desert. I can't look after myself. The HCC committee think I'm a joke. I can't sing well enough to be in a non-auditioning choir. I guess I wasn't even trainee of the month, was I?"

We propped Pete and Nancy, nearly asleep, on the cushions between us. I reached over the top of them and wrapped my arm around her, leaning my head on her shoulder.

"Possibly not. But you are a pretty amazing friend. You have no idea what you've done for me, Marilyn. I could be your cleaner for the rest of my life and it wouldn't repay what I owe you."

"Well, when you put it like that, you can start by dishing up a plate of that pasta."

* * *

I had been speaking the truth about the help-hole. Sometimes I wondered if it was Sam I missed, or being there for Sam. Being needed. I filled the hole with as much work as I could get, along with making plans for the Grand Grace Gala. I walked nearly everywhere, now that spring had really taken hold, and ate with Perry at his house or the club every few days. For the first time in years I was saving money, scraping together enough pounds each week to begin to ease the tension in my throat. I bought myself a new pair of walking boots and a couple of books. I stood a millimetre taller, breathed a little deeper, laughed a whole lot louder.

The last week in March, Larissa summoned the wedding party for another meeting. I wanted to get to HCC early to sign the contract for the gala, Perry having sweet-talked the manager into giving me a ridiculously cheap rate for hire of the ballroom, with a three-course dinner thrown in, so Marilyn picked me up.

"When are you going to pluck up the pluck to learn to drive?"

I shook my head. "My pluck's doing fine, thanks. Have you seen how much lessons cost?"

"Bah. You know Perry'll pay for them."

"If I asked him, he would."

"But you won't?" She stopped to let a couple of children use a zebra crossing.

"If I can't afford driving lessons, how will I afford petrol, or insurance, or road tax?"

"Faith, who do you think pays for my petrol?" she asked, waving at the children.

"That's different. You have Nancy and Pete. And you take care of everything while James is away."

"It's not different. When you're married what's his is yours. You can't be married and stay independent. The two are mutually exclusive. You can't keep a back-up plan, the expectation that things might not work out."

"I know that," I said, slightly narked.

I did know. I had no back-up plan. That was the whole point of getting married.

Contract gleefully signed, we met Perry and his parents in a small private dining room. After an hour sampling menus, and pre-dinner, during-dinner, and after-dinner drinks, we covered the topics of invitations (design: frumpy; wording: ostentatious; number: verging on panic attack), flowers (bleugh), and entertainment (an opera singer. Not for the service. For the evening reception).

I say discussed. Of course, by "discussed" I mean Larissa read out her plans, accompanied by numbered pictures, Perry agreed they were perfect, and I nodded feebly. My trusty wing-woman Marilyn, on the other hand, grew increasingly red in the face, alternately widening and narrowing her eyes at me and throwing in comments like, "But Faith, you hate fruit cake. Didn't you want chocolate?"

To which Larissa smiled her sharky smile and shot invisible death-rays across the table, hoping to cremate Marilyn's vocal cords. "Don't be ridiculous. If we don't have fruit cake we can't save a layer for the baby's christening."

Perry turned the colour of a plain sponge. "Mother. Faith is not pregnant."

"Precisely. You need a fruit cake to last until she is," she snapped.

"How long does fruit cake last?" Perry asked.

"Oh, a good eighteen months if it's done properly."

"Mother..." Perry sounded as though he had some eighteen-month-old fruit cake stuck in his throat.

"Oh, stop fussing. Wills and Kate did it. As did your father and I. We're not going to be the first ones to break generations of tradition."

Item seven on the agenda was bridal party underwear. Yes. Apparently my underwear was up for discussion in front of the bride's future father-in-law as well as the groom.

"Now, this is going to get tricky." Larissa tapped her pen on the table, to make sure she had our attention. "We need to create a smooth line for the *Nottinghamshire Life* shoot. However, due to the necessary contour adjustment, I think we go with a full body wrap. Not easy to find in the UK, but Milton's secretary made some calls and we can import one if we act sharpish. The question is how successful Anton is going to be at reducing your size in the next ten weeks. What are your current vitals?"

"I have no idea," I mumbled, avoiding everyone's eye. Did brides normally have this sort of conversation with their family? If my mum was still alive, would she be asking me these questions? Or would we spend a giggly shopping trip trying on bras and knickers together and making jokes about my wedding night?

"What did you wear, Larissa?" Marilyn asked. "I didn't think boob tape existed when you got married."

"I graduated from the Lady Rosalind Institute. I don't need

additional support. I am merely being considerate towards Faith's different physique."

"I think underwear is the least of Faith's challenges when it comes to this wedding. She's perfectly capable of choosing her own bra."

"Excuse me." I pushed back my chair, unable to leave fast enough to avoid hearing Larissa say, "I think we can all see that isn't the case."

I dived into the ladies' room, locking myself in a stall for a few moments and leaning my head against the wall, deep breathing, Hester-style.

I squeezed back the ache in my eyeballs, all too aware I had no frame of reference when it came to family, no idea what the boundaries were. Confused, slightly overwhelmed, I allowed the grief to wash over me. Grief for my mother, and for my absent brother. I felt hopelessly alone.

Someone opened the main door, moving across and tapping on my stall.

"Are you okay?" Marilyn, of course.

"I'm fine."

"Are you leaning on the door and trying not to cry?"

"Maybe." I smiled, despite myself.

"Would you like to lean on me instead?" She poked her fingers around the crack at the side of the door.

"If I do that, I'm definitely going to cry."

"Open the door, you muppet. I want to show you my impression of Milton when Larissa started talking about underwear."

I blew my nose and pressed the palms of my hands into my eye sockets until the pain became bearable, then opened the stall door to find Marilyn, arms twisted together in mock horror, pulling the strangest expression of confusion, glee, and disgust as her eyes rolled about in their sockets.

I couldn't help laughing as she then straightened her features and peered at me down her nose. "Agenda item one hundred and sixty-five. Consummation of the wedding vows. Now, traditionally the Upperton males have used the position demonstrated by Milton's grandparents in diagram seven."

"Stop it!" I giggled. "I'm trying really hard to respect Larissa. She's put a huge amount of effort into this."

"What? She doesn't respect *you*. She's being downright mean."

"I don't think she meant to be."

"Don't be naïve, Faith. Everything that woman does is calculated." Marilyn folded her arms.

"Is she trying to drive me away?" I asked, all trace of laughter gone.

"Possibly." She pulled a wry face. "But that could mean even greater public humiliation than if you stayed."

"Public humiliation: a fate worse than death to all true Uppertons."

Marilyn turned round and began examining the profile of her stomach in the mirror. "I think wielding such wedding power unchallenged may have tipped her over the edge into megalomania."

"I have a suspicion she's always been like that, and this wedding has just brought it to the surface. Perhaps they teach passive-aggressive control freak lessons at the Lady Rosalind Institute." I moved next to her and turned on the cold tap, splashing some water on my face.

"If they did, I think she must have failed on the passive part. She needs to be stopped before things get even more out of hand."

"I'm not sure they've reached out of hand." I turned the tap off, and pulled out a paper towel from the super-expensive dispenser. "I don't actually care about the colour of the writing on the invites. It's not as if I'll be needing that many."

"Faith. Nobody lets their mother-in-law choose their wedding ring." Marilyn stopped examining herself and turned to focus on me. "The Ghost Web is for one dreadful day. You have to wear that ring for as long as you stay married. As your friend, I'm rooting with you that it'll be a long, long time. Please choose your own ring. And flowers. And first dance. Only you can slay the beast. She'll thank you for it in the long run."

I took a deep breath. "I'm not being awkward? They are paying for it all."

"It is not awkward to want to choose what pants you wear to your own wedding! Hooten tooten, woman. You just negotiated eighty per cent off the price of a swanky banquet. Get out there and wield some personal power!"

And guess what? I did.

Marilyn and I strode into the dining room like Thelma and Louise. I stood behind my chair, back straight, chin up, and announced that I wanted giant daisies in my bouquet, would rather perform the can-can than dance to opera, and the only person who was going to choose my underwear was me. Before Larissa had time to close her gaping mouth and respond, I swung my bag over my shoulder and marched back out.

Sweeping down the corridor and through the main bar area, swinging my arms in time to the Rocky theme tune playing in my head, I kept the smile on my face subtle enough to hide the fireworks popping in my ventricles. *Go me!*

I swished through the foyer, tossing my hair over my shoulder and throwing out a confident glance that said *Yes, I am an awesome woman who rocks* to the three men waiting to be seen by the receptionist. Wow. It had been too long since I'd stood up for myself. London Anna was back. No. This was new, post-London, post-HCC Faith. London Anna could stand up to sleazeballs. Post-London Faith could stand up to *rich, crazy* sleazeballs. Da da duuuuh, da da duuuuh!

I winked – yes, *winked* – at one of the admin staff, Luke, as he spotted me from across the room, too go-getting and poised and cool to slow down and check out his response.

Decisively pulling open one of the grand front doors, I barrelled through, colliding with a man who had been about to enter from the other side. Caught up in my mini power trip, I failed to notice his face. Then he spoke.

"Watch it!"

The Rocky tune screeched to a stop, replaced by deafening silence. I think my liver nearly jumped out of my mouth.

After a horrifying moment where his red, wrinkled, menacing eyes met mine and held me there, survival instinct kicked in. I pushed past the monster that was Kane, stumbled down the entrance steps, and fled for my life.

Chapter Seventeen

arilyn's car caught up with me halfway down the HCC driveway, assuming my trembling, half-frantic state was due to having confronted Larissa. Perry called a few minutes later, as Marilyn drove me home. Struggling to be coherent, my mind spinning with thoughts of Kane, I babbled an apology, blaming pre-wedding nerves combined with pre-five o'clock wine tasting. The next few days were a plummet back into nightmares and constant nausea, and yes, I did spend one evening weeping in the back of my wardrobe.

I left a rambling message for Gwynne.

She called back the next day. Kane had attended his latest parole meeting. He had no car, a minimum wage job, no means of gallivanting about the country terrorizing past victims. Could I be sure it was him, after all this time? Could my fear have taken the splintered memories of a man I hadn't seen in twenty years and superimposed them onto someone else? Could I accept the possibility I had been mistaken?

Yes. No. Maybe. Urgh. Yes.

No.

Having asked Marilyn for a lift to choir practice that Wednesday, I fumbled my way through the new songs we were learning in preparation for October's national final. Hester had asked us to pick songs that made us feel strong. That evening they simply reminded me of how vulnerable I felt.

Songs about independent women were banned, on the basis we were "fools" if we still hadn't realized we were stronger together. Ebony shyly played us a country song: "This One's for the Girls". It was snappy and fun, and Hester could hardly refuse lyrics about being beautiful the way you are, standing your ground when everyone is giving in, and dreaming with everything you have. She probably would have written that song herself if Martina McBride hadn't got there first.

There was an overwhelming vote in favour of Katy Perry's "Roar", but then an argument broke out about whether we needed a song with some spiritual context. Yasmin stole Millie's bobble hat (red, in the shape of a strawberry), and in the ensuing scuffle no one noticed the new arrival until she reached the front of the room and whacked the music stand with Hester's baton.

"Hey."

Polly. A tiny, scrunched-up baby strapped to her chest.

"Where did you come from?" Uzma asked.

"Marilyn's house."

Marilyn coughed. "Ahem!"

"Sorry. *Our* house. I wasn't sure if she'd finish her feed in time, so Marilyn left me the money for a taxi."

We crowded round to see the baby, still unnamed at a month old. If Polly waited any longer, she'd have to register her as "Baby", like the girl from *Dirty Dancing*. We petted and aahed, asking all the usual questions. Yes, Baby was putting on weight, no she wasn't sleeping well, yes Polly was eating properly and resting enough, no she wasn't going to miss the national finals.

There were some non-usual questions we didn't ask but wanted to. Was she still pressing charges? Had she seen Tony? Was she going to? Did her bashed-up hand and cracked ribs still hurt? Was she getting a divorce?

She offloaded a twitching Baby to Melody and waited for us to stop fussing. "I heard you're looking for a song. How about this?"

And then she started to sing "Listen", the Beyoncé song. About not being at home in her own home, and being more than what he made of her. Starting again, moving on, writing your own song.

Whew. We had not heard Polly sing like that before. Could breastfeeding affect your vocal cords? Could unwrapping the fear and anxiety and secrets and shame that wound so tightly around your whole body do it?

Of course we cried. Some (me) more than others. Cried, even as we joined in, stood with Polly, held her hand, rocked her baby, believed her, and believed in her. Sang her song.

A tentative answer to the biggest unasked question: Polly would make it. One day, she would be okay.

I grabbed a coffee at break time. Barely able to force down sips, I skulked in the corner, wanting Marilyn and Polly to hurry up and finish chatting so I could get home and stop having to fake being fine, wanting the evening to last all night so I didn't have to go home to a house empty save for dark crannies, mysterious creaks, and ominous shadows.

Eventually, Dylan extracted himself from the flock of broody women cooing over Baby and made his way over.

"Not into babies?"

I managed a crooked smile. "I love babies. Especially Baby. But I had a big cuddle when I minded Nancy and Pete yesterday."

"Marilyn's still training with Anton?"

"Twice a week."

"It looks like it suits her." He gestured at her grinning with Leona by the serving hatch.

"She's lost nearly four stone."

"No. It's more than that. She looks... happier. More comfortable in her own skin. When she first came along, Marilyn was mostly bluster. Now she seems like Marilyn."

"She did get a bit lost for a while amongst all those sleepless nights and nappies." I nodded at him. "You're a pretty perceptive man, Pastor Dylan."

"I've had a lot of practice." He looked at me and smiled, blue eyes softening. "So you won't dodge the question when I ask what has you so rattled?"

I studied my feet for a minute, unable to handle his gaze. "If I talk about it, I'm going to start blubbing. Or screaming. Either way, it'll make a scene. And you know how I feel about scenes."

"Do you want to come into the office? They could be passing Baby round for a while yet."

"No." I flapped a hand in the direction of everyone else. "If they caught me in the office with the minister I'd never hear the end of it."

"You mean Marilyn would want to know what was up."

"That too."

"What can I do to help?"

I shook my head and shrugged.

He gave my arm a fist bump, gentle enough not to spill my tepid coffee. "If you think of anything, or just want to talk, you know where I am."

* * *

The next day, I spent two hours on buses getting to a hotel that would have taken me forty-five minutes to reach along public footpaths, and then spent the whole journey on the verge of panic anyway. At least if I was walking I could run away. The thought of being trapped on a bus with Kane gave me palpitations. I waited nearly an hour for a taxi to show up at the end of my shift, and then forked out most of my tips on the fare.

As I climbed out of the taxi, the red car glinted in the evening sunlight. I stopped and looked at it for a moment. It had sat there useless on the road for months now. Was I being an idiot, resisting Perry's overindulgent present? If I daren't walk anywhere, that heap of shiny metal might end up being the only way to keep my independence. I bet it had really good safety locks to keep killers out. I marched inside, kicked off my work shoes, dumped my bag on the kitchen counter, and picked up my phone before I could change my mind.

Perry set up a driving lesson for me the next day with a guy he'd met at a business conference. Bob Chase, a forty-something instructor wearing a crumpled pair of shiny trousers and a Formula One cap, turned up in a Vauxhall Corsa. His eyes nearly popped out of his head when he saw my car. He had a change of heart about my first lesson being in his specially modified vehicle, spending the first twenty minutes driving the sports car to a suitable location to start me off (I suggested a few quiet roads and empty car parks nearby, but for vague reasons he picked one a good few miles further away).

Groaning with delight at every twist and turn, closing his eyes way more than the Highway Code must surely recommend, he slid to a stop in a large layby in the middle of nowhere. A couple of times he began explaining something about the driving process, only to get sidetracked by the apparent amazingness of the car.

Eventually, we swapped seats and he talked me through how to turn the engine on and get moving. Hands and legs trembling, I gave it a go.

Screeeech!

Bob yelled in alarm over the hideous sound of scraping metal, diving across to undo whatever I'd done. I opened my eyes to find the car hadn't moved a millimetre.

"Promise you won't do that again," he said in a strangled voice.

"Okay." I had no idea how to keep that promise. My frayed nerves were not coping well with being pushed further out of their comfort zone by a man they didn't know, and certainly didn't trust.

"Right. Let's have another try. Be gentle with her now. This princess needs to be stroked. She'll refuse to play if you treat her rough." He caressed the dashboard with his fingers.

I swallowed down my urge to vomit. Who knew what Bob would do if I threw up on the princess?

We tried a few more times, Bob's increasing distress at my ineptitude only pushing my stress levels higher, making things worse. When he let out a whimper, I'd had enough.

"I think we'd better call it a day," I said, climbing out of the driver's seat and moving back to where I belonged.

He didn't need to be told twice. Funny how the journey home took half the time.

He made a lukewarm attempt to book a second lesson, but even Bob wasn't convinced another drive in the princess was worth the pain of watching me mistreat her.

I stomped inside, whipping open the fridge door and taking out an enormous piece of Marilyn's butterscotch tart. Spooning off a huge chunk, I wolfed it down furiously before calling Perry.

He found the whole thing hilarious.

To be honest, if it hadn't been for my underlying urgency to be able to drive, I would have done, too. He did coax a smile out of me by the time I'd finished venting.

"Do you want me to find someone else?" he asked.

"No. I don't think learning with a stranger is going to work."

"Well, you know I'd happily do it, but the Hampton deal is reaching the crucial stages. I've got a load more trips coming up in the next month or so. Is there anyone else you can ask? Someone just to get you started, help you over the initial nerves?"

I thought about it: the few people I knew, the even fewer number who had a car and were available during the day, and the fewer still whom I would feel comfortable having driving lessons with. That left approximately two people. And there was no way on earth I could be in control of a moving vehicle with one-year-old twins strapped in the back seat. But hadn't the other one recently offered me help, with eyes so honest I genuinely believed he meant it?

With Perry's approval, albeit coated with a layer of bemusement, I called Dylan.

Knowing something of the situation with Kane, suspecting even more, and detecting the desperation in my voice, he cautiously agreed.

The following Saturday I had my second driving lesson. Sat in

Dylan's truck on a deserted back lane (he said the sports car would cost a fortune to fix if I happened to bump into anything, whereas the truck was so dented one more scrape wouldn't make any difference), I squared my shoulders, took a deep breath, checked my mirror, gingerly lifted one foot off the clutch while pressing down on the accelerator with the other, and stalled. Again.

"It's no good." I threw my head against the steering wheel. "I can't do it. This is a waste of time. I'm too old for this. You might as well take me home."

"And how old is too old to learn how to drive?" He tried to keep a straight face, but the smile showed in his voice.

I mumbled against the steering wheel. It was nice down here. The sun shone through the windscreen onto my hair. It smelled of leather and machinery. In fact, it smelled a lot like Dylan.

"What was that?"

Hello? Earth to Faith? I quickly pulled myself back up again. "I'm twenty-five."

"*Really?*"

"Why?" I turned to look at him. "How old did you think I was?"

"Err." He shifted in his seat, and scratched his stubble. "Well. Um. You don't *look* older than twenty-five. You just act like, well... you've got a lot of life experience."

My eyes narrowed.

"I mean, you're confident." He searched the roof of the truck, as if looking for inspiration. "Capable. Serious."

Eyes: tiny slits.

"Reliable?"

"Wow. You really know how to make a girl feel special."

"No, I really don't. Hence being single for the past hundred years." He ran his hands through his hair, making it even more dishevelled. "Look, what I mean is, you know who you are, and you don't try to be anyone else. That's unusual in someone your age. So yes, it is pretty special."

Hah! I started to laugh. "You are so wrong, Pastor Perceptive.

Most of the time I don't even know what to call myself." My laugh turned bitter and slightly maniacal. I squeezed my eyes together and swallowed, hard. For goodness' sake. Enough crying!

When I opened them again, he was watching me, his face blank. I wondered if this was going to be the moment Dylan realized I was internally unstable. About as far from confident and capable as it is possible to get.

"Right. Out."

Excuse me?

"Come on. Out you get." He climbed out his side and came around, opening the driver's side door while I still sat there, hands on the wheel. Was Dylan throwing me out of his truck? Had he decided to leave me here in the middle of nowhere? Had my laugh been so disturbing he couldn't risk taking me home? Or to a main road? Or a bus stop?

He held out one hand to help me down. Remembering how it felt the last time our hands touched, I ignored it and clambered out myself.

He jumped into the vacated driver's seat, and turned the engine back on. Too stunned to move, I watched as he began to drive forwards. What? Was he really leaving me here?

No Faith, you bag of nervous nerves. He's parking the truck on the verge.

Oh. That's okay then.

"Right. This way I think." He jerked his head in the direction of the road ahead, and began walking.

"Am I allowed to know what's going on? Is the driving lesson finished?"

He turned round, and started walking backwards. "No. But it's obvious even for Pastor Perceptive that you aren't going to be able to concentrate on anything while you're like this. You walk to calm down, and de-stress. So, let's walk. And if you can bear to talk, even better. Then we might actually get something done today."

We walked. Along prickled hedges that bore a sprinkling of fresh, tightly curled green leaves. Beneath a canopy of silvery branches, showering us with pale pink blossom in the breeze. After a while, we followed a signpost down a dirt track, the edges bushy with cow parsley.

I breathed in the pungent smells of spring – damp earth, new grass, the faint hint of pollen from the first flowers, the ripe warmth of the cows in the meadow beyond. I listened to the stillness – the faint hum of a tractor on the ridge above us, the whistle of brisk wind in the branches, the birds welcoming the change of season with their jubilant chorus. My heart began to slow as my mind eased and the tension that ached in every muscle gradually dissolved. For the first quarter of a mile, we just walked. Not that it was ever "just" walking in a place like this. But we didn't talk until, finally reaching a lopsided gate at the end of the lane, Dylan stopped, leaning back against it, and I figured I had better say something.

"I don't know where to start."

"The beginning'll do, if you can't think of anywhere else."

"Right." I leaned on the gate beside him. "So the man who killed my mum, the one Sam thought he saw in February? Last week I think I saw him at HCC."

I felt the gate creak as his body went rigid. Waited while he took a moment to take that in.

"Okay. I'm officially donning my pastor hat." Dylan mimed putting on a cap and straightening it up. I raised my eyebrows at him.

"I'm wearing it because I'm guessing you still haven't told Perry about this, and it is completely wrong for you to tell a friend before the man you're going to marry. But you need to talk about it."

"I know. Thank you."

"Plus, the caveman in me really wants to hunt this man down and smash his face in. My pastor hat reminds me that wouldn't be a wise or good thing to do."

"He'd snap you in half before you got a chance. No offence. He's seriously evil."

"And you think he's looking for you."

"I think he's just about found me." I told him about what had happened, about what I remembered of Kane from before he went to prison, some of how it affected me then, and now. I even told him about hiding in the wardrobe – then, and now.

"Is there somewhere you can stay? With a friend? A relative who owns a fortress? On the other side of the planet?"

"I did consider joining Sam in his treatment centre."

He turned back to stare out into the field, rubbing one hand over his face.

"Are you *crying*?"

"No. Absolutely not." His voice cracked. "Not that I would be ashamed if I was. Real men can cry."

"Because I'm holding it together by the wispiest of threads and if you are crying, tough man, I may collapse into a mushy pile of human jelly in this mud, and not only will that mess up your truck, I won't get any driving done. And as you now know, I have a very good reason to pass my driving test as soon as humanly possible. So buck up, pull yourself together, and don't you dare even think about crying."

"I'm not crying! A fly flew in my eye. Both eyes."

"Good. Now we're going to walk back and I'm going to get the whole sorry saga off my chest. You are not going to cry, I am not going to cry, and you are going to teach me how to drive a car without stalling and how to change gear. Got it?" I set off, stomping down the track.

Dylan called after me, "Now that's what I call a capable, confident, reliable woman."

Nearly two hours later I had reached the heady speed of fifteen miles per hour. Fast enough that anyone chasing me on foot would eat my dust. Not quite fast enough to be let loose in the sports car, yet. I wasn't sure my car could drive at only fifteen miles per hour. But it was a start.

Dylan drove us back to Houghton. We rode in silence, listening to a soft country music song about a man plucking up the courage to tell his girl he loved her. The gentle hue of dusk settled, bringing with it the nip of evening as we approached the village.

"Are you hungry? I accept driving lesson payments in pizza." Dylan slowed down to let a family with three small children cross the road.

"I can't tonight. I'm having dinner with Perry. But some other time?"

He nodded. "Sure. Do you want another lesson?"

"I don't think I'm quite ready for my test yet."

He smiled. "No, I meant do you want another lesson with me?"

"Do you have the time?"

"I can make the time. Tuesday's probably best this week. I have a meeting in the morning, but I could do after lunch if you're free."

"That's great, thanks. I really appreciate you doing this."

He turned into my little street, dodging the parked cars signifying the other residents were settled in for the evening.

"No worries. I enjoyed it." He pulled to a stop and I jumped out.

"Thanks again. I mean, not just for the driving."

He nodded, one sharp down and up of his chin. "Do me a favour?"

I waited.

"Talk to your boyfriend."

"Bye, Dylan."

"Have a nice evening." He waited while I let myself in, then disappeared into the sunset.

I went upstairs and took a shower, trying to wash away the vague sense of irritation that I suspected Dylan caused by wishing me a nice evening with Perry. Did I really want Dylan to feel jealous, knowing how completely that would screw everything up?

My head, absolutely not.

My heart? My hormones? They sat through a fancy dinner at the club, a moonlit walk along the green, compliments, and caresses, and all they could think about was pizza in a greasy two-seater truck with a man who smelled of leather and always looked as though he'd just finished a major demolition job. A man whose smile hit me right where it hurt and managed to make it feel better.

Did I think about telling Perry the truth about Kane?

A thousand times. With every bite of dinner, every sip of sparkling water.

Did I feel responsible for our relationship being built on secrets? Yes. One hundred per cent.

But, and this is the honest truth, if he had paused once to ask me how I was, how my week had been – *what's going on with you, Faith?* – I would have told him. I would have told him every darn thing.

* * *

Now he knew the real reason behind my wanting to drive, Dylan insisted on giving me lessons nearly every other day for the next two weeks. When I could shake off the spectre of Kane, stuff my wedding stress to the back of my brain, and stop worrying about the fact my brother had mentioned coming home, I actually started to find the lessons a lot of fun.

Concentrating on a new skill, like choir practice, became a useful distraction, as I focused on mirrors, signalling, and manoeuvres to the exclusion of everything else. Dylan was a good teacher, using all his minister skills of patience, kindness, and self-control to explain the same thing to me over and over again until I got it. Watching for the moment when the yuckiness started to creep back in, then ordering me out of the truck for a walk. Before long the walks became part of the lesson. One day, we met around lunchtime so Dylan brought a couple of sandwiches and a custard tart. The next time I brought a flask of homemade lemonade and a picnic pie, the recipe of which I'd been experimenting with and wanted an opinion on.

As we walked, and sometimes ate, we talked. About anything and everything. Dylan talked about his job. All the parts of it he loved, and the tough parts, the loneliness and the frustrations. How his faith somehow made it more than worthwhile. That led on to his past, growing up on one of the toughest estates in Leeds with a single mum working two jobs – getting into the kind of trouble that bored kids with no money and no parental supervision end up in. Finding himself running around with a crowd of boys who veered further and further into a life leading nowhere good.

"So how did you end up from there to here?" I asked one blustery day towards the end of April, as we paced through a newly ploughed field. "Something must have saved you."

"Fear, mainly. Shoplifting and fist fights I could handle. But men in dark glasses asking me to drop a package at some dump under the cover of darkness? That scared me. My mates loved it – they were ambitious, and saw joining a gang as the way to earn power. Called us the band of brothers. The day we went to get our tats, I watched them playing at being big men, branding themselves for life, and knew I didn't want that. Messing about as kids was one thing. But we weren't kids any more. I felt like if I got that tattoo there'd be no going back."

"And? What happened? Did you get it?"

"I'm stood in the back room of my mate's uncle's shop watching them go one at a time. Discreetly trying to wipe the sweat from my face, ready to claim a needle phobia if they see my hands shaking. To not go through with it would be unthinkable. Like, the worst kind of betrayal. And I had no escape route planned. No options left. So, I prayed. To a God I didn't believe in, or want to."

We had reached the river, and made our way to where a narrow bridge rose over the water. Leaning against the barrier, Dylan stuck his hands in his pockets, turning sideways to avoid the worst of the wind.

"I was up next. It was like one of those moments where your life flashes before your eyes. And I saw nothing to be proud of. My mum crying on her birthday because the police had been round again. Chucking the cake I'd nicked in the bin as she screamed at me to get out. I made a bargain with God right then. If he got me out of this I'd sort myself out. And then, just as the guy called me over, his phone started ringing. The shop was about to be raided. I went straight home, packed my bags, and caught the next train to my uncle's in Cardiff. I didn't go back for eight years."

"How old were you?"

"Seventeen." He raised his eyebrows in acknowledgment of how my life had been at seventeen.

Dylan pushed off the railing and began walking back. "My uncle set me straight to work in his renovation business. Flipping houses. He figured if he worked me hard enough I'd have no energy left for trouble."

"And he was right?"

He quirked up one side of his mouth. "Nearly. He also dragged me along to his church every Sunday. I pretended to hate it, but something about the people there got under my skin. They had that something my mates back home had been looking for. It was a real band of brothers."

"So you stuck around long enough to find God?"

"I stuck around long enough to find a pretty girl. God came later."

"So what happened to her? The pretty girl?"

"I messed it up. She ran out of patience. I moved my broken heart here." He paused to unlock a gate leading us back onto the road where the truck sat waiting. "Decided I needed some time out from pretty girls."

He looked at me then, only a couple of feet away, and I swear some kind of weird vacuum in his eyes sucked away every last drop of air between us. My heart stalled, and it was one of those clichéd movie moments when time stopped, the sounds of the birds and the wind and the rushing water vanished, and for one crazy, awful, fabulous second I thought he might kiss me.

He dropped his gaze abruptly, and cleared his throat. Yanking open the gate, Dylan gestured for me to go through first, those ocean eyes now only able to meet mine for a glance before darting away.

Get a hold of yourself, Faith. He pours out his broken heart to you, and you decide he wants to kiss you?

We finished the lesson, trying to act normal. Dylan laughed too hard at my jokes, and I responded to his tuition over-earnestly. The truck crackled with electricity, the heavy, tangy air before a summer storm. After dropping me off at choir practice, he didn't follow me in, or ask about another lesson. Nothing had happened, but it was something. And for the rest of the week, as I rushed about organizing Grand Grace Gala table decorations, chasing after the now toddling Nancy and Pete, addressing wedding invitation envelopes (one job Larissa actually trusted me with), and serving canapés to crowds of drunk, sweaty, over-friendly businessmen, my head swirled. Not with Kane, whose shadow had slowly begun to retreat, or with my future husband, busy working on his new deal. I thought about the nothing. And what I would have done if Dylan had made it a something. And I wondered what I felt most scared of – another nothing happening, or one never happening again.

I found myself trying to pray about it, asking God to take away these thoughts. These feelings. It didn't work. I think God must have known I didn't really mean it.

* * *

The following weekend, I packed up my rucksack with a change of clothes, my warmest pyjamas, a torch, a first aid kit, and a family-size bar of dark chocolate, and hitched a ride in Marilyn's car.

It was time for our next choir activity. Two nights camping in Sherwood Forest. The air was damp and the ground muddy. The temperature might drop to near freezing. Our seventeen-strong troop included a wannabe sergeant major, a cosmetic addict who cried if she split a nail, two pensioners, a teenage delinquent, and fifteen-month-old twins. Twelve of us were camping virgins.

What could possibly go wrong?

Chapter Eighteen

Marilyn and I were the last to arrive at the campsite early on Friday evening. Things were already descending into chaos. We quickly joined the rest of the group, trying to pitch the first of the three tents Hester had borrowed from other members of the church. Accompanying the canvas sheet were a bag of long, flexible poles that needed assembling, a load of tent pegs, and a distinct lack of instructions.

The slots for the poles were colour-coded, and it all seemed straightforward enough, except that the late April wind roared through the trees, whipping our hair in front of our faces and causing the tent to flap about like a wild bird entangled in a net. It took half of us to keep the tent from taking off, someone else to push an unsettled Pete and Nancy up and down in their pushchair, someone to poke a pole through the right hole in the canvas, someone else to pull the other end, another person to tell them they had got the wrong pole or the wrong hole, someone to push the tent pegs into the mud, two of us to try and start a fire, one of us to keep her hair from getting messed up, another to try to find a mobile phone signal, and all of us to yell suggestions into the wind, most of which didn't make any sense and none of which helped.

By the time an hour had passed, we had one wonky, half-erected tent, two extremely fractious toddlers, lashings of mud all over our clothes, our hands, and some faces, a pile of damp wood that refused to light, and a bunch of rather stressed out, fed up, hungry women. Not a great combination.

"Where are the bathrooms?" Kim asked, after we decided to leave tent one and move on to tent two, refusing to believe it could be any more of a challenge to pitch.

Hester shook tent two out of its bag, rolling it out across the mud. "About fifty paces into the woods, turn left and you'll see a clearing surrounded by blackberry bushes."

"Okay. I'll be back in a minute." Kim picked up a washbag that was not much smaller than my rucksack. "I need to sort my face out."

Hester pointed to a trowel, lying with the pile of cooking equipment. "Take that if you need to go."

"Eh?"

Hester smiled and said nothing. Kim picked up the trowel with two fingers, holding it at arm's length, and disappeared into the woods. We started wrestling with tent two, slightly more aggressively than last time, and had managed to hammer in a couple of pegs and get the basic frame up by the time Kim returned.

"Hester!" she whined, marching up. "I couldn't find them anywhere. It's starting to get dark in the woods and there are no lights or signs or anything. I've used up loads of the battery on my phone 'cos I had to use it as a torch."

Hester thwacked at a peg with the mallet a couple of times, while every hair remained in place on her head. "Did you walk fifty paces into the woods and turn left?"

"Yes. But how do you measure fifty paces? For a shrimp like Rowan, fifty paces would hardly get you into the woods. For Mags you'd be out the other side."

"Did you find a small clearing surrounded by blackberry bushes?"

"I found a small clearing. But I don't know what blackberry bushes look like. I didn't find any blackberries."

"Bushes covered in thorns? Like that one over there?" Hester pointed out a nearby bush.

Kim shrugged. "Probably."

"Then you found the bathroom."

"But I didn't though, did I, because there wasn't any bathroom!"

Hester stood up, slowly, and put her hands on her hips, just above her waterproof trousers. She looked at Kim, and waited. There were a couple of gasps from behind the tent.

"I don't get it," Kim pouted.

We all looked about for someone to break the news to her. Marilyn stepped forwards, but Melody dove in.

"Kim. You, ah, found no bathroom in the clearing because, if I am not mistaken, the clearing *is* the bathroom."

Silence for about ten seconds while nobody moved, breathed, or took their eyes off Kim.

"WHAAAAAAAAT?!" Kim screeched, sending all of the birds from the entire forest whooshing up into the sky en masse.

Her face turned dark purple underneath its faded foundation. She pulled a horrified, furious face at Hester, turned around, and hurled the trowel into the depths of the woods. "You... what... we... I... you cannot... no way... you total... THAT'S ILLEGAL!"

She turned to Ebony, who had driven her here. "You need to take me home. Now."

Ebony glanced at Hester. "Errr. I don't think that's an option, Kim. The weekend is compulsory."

"Compulsory! Hah! Polly's not here."

"Because she has Baby."

Baby had been officially registered as Esme a couple of weeks earlier. It was really time we started calling her by her name, otherwise she would end up Baby for life.

"Right! And it probably wouldn't be safe to bring a baby out into the middle of nowhere, in the freezing cold, with no house, no shower, no heating, no coffee machine, and a pile of dirt for a TOILET! I am not a BEAR!"

"No dear," Millie chipped in. "A bear wouldn't bother with a trowel."

She whipped out her phone. "Fine. You nutters can stay if you like. I'll call Scotty. There is no way I'm spending the night out here.

You can take your *choir bonding, competition winning, toughen you up, and make you champions camping weekend* and bury it with your trowel!"

"Kim, please stay," Rowan said.

Kim ignored her. "Eurgh! I can't even get a signal in this wilderness. Who does she think she is? Bear bloomin' Grylls?"

She stomped off to the treeline as best she could in a pair of pointy-heeled ankle boots. They were more effective at kicking over the bucket, a cool box, and the pile of firewood as she went.

"Should I go after her?" Leona asked.

"She'll come back when it's dark." Hester resumed hammering. "Which won't be long, ladies. So you'd better quit standing around gawping and get cracking. Once these tents are up you've got to find a source of running water. An inability to stick together spells certain disaster."

"What does disaster entail, exactly?" Uzma asked, poking a pole through the last slot in tent two. "Cold? Starvation? Death?"

"I was referring to the Community Choir Sing-Off," Hester said. "Oh."

"But I wouldn't rule any of those out, either."

Ten minutes after the last tent was stood up, precariously leaning against the wind with the others, the heavens opened.

Thankfully, Hester had stocked up on drinking water. We set out the buckets to collect some rainwater for washing up (and washing us).

We were getting there, but with dusk creeping across the site, the temperature plummeted. We huddled in the central area of the largest tent. Hester had left us to go and make "preparations", whatever that meant. We were abandoned, wet, filthy, hungry, and about ready to roast our choirmistress if it might provide the fuel to make a cup of tea.

"There is no way we're going to get a fire lit. What are we going to do about an evening meal?" I asked, cuddling Pete all snug in his baby sleeping bag.

"She's probably expecting us to catch it and cook it ourselves," Rowan huffed, her hands stuffed in her armpits. "I did *not* expect my first night away without Callie to be like this."

"We can't even forage for berries at this time of year," Uzma moaned. "I'm starving."

"You ate nearly a whole jumbo packet of tortilla chips an hour ago," her cousin Yasmin said. "I was saving that for a midnight feast."

"A midnight feast? What is this, an Enid Blyton book?" Uzma barked back.

"If it was an Enid Blyton book, we'd have lemonade, massive sandwiches, the sun would be shining, and there'd be a dangerous villain creeping about in the woods." Janice leered at us from beneath the bobble hat Millie had knitted for her. In the shadows from the torchlight, she could have passed for a dangerous villain.

"Stop it!" April whimpered. "I'm freaked out already. I hate it out here. The bats and spiders and badgers are bad enough."

"And what about Kim?" Rowan asked. "She's been gone for, like, an hour and a half now. What if she's lost? What if her phone ran out and she hasn't got any light, so she's stumbling about in the rain, freezing to death, and going round in circles all delirious?"

"Perhaps the dangerous villain will kidnap her!" Janice added.

"Ooh, I quite like the sound of that," Millie said. "Is he a handsome villain? One who turned villainous because of undeserved circumstances beyond his control, but is really an honourable rogue underneath?"

"The dangerous villains back in my home were not like that." Rosa wagged her head. "Nuh uh. If they caught a beautiful young woman wandering in the woods they would not have honourable plan in their mind."

"I don't think there are any types of villain out there. Honourable or otherwise," I said, trying to bring the conversation back to reality. Trying to ignore the fact that a dangerous villain might be wandering around looking for me.

"She could have fallen in a ditch! Or an abandoned well. Or been caught in an animal trap," Rowan said, enjoying the drama. "When people get bad hypothermia they think they're really hot and take off all their clothes."

"Maybe she's crawled under a fallen down tree and is slipping into a coma right now," April squeaked.

"We've got to go and find her!" Rowan cried. "We can't let her DIE out there!"

April burst into tears, swiftly followed by Nancy, who had been woken up by Rowan shouting.

There were various murmurs and mutterings in response to this. The rain pelted the roof. Shadows danced and jerked as the wind buffeted the badly pegged canvas. The group began to argue about who would brave venturing outside to search for Kim's naked, icy body.

"I don't mind finding her if it's natural causes," Millie said, stoutly. "But if the villain has done it? Stabbed her to death, or garrotted her with an ivy branch…" – she shuddered – "I'm not sure my constitution could take it."

"What about me?" Leona said. "I've got high blood pressure. Something like that could finish me off."

"That's if the villain doesn't," Rowan added.

"Stop it!" I tried to stand up, forgetting I was in a tent and whacking my head into the roof, causing the whole structure to wobble unnervingly. "There is no villain!"

"You don't know that," Janice sniffed.

"Why would there be a villain creeping about in the middle of Sherwood Forest in the pouring rain?"

"No need to get shirty."

"You're being ridiculous. We have eight torches on. We're the only light for miles. Kim couldn't miss us if she tried. She's phoned Scotty and gone home. It was ridiculous to think she would last more than a couple of hours out here. Right now she's probably up to her neck in a bubble bath, sipping a glass of wine. Can we please focus on what's important?"

Everyone looked at me.

"When's Hester coming back, what on earth is she preparing out there, and what are we eating? And can somebody please come up with some way to make a cup of tea?" I sat back down again, steam rising from my all-weather anorak.

"There's a gas camping stove in the boot of my car," Hester replied from outside the tent flap, causing April and Ebony to squeal in fright. We set about heating beans on one side and hot dogs on the other. After a short, sharp discussion, it was agreed we would be using bottled, not rain or river, water in our tea.

Halfway through my hot dog, Marilyn shuffled around to my side of the tent and whispered in my ear. "I need to find the blackberry bushes."

"Right." I took another delicious mouthful, wondering if the whole point of camping was its ability to transform sausages of highly questionable meat content and cheap white bread into heavenly manna.

"You're coming with me."

"Wrong."

"Faith! I gave birth to twins last year. My pelvic floor doesn't have time to argue about bladder matters. Have you seen Pete's head?"

"Enough!" I hissed. "That is too much information, Marilyn. Save it for your mum and baby group. I'll come if it means you stop talking about that stuff!"

I crammed in the rest of the hot dog, snagged a torch, and squeezed out of the tent behind Marilyn. After a few moments fumbling about, we orientated ourselves in what we hoped was the right direction.

The rain, which had eased off to a drizzle, barely penetrated the canopy of trees once we entered the woods.

However, two paces into the treeline we hit the darkness. The kind of darkness that makes our normal, urban, lamppost a plenty, glowing windows, and headlights darkness seem like the middle of a summer's day. This was a thick, oozing black that reduced the thin beam of torchlight to a feeble tendril. Darkness so solid and real it had a smell, like must and dirt and deep dungeonous caves. Marilyn grabbed my arm and we crept through the woods, jumping when our feet snapped twigs with a loud crack, letting out involuntary squeaks as we heard a rustle to one side, followed by what sounded like the call of a night bird. Or the manic giggle of a villain. Or possibly a werewolf.

"Has it been fifty paces?" Marilyn whispered.

"Not yet. Seventeen."

"Seventeen!"

"Yes. Concentrate on keeping the torch on the path, so we don't fall in any holes or end up in a bush."

"I'm trying, but I need to keep it straight ahead so we don't walk into any giant spiderwebs, or rip out our eyes on a stray thorn branch."

"Well, keep flicking it around then. Not that fast! That's better. Only fifteen paces left to go."

We shuffled forwards a few more steps.

"Why are we whispering, by the way?" I asked.

Marilyn tugged me a little closer. "I don't know why you're whispering, but I'm doing it so the dangerous villain doesn't hear and come to pick us off as easy prey."

"What?"

"Or wild boar. They're carnivorous. I saw it on a documentary. I don't fancy being gouged by a tusk this far from a hospital. How many steps?"

I ducked just in time to avoid a low branch. "Eight. And one, wild boar don't live in the UK, let alone Sherwood Forest. Two, they don't eat humans and three, are you saying you wouldn't mind being gouged by one if you were in the City Hospital car park?"

"One. Wild boars are currently undergoing a population explosion in the UK. There are thousands of them. Two. They might not hunt live humans but they can and do attack them if threatened. Three. They weigh twenty stone, can run at up to thirty miles per hour, and jump six feet. *Six feet.* Four. They are nocturnal. Which means they come out at night. Are we there yet?"

We paused to look around. "This should about do it. Shine your torch to the left and wave it about a bit."

We clomped about in the undergrowth for a few minutes, looking for the clearing surrounded by the blackberry bushes. Marilyn's search grew increasingly urgent, until she suddenly stopped dead, so that I crashed into the back of her.

"Hang on a minute. Why are we looking for a pile of bushes designated by Hester as the official bathroom anyway? Take this." She handed me the torch. "Keep an eye out for boars."

I turned away. "What are you doing? You can't just go in the middle of nowhere."

"Hello? Everywhere here is the middle of nowhere. Hester's pretend bathroom is the middle of nowhere. It's the dead of night. There's nobody here. It's not as though I'm going to need the trowel."

I shuddered. "Under no circumstances am I using the trowel this weekend."

"Tomorrow, we should hike through the woods until we reach the visitor centre. Or an actual campsite. There'll be a no-trowel-necessary toilet there."

Marilyn, job done, took the torch from me. I found a discreet spot a short distance away and took my turn.

"I bet Hester never even got permission for us to be here. Kim's right. It can't be legal to camp in the middle of the woods with no facilities, or running water or anything," I said.

"What I want to know is…"

I never did find out what she wanted to know. At that point, a *thing* hurtled out of the pile of ferns to my right, tripped over my crouching form, and tumbled head over heels into a patch of stinging nettles.

My goodness. A good job Marilyn had gone already. An elite SAS commando's pelvic floor couldn't withstand that sort of attack out in the middle of the pitch-black woods and caught in a compromising position.

"WILD BOAR!" Marilyn screamed, careening from side to side with the torch beam, blinding me and no doubt the creature, now thrashing about and making hideous screeching noises. "Find a weapon! Run for your life! Every woman for herself! If I don't make it back, tell the twins and James I love them!"

I quickly rendered myself decent. Marilyn picked up a broken stick and advanced towards the writhing, shadowy shape, now making distinctly un-pig-like noises like, "Ah! Aaah! Oh! Get me out!"

Definitely not a wild boar, then. And if it was a villain, they weren't very dangerous, judging by the pathetic wails and impractical boots.

"Keep still. You're only making it worse." I tucked my hand inside my anorak coat to protect it from the nettles, and grabbed on to one flailing hand. Marilyn dropped the stick and took hold of the other. Together we pulled, managing not to fall into the nettle pit, and stood the filthy, matted, semi-hysterical woman on her feet.

It was a good job there were no bathrooms with mirrors for Kim to take a look at herself. Even without the gazillion red and white nettle stings bumping out all over her bare skin, she looked as though she'd been living wild in the forest for a month, not a couple of hours. Wowzers. I had looked better than that after three weeks living on the street with an infected knife wound.

"Where have you been?" Marilyn asked, incredulous. "What happened? We thought you'd gone home."

Kim looked at her. A fat tear carved a white path through the mud on her cheek.

"Oh, it doesn't matter." Marilyn wrapped her up in a hug, and began walking her back through the woods. I waited for them to take a few more steps.

"Er, guys? I think you're heading in the wrong direction."

After a few false starts, we eventually found the path back to the tents. Once there, we stuffed Kim with hot dogs and hot chocolate, listening to her tale of woe about her search for a phone signal leading her further and further into the forest, until her battery ran out. Then the rain started, so she took shelter under a large tree. After a few minutes, she gave up waiting for the rain to stop and began wandering around aimlessly, trying to find any form of civilization, until she caught the glow of the torch in the distance.

"Do I look bad?" she asked, pointlessly running her hands through the nest of tangles on her head.

"No, no," we all murmured. "You look fine."

"Yeah." Rowan wiped her friend's face with a tissue. "You suit the *I'm a Celebrity* look."

"Really?"

"How are the stings?" Melody asked, changing the subject.

"I can hardly feel them any more. Those dock leaves really work. I'm just tired. Where are the beds?"

Good question. We looked at Hester. Were we to build our beds out of soggy ferns and clumps of muddy grass? String hammocks made of sycamore boughs? Our director stared back at us, unflinching.

"There are roll up mats in the back of my car and Ebony's, and spare sleeping bags for those who haven't brought one. Kim may go to bed in tent one. For the rest of us, it is time to get started."

"Get started with what?" We gaped at her. "It's the middle of the night."

"It is quarter to nine."

Quarter to nine?!

"It's also freezing, pitch black, and still drizzling, not to mention blowing a gale," Mags pointed out.

Get started?

What could Hester possibly have planned out here?

"First, we hike."

That did not go down well.

"What? Why are you moaning? I told you about the night hike." Hester bristled.

247

"We thought that was a joke," Uzma said in a dazed voice.

"Did I sound like I was joking?"

"You never sound like you're joking," Leona pointed out. "Is this a sensible idea?"

"I did this very same hike with the Girl Guides last year," Hester snapped. "We all had a marvellous time."

"What's second?" April asked, shivering with a combination of cold and fear. "You said the hike was first."

"Let's conquer the first, first. Then we'll get on to what's second. Now, stout shoes, water bottles, and torches, choir. It was all on the kit list. Hup two three four. What are you waiting for?"

In the end, after a discussion about who got to stay that nearly turned as nasty as a boar fight, Millie and Janice pulled the old and infirm card, getting to stay behind with Kim, the sleeping twins, a lamp, and a packet of mini apple pies.

We trudged through the mizzle, stumbling over hillocks and stepping up to our ankles in unseen puddles. Barely speaking, too tired, and too busy concentrating on where we were going, we plodded on through trees and fields. Not adventurous. Certainly not fun. I wondered what the weather had been like when the Guides had done it. It seemed as though Hester had gone too far this time, and the trip would break instead of make us.

Until we hit a particularly tricky stretch along the edge of a swampy meadow.

We had to shuffle along, clinging to twigs sticking out from the hedge running alongside, leaping from tiny, slippery stone to tinier, even slipperier stone as we tried to work our way to the end of the field without falling in and sinking to the bottom of the swamp. Marilyn, familiar enough with Anton's killer training sessions to take this walk in her stride (and even, quite possibly, enjoy being able to vault stiles and leap across brooks for the first time in years), led the way. She used the largest torch to navigate a safe path, making sure the person behind her could follow. We had to grip on to each other's hands, and shoulders, and rucksacks, watch carefully for those who began to wobble, and call out instructions to guide those behind us, and updates to those in front. In the end, we began to get the hang of it. We switched places so the stronger among us, those more used to hiking through swamps, flanked the weaker and more nervous members of the group. We organized a system with the seven torches (six, once Leona dropped hers in) so that everyone could see when they needed to. We offered encouragement, and advice, and cheered each other on.

Would you look at that? I thought proudly to myself, as I helped Rosa breach a particularly long gap between stones. *We've become a team.*

Then from the back came a piercing shriek.

April had fallen in.

"Woman down!" cried Hester, who'd been guarding the rear.

We all froze, peering anxiously back through the darkness in the direction of the squeals and splashes. The surprise sent Mags into a dangerous wobble, and it looked like there would be another woman down until Rowan hopped forwards and steadied her.

"Right." I looked up and down the line from my halfway position. "Marilyn, can you see what's on the other side of the gate?"

"There's a dirt road. I can't see far but it doesn't look too bad."

"Everybody who's already gone past me, keep going and get to the track. The rest of us can work our way back and help April."

"I want to help April!" Rowan said from her position three people in front of me.

"Tough. If there are too many of us we won't all fit on the safe spots and someone else will end up falling in. Come on, let's go!"

The back half of the line hopped, skipped, and shimmied back to find April thrashing about in the mud, now up to her thighs.

"Stop moving about!" I yelled.

"She's not listening." Hester squatted on a larger rock, holding out a branch towards April, who was a metre or so into the field. "She's panicking."

We tried a couple more times to get her to stop moving, as it only wiggled her deeper into the mud, but to no avail.

"Is someone going to have to go and get her?" Uzma asked, wide-eyed in the torchlight.

"They aren't going to be able to pull her back," Mags frowned. "She might even pull them under without meaning to."

"Hang on a minute." Uzma took off her coat, arranging it on top of the marshy mud. Slowly laying down, she spread her surface area out as much as possible. She sank several inches into the squelch, but keeping still seemed to be working.

"Hand me the stick."

Hester passed it over, and with a mixture of gentleness and urgency we ordered April to grab onto it. Somehow she had twisted around, in the opposite direction to the torchlight, her wails and gasps becoming more frantic.

"I'll go round the other side." I found a rock a metre or so into the meadow, and stepped onto it, holding on to Yasmin for balance. When I moved onto the next one, she followed me, and Rosa stepped into her place, so we were now holding on to and supporting each other like a human chain.

I managed to reach three-quarters of the way round before the stones ran out. Copying Uzma, I spread out my coat and gingerly started to lie down. The mud reached April's hips now. Things were starting to look seriously dangerous. And every second the job of pulling her out grew even harder. Yasmin passed me a torch.

"April. You have to stop moving!" I begged her, trying to keep the fear from my voice. "Keep still!"

No response.

"Reach forwards and lean on me!" I screamed.

Then, from beyond the gate, a hundred metres away, came the voice of an angel.

"Lean on me."

Through the mizzle, the wind, and the anxiety came a pitch-perfect harmony as the rest of the choir joined in with the next line.

As part of the stronger together theme for the competition, Hester had got us using this song for our "out with the stress in with the strength" breathing exercises and warm-up.

After several weeks, none of us could hear it without automatically dropping our shoulders, blowing out our no-good tension, and becoming still.

April paused in her struggling and cocked one ear towards the sound. Those of us near her joined in with the rest of the chorus.

"Keep breathing, April," I called out, my words stronger now. "In and out. Breathe with me, honey. I'm here. I'm with you. We're going to get you out."

She splashed around to face me.

"Faith!"

"I'm here. I'm getting you out. But you need to listen to me, April. You have to stop moving and follow my instructions. Ready?"

April looked at me sprawled on my belly in the mud, her face ghoul-like in the torchlight. "I think so."

It took about a hundred thousand hours, a swamp load of tears, and countless verses of "Lean on Me", but together we got her out and somehow carried her to the other side of the gate.

After several hugs, more tears, a change of clothes for April, and Hester's emergency chocolate bars for everybody, we were ready to get the heck out of the dangerous wilds of Nottinghamshire. Hester's hike had managed to make the tents seem inviting.

"Are you sure, April? You aren't hurt? We can call an ambulance as soon as we reach somewhere with a phone signal." Melody took her pulse one more time.

"I'm not hurt," April beamed. "I'm fine. You saved me. I was really scared. I thought I was going to be swallowed up into the swamp forever."

We all took a deep breath. At one point, we had thought that too.

"Then I heard you sing. And I wasn't scared any more. I wasn't in the swamp alone. I knew you'd help me out. You wouldn't leave me. So I felt happy."

"You felt happy? Stuck up to your waist in that mud?" Uzma boggled.

"I felt happy 'cos I knew I wasn't alone. I knew you'd get me out. All that time, that whole walk, I'd been scared in case something scary happened. But I didn't need to be scared. You were here. All of you. My friends. My sisters. You didn't leave me. I didn't need to be scared any more."

I thought about what April had told me about her family – her destructive relationship with her mum, leaving home to kip on friends' sofas, no job, no security, no one. Until she fell in love with a seriously ill man-child fighting a drug and alcohol addiction. And then he left her, too.

I mentally threw some more of my petty, ugly jealousy back over the gate and into the depths of that swamp right then and there. Squelching my caked feet across the path, I pulled her into a hug.

"You're not alone, sister. Don't be scared."

"I could say the same thing to you," she laughed, pressing her stinky face against mine.

Marilyn swivelled round and pointed one finger at Hester. "Did you plan this?"

Hester patted her head, every spotless hair in place. Was it actually a helmet? Made of some space-age dirt-resistant technology? "I'm choosing not to answer that question. But you know by now I do nothing without asking my boss first."

"What, Dylan?" Rowan asked. "Dylan planned this?"

Rosa rolled her eyes. "She means God, Rowan."

Some decades later, around midnight, we stumbled back into camp. Soggy, chafed, blistered, and utterly jubilant as we sang another round of musical classics. The notes our half-frozen lungs and exhausted voices produced were no longer pitch-perfect, or even in time. It sounded fantastic.

Every one of us slept for eight straight hours. *I* slept for eight straight hours. No nightmares, no sweats, no chattering teeth nor trembling bones. I was not alone. I was with my friends. My sisters. I was safe.

Chapter Nineteen

The sheep bleating in my ear woke me up. Either that or the sound of it ripping off a chunk of my sleeping bag.

Up close, sheep are massive.

Massive and filthy, smelly and sharp-hooved and massive.

Momentarily forgetting my friends, my sisters, not being alone and all that, I nearly peed my thermal pants.

"Sheep!" Marilyn called, from the other side of the tent.

"No kidding," I growled back. "Got any bright ideas?"

"I have to get Nancy and Pete out. Sorry. Mother's instinct."

There was a rustle as she scrambled for the entrance, a baby in a mini sleeping bag under each arm.

"Rosa? Melody?" I called feebly to my tent-mates. "Did you know there's a sheep in the tent?"

A bleary-eyed Rosa poked her head out of her blanket. "It's a sheep. I think it eat your sleeping bag."

"Yes. It's also blocking my exit. I'm stuck here until it moves."

"Did you try shooing it away? Like this, *shoo, shoo*." She made a flapping motion with her hands. "Or like this." She clambered to her feet and shooed again, waving her blanket up and down.

The sheep gazed at her across the tent before bending its head and taking another mouthful of my bed.

"Hang on. I go get a weapon. We can beat it out of the tent."

Beat it out? With its hooves pinning my sleeping bag to the ground?

"Melody," I called out, causing the sheep to waggle its head in my direction.

"Yes, my darling?" she replied, from within her separate compartment.

"There's a sheep eating my sleeping bag."

"Well, that doesn't sound very good. I wouldn't let it get away with that if I were you."

"I don't think I have any choice in the matter."

Silence.

"Are you coming to help me?"

I heard a zipping noise, but Melody's door into the main tent remained closed.

"Mel? Melody?"

My teammate, friend, and spiritual sister had scarpered out of the back entrance.

At that moment, I paused to consider how the sheep had got inside in the first place. Carefully, keeping the rest of my body still, I rolled my head to look behind me.

Yikes!

Another sheep, staring at me through an enormous rip in the back seam. Wearing a yellow and pink striped bobble hat.

I was surrounded.

And judging by the yelps and baas now erupting from all directions, I wasn't the only one.

Rosa poked her head back in through the tent flap. Her arm followed, clutching a mop.

"Here. Whack it with this. On the nose. It will soon be getting the message and coming out of there."

"Yes. Either that or it will lose its temper, bite my face, and make a smoothie out of my internal organs as it tramples me to death."

"Faith. It is a sheep. You need to do your breathing exercise. Then show it who is boss."

"We both know I'm not the boss."

"I do not know that!"

"I meant me and the sheep."

"Oh for mercy's sake! I come in there right now to sort this out."

"Wait! Let me get out of this bag first."

But every time I tried, the sheep began to wave its head around in agitation, moving closer rather than further away from my all-too-squashable head. In the end, after I stopped moving for what felt like an hour at least, it stepped off the sleeping bag. I hastily wiggled past and out of the entrance, like a caterpillar sneaking out of a bird's nest, and feeling just as vulnerable.

Straight into a scene out of a post-apocalyptic movie. Planet of the Sheep.

Tent one – admittedly our first, and therefore worst, attempt at pitching – was no longer upright. Tent three had a sheep standing in the entrance, chewing on a guy rope. The wet coats we had strung up to dry between a couple of trees now lay on the damp grass, all except for April's parka, which one sheep now wore on its back.

Uzma reckoned that with a pair of dark glasses it could pass for a '90s rock star.

The food supply, safely stored in tent one, now lay trampled across the clearing in various states of dishevelment.

"Honestly." Leona snatched a packet of crumpets from the mouth of one of the smaller beasts and nearly got her fingers nipped off. "You can eat grass. Look around, you dumb animals. It's all around you. More than you could ever need. Grass, grass, and more grass. We, however, cannot eat grass. We needed that loaf of bread. And you didn't even *eat* the butter. You just trod on it."

And the droppings? Someone needed to teach those animals how to use a trowel.

After a stressful hour herding the sheep into the next field, before cobbling together a makeshift barricade out of a fallen tree trunk, Hester rallied our soggy spirits by declaring an emergency trip to the nearest pub for hot food and running water. Some of the group didn't even bother getting changed, shoving on a jumper and wellies over their pyjamas before diving into the cars.

We sat in the pub like a bunch of wild women, plates loaded up from the breakfast bar as though we hadn't eaten a decent meal for a month. Whew. And I knew what that felt like. Glancing around at my cohorts, with their messy hair, grass-stained onesies, stale swamp stink, and smudged faces, I suspected some of them might know that feeling, too.

"Now I know why celebrities are so thin," Rowan declared, around a mouthful of limp bacon. "The more you slum it, the better food tastes. Rich people probably don't even notice what their breakfast tastes like. I bet some of them don't even have breakfast. Faith, does Perry eat breakfast?"

I nodded. "Yes. He eats granola with fruit and yoghurt."

"See. It's in our genes. If you're warm and dry, you're fine eating fruit. If you wake up in a sodden tracksuit 'cos a sheep's eaten your bedroom door, your body needs grease. It's like '*Dude! I'm going to need more fat deposits to keep warm in these conditions*'."

"You're not rich, Rowan, and you're tiny."

"Yeah. Well. I can't usually afford breakfast." She glanced up, suddenly embarrassed. "At least, I don't usually have time to eat it. What with getting Callie ready for nursery and starting college and everything."

"How's that going?" I asked.

"Not bad, actually. It's not like school. I call the teacher by his first name, and he talks to me like I'm a normal person, not a deadbeat. He says if I keep it up I can get a C first time."

"And then your beauty course?"

She nodded proudly. "Sherwood College say I can start in September if I pass maths and English. I just need to figure out how to pay for the fees."

"Would you like me to see if I can get you some waitressing shifts?"

She shrugged. "Maybe once Callie's at school full time. For now, it'll be enough to leave her with my mum while I'm training. Thanks anyway. Hester says if it's meant to be, something'll come up."

"I'll add you to my prayers," I blurted.

She beamed in surprise. I felt a little surprised myself. What prayers? Help, God, please don't let Kane get me or my brother? And please stop me feeling attracted to a man other than my nice fiancé?

I took a swig of tea in an attempt to quench the prickle of anxiety pointing out that here, sat in a grubby pub in yesterday's underwear with a group of women resembling a Neanderthal tribe, I felt more part of the family than I did nibbling on smoked salmon at HCC with those I would soon be legally related to.

When we returned to the field, the first thing I noticed was a bubblegum pink Mini parked up with the rest of the cars. Once Marilyn pulled over, I saw the bunting stretching between several trees towards the far side of the clearing. And balloons. A lot of pink balloons.

As I climbed out and started walking over to the wreckage of the tents, two pink people jumped out from behind a large oak tree.

"Surprise!" Natasha and Catherine were wearing pink wigs, pink cowgirl hats, pink wellies, and pink T-shirts that said "Faith's Final Fling!" in swirly, glittery letters.

"What?" I stood there, gaping like the fish out of water I knew I was about to become.

"Surprise!" they squealed again, flapping their hands about. "It's your hen do!"

"But I'm not having a hen do."

"Wrong, Faith. You *totally* are!"

I swivelled my head to face Marilyn, my matron of honour and therefore the one in charge of making sure I didn't have a hen do. She grinned at me. "Outnumbered, outmanoeuvred, and outvoted."

"What about this being *my* wedding? Where I get to decide what does *and doesn't* happen?" I hissed.

"That only counts where you're right. When you're being an idiot we get to overrule."

"Yes!" Natasha tipped out a bag of matching T-shirts onto the grass. "Outnumbered, outvoted, outmanoeuvred, and overruled. We are going to give you the best. Hen do. Ever."

My heart slipped down my trouser leg and plopped onto the grass in a sorry heap. Oh boy.

The itinerary for the best hen do ever?

To start with, a high-rise climbing, swinging, treetops, monkey-type "adventure". A stroll in the woods compared to our adventures the night before. Only Marilyn tried to back out, and that was because she couldn't believe she came under the weight restriction. Having worked herself up into a nervous frenzy when we arrived, the instructor didn't even blink at her size. I thought back to the rock climbing trip, where she had sat on the sidelines with Polly. It was fantastic that Marilyn had energy now, was fitter and stronger and healthier. But more than that, those months of sweat and tears and aching muscles and utter exhaustion with Anton had enabled her to become a fully participating member of life again. Take that, sidelines! It's the sidelines' turn to sit on the sidelines now!

I slung an arm around her shoulder. "I should charge you for all the extra dress material Rosa's going to have to throw away."

"This hen do T-shirt is a medium. I've lost so much weight I'm medium. In the middle. Non-large." She tugged at the top in disbelief.

"It's what you've gained that makes the difference."

"I'm going to smash everybody on this course. Even those gym-honed posh girls." She grinned.

"Everybody except me. You have to let the bride win, of course."

"I have to do no such thing. What, one hour into your hen do and you've gone bridezilla on me? Save the attitude for your mother-in-law."

"Speaking of Larissa, why isn't she here?" I looked around, as if expecting her to appear out of the trees. "I'd have liked to see her dangling off that bungee thing. Given her a helping shove down the zip wire."

"Unfortunately, the date clashed with her annual Lady Rosalind

Institute reunion." Marilyn shook her head in mock woe.

"Coincidence."

"No-incidence. Today has been planned with military precision. No attention spared to detail."

We reached the first obstacle, where the rest of the choir waited for me to lead the way.

I gave Marilyn a kiss on the cheek and whispered, "Thank you for ignoring my instructions. You go ahead and leave me happily eating your dust."

By the time we had finished the course, eaten a picnic lunch sprawled on blankets in the sunshine, and limped back to base, we felt optimistic enough to construct a bonfire. The afternoon was spent wandering around scouting out dry wood, clearing up the sheep damage, and munching on the cakes Natasha and Catherine had brought along. Kim and Rowan got out their cosmetic bags and had a go at untangling our rat's-nests and scrubbing up our outdoor faces. Not a lot they could do about the smell, but we were getting used to it.

"Are we going out later, then?" Yasmin asked, as Kim painted her nails for her in different colours.

"This is about as out as you can get," I smiled, waving at the countryside.

"No. I mean out, like in out where other people are."

"We're not," Catherine answered. "Why would we want to go anywhere else when we've got a rockin' group of women right here? Sitting under the stars with a bonfire, marshmallows, and Natasha's party playlist on her iPod..."

"Yeah. No shelter, no toilet, and no chairs... What more could a girl ask for?" Rowan looked up from brushing Leona's hair.

"I think the plan is to be back in your own beds tonight. Hester asked the church minister guy to come and pick the gear up at about eleven."

"Dylan?" Yasmin smirked. "So there's at least someone to get dolled up for then."

Kim pointed the nail polish brush at her. "You know better than that. Aren't we supposed to have learned we don't need a man to get dolled up for? Besides" – she pulled a sly smile, looking down and pretending to concentrate on Yasmin's fingernails – "I think for all of the women here, our appearance will go right over Dylan's head. Except for one. And she could wear a second-hand bin bag and he'd not be able to take his dreamy eyes off her." Half the women within hearing distance froze. The others jerked their heads towards Kim.

Apart from me, that is. I reacted by turning crimson and busying myself with choosing a shade of lipstick while pretending to ignore the awkward giggles. Had she really just said that? At my hen do?

"Get on with it, then," Yasmin urged Kim on, trying to change the subject. "Haven't you seen the state of my cuticles?"

I gave my engagement ring a squeeze, reminded myself that Dylan's behaviour had been entirely appropriate, up to and including the gate non-incident. Men didn't fist bump people they fancied, did they? He's a minister, for goodness' sake! I was ridiculous, over-analysing every look and smile, reinterpreting the kind words Dylan used all the time, and transferring my own stupid emotions onto his entirely rational ones. Once Perry had returned from wherever he was this week, and we were able to spend a bit more time together, my feelings would return to normal in good time for the wedding.

Ah, yes. And what were your normal feelings towards Perry, exactly? Strong enough to prevent any future crushes when a handsome, kind, funny, wise, lovely man comes along?

I took a deep breath. They were going to have to be.

* * *

We lit the fire as dusk began to fall and gathered round it on a motley bunch of makeshift seats – the folded-up tents, upturned buckets, and cool box. The twins oohed and aahed at the crackling flames from the safety of their pushchair. As the stars emerged in the purple sky, the scent of pine trees mingled with the warmth of the wood smoke, and the wood pigeons cooed their bedtime story. All of us agreed this was better than being crammed round a table in some city-centre restaurant.

To make things just about perfect, Polly and baby Esme arrived with four carrier bags of fish and chips. We toasted love, friendship, a memorable weekend, no broken bones and not too many bruised bottoms, and – to a lesser degree – marriage.

"To Perry, wherever he may be," Mags declared. "A man with excellent taste in women. May he fulfil all Faith's bodily, mind, and heart's desires, 'til death do them part."

"Bodily desires? 'Til death do them part? She should be so lucky!" Janice said, causing a ripple of laughter.

I bent my head, pretending to hide my blushes rather than the stab of anxiety. It had been easier, in the planning and the preparation of my wedding, to dismiss the reality of the marriage that came after.

Once the sun set behind the oak trees we brought out the blankets and sleeping bags that had managed to escape the sheep. Wrapped ourselves up in pink bobble hats and fleecy jackets, easy conversation and good company. Hester challenged everyone to give me a piece of marriage advice.

Looking around at the group, I braced myself.

Natasha kicked us off. "Go on a date every fortnight. That's what my parents do."

"Tell him you love him every day," Ebony said, her cheekbones pink. I nodded my thanks. *How about I start by telling him I love him once?*

"If you want to get the most out of a marriage, you can't go into it with a fifty-fifty attitude," Mags said. "If you both decide to give one hundred per cent and try to outgive the other, that's when you get a marriage that sings."

"Sex begins at the breakfast table," Janice declared. "Or sometimes on the breakfast table. But that's not what I mean. Don't leave all thoughts of romance until the end of the day when you're knackered and your brain is full of work, leaving you feeling about as sexy as a bowl of dirty dishes. Then, when his hand begins to creep across the bed what you want to do is sit up, clock him over the head with your hot water bottle, and ask '*Are you kidding me?*' "

Are you kidding me? That pretty much summed up how I felt about sex with Perry. Maybe we needed to start having breakfast together.

Millie nodded. "Then, before you know it he's going on business trips to conduct sneaky business with his thirty-two-year-old personal assistant and her fake boobs. That's my advice. Make sure his personal assistant has her own boobs."

We carried on. Rowan, whose only boyfriend had been Callie's father, told me, "Dance together. In the kitchen. Under the moon. Pull each other close and learn to move in time." She shrugged. "When I find a decent man I'm going to dance with him every night."

April solemnly advised me to stick with it; the bad times are worth fighting through to get to the good times on the other side.

"Grace," Leona added. "Grace is the oil that keeps the wheels running smoothly. When he leaves his underwear on the bathroom floor, forgets your birthday, snores, and snaps at the kids. Those days when you can't stop fantasizing about packing up a suitcase and running off to live a life of bliss on a deserted island, where nobody leaves an empty packet of tea in the cupboard, or burps when you are trying to enjoy your meal, or expects you to know where his rugby top is. On those days, you need to remind yourself – this is a good man, on the whole. He is faithful, and kind. He works hard, and means well even when he hasn't got a clue. He is decent, and he loves me as best he can. Take a deep breath and pray for grace."

After the others had taken their turns, Polly went second to last. She crossed her arms and pulled a face. "What can I say, Faith? I'm the last person who should be doling out advice. Just don't put up with any crap." A tear rolled down her cheek, as Melody reached over to give her hand a squeeze. "Marilyn?"

My best friend looked at me, her expression neutral. "Honesty. And trust. A good partner brings out the best in you, but that's impossible when you don't even let him know you."

I cleared my throat, more than a little overwhelmed by the prospect of what I was letting myself in for. Marriage sounded like hard work. So much more than two people sharing a house, and a bed, and some memories, maybe some kids.

That was okay, I decided. I could do hard work. I could learn to trust Perry. That took time, right? I could rustle up enough grace. We could dance in the kitchen. And his personal assistant was a man, so I felt pretty sure he didn't have breast implants.

I could make it work.

My phone rang, as a tiny flicker of signal managed to penetrate the forest depths. Sam. As I answered my phone, the twelve missed messages and countless texts beeped through. I excused myself, finding a private spot a short distance away to answer.

"Hi Sam."

"Faith! Why didn't you answer my calls? I need to talk to you."

I took a deep breath. I would make it work.

* * *

Having reassured Sam that I was fine, and reassured myself that he was as fine as could be expected underneath all the rambling waffle, I hung up and went back to the others. They had a gift for me. A set of china cups and saucers and matching teapot. I loved them, but I couldn't help thinking how out of place they would look in Perry's space-age kitchen. They'd look bloomin' lovely sitting on the bashed-up oak dresser in my kitchen, bought for thirty pounds from a charity shop, sanded down, and painted duck-egg blue to match my cabinets.

After the obligatory sing-song around the campfire, leaving my bridesmaids fairly bedazzled, Natasha turned up her iPod and set the playlist to party. We all kicked off our shoes and danced on the cold grass – even Hester, even Polly. *Especially* Polly, who danced as if the leg irons holding her back for the past few years had finally been hacked off. We boogied until we were breathless, then we had a drink, and some more food, and got up and boogied again.

During the middle of a particularly energetic reconstruction of the last dance from *Dirty Dancing*, high on endorphins, laughter, and two rare glasses of wine, I launched myself across the clearing into Marilyn's waiting arms, leaving us both in a heap on the grass. At that moment, Dylan strolled up.

"Hello, ladies." He grinned, hands in his pockets. "So this is what you get up to when no men are around."

"Dance with us, Dylan!" Rowan grabbed his hands, and started attempting a pachanga, or whatever it is Patrick Swayze and Jennifer Grey do in the film. To my surprise, Dylan went with it, with relish, adding some spins and even a dip as the song came to an end. Huh. Well. There you go then. How nice for Rowan.

He pulled her back up again, ruffled her hair affectionately, then looked across at me and winked.

Good job it was too dark to see my schoolgirl blush. And if I was the one he winked at, well, we were friends. It wasn't some secret signal, meant only for me, about how actually he was really pleased to see me...

Sheesh, Faith. This is why you don't drink wine.

"How's the hen? Fun weekend?" He wandered over while Hester began barking instructions for the evacuation.

"Today was great. Yesterday...? Probably best summed up as memorable."

He frowned, scanning the clearing. "Is there a problem with the drains here?"

"Um, no. There are no drains. But we've been using the woods. And Hester brought a trowel."

His nostrils flared. "I think you needed to dig a bit deeper. That is rank."

With horror, I realized what the smell was. "Actually, that's not what it is."

I leaned in a bit closer, screwing up my face in apology. Dylan veered back, covering his face with his hand.

"I don't mean to be rude, but what on earth?"

"I know. I ended up in a sort of swamp last night. A few of us did. Help me carry some of this stuff to the car and I'll tell you about it."

We loaded everything up, and searched the clearing for any last trace of litter or chunks of chewed-up tent. Most people had left by the time Marilyn started strapping her now sleeping toddlers into the car, and I had a moment to say bye to Dylan.

"Thanks for coming out here. I'm sure you've got places you'd rather be in the middle of a Saturday night." I checked my watch. "Sunday morning."

He smiled. "Nope, can't think of anywhere I'd rather be than here." A look of horror flashed across his face. "I don't know why I said that. I just meant, you know, otherwise I'd be sat on the sofa by myself watching a rubbish film and eating crisps. I didn't mean, um. Anything else."

"Right. Of course you didn't! I never thought... I mean. Of course." I kicked at a clump of grass in front of me. "I'll probably skip church tomorrow. But I'll see you in the week for a lesson?"

Dylan looked over at the truck, then straight back at me. "Yeah. About that."

Oh. I tried to brace myself.

"Have you told Perry yet?"

"Told him what?" *About the gate? Nothing happened! Why would I tell him that?*

"About the real reason you're learning to drive."

Ah. I folded my arms. "I haven't found the right time yet. He's been working away. And I'm not sure I need to tell him. I haven't seen or heard anything about Kane in weeks. Gwynne was probably right. Kane's been to all his meetings. It was paranoia."

Dylan looked at me. I could just about see his furrowed brow through the darkness.

"Look, I will tell him. But it's my decision when. What? Are you going to stop giving me lessons until I do?"

Dylan ran his hand over his head. "I think it might be a good idea if you found someone else."

I had known it was coming, but felt the slap of rejection all the same. "What? Why? I thought the lessons were going really well. I thought you were my friend."

"Faith." His voice hardened. "I'm a minister. I have a job to do. For people who rely on me. I need to get on with it."

"Oh." *I'm relying on you, you idiot!* "Well, I'm sorry for taking up so much of your time. Thanks for all the help. I'm probably better off with a professional anyway."

"Don't be sorry." He glanced at me, then looked away again.

"Well, I am sorry. I never meant to drag you away from your job. If I remember, you offered to help me. And it didn't have to be so often. That was your idea, too. But it's fine. I understand. You're a busy, busy man." Urgh. I sounded like a stroppy teenager. I hated, hated, hated accepting help from people. I didn't know how to handle it being withdrawn.

He sighed, closing his eyes for a moment. "Look. I want to help you. But Faith, I see you what, five times a week, with choir rehearsal and Sunday services? How often have you seen Perry in the past month? He should be teaching you how to drive – or at least paying for you to have driving lessons. He should be the one awake half the night worrying about the ex-convict who may or may not be hunting you down, praying and hoping that when this monster does he can be there to stand between you. I like being your friend, Faith." He stopped, swallowed, ran his hand through his hair again. "I love being your friend. But you're getting married in three months. This is your hen do. I shouldn't be the one here taking the equipment back."

"It was a choir weekend. I knew nothing about the hen do bit. And anyway, Perry's in Germany."

"That's not my point. You need to sort things out with him. He should be the one you go to when you need help, or a shoulder to lean on. He should be the one crying about your terrible past. You're in a potentially really dangerous situation and he deserves to know. If he did know, he probably wouldn't be in Germany. You aren't being fair to him. And when you confide in me about this stuff I have no right to get involved with, you aren't being fair to *me*." He was nearly yelling now. I'd never seen Dylan like this before.

"My relationship with Perry has nothing to do with you! With us being friends." I choked on my words, on the humiliation and the hurt. "Do you think because I'm getting married I shouldn't have any male friends? That's hogwash."

He looked down at the grass I had kicked again. "No. I think because you're getting married you shouldn't be friends with me." He grimaced. "I'll see you around, Faith."

He strode round to the driver's side of the truck, yanked open the door, and screeched into the night. I walked over to where Marilyn waited in her car.

"Everything okay?"

I nodded, afraid to speak.

"Want to talk about it?"

I shook my head.

"Well, you know I'm here if you change your mind." She started the ignition.

"No, it's fine. We were just talking about driving lessons. Nothing serious."

Nothing serious. So why did I feel as though my guts had been ripped out with a blunt camping knife?

Chapter Twenty

*I*nitially I put the headache down to another night twisting myself up in my tangled thoughts and tangled duvet, along with the alcohol, something I rarely touched. I got up around dawn, tried to shower off any last traces of stink, and forced down a cup of coffee.

Ten minutes later I threw the coffee back up again. Then the chills kicked in. My throat felt as though someone held a lighter to it. I made it halfway down the street, determined to get to church, where I could show Dylan I'd brushed off last night's conversation as the petty nothing it was compared to the important things in my life, like my wedding, and my brother. Rasping, quaking, my head spinning, I stumbled back home and hauled myself back up to bed.

Fever, virus, bacterial infection. My greatest fear after long-lost killers, having a bin for a bed again, and something happening to Sam. Or rather, something even worse happening to him.

If I couldn't get out of bed, couldn't stay on my feet for a five-hour stretch, couldn't carry four loaded plates without my hands trembling, I couldn't work. If I didn't work, I ran out of money. Running out of money spelled big trouble.

I could survive on pennies, eat six-pence tins of beans, wrap up in an extra duvet when the gas got cut off. But what I wouldn't be able to do was pay the massive debt I still owed from when, in desperation, I had booked Sam into a private treatment centre for the first time.

Three years ago, the overstretched, overstressed community

nurses told me Sam must prove to be a danger to himself or others before being admitted to the kind of NHS facility that would help prevent him becoming either of those things. Distraught at watching him slowly tumble into his own personal hell, certain a rope or a bottle of pills or a bridge lay at the bottom of that abyss, I took matters into my own hands, and a monstrous bill along with them. The private facility saved his life. I had been paying for it ever since.

Two years after that, I had fallen ill with tonsillitis, but kept working. Having missed too many days already due to "compassionate leave", I faced a final warning if I took any more time off. Sam was on the downward slope of his constant cycle, and the signs all told me he was slipping fast. Garbled phone calls in the middle of the night. Empty bottles no longer hidden but strewn in plain sight. The pinprick eyes and sweating hands betraying a man who had handed control back to the chemicals.

The mornings and evenings were unusually bitter that spring, even for April. I ploughed on through my illness, tramping the two miles to HCC and back, and the combination of the cold, the walk, and the ten-hour shifts tipped tonsillitis into the worst sort of flu.

I knew I couldn't keep working, that the only way to fight required giving in. But my brain was addled, full of virus and fever and fear. Sam, sensing my exhaustion, my weakened attention, slipped even further into the darkness.

For six days I battled on. Hitching a lift with a colleague where I could, half-crawling home when I couldn't, crashing asleep at my desk, ignoring emails, and avoiding customers. Vomiting repeatedly, chills shaking my body so hard my teeth rattled one minute, my clothes getting drenched with sweat the next. My boss, having run out of patience at my continual insistence I had a bog-standard cold, issued me with a final warning – pull it together or find another job.

On the sixth day, I used eighteen pounds' worth of my precious tips on a taxi home following a particularly horrendous late shift. It had been nearly twenty-four hours since I had spoken to Sam, which at that point gave me a mild sense of disquiet, but I felt too weak to feel anything more. I ran myself a scalding hot bath, falling asleep in it until the tepid water startled me awake, shuddering. I toppled into bed, weeping with relief that tomorrow I had a day off.

I slept for fifteen straight hours, waking to find myself the teeniest, tiniest bit cooler, the pounding in my head a fraction less insistent, the ache in my bones marginally less agonizing. So, taking my time, I heated half a tin of thin soup and carefully spooned in every mouthful, pleasantly surprised to find it settled in my stomach. I had another bath, dressed, and took the five-minute walk round to Sam's, feeling a faint ray of optimism that maybe I had weathered the worst of it. Another crisis averted. I would still have a job on Monday.

The flat was quiet when I let myself in. Nothing unusual about that – I expected to find Sam in bed.

I called out to him a couple of times, again unsurprised by his lack of answer. Kicking my way through the mess that had piled up since I had last found the energy to clear up, I opened his bedroom door.

Weakened legs collapsed underneath me. I sank to the floor, pulled out my phone, and dialled for an ambulance.

Later that evening, crushed, beaten, cornered, I made another call. To Perry. Whereby I formally accepted his offer of a proposal of marriage.

Did he make the link between my acceptance and my hour of need?

Perhaps. On the other hand, he lived in a world so carefree regarding money, so removed from the need to make choices based on the financial implications, that perhaps he didn't. Either way, he never mentioned it, and once Sam was home again, six weeks later, offering his hearty thanks with all the charm and charisma that befitted a future Upperton brother-in-law, from Perry's point of view it seemed as though the issue was done and dusted. His point of view, however, couldn't see addictions, or the murky past that went with them. Let alone the murky present.

* * *

The week after my hen do, I cancelled my three shifts, my babysitting for the twins, and my meeting with Larissa and the florist, and spent three days straight on the sofa, under a duvet, eating the chicken soup Marilyn had brought round, and watching drivel on television in between naps.

Tuesday evening, the doorbell rang. I shuffled down the corridor, expecting to see Marilyn with another tub of food, but unable to ignore the surge of hope that it might be Dylan, despite my unwashed hair, pallid complexion, and saggy pyjamas.

Perry stood on the doorstep, carrying a fruit basket, a bunch of flowers, and a stack of romantic comedies.

"I'm so sorry I couldn't get here earlier. The traffic back from Heathrow was a nightmare." He dumped the goodies on the kitchen table and turned to enfold me in a hug. "Darling, look at you. You must be feeling awful."

I tried to pull away. "I must be smelling awful, too."

"I don't care."

He scooped me up and carried me into the living room, gently laying me on the sofa before kneeling down on the floor beside me. "I'm going to take care of you. No arguments."

He started by running me a bath, then made cheese on toast, served with scalding hot tea, with a spoonful of honey and lemon stirred in. He stuck on a DVD and rubbed my now-clean feet while we laughed and groaned through to the happy ending. At some point during the second film I must have fallen asleep, waking in the early hours to find a flask of tea on the coffee table beside my favourite cup, a packet of flu medication, and a plate of cookies.

I sipped my tea in the glow of the street light, squinting to read the get well note he'd tucked underneath the cup. It tasted of horrible guilt, stung pride, and foolishness. I loved Perry. But I so wanted to be *in love* with him. Not with my whole heart. Not so much I needed him. But enough to make him – and me – happy.

Enough to be the kind of wife he deserved. I was sick of pretending. Of hiding. Of feeling ashamed of who I was and what I felt. I thought about Marilyn's advice at my hen do, about being honest, and letting him know me. I had started to realize marrying Perry would be all or nothing. If I couldn't give it my all, commit myself fully from the start, I owed him the courage to walk away.

As much as I hated to admit it, as the dawn light began to peek through my curtains, I accepted Dylan had been right. I would tell Perry. Everything. Well, something. Okay – I would at least get started, and take it from there.

I tried to reinforce my decision with a marathon run of Hollywood Happy Endings. Faith's Final Fling had killed off my brief, ridiculous mental fling with Dylan. There had been no sign of Kane for weeks now, backing up Gwynne's belief that my subconscious had been playing tricks on me. Sam was on the mend again, April seemed to want to stick it out, and I was managing to control my need for control. I had stood up to Larissa, and got at least something of the wedding I wanted.

If I cried a few times, that was understandable. These types of films were supposed to be tear-jerkers. Add in illness, tiredness, and anxiety about missing work and it was basically inevitable. For the first time in forever, someone had taken care of me, and done it with unexpected tenderness. If I got through a couple of boxes of tissues, no biggie.

* * *

Once recovered, I spent the next couple of weeks sticking to my new resolve. I avoided Dylan, which didn't prove difficult as he appeared to be avoiding me, signed up with a professional driving instructor (a woman), and started to get properly involved with my own wedding plans, rather than focusing all my spare time and energy on the Grand Grace Gala, due to be held at the end of the month. Perry was away again, but we spoke every couple of days on the phone. I spent a long time thinking about what I needed to tell him, and how I would do it once he returned.

I took April to see Sam. My heart leaped when I saw him. Clear eyes, glowing skin, glossy hair swinging below his chin. If my heart leaped, April's must have taken off and done a lap of the visitor's room. I felt tempted to push her jaw back up.

We chatted for a while about what he'd been up to, the people he'd met, the food, his painting. April mentioned the wedding first. I carefully monitored his reaction, before bringing up the main reason for my visit, and for bringing reinforcements along.

"Is it all going okay, then? Not too stressful?" Sam asked.

"No. It's fine. Rosa's making the most incredible dresses for the bridesmaids. They're genuine works of art. You'd love them."

"You know I'm going to be there, don't you?"

I nodded. "It would mean the world to me if you were there. But if it doesn't work out, you know I understand."

He shook his head. "I'll be there. I promise. August fifteenth. It's on my wall calendar. I know a promise from an addict means squat, but this is different."

No, it wasn't different. But if he could stay in treatment a while longer, I could begin to allow myself to feel optimistic.

"Well, I hope so. I have a job for you to do."

His mouth flicked up in a tight smile. "I'm not making a speech."

"No! We can do without a brother of the bride speech. I want you to give me away."

Silence settled on the table between us. We both knew the significance of the request. After a moment had passed, I glanced at April beside me. She took hold of his hand.

"You want me to give you away?"

We both knew what he really meant.

You want me to give you up.

"Yes." A tear plopped onto the vinyl tablecloth. "A new start, for all of us."

His eyes met mine, the conflict of emotions swirling in the soft brown.

"I'm not asking you to stop being my brother. You know how much I love you. I'm asking if we can try to find a better balance. I'll be here when you need me, but April and Perry are here now too."

He took in a deep breath, his knuckles turning white where they held on to April.

"Are you sure about him?" Sam asked.

I let out a choked laugh. "Why do people keep asking me that? We're engaged, aren't we?"

Sam shook his head sharply. "I'm not people."

"Yes. I'm sure. And I'm going to tell him. About Mum and, well, everything else. If that's okay with you."

"You haven't told him yet?" Sam frowned, looking over at April.

"I know, I've got issues."

"Haven't we all?" He smiled suddenly, and the sight of it banished the shadows. "It would be an honour to give you away, little sister. Perry can take his share of your issues. April and I'll come round for fancy dinner parties, where I will charm all your new hoity-toity friends with my brooding artistic personality, and April will stun them with her dazzling wit."

"I love you, Sam."

He stood up, leaning over to wrap his long arms around me. "Yeah, yeah. Now how about you go and find a coffee so I can talk to April without you hovering over us?"

* * *

May's marriage preparation class would be the final one. I messaged Perry, now home, earlier in the day to let him know I would make my own way there. I had tentatively resumed walking, at least in daylight. Partly in an attempt to convince myself Gwynne was right about Kane. Partly because I couldn't afford the cost of taxis or hassle of rural public transport. Partly because I needed the independence and pounding out those miles felt like the only way I would hold on to my mind.

For the whole of the first half of the class, I kept my eye on the door, waiting for Perry to show. It was slightly awkward, as we were meant to be doing couple work about positive communication. During the break, I tried to shrug it off with half-hearted excuses, no doubt leaving the rest of the group wondering how I could bear the shame of my lousy fiancé. I texted said fiancé:

Where are you?

Work

It's Tuesday! Marriage prep. Last one! You promised to be here.

There was a three-minute wait before my phone whistled a reply:

Sorry. Forgot. I'll be done in half an hour.

I hurried out into the foyer and phoned him.

"Sorry! Sorry, sorry. I've just got to wrap this contract up. I'll be there in an hour, tops."

"It'll be finished in an hour. You promised you'd be here."

"I know, I really am sorry. How about I pick you up and we can do the questions at mine? I'll order some food. Light candles. Put on some music. I'd prefer to spend our first evening together in two weeks alone, not in a crowded church hall."

"We have to attend the course if we're going to get married here, Perry. You know that. This could mess up our plans." I leaned against a radiator and closed my eyes.

"Your plans."

"*What*?" I stood up again.

"That church is your plan, not mine. I've contributed no plans to this wedding whatsoever. Just the money. Which I earn by staying late some nights and getting three point four million pound contracts done. I'm sorry if I don't have time at this exact moment to talk about which one of us should empty the bin, discuss our non-existent sex life or what makes you feel loved. I'll see you later."

He hung up. Stung, and slightly shocked, I said into the phone, "Actually, I feel loved if you turn up when you say you will and follow through on your promises. Maybe instead we can discuss whether this whole marriage thing is a great big, ugly, expensive mistake."

Jamming my phone back into my bag, I glanced up to see Dylan standing a couple of metres away from me, head down, hands in his jean pockets.

Crackling with humiliation, I hurried past him, in the direction of the toilets. As I reached his shoulder, he lifted his head and looked right at me. His eyes were like I'd never seen before. As though a storm – a tornado – raged in their depths.

I locked myself in the ladies' room, squeezed my eyes shut tight, and kicked the toilet a few times, bruising my toe on the porcelain.

"Right, Faith. Pull yourself together. It's a spat. Every couple has them. And you've been in way more humiliating situations than this in the past few months. Who cares what Dylan thinks?"

I took a deep breath, checked my flies were done up, poked my head around the door to make sure Dylan had gone, and marched back to the marriage course, dialling it back to a breezy saunter once inside the room.

"Right." Zoe, the lovely course leader, smiled. "I'm pleased to welcome Dylan, who you've all met, to the final part of our course."

Right, of course Dylan is here. Where else would he be?

"Now, in a few minutes Dylan's going to run through some of the practicalities of your wedding day, and give you the chance to ask any questions. But before that, we have a final exercise to round off the course. Are you all sitting nice and close to your partners?"

Of course the in-love, blissful, happy couples who kept their promises and turned up when they said they would were sat together, as close as they could get away with, considering we were in the house of God.

"Ah. Is Perry not going to make it, Faith?"

The other couples untangled themselves enough to turn and peer at me, sitting bolt upright in my chair near the back.

"He got caught up at work. When he picks me up, we'll go

through everything together. I've been making notes for him."
I waved my notepad, fast enough that no one could read my
sprawling message to Perry, which included my opinion of his late-
night money making, and where exactly he could stick his gazillion,
gatrillion pound contract. "You work away; don't worry about me."

Gavin, who generally remained silent until Zoe nudged him,
frowned.

"Well, we can't have you sat there on your own. The whole point
is you articulate your feelings."

"It's fine. Like I said, we'll do it later."

"Why don't you work with Dylan for now? I'm sure he'd be
happy to stand in."

I shrivelled up in my seat, stealing a look over my shoulder at
where Dylan stood, leaning against the back wall. He did not look
happy to stand in. Arms folded, eyes narrowed, jaw clenched, he
looked like a pirate facing down a flotilla of the British navy.

"What do you think, Dylan?" Gavin asked.

"No."

"Oh, come on now!" Zoe laughed. "It'll only be for a few
minutes."

"It wouldn't be appropriate," he practically growled.

Zoe put her hands on her hips. "Don't be silly. It's just an
exercise. You don't have to pretend to be Perry, just help Faith think
through the questions."

His scowl, if possible, intensified.

"It's fine," I said, trying to press myself as deeply as possible into
the chair fabric. "I can sit here and think about them by myself. I
don't mind. Or, or maybe I should just go?"

"You can't go!" Zoe slapped Gavin on the arm.

He coughed. "No. You can't go. Isn't Perry picking you up?"

"And?" Zoe said.

"And we haven't given out the gifts yet. Please stay."

I looked down, feeling the eyes of the class on me. Well, nearly
all of them.

Zoe sung out, "Allie and Tom, please save it for after Dylan says, 'You may now kiss the bride'!"

A sheepish Allie and Tom unlocked lips.

"Look, I'll just sit here. It's fine. I can go over my notes."

I opened my course workbook and began reading it furiously, pointedly ignoring the angry bear behind me in the corner.

"What does it say then?"

I rolled up my eyes to see him pulling up a chair and sitting on it backwards, leaning his arms across the top.

"You don't have to do this." I flapped my hand at the book weakly.

He leaned his head forwards in one fluid motion that betrayed something of the energy contained.

"I *shouldn't* be doing this," he muttered, running his fingers through his mop of hair, a sure sign he felt awkward.

"Then don't. I said, it's fine."

"It's not fine. You look like the girl at the party nobody asked to dance, reading a book in the corner and trying to pretend she doesn't care." He squinted at me, the storm clouds in his irises dissipating. "You weren't that girl, were you?"

"I didn't go to many parties."

"Well, I went to a few. And I could never leave her sitting there. Even if I did get grief for it later."

"Grief? From who?" I asked.

"From my mates, who couldn't believe I always asked the least popular girl to dance. From the girls, one of whom developed a terrifying obsession about me. From Jennifer Jones, who I actually wanted to dance with for about three years." He shook his head, sorrowfully. "She wouldn't look at me because I chose another girl over her."

"So you were always this noble, even in your wilder days? Rescuing the damsels in distress?"

"I was. I can't help myself. Ask me the first question."

Rattled by his presence, I gabbled out the question without

thinking. "What are the three things you love most about your partner?" A rush of prickly heat engulfed my neck and chest.

Dylan didn't pause. "You're incredibly brave. And make a mean turkey pie at a moment's notice. You're the kind of inside and out beautiful that makes men want to forget everything that matters and go on some crazy quest to conquer the world, just to lay it at your feet."

Oh my. I gaped at him. Utterly undone.

He smiled and shrugged, resting his chin on folded arms, still on the back of the chair. For a moment I had a sudden fantasy this might be real – that I was here on the marriage course with Dylan, preparing to spend the rest of my life with him – kind and gallant, and who rescued lonely, unloved girls who didn't feel beautiful.

"Your turn."

I tried to get the cogs in my brain turning again. "The three things I love most about you?"

He raised one eyebrow at me and said nothing, but I caught the faint flush of pink rise up his cheeks.

"Perry! Of course, Perry. The things I love about Perry. My fiancé. I knew that. I'm a little bit flustered. You were answering as Perry. I knew that. Obviously. Perry. Right. What was the question again?"

Rescued lonely girls, even though he didn't really want to dance with them. Get a grip, Faith.

"That's it! What do I love most about Perry? Well. I love that Perry, um, likes to take care of me…"

Dylan narrowed his eyes. He was right. I didn't especially like being taken care of.

"And he makes me laugh. And, well, if I'm honest I don't know what I'd do without him. Does that count?"

"I wouldn't know." Dylan stood up so fast he had to grab the chair to stop it tipping over. He shook his head, lowering his voice so I could barely catch it. "You were right. This was a stupid idea."

He strode over to Gavin and Zoe, smiling at them and saying something too quiet for me to hear. After nodding at the clock on the wall, Zoe clapped her hands to regain our attention and we moved on.

After a brief talk from Dylan, and a short "Q and A" session, Dylan made a hasty exit, and Zoe and Gavin closed the marriage course by giving out gifts to each of the couples, and me, then praying for us. Their prayer for me included requests regarding Perry's work–life balance, valuing our commitments to one another, and making wise decisions. Gavin then asked God to make sure Perry turned up on time for the wedding. Everybody laughed, so I guess he meant it as a joke, but I'd never heard anyone make a joke prayer before. I couldn't wait to get out of there. Those prayers about lifelong commitments, giving ourselves to each other, being *devoted* and *loving each other more and more every year*, and becoming *as one*. Really? I mean, *really*? I didn't know a single couple like that. Except for Zoe and Gavin, who were now gazing at each other as they reminisced about their forty-odd years *as one*.

Class dismissed, the others giggled and smooched their way into the night, while I stayed behind and helped stack chairs and wash mugs. Relieved the mortification was over, I still felt sort of sorry to leave. I liked Zoe and Gavin. I liked coming to Grace Chapel's easy peace the first Tuesday of every month. I liked it when they prayed for me and the easy peace nestled round my shoulders and came home with me for a while.

I did not like waiting half an hour after the class had finished for Perry to pick me up.

Not wanting to seem like a nag, or as if I suspected I'd been forgotten by my husband to be, definitely not wanting to be the first to call after Perry had hung up on me, I loitered for another fifteen minutes until Zoe and Gavin were packed up, coats on and ready to leave.

"Have you rung him, checked he's on his way?" Zoe asked.

"It's fine, he'll be here in a few minutes. You go. I'll wait in the car park."

"You can't do that! It's bucketing down. We'd give you a lift, but we don't have a car. And then when Perry comes to get you, he'll think you've run off with someone else! Or been abducted!"

Zoe and Gavin laughed *as one*.

"It's okay. I don't mind the rain."

"Well, at least let me get you an umbrella; there's a spare one in the kitchen."

As she went to fetch it, the office phone rang.

"I'd better get that. Maybe it's Perry." Gavin went into the office and spoke briefly to whoever it was, coming out again just as Zoe returned, brandishing a purple Peppa Pig umbrella. "Here we go."

She handed it to me, taking the opportunity to give me a hug at the same time. "God bless you, Faith. And that man of yours. It's been lovely getting to know you. Just leave the brolly propped up by the door when you're done." Pulling back, she took Gavin's hand as they walked me out. "All right, Gavin? Why were you sneaking about in the office?"

"The phone rang."

He opened the door to let me and Zoe out, as we braced ourselves against the wet wind attempting to blow us back in again.

"Who's calling at this time?"

"Nothing important." They began to hurry down the steps, while I stayed huddled beneath the overhang of the roof. "Just that bloke again, asking about a redhead called Rachel."

"Well, I think the only redhead who comes here is Faith."

"I told him that."

"Right. Bye Faith!"

They disappeared into the stormy night, just about the same time the world shattered inside my skull.

Chapter Twenty-one

$\mathscr{I}$ stood frozen, a deer in headlights, panic running through my veins like a stampeding herd of buffalo. When I finally managed to steady my hands enough to phone Perry, it rang straight through to voicemail. I didn't leave a message.

"Okay. No need to panic. He's not phoning the chapel if he's hiding round the corner, is he? Lurking behind that bin over there, or in the shadow of that massive, creepy tree. Argh! Stop scaring yourself and think of a plan to get home. Or at least out of the rain until Perry turns up."

I ran through my options. Out loud. It helped drown out the sound of my terror.

"One. Phone Perry. No, tried that. Two. Phone a taxi. Only there aren't any taxis for miles. And I haven't got any money. Three. Phone a friend. Ooh yes. I have some friends now. How about Marilyn? No. The twins'll be asleep and Polly's gone to stay with her parents. Who else?"

I thought about the other choir members, but the few I knew best had no transport, or had to get up early in the morning, or, let's face it, weren't the level of friend I could call up at eleven o'clock at night to pick me up, ferry me six miles through a storm, and then drive home again. Even if I did have any of their numbers, which I didn't.

Yes, there was option four. Someone who happened to live in the manse right behind the church where he worked.

But I couldn't.

Not after the weirdness of the evening, pretending to be on a marriage course together, with the new, growly, pirate Dylan, and the *you're so beautiful I would die for you* thing. The way that thing made my newfound resolve melt, along with my insides, I could not turn up on his doorstep, sopping wet, and beg for his help once again because Perry had let me down.

I would rather fight off Kane with the Peppa Pig umbrella.

Come on, Peppa, we're tough stuff. We can do it!

I huddled against the door, wishing, hoping, *praying* Perry had not forgotten me. The longer I waited, the worse it would be if I did knock on Dylan's door. What if he had gone to bed?

Enough! I'm walking home. So I get a little wet? What's the worst that could happen?

My rational self gave my ridiculous, mixed-up, more-scared-of-knocking-on-Dylan's-door-than-a-murderer-on-the-prowl self a mental slap around the chops. *It's dark, and raining, and the footpaths will be a bog. Remember the camping hike. You could* actually die *if you try to walk home. Kane won't need to come and find you. Your own stupid pride will do the job for him.*

I stopped for a minute at the bottom of the steps, an enormous puddle lapping at my ankle boots, and wrestled with common sense.

What if I catch the flu again?

Furious at Perry, the storm, Dylan, marriage classes, my ugly past and confusing future, and of course mostly myself, I kicked a nearby lemonade can against the metal gate securing the far side of the chapel from the car park. Once wasn't enough, so I kicked it a few more times. Then I used a tissue from my bag to pick it up and deposit it in the recycling bin.

Ducking my head into the rain, wielding Peppa Pig in one hand, and using the pathetic glow from my cheapo phone as a torch in the other, I began making my way along the side of the building, in the direction of home. I crept towards the end of the wall. Heart hammering. Eyes straining. Feet squelching.

Suddenly, someone burst around the corner and, with no time to alter course, slammed into my chest, pitching me stumbling backwards.

I landed with an *oomph* in a stream of gravelly water, the umbrella and phone clattering to the ground as I instinctively reached back to protect my fall. All light now extinguished, I sensed as much as saw the person who'd knocked me over looming over me. Scrabbling for the umbrella, I sucked in as much air as my petrified lungs could muster and screamed.

Whew. I could *scream*. Somewhere behind the paralysing, hysterical fear, I impressed myself. And as the long seconds – one drawn-out, endless, Munch-type scream – passed, and my brain began to slowly unscramble, I knew that if what loomed over me was indeed the monster of my nightmares, the best thing to do in this village chapel car park was to make as much noise as possible.

If nobody came to my aid, they'd at least come to complain.

And if I thwacked the monster a couple of times in the face with the umbrella, so much the better.

Or so much the worse, as the man – and it was a man judging by the size and the shape of his shadow – grabbed the umbrella and wrenched it off me, tossing it aside before trying to take hold of both my arms as I lay there on the wet ground. I fought with him. Fought for my life. Fought like I should have fought Snake, the memories crashing over me. Eventually, he gave up trying to wrestle my arms, and pressed one hand firmly over my mouth. While I tried to prise it off enough to bite down, he yelled into the vacuum created where my scream had been.

"Faith! It's Dylan."

It took a few more seconds for my neurons to process those words. Dylan.

Oh.

Ah.

Whoops.

"Are you going to let me help you up?"

I nodded. He pulled me to my feet, the rain running off his brow as he peered through the darkness.

"I thought you were kids causing trouble. I really didn't mean to crash into you. Are you hurt?"

As soon as he let go, I fell against the wall, my bones like water, and began to slide back down to the ground.

"Ah, no. Don't do that." He swept me up against his chest, and when my legs refused to steady, he scooped me up and carried me. I must have weighed twice as much as usual due to the gallons of water in my clothes. Burying my head into his shoulder I clung on as he jogged across a stretch of grass before dumping me onto a welcome mat and unlocking a bright red wooden door into a cottage.

"Faith? Come in out of the rain."

"Urhh. Right." More than a little disconcerted, I staggered through the door into Dylan's man cave.

"Are you okay to wait here for a couple of seconds?" I nodded as he disappeared into the main house, leaving me stood in the tiny entrance hall dripping rain onto the wooden floor. The stairs were to my right, steps piled high with books, papers, a jar of nails, a hammer, a sports bag, and various other clutter. Judging by the slamming and rattling sounds, I guessed Dylan was trying to make the place presentable. Given some of the places I had lived in during my younger, scarier days, I really wasn't bothered about the mess. I was however in need of a moment to compose myself following the sweeping off my feet thing, let alone what had led up to it.

And after our previous argument, now I had ended up here, alone with Dylan in his house, the storm raging all around us.

* * *

I was wearing Dylan's clothes! His *clothes!*

A pair of bunched-up tracksuit bottoms and a navy sweatshirt with a furry inside. They smelled of pine trees.

CHAPTER TWENTY-ONE

Oh dear. I had been doing so well.

He handed me a mug of steaming hot chocolate. I took a tentative sip, pretending that the warmth oozing through my insides was purely down to the drink. We sat down on opposite sides of his breakfast bar.

While my clothes dried, I recounted what had happened.

"I can't think of anyone asking about you, or about someone with red hair. I would have remembered that because of the guy at HCC."

"He wasn't asking for Faith."

"No? Who was he asking for?"

I took a deep breath. Remembering that little girl, the person I used to be, her hopes and fears, her confusion, and the terrible things she grew to understand. Remembering how it sounded on her lips, what it meant – the name my mother gave me. The name I used to call myself. The name Kane knew me by.

Pressing my hands against my eyes, I offered the most precious part of my past to this man who made me feel so treacherously safe. Opened myself up to him in a way we both knew crossed a line.

"My name was Rachel."

Dylan went very, very still. He got up and carefully placed his mug in the empty sink, then stood staring out of the window into the pounding rain.

"You've spoken to him." My voice trembled.

He sighed, gripped on to the edge of the work surface for a minute before turning back around. "Yes."

"And?"

He grimaced. "He came to church the other week, when you were ill, and asked around for Rachel then. Said he used to live in the area, a long time ago, and was trying to catch up with his wife's family. His wife attended the chapel, and he'd heard her daughter – his stepdaughter – was still around. He didn't mention hair, or I might have made the connection."

"She wasn't his wife." As if that mattered. The room went black.

I couldn't hear past the clanging in my ears, but felt Dylan's hands pushing my head down between my knees, his firm arm gripping my shoulders as he urged me to breathe.

I managed not to faint, but it took a lot longer for the panic in my chest to subside.

"He's here. He's been here. He's looking for me. He phoned tonight. I have to go. *I have to go!*"

"You can't go home like this."

"I can't stay here." I tried to get my breathing under control.

"Call Perry. You can stay at his tonight. Wasn't he supposed to be picking you up anyway?"

I nodded. "My phone's in the rain. It fell when you ran into me."

"Here." He handed me his.

The phone rang for a long time before Perry picked up. I could hear the sound of heavy music in the background and people talking.

"Where are you? Why didn't you come and pick me up?"

"What? Faith?"

"Yes it's Faith!" Fear made me snap. "Who else would it be?"

"Faith! Lovely Faith. Didn't you get my message? I can't come and pick you up. Eddie stole my keys, the thieving scoundrel."

With a flash of awareness, I realized he was drunk.

Great timing, Perry.

I clenched my jaw so tight I'm surprised my skull didn't crack.

"How am I going to get home?"

"I don't know. Maybe your little vicar man will drive you in his Popemobile. Or you could walk. You like walking. Walking up and down everywhere, walk walk walk."

"I thought you were working." I didn't bother hiding my growing anger.

"I was. We finished. Decided to celebrate. Come on, Faith; don't be that woman."

"What woman?" A woman terrified at the effect of toxic substances on the people she cares about?

"Nags. Nags who expect me to come and get them. And don't even invite me in afterwards. I bought you a car, didn't I? Learn to drive."

I hung up, smarting.

Dylan said nothing.

"He's just finished the business deal he's been working on for the past month. They're out celebrating."

He furrowed his brow.

"He's in no fit state to drive. Or listen to my problems."

"You haven't told him."

I closed my eyes. "I'm going to. I planned to. But then this deal came up, and I've barely seen him. And when I have it's been with his parents there, planning wedding stuff, or for a quick lunch. Hardly the right time to tell him, by the way, my mum got murdered by her pimp boyfriend, I got fostered by my grandma, who then died, leaving me in the care of my brother – who incidentally, I never mentioned, happens to be an addict as well as mentally ill. Oh yes, and his dealer also came to join our family. That's how I happened to get the scars you haven't seen because I freeze every time you touch me thanks to my history of abuse. Then, over coffee I could mention my time on the streets, working in the strip club, and how the man who started all this is now on the loose and hunting me down in order to, I don't know, kill me and Sam. Hardly the usual topic of conversation for the HCC lunchtime crowd."

"I'm so sorry." Dylan quieted my flapping hands by placing his hand back on my shoulder, standing beside me where I perched on the stool. I resisted the urge to collapse into him and bury my head in his chest. His careful distance enabled me to see how that would make me simply another one of those women: the clichéd woman in distress let down by her idiot fiancé, throwing herself at the handsome, morally unavailable rescuer.

But the truth was, I wanted to feel the security of Dylan's hand on my shoulder all night, and for every night until Kane was back behind bars. And for every night after that.

Dylan, however, was made of stronger stuff. He pulled away, putting enough distance between us to allow my head to start working again.

"Right. I'll fetch your phone and then drive you home. I can watch TV on your couch until morning."

I took a deep breath. "Is that a good idea? I don't think the other church leaders would approve."

"Right now, I'm more concerned with keeping you safe than what anyone else thinks."

"I'm not having you get into trouble because I've had a shock. I've survived a lot of nights knowing Kane was looking for me. He isn't going to turn up at my door tonight." I managed a wobbly smile. "Everything you said at the campsite is still true, Dylan. Perry was out of order, but it's the first time he's ever spoken to me like that. If you would be kind enough to drive me home, I'm going to try to get some sleep, then call my Family Liaison Officer first thing tomorrow. And then I'll tell Perry everything."

He nodded. "Okay. I'm sorry."

"Don't be sorry. I'm glad you've got my back."

"If anything happens, the slightest thing, promise you'll call the police first, then me?"

We drove home in silence, as I wondered what the evening's events would mean for our friendship. I let Dylan check the tiny back garden and the inside of the house.

"What is it?" I asked before he left.

He had paused by the front door, and I could see him debating whether to say something.

He shook his head. "It's not really the right time."

"It's not really the right time to leave me wondering, either."

It had been a weird night. One where boundaries had shifted and consequences taken a "time-out".

Stepping onto the path, he squinted through the rain, glowing orange in the street light. "You freeze when he touches you? That's not good, Faith. Maybe you ought to talk to Zoe about it, or something."

"Excuse me?" I scrabbled for an answer, trying to remember what I'd said when my brain was still in panic mode. "I said… no, um, I said I freeze when a man touches me. Not Perry. Well. Not just Perry. Man. Men. I'm working on it. We're working on it. It's fine."

He nodded, a faint frown creasing his brow. Then, walking to the end of the path, he turned and said, "But that's not true. You don't freeze when all men touch you."

No, but I did freeze then.

He watched me for a long second, the rain running down his face. "Take care of yourself, Faith." Opening the truck door, he climbed inside and drove into the storm.

I didn't sleep that night. For lots of reasons. All of them scary ones.

I called Gwynne as soon as I deemed it a respectable hour. She listened, as always, said little, but I could hear by her tone of voice that the game had shifted. She promised to get back to me as soon as she had any news.

I didn't bother calling Perry, instead walking round with the intention of serving him a strong coffee with bacon and eggs to soak up his hangover while I talked.

To my surprise, he was already up and looked about to head out.

"I thought you'd be taking the morning off," I said, stepping inside.

He had the decency to look sheepish. "Yeah. Things got a bit out of hand last night. I'm sorry I forgot about your thing. The guys have worked so hard I couldn't refuse their invitation to blow off some steam. It would have looked bad if the boss hadn't joined them for a couple of drinks."

"A couple?"

He took hold of my hand, and kissed it. "I'm sorry. It's a bit vague but I'm guessing I said something stupid, quite possibly crude, and almost certainly disrespectful. It's one of the reasons I don't get drunk very often."

I nodded my head to indicate my acceptance of his apology. "Can I talk to you?"

He glanced at his watch. "If you make it quick. The review meeting's in thirty."

"Ah. This won't be quick. Can I make you dinner instead?"

"No. Let me do it. You can fill me in on what I missed last night." *Or not…*

He kissed me goodbye, and left, leaving me standing on the doorstep with all that energy I'd worked up and nowhere to vent it. My instinct was to march it out along the fields, but there was no way I would go tramping through the countryside like a deer waiting to be picked off by a bullet.

I did, however, know another great way to use up excess energy only a six-minute walk away.

"Faith." Marilyn waved me inside. "Is it Thursday? I'm not fired up for Anton this morning. I thought today was yesterday."

"It is yesterday. Well, Wednesday. I'm not here to babysit. I just wondered if you fancied a coffee."

"Excellent! Polly's topping up the machine as we speak."

I settled on the floor and built towers for Nancy and Pete to knock down while we talked.

"Is it working out okay, then? The place still looks tidy since the big clear up."

"Polly is a godsend. I can't believe I ever managed without her." Marilyn nudged Polly, sat beside her.

"You didn't manage," I laughed. "This place was a disaster zone."

"I was a disaster zone, you mean," she said.

"You were a woman coping admirably in highly challenging circumstances."

"And you've helped me out way more than I helped you," Polly said. "Letting me stay has been the kindest thing anyone's ever done for me."

"So you're going to stay, then?" Marilyn asked.

"No." Polly picked a squirming Esme out of her bouncy chair. "I won't stay once James is back. You've had the best part of a year apart. I'm not going to be gooseberry for your three months together."

"You won't be a gooseberry. You can babysit while we go out on hot dates. I love having you here, Poll. Please stay."

"No. Your house is lovely. It's been a home when I needed one most. I love being part of your family. But one dream has kept me going these past few years. That I'll get a house, and paint the kitchen cabinets yellow. I'll sew green and white striped curtains and put up shelves for ornaments I've found in gift shops and car boot sales. I'll be able to walk around in my tatty old dressing gown eating ice-cream out the tub, leaving dirty mugs on the table, and watching MTV shows about teenage pregnancy and celebrity gossip."

"What? You can do all those things here. I'd love a yellow kitchen." Marilyn looked at her, eyes round with intent.

"I know that. But this is your house. And James might not appreciate it as much as you do."

"I understand," I said. Boy, did I understand. "You need to make yourself a haven, a nest. A place that's yours, where you can be Polly and feel beholden to no one."

She sighed, her eyes dreamy. "I never, ever thought that could be possible. It sounds like heaven."

"You could have my place."

Um, excuse me? What? Whose place? Did somebody just open their mouth and offer Polly their house?

Marilyn and Polly both gaped at me.

"What?" Polly's eyes widened. I could see the tiniest flicker of hope spark amongst the blue-grey flecks.

"I'm moving out in August. The landlady's lovely; she'll be pleased I've found someone to take over the lease. And she's fine about decorating, as long as you aren't too radical."

I told her what I paid in rent.

"I can manage that. Once my maternity leave is up I'm working three days a week. With tax credits and everything, I think I can afford that. It'll be perfect. Faith, I can't believe this! You're giving me your house?"

"You might want to look at it first. It is tiny. And the bathroom is an homage to the eighties." I cleared my throat. "You also might want to think about moving further away, depending on what happens with Tony."

"Maybe once he's out of prison. But right now I want to be near my friends, if I can. And my new family. My job is here. And I wouldn't miss the next round of the competition for anything."

We agreed she'd call in that afternoon to have a look round. I had something else I needed to do first. After a nervous ten minutes waiting for the bus to Brooksby, I scurried the quarter of a mile to Rowan's house.

She lived in one of the old coalminers' homes. A generous size for the average family. For the four generations who currently lived there, including Rowan's grandfather, her parents, three older sisters, Callie, and two huge dogs, it felt distinctly overcrowded.

"Come into the back." She led me through a front room, furnished with a sofa bed, a chipped white chest of drawers, and a giant television, into a decent-sized kitchen. "Right. We've got just under an hour before Mum brings Callie back from nursery, and Grandad'll want his lunch. What are we doing?"

I took a deep breath, and told Rowan what I wanted doing. She stuck one hand on her jutting hip and wagged her chin at me.

"Are you nuts? No offence, but that idea is rank. You'd look so bad. They probably wouldn't let me start my training if college got wind of it."

"Nobody will know it was you."

She shook her head. "Nah. Can't do it. Why on earth would you want to anyway? You're getting married in a couple of months. You'd look like a troll on your wedding day."

"You're probably right. But I'm looking for a complete change. What would you suggest?"

"I'd suggest keeping your amazing hair and buying a new top."

"I need to change my hair. Please. I know you can think of something that will look bearable."

Rowan studied me for a few moments, her gaze assessing more than simply my hairstyle.

"Okay. We'd best get started."

Chapter Twenty-two

When I opened my front door to Polly that afternoon, she looked at me in confusion until I said hello.

"Faith! I thought it must be your sister or something. You look like a different person."

Excellent. Mission accomplished.

"Oh, you know. I fancied a change. One of those flippant moments when you do something crazy. I figured it's hair. It'll grow back. Better than getting an impulse tattoo and being stuck with it."

We smiled and rolled our eyes. Leona had returned from a girls' weekend in Blackpool with a five-inch portrait of Benedict Cumberbatch on her upper chest. Her husband was not happy at confronting a scowling Sherlock every time he got near her.

"Well. It looks great. Kind of surreal. But it's nice. You seem... not older exactly, but more sophisticated. Perry will love it."

I showed Polly round, pointing out the foibles that never fail to accompany an old house. She nodded and smiled, and asked questions about what I would take with me to Perry's, and what would stay, her brain whirring with plans and ideas.

I called the landlady to seal the deal, and after a breathless hug of thanks she rushed back to Esme, who would be getting ready for a feed.

I ignored the feeling of dread in my guts at the prospect of giving up my house. My safe place. My independence. Perry's house had a fancy lock system, burglar alarm, security lights, and Perry. Time to let go of the "needing my own house" issue. Even if I did have to prise it off with a crowbar.

I changed into one of the designer dresses Perry had bought me, attempted to cover up the haunted look on my face with dabs of make-up, slipped on a pair of obscenely expensive shoes, and braced myself to look in the mirror.

Yikes.

I closed my eyes, took a few fortifying breaths – out with the stress, in with the calm, Hester style – and took another peek.

It was only a haircut. But Polly was right. My hair had been such a defining part of me, without it I felt more vulnerable, not less. Like a turtle without its shell. I probably weighed a lot less, too. Instead of my usual mane a razor-sharp chocolate bob swung an inch above my jawline. It brought out the green in my eyes, contrasting dramatically with my creamy complexion.

"Come on, Faith. You can pull this off."

I straightened my spine and pulled my shoulders back. Tipped my chin up a couple of millimetres. Remembered the timid little girl with her cloud of red curls, cowering as she tried to make herself invisible. The reflection in the mirror scowled. This woman had poise. She looked striking. Anything but invisible. This woman commanded a second look.

A perfect disguise.

I marched round to Perry's in my high heels, swishing my hair and tossing cool glances at the young men lingering outside the shop who whistled through their teeth at me. I did need to duck behind a tree a couple of times to tug my dress back down, as the silky material kept riding up. I also skidded on a patch of slippery wet pavement, tumbling into a wall and laddering my tights. The wind played havoc with my hair, too short to tuck safely behind my ears, and the tiny handbag I'd brought instead of my rucksack kept sliding off my shoulder, so I had to hitch it back up every few steps. I had a way to go in perfecting my new persona, but nevertheless I could stride through the streets with some confidence, sure Kane would see nothing of Rachel if he happened to see this new Faith.

* * *

Perry looked surprised when he saw me, but quickly regained composure. Encouraging, as it was nothing compared to the shock he would feel once I started talking. He beckoned me into the living room, giving me a chance to steel my nerves while he fetched me a drink.

He handed it to me with a kiss. "You look gorgeous. I'll miss those curls, but it's kind of sexy having you look so different. Like a whole new you."

"I hope there wasn't too much wrong with the old me."

"There could be nothing wrong with any version of you. Red hair, brown hair, scruffy jeans, or a ballgown. That's just the wrapping. It's the you underneath I love."

I took a deep breath. "What if the person underneath isn't what you think?"

He tugged on a strand of my hair. "Half the time I don't know what I think. You are a mystery to me, Faith. An enigma. It's part of your appeal: the challenge to find out what lies beneath. Discover what makes you tick."

If this was true, he'd done a brilliant job of hiding it.

"I said this morning I need to talk to you, and part of that might help explain. I want to tell you about my family."

"Great. You can tell everyone. I'm sure they'll be dying to know. And don't worry, nobody's expecting to hear you're actually twenty-fourth in line to the throne, or have an ancestral home hidden away somewhere. It doesn't matter how humble your beginnings, we Uppertons are a welcoming lot."

"What?"

"No, really. One of Mother's grandparents worked as a housemaid, and nobody thinks any the less of her."

"Perry, slow down a minute, please. This isn't about my social status."

The doorbell rang. Perry stood up. "That'll be them. Fantastic. You can regale us over dinner."

A minute later he ushered "them" in. Larissa and Milton, of course. Aunt Eleanor to make things even better.

"My goodness." Larissa pecked the air to the side of my face. "You look almost like one of us." She scrutinized my head. "Not a bad job either. Is this the girl you've booked for the wedding?"

"Yes."

"Hmph. Milton, will you remind me to let the stylist know we don't need him for Faith? It'll give him more time for the others." She turned back to me. "Is she doing the bridesmaids?"

"Yes. You knew this. We talked about it ages ago."

"Well, seeing is believing and all that. She might not have been quite *Nottinghamshire Life* standard."

No point, Faith. Say nothing. Keep blowin' it out.

Perry, ever the perfect host, made more drinks and settled everyone down before throwing me to the wolves.

"Faith was just going to tell me some more about her family. Isn't that marvellous?"

I choked on my orange juice.

Aunt Eleanor raised one eyebrow. "Well. That would depend on what she tells us."

I tucked a strand of my new bob behind my ear. Looked at these people I would soon be a part of. I felt tired and scared and utterly fed up with these ridiculous games. There were parts of my past I would never share as they belonged right there, in the past. But I already fell below Upperton standards. That was their problem, not mine.

"I didn't used to be called Faith Harp. My name was Rachel."

And I told them – the short version – of how my mother had lived, how she died, and why I changed my name.

Talk about awkward. Larissa and Aunt Eleanor stared at each

other across the table, sending silent posh messages regarding what they thought about *that* revelation.

Milton folded and unfolded his napkin a few times. He muttered, "Change of name. That explains why Google drew a blank."

But Perry, he looked straight at me. He took hold of my hand. Cleared his throat.

"I wish you'd told me."

I shrugged, glancing at his family. "I think you can understand why I didn't."

"So." Larissa took a large swig of wine. "You lived in Chester. Did you ever go to the racecourse?"

"No."

Perry sighed. "Of course she didn't, Mother. She left age six."

"No." She pulled a tight smile. "I suppose even if you had you wouldn't remember."

"I never went."

"We were last there… remind me, Milton. Seven years ago? No. It must have been eight, as Hugh hadn't graduated yet."

"No, Larissa." Eleanor shook her head. "It couldn't have been more than six. It was before my operation."

My phone rang. I looked at the screen. Sam. Calling from his own phone, not the hospital line.

"Excuse me." I stood up, interrupting the discussion about which horse had won what race. "I need to take this."

Perry frowned at me. "Sam?"

I nodded, hurrying out of the room. Moving into the kitchen, I answered the call. "Sam?"

"Hi. Yes, it's me!"

"What's going on?"

"I'm home."

"*What?*" I sat down, hard, on one of the chairs.

"I know! I can't believe it. But I'm doing really well. Feeling great." He sounded it, too.

"How did you get home? Why didn't you call me?"

"April came. I wanted it to be a surprise."

I rested my head in my hands, tried to keep my voice positive. "Well, you managed it. I'm surprised."

* * *

I left Perry's as soon as I could without seeming rude. I knew the story about my family remained half told. If anything, I'd left the most important bits out. But trying to keep up the pretence of happiness at Sam's return exhausted me. A hurricane raged through my aching brain. All I could do was hope and pray the police found Kane before he found us.

I spent the following week on red alert, scurrying round to visit Sam, quaking my way through a few work shifts, and overseeing the final preparations for the weekend's Grand Grace Gala. I didn't tell Sam that Kane had been to the chapel to look for me. Or that he'd phoned the office there. I didn't tell him that when I left choir practice, a bashed-up green car parked across the street pulled out behind Marilyn and me, keeping right behind us until we lost it at a level crossing.

I marvelled at his latest painting, listened to his future plans, politely declined his invitations to go walking with him and April, and kept on hoping, praying, begging that somehow this would all end without destroying us both.

I pestered Gwynne almost daily. Kane had been at work all week, she reassured me. It would have been nearly impossible for him to have been in Nottinghamshire on Wednesday afternoon to follow me home.

"What about Saturday?" I asked. "Does he work weekends?"

"Lock your doors, keep your phone charged, don't do anything stupid, and try not to worry. We're keeping an eye on him."

I spent Saturday at HCC, supervising the layout of the ballroom, hanging up fairy lights, decorating tables with tiny black musical notes, and filling glass centrepieces with flowers wrapped in cones of sheet music, only pausing for one last brutal rehearsal with Hester.

The tight coil of tension in my guts never quite left, but the Grand Grace Gala, those lively, hilarious, excited choir members, and a whole day doing what I did best went some way towards providing a distraction.

At seven, the first guests began to arrive. All spruced up in our choir dresses, we welcomed them in, trying not to feel too daunted by the flash of diamonds, the glint of gold watches, and the swish of dresses that cost more than we were trying to raise for the whole trip. Perry and Marilyn had come up trumps in working their HCC connections. Each choir member had been allowed to bring one guest at a discount price, while the other eighty tickets had been sold for a preposterous amount. We had better make it worth their while.

Thirty minutes in, Mags took the microphone to welcome everybody and invite us to take our seats.

"Who's your guest, Marilyn?" Leona asked, as we all sat down.

"I haven't got one." Marilyn shrugged. "My sister's babysitting. I wanted to ask Anton so he could sit next to Polly but she wouldn't let me. And most of the other people I know have paid full price to come here."

"Poor you," said Kim, half sitting in Scotty's lap. "It's rubbish James couldn't be here."

Marilyn shrugged. "He'll be back in a week. I'm expecting Faith to dance with me instead, seeing as Perry is over persuading the rich boys to get their wallets out. I'm more interested in Hester. Did anyone manage to find out who her plus one is?"

We all looked at Hester, still deep in conversation with the Mayoress on the other side of the room. There had been much speculation about Hester's guest. Rowan had even tried to start a sweepstake before someone pointed out that might not be an appropriate way for a church choir to treat its director.

Suddenly Rowan, sat with her grandad, gasped. She looked around at us, eyes glittering and mouth hanging open. "Get. A load. Of this, girls. I can take credit for the hair. But the rest? Like, wow."

We swivelled our heads around to see.

Kim let out a long whistle. "Check him out!" She pulled a wide grin before suddenly remembering Scotty. "Not that I'd want to, of course." She leaned in and nuzzled his neck. "You know I've only got eyes for you, babe."

"That is one fine figure of a man," Melody murmured to her sister.

Millie started flapping her hands in front of her face. "Whewie, Janice. If I was ten years younger…"

"Try forty years," her son said, turning crimson.

He wasn't the only one feeling disconcerted. Dylan, who had waited to escort Hester to our table, sauntered up, breaking into a grin as he approached.

Like every woman on the planet, I think all men scrub up well in a tux.

Some men have a lot more scrubbing up to do than others. For example, those who usually wear faded T-shirts and paint-splattered jeans, forget to shave, and walk about in work boots with sawdust in their unkempt mop of hair.

It was universally accepted that Dylan was a hunk.

With his hair cropped, clean shaven, and a slick suit on?

Well – hooten tooten as Marilyn would say.

Which she did, several times, as she kicked me under the table.

Oh no. He was coming to sit next to me. *Pull yourself together, Faith! Lungs, stomach, hormones – control yourselves!*

"How are you, ladies? Having a good time so far?" Dylan pulled out Hester's chair for her, then sat down. "You've done an amazing job. The place looks incredible."

He looked round the table with a smile, then turned in my direction. "Hi, I'm –"

He stopped, his turn to stare. "*Faith?* Wow. Your hair. I didn't even realize it was you."

CHAPTER TWENTY-TWO

I pulled a face. "Well, that was sort of the plan."

He studied me for another minute before nodding. "How are you doing?"

"Okay. Perry's taking care of me. I'm fine." I couldn't look at him.

"Right."

Throughout the whole of the meal I concentrated on making conversation with Marilyn, on my other side, and the rest of the table. Dylan, too, made no attempt to speak directly to me again. And yet. All I could think about was him. His arm, only a few inches away from mine. His beautiful face, that I carefully positioned just outside my field of vision. Sometimes when he moved his hand to accompany an anecdote I caught his scent, the usual pine and leather overlaid with a hint of aftershave.

I wondered if this was still the teenage crush I had never had. One last (and first) hurrah before I committed to a lifetime of comfortable, steady, safe.

Or was it more? Was this what falling in love felt like? Had these past few months of choir, and letting go and breathing out, of gradually, like a flower bud, opening up to this new life of friendship and fun and acceptance, had it produced the unexpected – and totally unwanted – side effect of repairing my heart to the point where it could fall in love?

And if so, why had I gone and fallen for the wrong person?

And if he was the wrong person, why was being near him the only time everything seemed right?

And what on earth was I going to do about it?

April and Sam arrived moments before we were due to sing. Not yet up to a whole big night out, Sam wanted to hear the choir. He planned to stay for half an hour or so, then catch a taxi back with April.

We took our places on the stage at the front of the room. Hester checked our posture, pointing to her face to remind us to smile and giving us a discreet thumbs up before turning to address the crowd.

"Ladies and gentlemen. May I please express my thanks on behalf of the Grace Choir at your being here tonight. I started the choir eighteen months ago with one purpose in mind. To bring together a group of ordinary women and, by teaching them how to create something beautiful and magnificent, I would show them that they, in fact, were beautiful and magnificent.

"Ladies and gentlemen, as our lovely soloist Rowan would say – epic fail!"

She paused, scanning the room. "Not one woman who came to join our group was ordinary. I am ashamed for thinking otherwise. And they have taught me far more than I could ever teach them. I am proud –" Hester paused to clear her throat. Almost as if she held back tears!

"I am so very proud to introduce the bravest, strongest, kindest, and quite possibly strangest bunch of *extraordinary* women I have had the pleasure to know. Put your hands together for the Grace Choir!"

At that point, as the ladies and gentlemen put their hands together, Marilyn, standing at the end of the back row, suddenly ran to the front of the stage, elbowing Hester out of the way, and launched herself off the edge.

Sailing through the air, she landed with a skid on the wooden dance floor, before sprinting across the room and into the arms of James.

James caught her, spinning her around a few times before placing her back on the ground, holding her at arm's length while he took her in.

"Excuse me," he said, looking round at the crowd with mock horror. "I seem to have made a terrible mistake. For a moment there I thought this woman was my wife. It's been a few months since I've seen her. Please don't take offence."

"I'll take *this*," Marilyn said, wrapping her arms around his neck and giving him an enormous kiss that went on so long a couple of people wolf-whistled.

They broke off and stood there, foreheads pressed together. I couldn't catch what James said to his wife as she glowed with health and happiness, but his grin, his tears, his hands firmly planted on her backside said it all.

Hester coughed into the microphone. "Shall we continue?"

James stood back, to let Marilyn rejoin us on stage.

She shook her head. "It's fine. They can manage without me."

"No," James frowned. "You have to get up there. I want to hear you sing."

"Trust me," Marilyn smiled. "You don't."

James looked at Hester for back-up.

"Trust your wife, James. She knows what she's talking about."

So the Grace Choir sang without their top lip-syncher, and, no offence to Marilyn, we sounded our best yet. Nearly everyone stood to their feet by the end. We bowed, graciously, and took a much-needed break to catch our breath, quench our thirst, and steel ourselves for the next part of the evening – the auction.

Did we really have anything these people who had everything would want to pay good money for?

Had they loosened up enough to bid high anyway?

Aha. We had forgotten one thing.

Those good old fashioned posh-people traits of one-upmanship, competitiveness, and mob mentality.

Yes, at times the bidding became so frenzied, we indeed seemed to be on the verge of a mob.

Guided – and goaded – by Hester's forthright use of the auctioneer's gavel, the bids began to rise. Somebody paid over three hundred pounds for a hair styling session with Rowan. After seeing the before and after photos, two members of HCC paid a monstrous amount for Marilyn to give their wives a workout training session. From the looks of them, as they slapped each other on the back, red-nosed and sweaty-faced, they could have done with the training themselves.

Throw in a singing lesson from Hester, a custom-made outfit

from Rosa, a technology masterclass from Uzma, and a set of children's bobble hats, hand-knitted by Millie, and we were well on our way to reaching our target.

Eek. My turn next. Whatever the lot sold for had to cover the cost of the four-course meal I would cater, so it needed to be a decent bid or someone (me) would be out of pocket.

Hester did another grand introduction, nudging beyond embellishment, past exaggeration, and into plain fabrication a couple of times, but I guess it was all in a good cause. She finished off by mentioning my outstandingly awesome organizational skills, as demonstrated by planning the gala.

"Who'll give me one hundred pounds for a fully catered dinner party for six, to start us off?"

An HCC committee member at the back raised her hand.

"One hundred and twenty!" called out another one.

And we were off.

A couple of minutes later, someone upped the bid to two hundred and fifty pounds if I made it for eight people and threw in party favours.

"Anyone else?" Hester barked.

There was a brief silence.

"I'll give one thousand pounds if she organizes my daughter's eighteenth birthday party." Eddie, Perry's partner, waved so we could see him.

Hester looked at me, eyebrows raised. "Faith?"

I sidled up to the microphone. "Um, will that include the cost of the party?"

Eddie shook his head. "No. Expenses are extra. The grand is for you."

"Okay." I nodded at Hester and stepped back, trying to appear nonchalant.

"What do you say, then? Any more? Who can top that?"

Nobody would top that. Eddie was Perry's partner. Perry had probably offered to give him the money.

"One and a half if she can sort out my parents' wedding anniversary without bloodshed," a man on another table called out.

"My fiancé says he'll give two if she can plan my wedding without sending him bankrupt," a young woman in the corner joined in.

We were off again.

Hester had her gavel poised, on the second "going", about to say "gone", when a raspy voice called out, "Ten thousand."

Everybody sucked in a deep breath. I knew this because when I saw who spoke, staring at me while raising his hand in a salute, I couldn't find an ounce of oxygen left for me.

Without even bothering to ask what it was for, Hester slammed her gavel onto the wooden block. "Sold to the man at the back for ten thousand pounds!"

The crowd broke out into uproar.

I couldn't hear any of it. I felt as though I wore a space helmet.

Hester had sold me for ten thousand pounds to the man who murdered my mother, ruined my life, and nearly destroyed my brother.

My brother. I clutched my chest, willing it to start working again, frantically searching the crowd with my eyes as the applause went on.

Where was Sam?

Chapter Twenty-three

I left the stage as quickly as I could without appearing conspicuous. Hester began calling everyone's attention back for the final bid, and I took another moment to scan for Sam. Or Kane, who had vanished in the excitement.

Slipping along the outside of the room, I reached Perry's table.

"Perry. Have you seen Sam or April?"

He swivelled slightly in his seat to look at me. My heart sank at his drooping eyelids and sloppy smile. "No. I'm talking to Eddie and Jones about your legendary cooking skills."

"Right, well —"

"Say hello, Faith," he said, the words spilling out on a wave of alcohol fumes.

"Pardon?"

"Say hello to Eddie and Jones."

I gave them a tight smile. "Hi. Thanks for coming. But Perry, I really need to talk to you about Sam."

He groaned, shaking his head. "I'm talking to Eddie and Jones at the moment. Sam's better now. April's looking after him." He paused, slowing his speech down as though worn out. "Let it go, Faith, for one blessed night, can't you?"

"Please. I need to speak to you for two minutes." I put my hand on his arm, trying to suppress my panic.

"No!" He shook it off, clumsily. "Just for once let him take care of himself. He's back five minutes and straight away retaken the

311

number one spot in Faith's affections. What about me? What about my needs and affections? I'm not interested in talking about your nutjob brother tonight."

Eddie gripped Perry's arm. "Steady on, man." He looked at me in apology. "Ignore him. He's a horrible drunk. He'll feel wretched in the morning."

I nodded, unable to speak, and left them, the sounds of the auction buzzing in the background as I hurried round to my own table near the far end of the hall. My eyes still hunting, pointlessly, in every direction.

Dylan stepped out from an alcove as I moved past, taking hold of my arm.

"That was him." His smooth skin had turned white.

"I can't find Sam." My voice sounded hoarse.

"He left, about ten minutes ago."

"By himself?"

"I don't know."

I turned to the two tables taken up by choir members, but couldn't see April. The final bid had been sold, and the guests rose to their feet, applauding Hester as she thanked everybody for their generosity.

Dylan loosened his grip on my arm, sliding his hand down to squeeze my hand, briefly, before letting go. He led us through the crowd as he searched for April, pausing every now and then to ask somebody if they'd seen her, or the man who made the big bid.

By the time we reached the door, Marilyn had hustled round to join us.

"What's happening?" she asked. "Is it Sam?"

"Possibly," Dylan said, ushering us into the ballroom foyer. "Have you seen April?"

Marilyn looked at me. "When I nipped to the loo after your moment of glory she was talking with the guy who made the bid out here."

Sensing my legs crumple, Dylan braced me with his arm. "Did you see what happened next? Where either of them went?"

Marilyn's eyes were like saucers. She put one trembling hand up to her face. "They left out the front door. I thought she must know him. Who is he? What's happened? Is April messing about with that old bloke? They looked pretty grim, to be honest."

Gasping, I clutched at Dylan as if I was drowning. "Call the police."

He'd already dialled the first two nines by the time I hit the floor.

As soon as I knew police cars with lights flashing and sirens wailing were speeding to Sam's flat, I dragged myself up and stumbled outside, where the gusting downpour hit me like a slap.

Dylan came right behind me.

"Where's your truck?"

"In the other car park. But Faith, I've had three beers. I can't drive. Especially in this weather."

I whipped around, grabbed the lapels of his jacket. "How long is it going to take the police to get to Houghton? You could get me there in six minutes. Less, if you break the speed limit."

He shook his head, his eyes pleading with me. "No, Faith. What about Perry?"

"Perry's been drinking a lot more than you. I don't have time to explain to anyone else. Please, Dylan. I am begging you. Everyone else's come in taxis. Put your moral principles to one side for six minutes. Drive me to Sam's."

He closed his eyes for a second, before shaking his head briefly. Then, pulling away, reached into his pocket. I breathed a whoosh of relief.

"No. I'm sorry."

What?

"Here." He threw something at me. Automatically I reached up my hand and caught it. His keys.

"You drive."

"Do you want me to tell Perry what's happening?" Marilyn had managed to gather something of the situation from hearing Dylan's 999 call.

I paused for a tiny moment. Flashed back to the ballroom. "Right now, I really don't care."

I ran to the truck. Clambered in. Dylan grabbed the magnetic learner plates out of the glove compartment and stuck them in the windows.

"Take it slowly now. If you reverse back in a straight line you can turn around by the trees."

I looked at him, overwhelmed with panic. "I can't. I can't do this."

He smiled. "Yeah you can. Remember that turning by Little Farm? It's just like that. You could do it with your eyes closed."

I shook my head, my hands shaking so hard I could barely grip the steering wheel.

Dylan kept on talking, his voice calm and steady. "You can do this, Faith. You can do this for Sam. Take a deep breath, blow out the fear or whatever it is Hester taught you. Breathe in."

I let out a trembly breath, sucked in some courage, some strength, whatever the heck it was I needed to get this truck to my brother.

"Okay?" Dylan pulled on his seatbelt.

"Okay." I let out a weak laugh. "Do you mind if I sing? It kind of helps."

"As long as you don't mind if I pray. That definitely helps."

So, slowly at first, oh so carefully, I backed the truck out and swung it around. Picking up speed as we headed down the drive, I decided to ditch the singing and joined Dylan in praying instead.

When you think your brother's life is at stake, a two-mile drive through a rainstorm is nothing, however inexperienced a driver you are. What you do when you reach him is another thing altogether. When I came to a juddering stop outside Sam's flat, there were no police cars outside. The lights were on in the windows above our heads.

Dylan and I exchanged glances. I knew he wanted me to stay in the truck, or at the very least to stay behind him. He knew better than to tell me that. I did feel a moment's reassurance that there were worse people I could be sprinting up the shabby staircase with than a Northern ex-gang member with God on his side.

As we rounded the top of the stairwell we could hear it. Thuds, scuffles, a deep rasping voice dripping with menace. My brother's garbled cry. I burst in through the open door. Sam flailed against one wall, Kane's vengeful hands around his throat.

Screaming, I leaped towards him. Strong arms pushed me aside. Dylan threw me onto the sofa as he moved in front of me. He called out. Kane tightened his grip. Sam's face turned a hideous purple. His eyes bulged as his legs kicked and bucked against the wall. It must have been seconds – less than a second – before Dylan picked up a plant pot – a recent addition from April's garden centre job – and smashed it into the back of Kane's head. Kane dropped like a marionette with snapped strings. Sam slid to the floor behind him. I scrambled off the sofa and fell to his side.

That was how the police found us, a few minutes later.

Sam, choking and sobbing, cradled in my arms. Dylan with April, trying to assess the damage to her unconscious body, sprawled out by the fireplace.

Kane, motionless, a pool of blood as black as his heart creeping across the carpet. After all these years, all the phone calls, the middle of the night emergency visits, the job losses, the shopping, the cleaning, and the dropping everything to be there for Sam: after all this, I hadn't been there when he really needed me. I hadn't saved my brother.

My debt remained unpaid.

After a few hours and numerous tests, the doctors discharged Sam from hospital. Bruised, hoarse, battered, there was no physical damage time wouldn't heal. A nurse brought me to his bay to help gather his things together – a ripped shirt, a box of painkillers, the loose change from his pockets. I took his hand, leading him out towards the exit, but he stopped a few paces down the corridor.

"April?"

"She's been taken for a scan. They'll keep her in tonight, at least."

"I want to see her." He turned back towards the direction we had come.

"We can't see her now. The doctors are doing tests. We can come back first thing in the morning and see her then."

He looked at me, and my insides withered at the dead light in his eyes. "I can't leave her."

"You're no good to her hanging around here, Sam. The best thing you can do for April is go home, clean up, get some sleep, and visit her in the morning when she's woken up."

"I won't leave her alone."

Letting out a long sigh, I began tugging him in the direction of the waiting room.

"Look, Dylan's down the hall. He can stay with April until we get back. And they're trying to contact her mum, so she'll be here soon, too."

"She hates her mum. And she barely knows Dylan. He won't protect her from Kane. He doesn't get it."

"Doesn't get what? Kane is in another hospital under police guard. We don't need protecting from Kane any more."

Sam laughed, shaking his head. It sent chills through my bones.

We reached the waiting room, where Dylan sat in one corner, nursing a cup of brown sludge.

After another five minutes' weary discussion, revealing the wreckage of Sam's emotional state, we agreed a compromise. Dylan would take Sam back to his house. I would stay with April overnight, protecting her from both her mum and Kane.

Sam made me swear to watch April, to take care of her. He muttered something about how April would be better off without him, that he was the problem. I remembered those words from the day he had packed my bag for London. However, too exhausted to understand what they meant, now I hugged my brother and told him goodnight.

Why did I decide to trust someone else with my brother's welfare at his weakest, most vulnerable moment?

I may keep asking myself that question until the day I die.

* * *

The cavalry arrived at nine the next day. I un-crunched my aching muscles, tried to wipe the sleep from my eyes, and accepted the freshly ground coffee, steaming doughnut, and warm embrace from Mags, Melody, and Rowan with gratitude that brought fresh tears to my eyes.

I had forbidden Marilyn from coming to the hospital, vowing to ditch her as my matron of honour if she left her husband's side the day after his return.

I filled them in on the latest news, i.e. nothing. No one had managed to get hold of April's mum, which may have been for the best. April remained in a stable but critical condition, accompanied by long words and medical jargon my brain had no capacity to comprehend at that moment.

"Come on, darling," Melody clucked. "I'm taking you home."

"Can you drop me off at Dylan's instead? Sam's there."

"Of course. No problem."

Only there was a problem. Sam was not there.

After banging on the door for longer than my nerves could stand, a rumpled, dishevelled Dylan let us in.

"Sorry. I must have dozed off. We sat up most of the night, but Sam went to bed around five."

"You dozed off?" My heart started hammering. "You weren't watching him?"

"Only for an hour or so. He was sleeping. I checked on him first."

I pushed past him, through into the tiny living room. Whirling out again, I confronted Dylan in the kitchen.

"Where is he?"

"Upstairs, in the spare room. Calm down, Faith. It's okay."

"No." My voice was loud, angry. "It is not okay."

I raced up the stairs, banging all four doors open until I located what had to be the spare room.

My howl rattled the window frames. Dylan found me on my knees in the doorway. He said nothing, but I heard him searching the house, opening the front door, and no doubt doing the same in the garden, the car park, the side alleyway.

I remained on the floor, bent double as the numbness set in, creeping over my body like a cloud across the sun.

It was too late. Searching was pointless. Dylan had fallen asleep, and now my brother, my family, my heart, had gone.

* * *

The next week or so passed in a haze. I clung to the numbness for dear life. I answered questions, signed official statements, gave out information, went through the motions. Gwynne came to tell me how Kane had managed to keep travelling to Nottinghamshire undetected. Stolen cars, old contacts, forged ID. None of it mattered. None of it could change anything. None of it could penetrate the grey.

Perry moved in, bringing flowers and fruit and more films to watch, as if any of that could make things better. He even took a few days off work, before fetching his laptop and setting up an office in my kitchen. I kept my new phone switched on, at the authorities' request, in case Sam got in touch. It made no difference to me. I knew there would be no call.

After two days Perry told Dylan to stop leaving messages and sending texts. When he called round, I listened from the bedroom as Perry politely told him to leave me be. I felt nothing. All-encompassing grey nothing.

Cards came through the door, more flowers were dropped off. And food – pasta bakes and casseroles, cakes and steaming pies. Perry ate what he wanted, the rest I calmly scraped into the bin.

Larissa and Milton called round. Again, I stayed in bed, listening detachedly as the voices rose to penetrate the ceiling.

She's a liar, Peregrine.
How can you trust her?
All this time, and not a word...
He's an addict. *Do you really want to take that on?*
No wonder she...

I brushed off the flicker of curiosity at whether Perry would stay, and sank back into the grey.

After a week, a soft-spoken doctor with sharp creases between her eyebrows came to my bedroom, perching on the empty side of the bed. She asked me more questions, most of which I forgot as soon as I answered them. I laughed when I saw the familiar name of the pills she prescribed, startling myself with the bitter cackle.

Eleven days in, I lay alone in bed, Perry having nipped to the office for a meeting. As I stared at the ceiling, embracing the grey, somebody knocked on the door.

A minute later, I heard the sound of the lock unclicking and the door opening as the somebody entered my house. I tugged the duvet up over my head and tried to ignore them.

There was a louder knock. My bedroom door. I had a second to regret not wedging a chair under the handle before the door swung open, footsteps crossed to my bed, and came to a stop beside my head.

"Faith."

I groaned.

"Don't groan. I'm not here to ask how you are. Or try to cheer you up. But I'm not going away until I've looked you in the eye."

I groaned again, flipping off the duvet. It was suffocating under there, anyway. I squinted at Hester in the afternoon sunshine poking round the edge of my curtains.

She squinted back at me for a few seconds before nodding firmly.

I mumbled a rude word, edging the covers back up in anticipation of what was coming.

"Right. Up you get, then. Rehearsal is in forty minutes and you know how I feel about lateness."

"Ungh." I let my hand flop back onto the mattress beside me.

"Come on, girl. We know how this is going to end. Spare us both some pain."

"I can't." I moved my head a couple of inches to look at her, so she knew I meant it.

"Hmm. I don't like that word. It makes my scalp itch."

"All right. I don't want to."

"Why?" She sat down on the end of the bed, the gesture so tender from one so steely it knocked the grey off balance.

"You know why. Those songs. The way we sing them. I can't feel that now. It'd kill me."

She twitched her shoulders. "Bah. You've got to feel it sometime. Makes no difference to how much it'll hurt when you do. Come and face those feelings with your friends. Start the process."

"That's not the only reason."

"I know it isn't. I want you to talk to me about the other reason."

"I can't see him, Hester." I closed my eyes.

"That word again." She lowered one eyebrow at me.

"I don't want to see him."

"Well, you might as well get up and put some clean clothes on then. Dylan's on leave."

I slowly pulled on some jeans and a short-sleeved top and accepted the cup of coffee Hester brewed. I even managed to swallow half a sandwich while she brushed my hair, an act so gentle it dissolved a dangerous amount of grey in the process.

Once we reached Brooksby, we took a sharp right turn onto a side street instead of heading to the chapel.

"Where are we going?"

"Here." She pulled to a stop outside a modern semi-detached house, beeping the horn a couple of times before climbing out and walking round towards the pebbled driveway. As she approached, the front door opened and April gingerly stepped out. Hester offered her arm, helping her take slow, careful steps to the car.

I leaned my head against the seat rest and tried to burrow myself back into oblivion.

"Hi, Faith." April manoeuvred herself into the back seat and promptly burst into tears. "I'm so sorry!"

"Me, too." I reached around and patted her knee.

"It's not the same for me as it is for you, but I miss him so much."

"I know."

So five minutes later, the physical and emotional casualties of Kane's vengeance limped into Grace Chapel. We sat at the back, acknowledging the smiles and waves and expressions of sympathy with gracious nods. We kept our mouths closed, but our ears open, and found some semblance of peace in the beauty of the songs sung, took our first steps on the long road to healing as we listened to those awesome women sing them.

We did all anyone could do in the face of unbearable loss: we kept on breathing, our hearts kept beating, our brains kept thinking, and we carried on living for one more day.

Three days later the news finally arrived, as I sat drawing rainbows with Nancy and Pete on my living room floor. I wasn't shocked. I didn't wail, or weep, or try to explain it away. To me, this was old news, announced as the howl ripped from my soul, kneeling upon Dylan's floor a lifetime ago.

So when I stood over my brother's body, kissed his once-beautiful brow, and whispered my goodbye to him; as I chose his coffin, waited for the results of the post-mortem, collected his death certificate, did the hundred and one things that need to be done in these situations – to my mild surprise, my aching lungs kept breathing, my broken heart continued to beat, my mashed-up brain kept on going. I carried on living for one more day. Two days. A week. A month.

The only other thing I will say about that time is, when the choir sang my darling brother goodbye with the words of "Amazing Grace", it sounded like the very angels were welcoming him into heaven.

The Name I Call Myself

* * *

I started walking again, with April as her strength returned, or with Marilyn. Sometimes heading out on sweet adventures with Nancy or Pete, joining them in examining every ladybird, or fallen leaf, or dull grey stone that looks to adult eyes like every other stone on the path, because we have lost the magic of a toddler's world view.

I found comfort in the small things, the vulnerability of grief creating the necessity for narrow, simple, safe. I felt as though several layers of skin had been stripped away – leaving me so raw that a word, a waft of scent, a time of day, a memory would overwhelm me with the pain.

I put Sam's flat on the market. April had decided it would be too painful to move back in, instead finding a little place to share in Brooksby with Rowan and Callie.

I revelled in choir practice – those afternoons a precious solace when I stepped out of grief for a time, became no longer a woman bereaved, ravaged, alone. I joined with my friends, my sisters, in embracing something bigger than me, than my life or my problems or my sorrow. I became a vessel, an instrument, a part in a machine that created beauty and light and hope as it freed our spirits to soar.

I returned to work, finding respite in the familiar rhythms of chinking glasses, scraping plates, the hiss of steam and impatient chefs.

I allowed my fiancé to love me, as best he could. He moved back home once I felt stronger, gradually slipping back to his workaholic hours. He showered me with gifts, compliments, and tender-hearted gestures. Listened to the hidden story of the past few months with dismay and frustration at my secrets. Heard a little, just enough, about my time as Anna.

I started to cook again, experiencing sparse pleasure of my own from what I produced in Perry's kitchen, but finding satisfaction in his. His parents kept their distance. Wedding plans rumbled on.

But. At every step along my journey back to life, I carried the awareness that the black hole inside me was a tiny bit bigger than Sam. There was an extra space. An additional aching gap.

I missed my friend.

However angry I felt about it. However fearsome my rage towards him. However much I tried to slap the missing him feelings down, rip them to shreds, bury them under the blame. I liked walking with April – together we talked about Sam, and it helped us both. I loved that my friends were there to listen, to give me lifts, to provide distractions. It meant so much to realize Perry knew nearly all of my secrets, and still wanted me to be his wife.

But I missed my friend. I missed his eyes, his smile, his gentle teasing. I missed his stories, the smell of his truck, knowing he would catch me when I fell off a cliff. I wondered if his hair had grown back, or if he had decided to keep it short. If the reason he hadn't come back to choir rehearsals was to avoid me, or enable me to avoid him. I wondered why he'd gone on holiday when I needed him most. If he'd believed me when I said I would never forgive him for what happened.

Two weeks before the wedding, while I was sorting through some of my meagre possessions, wondering what to pack up and what to leave behind for Polly, my phone rang. The minister who called explained he would now be conducting the wedding ceremony, if I didn't mind, as Dylan had taken a sabbatical. I thanked him, and sat holding my phone for longer than I care to admit.

I then took out a piece of paper from my desk drawer, and wrote one more wedding invitation. Sealing it inside an old brown envelope, I tucked it back inside the drawer. I had a little bit longer to decide whether to send it.

Crunch time. After a week of tying bows around two hundred party favours, carefully inscribing names on place cards, and enduring my bridesmaids' tour of beauty salons, Rosa arrived for a final dress fitting.

The bridesmaids went first, of course. Marilyn's poofy dress now took up about half as much space, the butterflies fewer in number but still fluttering as she twirled the flowing skirts. Rosa did one final pinning, and ordered Marilyn to do no running, and eat plenty of her delicious cakes all week so the dress wouldn't fall down and steal my thunder.

"I'm joking, of course." She winked at me in the mirror. "Nothing is going to steal the thunder of you in your dress."

"Depending on which dress she picks, that could be either in a really good way, or a reeeaaaally bad way," Natasha said, already slipping out of her tiny skirt in her haste to get on the dusty aqua shell dress.

I smiled back at them all, waiting for Natasha and Catherine to check their dresses were still fantastic before giving anything away.

"Now, then." Rosa peered at me over the top of her glasses. "What is it to be?"

I wagged a finger at her. "You know full well what it's going to be. Give it here and stop smirking."

* * *

I spent the night before my wedding day alone with my tears. People understood my desire to set aside this time to mourn for my lost family, both my brother and my mother and grandmother. That afternoon, Perry and I had gone over our vows with the stand-in minister. He whizzed through the content of the service, chuckling as he asked if we knew of any lawful impediment why we should not be joined together in holy matrimony.

I sucked in a lungful of grey. I had continued riding along the conveyor belt towards marriage throughout my grief, too tired, too weak, too lost to think about getting off. Also, too numb to think about the practicalities beyond packing up my things, agreeing with whatever decisions Larissa came up with, and nodding along with Perry's plans for our future. I had no idea what was waiting for me at the end of the ride, but when the panic of my aloneness pressed in, I longed to belong to someone again. To be part of a family, with history and structure and a place for me, however lowly.

Sam had been instrumental in my decision to marry Perry. The reason I would take my fondness and determine to coax it into something I could call love. However, the loss of Sam had only strengthened my need to be Perry's wife.

I took the extra invitation, the one sealed in a plain brown envelope, and tore it up.

Somewhere, underneath all the grey, I knew getting married was a really stupid, selfish idea.

Grief had made me stupid.

With my bridesmaids on hand, I took the morning of my wedding one step at a time. Eat breakfast. Shower. Sit for two hours while Rowan tries to work her magic on my overgrown bob and Kim vainly attempts to conceal the toll the past few weeks have taken on my face. Conjure up a smile for the photographer. Do not think. About him, or *him*. Get dressed. Get in the car. Get out of the car. Smooth the skirts of what is quite possibly the most beautiful dress in the universe. Lift up my head, throw back my shoulders, breathe out the bad, suck in the good. Take one step forwards, and another, and another.

Halfway down the aisle it hit me.

I had planned to have Handel's "Arrival of the Queen of Sheba" playing as I entered the church. Something innocuous and safe. But the notes had changed, evolved into something entirely different. And as I reached the back rows, the unmistakeable sound of thirteen women singing in perfect harmony broke out from the side of the room. Glancing across I saw them, lined up in blue summer dresses along the wall. Rosa gave me a grin and a thumbs up. Melody winked. April broke all the performance rules by wiping her hands across her face.

Flicking my eyes forwards I saw Catherine and Natasha beaming at me from the front of the chapel. I felt the strength and the solidarity of Marilyn's arm as it gripped mine, refusing to let me take this walk alone. Pete called out "Mummy ah Fai!" and clapped his pudgy hands together.

As the love bombarded me, I had to stop. My fingers sought for something more to steady me, clutching on to the back of the chair to my right. The person sat behind there placed a warm, rough hand beneath my elbow to support me.

These were my family. My sisters. My friends. I was not alone. Since I had stepped into the Grace Choir rehearsal eleven months earlier. Before then, even – since that first afternoon eating cake and giggling in the Cottage of Chaos – I had never been alone.

What on earth was I doing marrying a man I wasn't in love with to try to fix a problem that didn't exist?

How could I do that to him?

What had I been thinking?

"Are you okay?" A deep voice, with a gentle Northern accent, jolted me out of my whirling thoughts.

I turned to see Dylan gazing up at me. "Faith?"

"Your hair's grown back."

The corners of his mouth curled up, ever so slightly. It didn't hide the sadness in his eyes. We looked at each other for a long time.

"Perry's waiting for you…" Dylan left the sentence hanging, dropping his hand. I broke his gaze, sure something else lay behind the sadness.

I nodded, and continued what must have been the longest walk of my life.

Men are supposed to smile as their wife-to-be walks down the aisle, I think. Or maybe cry. Perry watched me as I stepped up to join him and let out a long sigh. Frowning, he took hold of my hand.

"Perry, I'm so sorry, but we need to talk –"

"I know," he cut me off, nodding curtly. "Give me one minute."

And then he stomped down the aisle, yanked Dylan to his feet by the scruff of his shirt, and smashed his fist into his face.

"Hooten tooten!" Marilyn whistled, as the room went deathly still. "I guess this means the wedding's off."

Chapter Twenty-four

Three months later, I decided one of the absolute best sounds in the entire world is the rustle of an audience from behind a stage curtain. Throw in the murmur of anticipation and the squeaks and hoots of the orchestra tuning up and you cannot beat it.

The Grace Community Choir waited on the left half of the stage, in tiered seating allowing us to perch above our competitors sat on the front three rows below. Two more choirs took up the middle section, and the final two filled up the right hand side. Melody, sitting next to me, slipped her cool hand into mine.

"Peace, woman," she whispered out of the side of her mouth. "You're setting my nerves all a-twitter."

"I'm sorry. I'm so anxious. Look!" I pointed my chin at my chest. "You can see my heart thumping through my dress! How much longer?"

She elbowed Rosa on her other side. "Rosa! How much longer?"

Rosa shrugged, before twisting round to April behind her in the soprano seats. "April! What's the time?"

But before April could answer, a hush fell over the one thousand strong crowd as the curtain began to open in the Derry Millennium Forum.

"Ladies and gentlemen!" the evening's host announced. "Welcome to the Community Choir Sing-Off national finals!"

We were fifth to perform. A good slot, according to Hester, as it left you fresh in the judges' minds. An excruciating slot, according to the rest of the choir members, as it meant sitting and listening to four of the best community choirs in the kingdom smash it, rock it out, and bring the house down.

We had a twenty-minute interval before going on. This resulted in a sudden panic when, as we lined up in preparation to take our place centre stage, we realized Janice was missing.

"She's in the loo again," Millie declared. "I told her not to eat that packet of fig rolls. 'It can only mean bad news,' I said. But, oh no, what do I know? 'Sound as a pound, Mille,' she said. 'Solid as a rock,' she said, 'intestines of steel', apparently. Well, I said –"

"Enough!" Hester glowered down the line. "Can somebody please go and see what's happening? Rowan. You're at the back. Go."

Rowan curled her lip up. "Urgh. No chance."

A toot of steam escaped from Hester's ears.

"Fine!" Rowan sprinted off, as easily as she could in a slinky red dress and six-inch heels, calling back, "I'm an Internet sensation, you know. Internet sensations aren't supposed to sort out old ladies stuck on toilets with fig roll issues."

Rosa shook her head. "Oh my goodness. Since she went virus that girl getting too big a head. By the time that tour finished she'll be going Robbie Williams."

"Eh?" April wrinkled her nose.

"Like Zayn from One Direction." I helped her out with a twenty-first-century example of a band member leaving to pursue a solo career.

Kim shuffled in front of me. "Actually, if we're waiting for Janice, I think I might pop to the loo…"

Hester zoned in her laser beam glare.

"I can't help it, Hest! I'm dead nervous!"

"No one else is leaving this line."

We muttered and wriggled for a few seconds as we waited, adjusting dress straps and tucking stray curls of hair back into place. A ripple of applause welcomed the host back on stage to announce our appearance, and we froze, all eyes on Hester.

"She's not gonna make it," Rowan huffed as she clacked back into the wings. "Said it's like Mount Vesu–"

"Stop!" Mags begged. "I'm feeling sick enough as it is."

"Well. Anyway, she isn't leaving that bathroom anytime soon."

A larger round of applause, and one of the stage crew beckoned Hester forwards.

"What are we going to do?" Leona gaped. "We might get away without her voice, but we've got to have an even number or the moves won't work."

"Someone else could drop out," April said, wincing as the rest of the choir launched optical daggers at her.

Hester closed her eyes momentarily, sucked in a deep breath, and held up one finger to indicate she needed a minute.

Whipping out her phone, she jabbed at the screen. "How fast can you get here?" she barked down the line. "Make it two and you're on."

Baffled, we exchanged glances while Hester marched over to the crew member and muttered briefly at him. He stepped forwards and signalled to the host that there had been a slight delay.

The door behind us slammed open, and Marilyn burst through. "Ta daa!" she yelled in a sort-of backstage whisper. "Look, girls, I knew wearing red was a portent!" Spinning around to show us her dress, her smile nearly split her face in two.

"I can't believe it!" She dashed up and down the line. "Where do I go? Here? Hester, you are awesome. I knew you'd let me sing in the end. I prayed for it and everything. Hooten tooten! This is one of the best days of my life!"

Hester coughed, a look of panic flitting across her face. We needed Marilyn's moves, not her toneless voice. Polly reached out and pulled her into the line. "Yes, well," she said, pointedly. "You've been one of our best members, Marilyn. Truly embraced the spirit of the choir. *Grace* – that's what it's all about, isn't it, Hester?"

Hester blinked a couple of times. "Yes," she said, her voice squeaking on the word. "Grace. Right. Let's go." As Marilyn skipped past she leaned forwards and said, "You can sing, as long as you keep it quiet."

Marilyn smacked Hester on the backside without pausing. "Don't worry, Hest. I'll make you proud."

Hester shook her head as she took her place at the back of the line. "You always do."

We ended up coming in third, according to the judges. First, according to the unofficial vote of the Grace Choir and its equally unofficial fan club. First, if you rate our position on how much fun we had, how far we had come, how much passion we threw into it, and how many bows we took before the host herded us offstage.

The fun continued in the hotel lounge afterwards. My, those Grace women knew how to party. Throw in the actual winners, a group of ex-factory workers from Glasgow, staying in the same hotel, and the fact that the Irish need no excuse to party, and it looked as though we would be singing and dancing well into the night.

After all those years of organizing other people's special occasions, watching them go wild on the dance floor from behind the bar, I lingered on the fringes, not quite sure how to join in without Perry to hold on to.

"Come on, Faith!" Rosa wove through the other people currently jiving to some sixties classic and stopped in front of me, hands on hips as her chest heaved from exertion. "Come and dance!"

I scuffed my fancy shoe against the edge of the carpet. "Maybe later on."

"What? You don't like dancing?" She shimmied in place for a couple of beats.

I shrugged. "I'm not used to this type of music. The kind of parties I've been to were a bit more... sedate."

"Phooey. Even babies know how to dance. Come on, strut that funky stuff!"

She grabbed my hands and yanked me into the middle of the dance floor, where I stood swaying self-consciously to the music.

"Nah-ah!" Rosa shook her head. "Not like that. Copy me." She did a few shimmies, and I tried to follow along, stumbling into one of the factory workers behind me.

"Okay. No. That's not working. Try this." She stopped bopping and stepped right in front of me. "Close your eyes. Do it! Close them!"

I closed my eyes.

"Now, listen. Feel the beat. Start to move your body. Don't worry what it looks like. Pretend you are in your living room at home alone."

I tried, sort of. I didn't dance in my living room at home. And I had rarely had any time there alone since Polly and Esme had moved in, giving Marilyn and James space while I waited for Sam's flat to sell so I could afford to move somewhere else.

I suffered until the song finished and made my excuses, finding a comfy sofa in the corner to sink into while recovering my dignity. A minute or two later Marilyn came and plopped herself down on the seat next to me. Wiping the sweat from her brow with a napkin, she took a large gulp of the glass of water in her hand.

"I thought I might find you sat on your own in the corner."

"I'm soaking up the ambiance. Savouring the moment."

"It was awesome, wasn't it?"

I smiled. "It was. Are the twins in bed?"

"Yeah. James took them up. He's making the most of some time with them before starting his new job."

"Is he looking forward to it?"

"*I'm* looking forward to it. It's been great having him around these past few months, but I'll be happy to have him out of the house during the day so we can get back to some sort of routine. The place is a tip since he got back. Having said that," she nudged me, "I still haven't got used to waking up every morning and finding the love of my life there next to me. Let alone him coming home to me every night. A good man is hard to find. We need to keep 'em close once we do."

I gave her a sidelong glance, but she ignored me, taking another drink. We sat there watching the dancers for a while. I thought about good men. One good man.

"Are you missing him tonight?"

I somehow managed to choke on my own breath.

Marilyn kept her eyes on the dancers in front of us.

I shrugged, ready to brush her off with a bland reply. Then she lay her head gently on my shoulder and my heart cracked open.

"Yes. I'm missing him. I keep expecting to see him being chatted up by Millie, or laughing on the dance floor."

"It'll take a long time to get used to him not being around."

I sighed. "I feel like I should be over it by now."

Marilyn sat back up again, and turned towards me. "What? That's ridiculous. You'll learn to live with it, but you'll never be over it. You'll always miss him. Why are you always so hard on yourself?"

I frowned. "How long should it take to get over a minor broken heart? It wasn't like we'd known each other that long. Compared to losing Sam…"

She screwed up her face in apology. "Oh, I'm sorry. I was talking about Sam. I thought you were missing Sam, and that's why you were looking so sad. Sorry. I should have realized you meant Perry."

My eyes widened in surprise. Marilyn peered at me.

"Wait. You didn't mean Perry. You weren't sat here thinking about Perry. So who were…? Dylan!" She gasped. "You were sat here in the corner like a loser, dreaming about Dylan! Pining for him! Perry was right – you're in love with Dylan!"

"Shhh!" I hissed. "Keep your voice down. Dylan was a good friend, and part of the choir. It's only natural I'd be thinking about him for *a couple of seconds* tonight."

A sly grin broke out across her face. "Have you spoken to him since the wedding?"

I shook my head. "You know I haven't. He's been on sabbatical. And I hardly think he wants to see me, given how I treated him after Sam went missing. And then the next time I saw him he got punched in the face."

"Of course he wants to see you. He luuurves you. I think what he did after Sam went missing, despite the awful stuff you said to him, proves that."

"He went on holiday. What does that prove apart from that he wanted to get away from me?"

Marilyn gaped at me. "You don't know."

"Don't know what?"

"I can't believe nobody told you."

"Nobody told me what?" I pushed her gently, but hard enough to convey my irritation.

"He didn't go on holiday."

"What?"

"Faith." Marilyn took hold of my hand, deadly serious now. "He went to find Sam."

Those words were like a bomb going off in my head. In the smoking aftermath, I couldn't speak. Couldn't think. My head filled with white noise. Marilyn appeared to be watching me, her forehead creased, from the other end of a tunnel.

"He spent all those days looking, trawling through the worst sorts of places. Using all his contacts in the homeless shelters and the rehab centres to try to find someone who knew anything."

She gave me time to let this sink in.

"I can't believe this. I can't believe I didn't know. Why didn't he tell me? Why didn't he take me with him?"

"He told Perry. He actually asked him for help. Perry told him you didn't want to know where Sam was. You couldn't cope with it."

I might feel angry about that later. Right then I was too overwhelmed about Dylan.

As the shock sank in, my throat closed up, my eyes burning. "Did he…?"

Marilyn nodded. "He found him in a squat in Nottingham. Near the Ice Arena."

On that sofa in Northern Ireland, as my friends danced the Macarena around me, I felt as though I lost my brother all over again. The pain crushing me almost double, I fumbled for my bag on the floor.

Marilyn reached down and picked it up. "What do you need?"

"My phone. I need to speak to him. I need him to tell me everything. And I have to apologize. And thank him. How can I thank him? He really went to find Sam?" My tears were streaming onto my lap now, as sobs prevented me from saying anything more. Instead of handing me my phone, Marilyn put my bag to one side and simply hugged me, holding on tight until I began to steady my breathing again, and managed to stop making ugly hitching noises.

Patting me on the back a few times, she drew away. "Okay?"

I closed my eyes, took another deep breath. "Nearly."

"Right, now don't freak out when I tell you what I'm about to say."

I released a shaky laugh. "Well, that's making me freak out already."

"Nobody said anything because they don't know how you feel about it, and we know you've had a really awful time, but –"

Her phone rang. She paused to read the screen. "James. I'd better answer. Don't go anywhere!"

She twisted her body round to face the wall in order to drown out some of the noise, pressing her finger over her free ear. I took the opportunity to sneak off. Wandering out of the room, I paused in the hotel foyer. I was sharing a twin room with April, who'd gone to bed with one of the headaches that still plagued her since her injuries, so didn't want to go to my room. The bar on the other side seemed busy, and not being the kind of woman who feels comfortable sitting and drinking alone late at night, I turned towards the rear exit, which led to a courtyard area.

Initially the cold night air was a soothing balm against my feverish skin, but as I strolled aimlessly between the empty chairs and tables, I soon needed the shawl in my bag. Fishing it out, my phone came flying out with it, clattering onto the flagstones. I scooped it up, about to zip it safely into the side pocket when something stopped me.

I checked the time. Nearly midnight. Pacing up and down I tried to decide what to do. Leave it, and spend a sleepless night wondering, questioning, stressed out? Or phone him, and maybe get some answers, even if they weren't easy to hear? I dismissed the lateness of the hour – once Dylan knew why I was calling he would understand. And the chances were high he would be at home, wherever that was for him now.

Finding a seat at the far end of the yard, looking out across the river, I dialled his number, holding my breath. It rang for so long, by the time it clicked through I expected the answerphone, so was about to hang up.

"Hello?"

"Hi," I whispered. I could hear noise in the background – the thump of music, and people talking.

"Hang on a minute." After a few seconds the background sounds diminished. "Hello? Is that Faith?"

I closed my eyes. His voice – oh, I had missed that voice. "Yes."

"Well, hi." He sounded surprised. Maybe a little pleased. "Um, how are you?"

"Marilyn just told me. What you did for Sam."

"Oh. Right."

"I just wanted to say…" I stopped. If I spoke any quieter he wouldn't be able to hear me. Clearing my throat, I tried again. "I wanted to say thank you. And I'm sorry."

"You're welcome. And I'm sorry, too." His voice grew soft now. Something hard and ugly disintegrated inside me. I swallowed back the tears and kept going.

"And, I'd really like to talk to you about it sometime, if that's okay. Not now, I mean; I'm supposed to be celebrating. But when I'm home, if you don't mind."

335

"I don't mind at all."

"Right. Well, it sounds like you're busy, so I'm going to go, try to pull myself together, and get back to the party."

"Okay."

"We came third, did you hear?" I asked, suddenly reluctant to end the call.

"I heard. You were amazing."

I couldn't help smiling. Swinging my feet back and forth like a teenager talking to that boy she dreams about. "Well, I don't know about that. Marilyn had to step in for Janice at the last minute, and while she got most of the dance moves down, some of those high notes had an added twist I hadn't heard before."

"I thought it was the best you'd ever sung."

"What?" A spurt of adrenaline whooshed into my bloodstream.

"Breathtaking. I may have even cried. Which I'm allowed to, because I'm a minister and therefore kind of feeble."

If it was possible, my heart pounded even faster.

"I also thought you looked fantastic. Far better looking than the Glaswegians. If they were judging it on entertainment factor, Millie's hat should have swayed it in your favour."

I laughed. There were tears still mixed up in there too. "She knitted it especially. Actually, she knitted us all one, but the rest of us politely declined."

"And that routine you came up with for the last song? I'm sorry I missed all those rehearsals now."

The moonlight, the lights dancing across the river, they made me bold. "So, why did you miss them?"

"I thought you needed some space. I didn't want to be an unwelcome distraction in the lead up to the competition."

"And is that why nobody told me you were coming to watch us today? Why you snuck around so I didn't know you were here?"

He laughed now. "I didn't ask them not to tell you. And I didn't sneak anywhere. I had to catch a later plane and only just got here in time."

CHAPTER TWENTY-FOUR

"But you weren't at the party."

"I'm here now."

My breath caught. Those words had not been spoken down the phone line. I hung up, and turned around.

"See," Dylan said, pulling out the chair next to mine and sitting down, loosening his tie as he leaned back, looking out across the water. "I have this thing about girls who sit on their own at parties." He glanced at me. "Sort of a rescue complex thing."

"Ah yes." I nodded. "I've heard this about you. Your need to step in and save the non-beautiful girls from their terrible, lonely fate."

I peeked at him out of the corner of my eye. I could see his mouth twitch as he tipped his head to the side. "Yeeah... I've been working on that. Trying to cut down, as it were."

I kept quiet, wondering where this was going. Finding it hard to breathe, speak, or swallow, quite frankly.

"I've decided only to rescue those rare girls who think they're non-beautiful, but are actually so incredible you can't think properly when you're in the same room as them. You risk life and limb to catch them when they fall. Bunk off church to help their brother. You turn into an idiot who blabs stupid comments at really inappropriate moments. You offer to, I don't know, give them driving lessons or something. Even though you know it's a really bad idea because they're already engaged to a rich, handsome guy – which of course they're going to be.

"But even though you keep promising yourself to stay away, to stop killing yourself over her, you can't help finding chances to make her smile, or help her out, or turn up uninvited to her wedding. Because she is absolutely the last girl in the world who should be sitting by herself in the freezing cold at a party. So, yeah. I'm sticking to that kind of girl. Well. The one girl. Woman. Who makes me feel like that."

Nope, still lost the ability to speak. Or move. Just about managing to breathe, although the icy air will soon put an end to that.

"So." Dylan jiggled his chair round to face me, producing a

horrible screech as it scraped the stone. "Do you want to come inside and have a dance?"

He ran one hand through his hair, his face taut.

I bit my lip. "I can't dance to this music. It's just, well..."

Right on cue, the tempo pulsating through the wall slowed as the song changed to a love song.

Dylan gave a shaky grin, raising his eyes to the sky. "And who said God doesn't answer prayers?"

I still hesitated – flummoxed, overwhelmed. Terrified.

He held out his hand. "Okay. You don't have to dance with me. But can we please go inside before we turn into ice sculptures?"

I took his hand, allowing him to pull me up. We stood, so close together I could feel the heat coming off his chest. Seriously, how had I ever thought I could somehow conjure up this kind of feeling for Perry? He put out one hand, and tucked a stray lock behind my ear. I couldn't tell if it was me trembling, or him.

"Your hair's grown back." His mouth flickered as he softly ran his finger down my cheek and along the bottom of my jaw, never taking his eyes off mine. "I think we'd better go inside before I do something we regret."

I took a huge breath in, blew it out along with my doubts, my anxieties, and my messed-up, mixed-up mentality, and sucked in some personal power, right down to the bottom of my lungs, where it whizzed through my bloodstream, along my arteries, and into every cell. Up into my brain and right down to my feet, as I bent them to stretch up on tiptoe.

"Hmm." I placed my hand over his, where it still lingered near my face, and pressed it to my cheek. "I think the only thing I'm going to regret about tonight is if I let you go inside without kissing me."

So, when Dylan had managed to control the jaw-splitting grin on his face, he did.

Hooten tooten. We were going to have to do that again.

The Name I Call Myself

Reading Group Questions

1. There are two men in Faith's life. What were your first impressions of Perry and Dylan? Who did you warm to first?

2. What is your favourite scene in the book? Why?

3. Do you think it is ever right to marry someone for security? Do you think Faith could have been happy with Perry?

4. What did you think when Hester asked all the members of the choir to take off their make-up and put on a plain white T-shirt? Would you ever do anything similar?

5. What do you think about how Faith handled the fact she had to change her identity and her name? Do you think she told the truth to the right person?

6. Female friendships are a key theme in this book. Did you find watching these friendships develop empowering?

7. How did Sam's storyline affect you?

8. What does Faith and Dylan's relationship say to you about the importance of being open? Do you think their story ended in the right way?

9. If you could ask the author one question, what would it be? Why not tweet her your question @bethcmoran!

10. Has this novel changed you or broadened your perspective?

Loved
The Name I Call Myself?

Try a chapter of Beth Moran's captivating
Making Marion...

ISBN: 978 1 78264 099 8 | e-ISBN: 978 1 78264 100 1

Chapter One

"*W*ho are you?"

My first thought was to lie. To not be me. I hesitated.

The girl in front of me, so desperately trying to be an adult with her dark make-up and uneasy piercings looked up for the first time. Her expression from behind the counter said it all. What type of person doesn't know who they are?

A dozen names zipped through my brain. The women I wished I could be. Amelia Earhart. Emmeline Pankhurst. Lady Gaga.

The girl began tapping her biro on the book in front of her, jabbing angry marks on the white page.

"Marion Miller." This is my real name. I was here (and not standing behind my own counter at Ballydown Public Library) to discover what that name meant.

She checked her book. "You aren't on the bookings list. Did you reserve a pitch or a caravan?"

"No. I haven't reserved anything –"

She slammed the book shut, shoving it to one side. Scowled through the inch-long spider legs glued to her eyelids. "It's August. We're full."

I was about to explain that I only wanted directions to the Sherwood Forest visitor centre. But before I could, the outside door opened and a woman *sashayed* in. Apart from her tiny frame, nothing about her appearance said "girlish". All of her, from the top of her platinum blonde chignon to her sleek heels declared her a lady. Her simple red dress wrapped her perfectly, emphasizing curves where curves are meant to be. I couldn't guess her age. Thirty-five? Forty? Fifty, even? It felt crass even to consider how old she might be. For a woman like this, years and the passing of time are irrelevant. She was breathtaking.

She turned to me and smiled. "Hello. Welcome to the Peace and Pigs. I am so sorry, but an emergency has occurred and I require my daughter's assistance immediately. Have you booked in yet?"

A voice of pure honey. Made with pollen from the sweetest of North American flowers. Deep and rich. A Southern Belle.

As I opened my mouth to reply, the girl who must be her daughter answered. "She hasn't booked."

"I'm not here on holiday. I…"

The woman grabbed my wrist with her French-manicured nails. "You must be Becky Moffitt's niece – Jenna? You made it! I'm Scarlett. You are so very welcome! To be honest I was beginnin' to think you decided not to show up, but better late than never, today of all days. Now please, I don't mean to throw you in at the deep end, but as I mentioned, we are in the grip of an emergency. Would you mind very much taking over from Grace and supervisin' check-in? All you need do is welcome arrivals, find their pitch number in the book, make sure they've paid and hand them the information leaflet."

As she spoke, the woman steered me behind the desk. She patted my arm and turned back to her daughter. "Little Johnny escaped again. Valerie has him cornered with a broom by the bottom wash block, but he is squealin' like a great big baby; we need an extra pair of hands."

For a few beats of silence, Grace didn't move. I could feel tension swinging like a pendulum between them. Scarlett reached up her hand to smooth a non-existent stray hair back into place.

"Please, would you come and help?"

Grace rolled her eyes and plodded out to join her mum. The door slammed shut behind her, leaving me standing on the wrong side of the counter. A prickle of sweat popped out on my forehead, due to a lot more than the stifling August heat.

For the first few minutes, nothing happened; the only sound my breathless prayer, muttered over and over again, as if saying it more times made any difference. "Please God, let no one turn up. Don't make me have to speak to anyone else."

The problem was this. I knew and God knows that I prayed a bigger prayer only the day before, not formed in a moment of panic but wrung from the very marrow in my bones. God chose to listen to my first prayer.

The bell on top of the door jangled, and my heart accelerated to triple time as a man and woman stepped in. Crumpled and sticky, like the old sweet wrappers inhabiting my car footwells, they barely glanced up as they handed over their reservation details. I checked the name on the piece of paper against the entry in the book.

"Pitch fourteen." My voice had been replaced with that of an elderly toad.

"Excuse me?"

I coughed to clear my throat. "Pitch number fourteen." I pointed out the map on the back of the welcome leaflet I had been memorizing for distractional purposes. "Just here, by the play park."

"That's great." The woman swiped at the hair drooping in her eyes. "The kids have been stuck in the back of the car for five hours. They can play while we put the tent up. You might have genuinely saved us from committing murder. You know what it's like."

Nope.

They had already paid in full and I couldn't think of anything to say, but they stood there expectantly. I fought past the seven-year-old mute who grabs hold of my vocal cords whenever I am forced into making conversation with people I don't know. Remembered to do my mute busters: *breathe out, drop shoulders, pause. Breathe in, open mouth, speak.*

"Um. Have a nice holiday. And if you need anything, feel free to come and ask."

The couple smiled and nodded as they opened the door to leave. I held my breath the whole time and then, as the door swung shut, my mouth opened all by itself and yelled: "I'm not Becky Moffitt's niece!"

The man pushed the door back open and stuck his head around it. "Sorry?"

Shaking my head quickly from side to side, I tried to smile. It might have been more of a grimace. He raised his eyebrows, glancing back at his car impatiently. "You shouted something. I didn't quite catch it."

I swallowed, and managed to mumble, "I'm not Becky Moffitt's niece."

The man stared at me for a second. "Okaaaay. Well. Thanks for letting me know. I'll bear that in mind."

I waited for him to climb back into his car before banging my head a few times on the reception desk.

An hour or so later, Scarlett poked her head around the door. Her eyes swept the room before coming to rest on me. I hadn't yet died of fright or done a runner. This is despite the fact that every time the bell jangled, my central nervous system pumped out an adrenaline rush big enough to send a shuttle into orbit. I could, by now, smell my own body odour and had agonized for a very long forty minutes about whether or not to take a cold drink from the fridge behind me. What on earth was I doing here?

"Y'all okay in here?"

I nodded yes.

"Anybody showed up?"

"Six."

"Helped yourself to a drink and an ice-cream?"

"No!"

"Well then, how can you be all right, sat in this sauna in *jeans* with nothin' to cool you down? Take somethin' quick before you pass out on me. I don't want suin' for maltreatment of my employees."

Tentatively, I pulled a bottle of water out of the fridge and held it in front of me in both hands, trying to find the courage to own up before the real Jenna walked in the door. Embarrassment won out – I smiled instead.

"Well, just wanted to check you were still here, and managin'. We're chock-a-block busy this weekend, and I could do with Grace stayin' out here with me, so you just carry on here and I'll come by later. Reception closes at seven."

She'd gone. There were three more hours until seven. I hadn't eaten since my emergency lunchtime banana. At six, I plucked up the courage to take a flapjack from the shelf of food items that made up the campsite shop, but I also had nowhere to sleep that night and only seventeen pounds left in my purse. If I confessed to being Jean O'Shay, Maureen Sheehan, Paula Callahan, Aoife Briggs, Danny O'Grady and Liam O'Grady's niece but not Becky Moffitt's, would Scarlett pay me enough to rent one of her caravans? Or report me to the police for impersonation of a holiday park employee?

At five to seven, Scarlett swung in through the door. I don't know what she had been doing all day, but her appearance suggested she spent it being pampered in an air-conditioned beauty salon. Must be something they teach you in Southern Belle School. How not to wilt. In Ballydown, we call it a hot summer's day if it stops raining long enough to dry a load of washing, and if the wind is strong enough to give you chilblains but stops short of frostbite. So I had past my best after a long afternoon in the Peace and Pigs Holiday Park complimentary steam room.

But when she came to stand next to me, I saw that in fact her eyes were creased with tiredness. Opening the book, Scarlett scanned the page. "How'd it go?"

I garbled my answer, wound up so tight my muscles were humming.

"I'm sorry," Scarlett drawled. She looked right at me, emphasizing each word. "I only speak English."

I repeated myself, replicating her slow enunciation. Trying to iron the Irish out of my vowels.

"All the reservations in the book have arrived. There were no problems."

Scarlett narrowed her eyes. Not mean. Suspicious. "Where you from, honey?"

"Northern Ireland."

"Hmmm." She examined me sideways on, starting with my dark, scruffy ponytail and moving right down to my supermarket trainers, via an ill-fitting pair of jeans that I had stolen from my cousin Orla when she put on two stone after having three babies in four years.

It is a rare day that doesn't have me believing I am a little girl trapped in a woman's body. Under Scarlett's gaze I shrank down to even less than that. An adult who has taken neither the time nor the effort to learn how to become a woman. An insult to my gender. A disgrace to females throughout the globe. I felt sure she could see through my "I'd rather be reading!" T-shirt to the body armour of my grey and sagging underwear.

She let out a long, smooth sigh. An iced tea of disappointment.

"I was led to believe the Troubles were over. You are something akin to a war zone, sugar."

About ninety-eight per cent of my red blood cell supply rushed up to my cheeks and neck.

Scarlett's face softened. For one fraction of a second, I glimpsed what it must feel like to be her daughter. To be Grace.

"Well. If you are plannin' on stayin', better start to slow down your words some. And Scarlett's lesson number one: dress that pretty face with a smile once in a while. Peace and Pigs' people do not want to be greeted at the reception desk with your broken heart."

"Are you…" I took a breath. Slowed down my words some. "Are you offering me a job? Because there is something I have to tell – "

"Sugar, I know you ain't Jenna Moffitt. I don't need to know who you are if you don't want to tell me. Although it might make things easier in the long run. I do everything by the book here, but if you want to work for your board and keep, we can work out the rest."

"No! I don't mind telling you my real name. I'm not running away." I became flustered under Scarlett's raised eyebrow. "Well, not from anyone who matters. I mean, everybody matters, of course, but not anybody – um – legal. I mean…"

Scarlett held up her hand. She waited for me to look up and meet her eye, then moved her hand forward to shake mine. A business gesture. To seal a deal. But with one infinitesimal squeeze, Scarlett said much more than that. She told me I was welcome. Even with my awful clothes and clumsy words. My undisclosed past and shattered spirits were invited to rest on the porch swing of her hospitality for as long as they needed. A tiny whisper, faint as a last breath, dared to wonder if I might find a home here, under the oak trees where the sunlight dappled and the air carried a scent of honeysuckle, and with it hope.

My new employer, gracious and charming to a fault, left the room. In her absence, my tears spilled over, carving clear, clean pathways through the grime of my facade.

I managed to calm down after about twenty minutes. Only after I had wiped my face on my T-shirt, blown my nose and stepped outside did I realize Scarlett had been waiting for me the whole time. Sitting on the stylish oak bench outside the reception building, she could have been a classic sculpture. A masterpiece carved from a single block of marble by an impassioned master craftsman. I stood hovering for a few moments until she looked at me.

"Better?"

"Yes, thank you."

"Come on then. I need to eat."

I fetched my bag from the car, introduced myself properly, and we began walking across the site. The whole park had only ten vans for visitors and three for staff, but throughout August it would accommodate one hundred tents. We strolled past the wash blocks, laundry room and playground, locations I had memorized on the map. The pitches were dotted in between the oak trees, clustered in friendly groups around brightly coloured flowerbeds, tucked away in seclusion by the edge of the forest – nothing regimented into grim rows. On the west side, where the sun would be setting in a couple of hours, Scarlett pointed out Hatherstone Hall. Maybe a quarter of a mile from the park's boundary, beyond a field full of sheep, it rose magnificent on the skyline. Built of eighteenth-century grey stone, it appeared solid and unfussy, but beautiful nonetheless. Though trees shadowed the front of the house, I could make out three storeys, the second complete with balconies in front of the two largest windows. Ivy covered all the ground floor.

"Does anybody live there?"

"The Hall? Oh, yes. Lord and Lady Hatherstone spend most of the year here, with their son. Reuben runs an organic veg box business from produce grown on the estate. And there are two employees living in the annexe behind the main house with their three kids. Still – a big enough place for eight people to be rattlin' around in, if you ask me. More trouble than it's worth. That place positively eats money."

Scarlett continued to fill me in on the details of the estate until we reached a smallish static caravan, set apart on its own at the borders of the woodland, surrounded by a white picket fence. Next to it grew a flourishing vegetable garden, probably three times the size of my ma's yard back home. I recognized lettuce and some raspberry canes. Besides that I was clueless. Ireland might be green, but it rains far too much in Ballydown for anybody I know to consider gardening as a hobby. Not when you can get a tin of peas at Joe's Food and Fancy Goods for twenty-nine pence.

"This is all we have, so I hope you ain't fussy. I kept it back for Jenna Moffitt, but I'm assumin' she won't be requirin' it. It's clean, and there are some basics in the fridge to see you through to next weekend. Payday's Friday. It only takes one eye to see you need some time, honey. But Grace and I are in the blue home. Stop by whenever you're ready for company."

She handed me a key, and turned to go. I had a million

questions, but managed to find the courage to ask just one: "How is Little Johnny?"

"That hunk of ham! I could cook and eat him as soon as spend half my life in swelterin' heat chasing him around the wash block. Don't worry yourself, Marion. That pig will outlive us all."